Margaret Thornton was [illegible] there all her life. She is a q[illegible] order to concentrate on her writing. She has two children and five grandchildren. Her previous Blackpool sagas, *It's a Lovely Day Tomorrow*, *A Pair of Sparkling Eyes*, *How Happy We Shall Be*, *There's a Silver Lining*, *Forgive Our Foolish Ways*, *A Stick of Blackpool Rock*, *Wish Upon a Star*, *The Sound of her Laughter*, *Looking at the Moon*, *Beyond the Sunset*, *All You Need is Love* and *Sunset View*, are also available from Headline and have been highly praised:

'A brilliant read' — *Woman's Realm*

'A gentle novel whose lack of noise is a strength' — *The Sunday Times*

'A delightful first novel' — Netta Martin, *Annabel*

'A delightfully compelling story' — *Coventry Evening Telegraph*

'Thornton's love of her hometown Blackpool shines through' — *Lancashire Evening Post*

'A heartwarming and intriguing story' — *Sunday Post,* Dundee

Also by Margaret Thornton

It's a Lovely Day Tomorrow
A Pair of Sparkling Eyes
How Happy We Shall Be
There's a Silver Lining
Forgive Our Foolish Ways
A Stick of Blackpool Rock
Wish Upon a Star
The Sound of her Laughter
Looking at the Moon
Beyond the Sunset
All You Need is Love
Sunset View

Don't Sit Under The Apple Tree

Margaret Thornton

headline

First published in 2003
by HEADLINE BOOK PUBLISHING

First published in paperback in 2004
by HEADLINE BOOK PUBLISHING

10 9 8 7 6 5 4 3 2 1

ISBN 0 7553 0036 X

Typeset in Times New Roman by
Letterpart Limited, Reigate, Surrey

Printed and bound in Great Britain by
Mackays of Chatham plc, Chatham, Kent

Papers and cover board used by Headline are natural, recyclable products made from wood grown in sustainable forests. The manufacturing processes conform to the environmental regulations of the country of origin.

HEADLINE BOOK PUBLISHING
A division of Hodder Headline
338 Euston Road
London NW1 3BH

www.headline.co.uk
www.hodderheadline.com

Once again, for my husband John, with my love; thanking him for his support and encouragement and for his faith in me.

Chapter 1

May 1993

Eunice was awakened by a loud rattling sound. For a moment, as she stared around the room, she wondered where on earth she was. The bed felt strange too, the sheets much stiffer and unyielding than the ones she was used to. Then she remembered. Of course, they were on holiday. They were in Calais and this was the second day of their continental coach tour. There was the noise again; it seemed to be coming from the street outside.

'What the bloody hell's going on?' Ronald leaped from the other single bed a couple of feet away from her own and dashed across to the window. He flung back the curtains and gazed down at the street below. 'Who the devil's making that infernal din? Eunice . . . Eunice . . .'

'Yes, what is it, Ronald?' she asked with a small sigh of resignation. She glanced dazedly at her alarm clock: five o'clock. She should have been able to have another hour – well, almost. She had set her travelling alarm clock for five forty-five, a quarter of an hour before the routine call from the reception desk was due. But now, if the row outside didn't keep her awake, then Ronald would make sure she didn't go back to sleep again. She sat up, reaching for her dressing gown. 'What's going on?'

'That's what I'd like to know. Come here and have a look. You know I can't see properly without my glasses. There seems to be a crowd of people over there, shouting and carrying on. God knows what they're doing.' He peered short-sightedly in her direction, a comical figure with his boldly striped pyjamas rumpled round his middle and what little hair he had sticking up on end.

'Oh, Ronald, don't look so cross! And don't frown like that.' She was wide-awake now and in spite of feeling slightly irritated she couldn't help being amused as well.

He was always like this at the start of a holiday. Nothing was ever right, away from England. These bloomin' foreigners with their goddamned outlandish ways! Why couldn't they behave as we did? And so on and so on . . . She had heard it all so many times.

Eunice too stared out of the window. The hotel opened on to the main street and across the road there was a *boulangerie*. As she watched, a heavy metal shutter was pushed up – it must have been the sound of the first shutter that had awoken them – and she could see a man in a voluminous white apron stacking loaves of all sizes in the window. A crowd of ten or twelve young people was emerging from the shop, all carrying those incredibly long loaves of bread, some of them nibbling at the ends, others breaking off pieces and cramming them into their mouths. Other folk, women with baskets and men in berets, were either approaching or leaving the shop.

'They're buying bread, that's all, Ronald,' said Eunice.

'What? At five o'clock in the bloody morning!'

'You know they buy fresh bread every day here,' said Eunice, 'and the bakeries open early. It looks to me as though those young people have been having a night on the town, and now they're having their breakfast. They look as though they're enjoying themselves.' Her crossness at being rudely awoken was fast disappearing in her delight at the typically French scene in front of her.

'Huh! Don't know why they can't have sliced bread like normal folk do.' Ronald flopped down on the bed, scratching his head. 'And why can't they do their shopping at a reasonable hour? Bloomin' Froggies! Waking folks up in the middle of the night. Not that I've had much sleep, I can tell you. I was awake half the night with indigestion. Must have been that chicken they gave us last night; it was far too greasy. Then the cistern was rumbling like a giant with bellyache. Why their plumbing has to make such a confounded row I'll never understand.'

'Ronald, you don't half tell some whoppers!' Eunice laughed out loud. 'Not had much sleep? That's why you've been snoring half the night, is it? Keeping me awake—'

'Snoring? I've hardly slept a wink, I tell you . . .' He was smiling, though, and she knew his grumbling and early morning crotchetiness was largely an act for her benefit. He did snore, though. Often, at home, she escaped to the solitude of the spare bedroom, but on holiday she just had to grin and bear it. 'Come on, love – make us a cup of tea,' he said coaxingly. 'It's no use trying to get to sleep again now.'

She smiled back at him. After fifty years of marriage she was used to his little ways. She knew that after the first couple of days he would be much more relaxed and complacent about things, enjoying the holiday just as much as she was.

'Yes, a cup of tea's a good idea,' she said. 'I don't know how we managed before I bought this little kettle.'

A mini-kettle that held just enough water for two cups, tea bags and powdered milk were now essential items in Eunice's large travelling bag. Continental hotels had still not got round to providing tea-making equipment in the bedrooms, as had their British counterparts. Eunice couldn't imagine starting the day without their early morning 'cuppa'. At breakfast time on the continent it was invariably coffee, dark, strong and bitter, but just the thing to drive away any cobwebs lurking in the brain. Eunice always enjoyed it – provided she had had her cup of tea first – as it made her feel part of the scene. The tea that some of the English holidaymakers insisted on ordering was so weak it could hardly crawl out of the pot.

She made the tea and added the powdered milk, mixed with a little water to make it more palatable, then a minuscule packet of sugar shared between Ronald's beaker and her own. She unashamedly helped herself at motorway service stations to a couple of extra packets of sugar, secreting them away in her large handbag. The charges at such places were outrageous, so she considered it was no more than her due.

They drank the tea in a companionable silence. Ronald had recovered from his burst of annoyance and he hummed tunelessly as he rooted through their overnight case to find clean socks and underwear.

'I'll have first turn in the bathroom,' said Eunice, 'if that's all right with you. Then I'll see to the suitcase. Get everything out you need, love, then I'll lock it and leave it outside the room, as we've been told to do.'

'I can't say I'm all that keen on this living out of a suitcase, Eunice. And we've two more nights before we get to where we're supposed to be going.'

'Never mind, love. When we arrive we've got a whole week in St Wolfgang, and we've both been looking forward to it so much, haven't we? Anyway, you knew how much travelling there would be before we booked.' She reflected for a moment now about how much she still loved him after all this time. They had had their ups and downs, but she knew their troubles in the end had only served to make them stronger as a couple and more devoted to one another. She recalled the upstanding ginger-haired lad with the twinkle in his eye; the boy who had been a childhood friend and with whom she had, so unexpectedly, fallen in love.

He had aged, to be sure, but that was inevitable. And if, at times, he was a little irascible she knew it was only his concern about his health that was making him so. Ronald was not used to being ill. He had never been ill in his life, apart from when he was injured in the war; and then he had suffered from recurring depression as a result of the traumas he had experienced. But all that was ages ago and he had been unprepared for the two mild heart attacks he had had in recent years. He must take care, the doctor had told him, and Ronald was not too keen on that idea.

As Eunice glanced at him now he grinned at her, and she could see again the familiar twinkle in his grey eyes. It reminded her of when they were young and so much in love. And she knew that though they might be no longer young in years they were both still young at heart.

'Yes, so I did . . .'

'And we've been on coach tours before, so we know by now what it involves. And you know very well that you don't like flying.' She did not mention that it would not be wise to fly now, since his minor heart attacks; he did not like to be reminded of them.

'Fly? I should damn well think I won't! Not after that last pantomime we had. Ten hours' wait at Palma airport! No, thanks very much; my flying days are over. I was never all that keen on it anyway.'

Ronald was not overendowed with patience nowadays and the delay they had endured at the airport in Majorca had, as he had said, 'put the tin hat on it' with regard to flying. Eunice had thought at the time that it was just as well that they had had their holiday – and enjoyed it too. She had had the sneaking feeling that if the delay had been at Manchester airport, at the start of the holiday, then Ronald would have called it a day and gone home.

'We're going to have a lovely holiday, you'll see,' she said cheerfully, disappearing into the tiny bathroom. At least she called it a bathroom, which was what they had at home, but, of course, it wasn't. All the small cubicle contained was a loo, washbasin and a shower. Eunice disliked showers; she was definitely a bath person, and at home she loved to soak in perfumed bubbles of lavender or sandalwood essence. They did own a shower, a hand-operated one over the bath, which Eunice used to wash her hair; only on very hot days did she use it on the rest of her body. She had to admit that it was pleasant and refreshing in the summer time, but she would not like to be without her bath. That was one of the very minor inconveniences of continental travel. More often than not it was a shower rather than a bath, particularly en route, in the overnight hotels.

This one, however, was not too bad, she noted, as she adjusted the temperature and directed the warm water from the hand-held spray all over her. Sometimes it was a fixed one that drenched you, hair and all, as you stood beneath it, and she did so hate shower caps. She dried herself with difficulty in the cramped space, dusted her favourite Yardley's lavender talc over her body, then put on her new underwear. Always before going away on holiday, she treated herself to a few new pairs of knickers and a bra from Marks and Spencer. It was an indulgence, really, because she already had a drawerful; and who was going to see them apart from herself? Ronald took no notice, not after fifty years of marriage! But it made her feel good and she took a delight in these little luxuries.

She changed places with Ronald, then put on the rest of her clothes. Her grey polyester skirt was ideal for travelling as it did not crease and would not show the odd smear of dirt or spilt coffee. The two drivers took it in turns to serve hot drinks – tea, coffee or chocolate – to the passengers whilst the coach was on the move. An excellent idea, but it was almost impossible to drink at high speed from the polystyrene beakers without the occasional mishap. Eunice put on her blouse – or top, as they seemed to call them nowadays – with the vertical mauve stripes that almost matched the colour of her hair. She had been a brunette when she was younger, but when her hair had turned grey in her mid-fifties she had started having mauve tints. She knew the colour was possibly a little outdated now, but her friends had told her that it suited her, toning so well with her bright blue eyes, and so she had kept to the colour and the same bouffant style that she had had for several years.

She combed and patted her hair into place, then applied a little moisturising cream and solid powder, then lipstick in her favourite rose-pink shade. Eunice was not dissatisfied with her appearance. She might possibly be termed buxom, she supposed, with the extra weight that had appeared around her waist and hips; and she had always, even as a girl, had a generous bust. All the same, she considered she did not look too bad at all, bearing in mind that she would be seventy in a couple of months. As she smiled at her reflection she recalled her mother's words of long ago. 'You're vain, Eunice, that's what you are; always prinking and preening in front of the mirror.'

She sighed a little. Yes, she had been a bonny girl, sure enough. Ronald had thought so, and others as well. One certain young man in particular . . . Thoughts of him had often strayed into her mind over the last couple of months – ever since they had booked this holiday – although before that she had not thought of him for years.

Breakfast that morning was a self-service buffet, the time being somewhat early for more than a skeleton staff to be on duty. There was coffee in large vacuum jugs and a selection of cereals, fruit, rolls, butter and jam laid out on a table at the side. After a general murmuring of 'Good morning . . . Good morning . . . Have you slept well?' as they all smiled around the buffet bar, they sat down at the same tables they had occupied the night before.

The middle-aged couple they had met the previous night were already seated at the table, and the woman, Jean, smiled at Eunice and Ronald in a welcoming way. The two women had already remarked, as they helped themselves to the rolls and butter, that they had spent quite a comfortable night. It was the men who appeared to be less than satisfied.

'I never sleep well in a strange bed,' Jean's husband, Jack, observed. 'Not the first night at any rate. I'll probably do better tonight.'

'Depends on what we have to eat, doesn't it?' said Ronald. 'That greasy chicken kept me awake half the night, and what do you bet it's chicken again tonight? It's all they ever seem to come up with in these one-night places.'

'Oh, I don't think so,' said Eunice. 'It will probably be Wiener schnitzel tonight, Ronald. We'll be in Germany, remember.' She turned to Jean. 'I'm looking forward to seeing the Rhine Valley, aren't you?' Jean agreed that she was.

Ronald gave Eunice an odd look. 'I saw enough of the bloomin' Germans fifty-odd years ago to last me a lifetime.'

Eunice glanced a little apologetically at Jean and Jack.

'You've got to live and let live, Ronald. It's all a long time ago. My husband was in the Desert War with Monty,' she explained to the other couple. 'He was wounded out there.'

'And Eunice was in the war as well,' said Ronald. 'She was a land girl, weren't you, love?'

'Yes, that's right, dear.'

'You were fighting Rommel then?' Jack remarked to Ronald.

'Yes; he was one of the better ones, I must admit,' replied Ronald. 'But as my wife says, it's a long time ago. Best forgotten, I dare say. But those of us that were in it . . . well, we have long memories.'

'You look very nice, dear,' Eunice whispered to Jean, as they all stood in little groups near the coach while the drivers, Mike and Gary, with the help of one or two willing men, stacked the luggage in the boot. 'That blouse really suits you, if you don't mind me saying so. And those trousers – goodness, I wish I could wear them.'

'Oh, thank you. Do you really think so?' Jean's face lit up with pleasure. 'I'm never very sure of myself in trousers. I don't wear them very often. But it's different on holiday, isn't it? I wondered if they might be a bit too . . . young?'

'Nonsense, of course they're not,' Eunice assured her. 'Anyway, you're only a youngster, aren't you?' She guessed Jean might be in her late fifties. Hardly a youngster – that was a bit of friendly flattery – but youthful enough compared with Eunice herself.

Jean laughed. 'I'm fifty-six,' she said in a confidential tone.

'Well, I'd never have believed it. If I had a figure like yours I'd be wearing trousers . . . even though I will be seventy next birthday. As it is I'm a bit too broad in the beam and I like to dress – well, you know – suitably, not as mutton dressed up as lamb.' Eunice glanced around as she spoke at some of her fellow passengers, some quite as old as herself, with stomachs and bottoms bulging alarmingly in unsightly Crimplene. 'I mean, you've got to be careful, haven't you, when you get into your seventies? But some of them don't seem to care,' she added in a whisper.

Jean smiled. 'I suppose they think they're on their holidays, so what does it matter. You don't look seventy, Eunice.'

'Thank you. Yes, people tell me I don't look my age.' Eunice preened a little. 'Fortunately I'm in good health, so that helps. Of course, Ronald is a couple of years older than me . . . I do hope you'll excuse him, Jean, for being so niggly this morning.'

'That's all right. I didn't notice . . .'

'You didn't? No, I suppose I'm more aware of it than other people. His health isn't too good, you see.'

'Yes, you mentioned he was wounded in the war.'

'Oh no, it's not that. That was just a shoulder wound and minor burns. He soon recovered.' She did not mention the bouts of depression that had troubled him for several years. Fortunately, though, they had ceased, long ago. 'No, he has high blood pressure and his heart's not too good. But as long as he keeps on taking his tablets he'll be all right.'

'Oh dear.' Jean looked concerned. 'Won't this holiday be rather strenuous for him, travelling such a long way by road?'

'Not if he takes care,' said Eunice. 'We got the go-ahead from the doctor and we've both been looking forward to it, in spite of what Ronald says.' She smiled. 'I know he grumbles – he doesn't realise he's doing it at times – but he's enjoying himself all the same. And I'm here to take care of him, aren't I? That's the least I can do; take care of him . . . After all he did for me,' she added quietly. She had been talking half to herself as she uttered the last few words and she was aware of Jean looking at her questioningly. 'I mean – he's my husband, isn't he? In sickness and in health and all that. As a matter of fact,' she said confidingly, 'it was our Golden Wedding earlier this year. That's why we've come on this holiday. We both wanted to see Austria again. We had a lovely holiday there several years ago.'

'Oh, how nice,' said Jean. 'Congratulations! Have you let Galaxy know?' That was the name of the tour company. 'They usually have a bit of a celebration if it's someone's anniversary or birthday.'

'Oh no, dear. I don't want any fuss, and I'm quite sure Ronald wouldn't—'

'Come on, folks, let's be having you. All aboard, please.' They were interrupted by Mike ushering them into the coach; Gary was already in the driving seat.

'It's been nice talking to you, dear,' Eunice said to Jean, as Ronald rejoined her. He had been deep in conversation with Jack several yards away. 'We'll see you later, no doubt.'

They left Calais, heading east on the motorway that linked northern France with Belgium. Ronald soon dozed off – Eunice only hoped he would not snore – and she stared out of the window at the passing scene. It was an attractive tree-lined motorway, comparatively quiet compared with the M1 or M6, for instance, probably because motorway users had to pay tolls on the continent and many drivers preferred to find alternative routes. Coach drivers, however, usually had to choose the shortest distance between two points unless there was something of outstanding interest for which they must make a diversion.

Eunice was thinking of the unguarded remark she had made to Jean, about taking care of Ronald after all he had done for her. She knew what had prompted the remark. It was because they were approaching Germany. This afternoon they would be in the Rhine Valley. Yes, Ronald had done such a lot for her and he was still unaware of it. But she knew it was best to keep it that way. There had been many times when she had wanted to unburden herself, but she knew it had only been because she wished to get rid of the guilt she was still feeling. Hers was a secret known only to two other people, she mused. Ronald must never know about it.

It was incredible to think they were celebrating fifty years of marriage. They were so very happy together, she and Ronald. They had weathered the storms and were now quite a Darby and Joan sort of couple. It was only since his minor health scares that Ronald had become more niggly and, at times, dispirited, imagining that each little ache and pain was going to carry him off. Eunice had made up her mind a while ago that they must make the most of every year, every week, every day they spent together, living life to the full. Who could tell how much – or how little – time they had left?

She wasn't usually given to such introspection; she gazed out of the window again, trying to concentrate on the scenery instead of on her rambling and rather disturbing thoughts.

The motorway signs they were passing now listed very familiar places, not because Eunice had ever been there, but because they evoked such poignant memories. Everyone, over a certain age, had heard of Mons, Ypres, Armentières . . . How did that song go that the soldiers used to sing in the First World War?

Mademoiselle from Armentières
Never been kissed for forty years . . .

At least that was the polite version. Eunice didn't doubt that there was a bawdier one, but women in those days had not been allowed to hear such things. Times had certainly changed.

Here and there through the trees they caught a glimpse of war graves, hundreds of gleaming white crosses in serried rows, for the countryside they were passing through was where those bloody battles had been fought, where so many British Tommies – and German soldiers too – had perished in the trenches. Now it was a peaceful scene, with field after field of bright dandelions lifting their heads to the sun. But here and there by the roadside were clumps of blood-red poppies, a grim reminder of what had taken place there.

Mike pointed out to the passengers the fields that still contained tank traps – triangular concrete blocks like miniature pyramids – and he reminded them that they were travelling along what had once been the Siegfried line: a German line of demarcation, but to most people, Eunice included, a place where British soldiers threatened to 'hang out the washing'.

Now and again there was a brief view of tall poplar trees evenly spaced along a cart track with a red-tiled farmhouse in the distance, looking just like that familiar painting of *The Avenue at Middelharnis*. They stopped for mid-morning coffee at a Belgian motorway café, and the lunch stop, also, was on the Belgian side of the border.

They dined on vegetable soup and crusty bread. 'That's all we'll need, Ronald,' Eunice told him. 'We had quite a nice breakfast and it will be a good meal tonight, you'll see.' But Ronald insisted on finishing off with apple pie and cream and she didn't argue. She plied him with indigestion tablets, reminding him at the same time to take the rest of his medication.

It was a pleasant service area, where they sat in cosy little alcoves interspersed with potted palms and flowering plants. They seemed to take so much more care about their motorway cafés over here, Eunice observed, than they did in those huge impersonal places back home. The large windows overlooked a stretch of grass with attractive flowerbeds and there was a children's playground with brightly coloured swings, slides and roundabouts – an agreeable place affording a short breathing space on the journey. But short it had to be as there were still many miles to be covered before they reached their destination. Gary had told them they should be in Rüdesheim, the popular resort on the banks of the Rhine, by five o'clock. That would be after they had taken their short trip on a Rhine pleasure boat.

Soon after the lunch stop they crossed the German border and by early afternoon they were approaching the Rhine. Ahead of them loomed the twin spires of the huge Gothic cathedral of Cologne, but they by-passed it as they took the road towards Bonn.

'The birthplace of Beethoven,' Mike reminded them, putting on a tape of Beethoven's Fifth Symphony to add to the atmosphere. The views needed no commentary to enhance their beauty as they drove past riverside towns and villages – Königswinter, Bad Godesberg, Oberwinter – with houses painted in pastel shades of pink and cream. Above them loomed turreted castles, and vineyards swept down the hillsides to the river. The Rhine was the lifeline of this area, the broad silver-grey ribbon of river with parallel roads and twin-track railways running alongside either bank.

Ronald was wide awake now, viewing the scenery along with Eunice. She was glad he was not sleeping through it all, but she was relieved that he was not an inveterate chatterer because she wanted to be alone with her thoughts. They were approaching Remagen now, famous for the capture of the bridgehead by the Americans at the end of the war . . . but it was significant to Eunice for another reason. Heinrich's home had been there . . .

Chapter 2

1941

'Mother . . . I've decided to join the Land Army.'

Eunice had been trying for ages to pluck up courage to break the news to her parents. Edith and Samuel Morton were both there at the breakfast table, but, as always, it was her mother to whom she addressed the remark. The response she received was predictable. Her father scarcely glanced up from his tea and toast and did not bother to comment, but she knew he had heard her. He was shaking his head and frowning and she could hear a faint sigh of irritation escaping from his lips. It was her mother who spoke – for them both, Eunice guessed – as was usually the case.

'The Land Army? Whatever has put that crazy idea into your head? You don't know one end of a cow from the other! You're a town girl, Eunice. You haven't a clue about what goes on on a farm.'

'Then I'll have to learn, won't I? It's no use, Mother; I must do something for the war effort. I feel as though I'm wasting my time, stamping library books. It seems so . . . so trivial, such a waste of time when girls of my age are joining the forces or working in the aircraft factory.'

'You're only just eighteen, Eunice, and you're perfectly all right where you are. And it was what you insisted on doing when you left school. Surely I don't need to remind you of that. You refused to work here with me.'

'That was two years ago, Mum. It's different now.' Eunice was doing her best to speak calmly and not to raise her voice, or her mother would accuse her of being cheeky. 'Don't use that tone of voice to me, young lady!' was a favourite retort of Edith Morton, and Eunice knew she had to try to get on the right side of her now. 'You know how people were saying the war would be over in a few months? Well, it wasn't, was it? It's getting worse and I want to do my bit . . . And I didn't think you'd want me to join the ATS or the WAAFs,' she added, feeling she might score a point there. Her mother had even refused to have RAF recruits billeted in their small Blackpool boarding house, fearing that her daughter might be led astray. Instead, she had opted for Civil Service women from the Ministry of Pensions, the offices of which had been moved from London to Blackpool.

'I should think not, indeed!' replied Edith, bristling a little. 'The army or the airforce is no place for a young girl – or for women at all, in my opinion. It's a man's job, fighting for his King and country.'

'But they're calling the women up as well now; you know they are. Chrissie Iveson has joined the WAAFs, hasn't she?'

'She's older than you, Eunice; she's twenty-two. Listen, love . . .' The endearment sounded a little forced and was not one that Edith often used. 'Why don't you wait until you have to go? They won't call you up till you're twenty; women between twenty and thirty-one; that's what they're saying at the moment. And by the time you're twenty it might all be over.'

'And I'll have missed it,' cried Eunice. 'Oh, please, Mum! I do want to go. I want to feel I'm being some use.'

'You want to get away from home, you mean,' said Edith, giving her daughter a meaningful look.

'No – of course I don't,' Eunice protested, but she knew her mother had hit the nail right on the head.

'It might not be such a bad idea, Edith.' Eunice was surprised to hear her father speak. Samuel Morton was a man of few words. He usually left the talking to his wife – something she was very good at – but when he did speak his comments were generally terse and to the point, if sometimes tinged with bitterness. 'She won't come to much harm in the country. It's not like being in the blooming trenches in the last lot.'

Eunice knew that that was something he had never forgotten. He fell silent having given his point of view. His wife and daughter waited to see if any more words of wisdom were forthcoming, but it seemed they were not.

'Thanks, Dad,' Eunice said.

Very rarely did she have a conversation with him, any talking to him usually being done through her mother. She even found it difficult to address him as Dad or Father. It was not that she was afraid of him, not exactly, but never, since she was a little girl, had he made any attempt to build up a friendly relationship with her.

Her mother gave him an ominous glance and sniffed loudly. 'We'll see. I'm not saying she can go. Come along now, Eunice, get these pots cleared away before you go to work. And I'll go and see if their ladyships have finished.' She gave another audible sniff and swept out of the room.

The family, which consisted of just three of them – Eunice, to her great regret, was an only child – dined in their small living room at the rear of the house. The larger front room was given over to guests: in peacetime, holiday-makers, but now to the Civil Service women from London. There were eight of them and they occupied the four largest front-facing bedrooms. Eunice had a smaller room at the back, and her parents, also in an inferior back bedroom, were next door to her.

She sometimes wondered why her parents had bothered to get married at all. The bedroom walls were thin, but she very rarely heard the two of them conversing, or doing anything else, for that matter! It was hard to believe they ever had, and she had even wondered, after she became old enough to think about such things, whether she might have been adopted. But no; people said she was the image of her mother, with the same dark curly hair and blue eyes. And when she looked at herself in the mirror, her face in repose, she could see a certain likeness to her father too, in the set of her mouth and the angle of her cheekbones. She was their daughter all right, but she hoped she had not inherited the nature of either of them.

She watched her father now as she cleared the table and carried the pots into the kitchen, in preparation for washing up. This was the job she did every morning before setting off for work. Her father made no attempt to help her – in fact, she had never seen him lift a finger to help her mother at all, and Edith Morton seemed to accept that this was the way it should be, that she was there to see to the needs of her husband. His slippers were always ready for him on the hearth and a hot meal awaiting him on the table the minute he came home from work. He put on his raincoat now and his trilby hat, even though it was the middle of June, and, with the merest grunt of 'Ta-ra, then,' in his daughter's direction, he went out of the door. She did not hear him say goodbye to his wife, who would be clearing away the breakfast pots of the women from the Ministry of Pensions.

Eunice knew that, of the two of them, her mother had by far the harder job. Her father worked at the local Water Board office in what, she guessed, was a very menial position. She had heard her mother refer to him, somewhat disparagingly, as 'only a penpusher'. This was to her friend Mabel Iveson, and she had not known that Eunice had overheard. To her daughter she always spoke of him as 'the breadwinner', and pretended that he was also 'the boss', but Eunice knew that this was not the case. Although their North Shore boarding house was small, consisting of six bedrooms and a couple of small attic rooms, it was quite enough for one woman to look after single-handedly, and this was what her mother managed to do most of the time. Only occasionally, when they were extra busy, did she employ casual labour – a woman cleaner, for instance – to help out. Even now, although there was a war on, she took the occasional visitors. People were being encouraged by the Government to spend their holidays at home, but there were always some who managed a few days away at the seaside. And Blackpool, way up in the north of England and away from the threat of invasion, was one of the few towns whose beaches were not covered in barbed wire or booby traps.

When the house was full, Eunice and her parents would occupy the tiny attic rooms. From there, if you stood on tiptoe, you could just about see the sea, although the boarding house was ten minutes' walk away from the promenade. It was an ideal place to stay for those who could not afford very much, but who wanted a place that was clean and comfortable, and where good wholesome food was put on the table. In peacetime the same families had come year after year and, in the main, it was these people, though only a few of them, of course, who were coming now, in nearly the third year of the war. Edith had room for only a couple at a time as the billeting of either RAF recruits or Civil Service personnel was obligatory.

Only last week there had been a couple from Burnley, whose son was now in the RAF and daughter in the WAAFs, and the parents, feeling lonely, had decided to have a few days' holiday. They had remembered Eunice as a little girl and had remarked on how grown up she was now. This was something visitors always did, expecting, somehow, that you would stay the same for ever, in a time warp. Eunice had smiled, graciously, she hoped – her mother would tell her off if she was offhand with people – and had enquired about Billy and Mavis, the son and daughter who were now in the forces. She had remembered them, both a few years older than herself, with their buckets and spades and little round sunhats; they had been with their parents several times.

That had been in the late twenties or early thirties, of course, when her Grandma Gregson had been alive. The boarding house had belonged to her, and Edith, her only daughter, who had always worked for her mother, had inherited it upon the old lady's death five years ago. Not that she had been so very old when she died – only in her late sixties – but she had seemed old to Eunice. She had very happy memories of Grandma Gregson, a real old-style seaside landlady of the type caricatured on comic postcards: buxom and red-faced, with beefy arms, and iron-grey hair in a bun, she had habitually worn a voluminous crossover apron in a vivid floral pattern of blue and orange, edged with orange bias binding. The sight of her unsmiling countenance facing you on the doorstep might easily have intimidated many a visitor, but they all found that beneath her grim exterior there was what they often termed 'a heart of gold'.

All they wanted from a holiday was good plain food of the kind they were used to at home and a clean comfy bed to sleep in. Mrs Gregson had provided both of those requirements, but without any of the frills or niceties – starched serviettes, for instance, or a waitress in a frilly white apron and cap – that you might expect in one of the posher private hotels. Gertie Gregson – 'our Gertie' as she was often referred to, quite warmly, by the visitors, behind her back, of course – did not hold with all that sort of nonsense, or 'aping your betters' as she called it. She knew her place in the world; she was an unashamedly working-class woman who had been widowed early in life and had scrimped and saved to start the boarding house – or lodging house, as they were then called – in order to ensure that she and her only child did not starve.

In her establishment the food was 'plated up' as she termed it – no fancy tureens or dishes as that only made extra washing up – and placed in front of each visitor by herself or her daughter, dressed in their habitual spotlessly clean working clothes. If there was anyone who did not like cabbage or mashed turnips, for instance – and some children were dreadfully spoiled, in Gertie's opinion – then it was just too bad; they would have to leave it at the side of their plate and go without veg. There was no time to cater for individual fads and fancies.

Eunice remembered her grandmother telling her, however, that in what she called 'the bad old days', the landlady was expected to deal with all the visitors' individual requirements. In Blackpool, as in other seaside resorts in the early years of the twentieth century, the lodging houses had operated what was known as the apartments system. The visitors brought in their own food for the landlady to cook, and she would provide such things as bread, milk and potatoes, and hot water for tea, at a small extra charge.

Some landladies, Gertie included, had provided a pudding as well for those who wanted it, to round off the midday dinner. In addition to this, boots and shoes might be cleaned if required, although Gertie had drawn the line at washing visitors' clothes. But neither did she charge for the use of the cruet as some penny-pinching landladies did.

The apartments system had continued in Blackpool until the early 1930s, when the lodging houses had gradually given way to the boarding houses. In these establishments all meals were provided by the landlady at a fixed rate and to a fixed menu. This usually consisted of three meals a day: a cooked breakfast, a midday meal, always known in the north of England as dinner, and what was termed a 'high tea'. This was what the occasional visitors were still given now, in the boarding house run by Edith Morton, although the Civil Service ladies had a midday snack elsewhere and only required an evening meal.

Looking back, Eunice knew that her mother had changed since her own mother's death. Until then Edith – although she had always been a forceful character with a great deal to say for herself – had seemed almost cowed by the even greater dominance of Gertie. Eunice had attached little importance to them at the time, but as she walked to work on this pleasant June morning, she found herself remembering certain incidents.

Her mother had always been a good-looking young woman, but never had Edith worn a trace of make-up. Her face had always had that shiny, well-scrubbed look, and her glossy dark hair had always been coiled in a not very attractive roll around her head. After Grandma Gertie had died Eunice became aware of a change in her mother. She looked much nicer; very pretty, in fact. What had happened to her? Eunice realised that her mother was wearing lipstick, a bright red shade, although she had applied only the merest touch, and her usually shining cheeks had an unfamiliar pink powdery look. Her hair too was brushed loose and it curled in natural waves around her face and neck. Eunice had not commented; she had never been encouraged to make personal remarks. She realised now, however, that Grandma Gregson must have disapproved of make-up, that she may even have forbidden Edith, married woman though she was, to use it. Yes, Eunice had come to the conclusion that her mother may well have been afraid of Grandma Gertie.

She wondered now if that was why her mother tried to rule her with a rod of iron – to get her own back, as it were, for the way she had been treated when she was growing up. That didn't make sense to Eunice, though. She had already made up her own mind that if she ever had a daughter she would be tolerant and understanding towards her, and treat her more as a friend than as a child who had to be continually disciplined. Her mother did have her gentler side, of course, which manifested itself from time to time, and Eunice had never been in any doubt that her mother really loved her, but she had an odd way of showing it at times. There was no doubt that Edith's strict upbringing had had a lasting effect upon her, making it difficult to break out completely from the mould into which she had been forced.

Was it possible that she had not wanted to be a seaside landlady at all? Eunice did not know for sure. What she did know was that ever since her mother had left school at the age of fourteen – that would be around 1907, Eunice calculated – she had worked for her mother for a pitifully low wage. This was what Eunice had gathered from remarks her mother had made, such as, 'You young girls today don't know you're born; five shillings a week to spend on yourself!' Eunice gave the whole of her weekly wage from the library to her mother, as was the norm in most households, and this was the amount she was given back for her spending money. She had to admit she was reasonably satisfied as she was getting her 'bed and keep', as they called it.

'Yes, I worked for a pittance,' her mother had often told her. 'In fact, I didn't get any wages at all until I was twenty-one. Until then your gran used to give me a couple of bob a week to spend. And if I moaned about it I'd get a clip round the ear. You don't know how lucky you are, Eunice, and that's a fact.'

Eunice had no doubt that every word of it was true: that for her measly two shillings a week her mother had been chambermaid, scullery maid and waitress all rolled into one. Besides, she had seen for herself the way Grandma Gregson had treated her daughter. Edith must have been in her mid-forties when her mother had died, but she had still been regarded as a young girl who had to do as she was told.

The thing that had always puzzled Eunice was why her grandmother had always been so kind and loving towards her. She knew she had been indulged by her gran in a way her mother before her had certainly not been. She remembered, for instance, being given pennies to buy a Snow-Fruit from the ice-cream man, pedalling by on his 'Stop Me and Buy One' tricycle; or helping Gran in the kitchen, making her own little currant pasties out of scraps of pastry; or cuddling up on Gran's capacious lap by the fireside, listening to favourite rhymes from her Mother Goose book. Her mother had read to her as well, of course – never her father, though – but it was Grandma Gregson's soothing presence that Eunice remembered above all.

'You spoil the child, Mother,' she had sometimes heard

her own mother remark. 'It will only make it worse for me if you give her everything she wants. And one thing I can't abide is a spoiled little girl.'

Eunice had known only too well what she meant. When her mother took her to the open-air market in town, if they noticed a badly behaved child screaming by the sweet stall until she got what she wanted, Edith would always remark, not caring who heard her, 'She's short of a good smacked bottom! Don't you ever dare behave like that, Eunice!' And Eunice never did.

'Oh, leave her alone,' Grandma would say, whenever her mother suggested she was being spoiled. 'She's my little pal, aren't you, Eunice? And she's as good as gold. Anyroad, it's a pity if I can't indulge my only grandchild, isn't it? It doesn't look as though I'm going to have any more.' Yes, Eunice and her grandmother had been good pals and she had been heartbroken for a long while when the old lady died.

She had left school three years later at the age of sixteen, after gaining quite a reasonable pass in her School Certificate exam. There had been no question of her staying on in the sixth form as a few of her friends were doing. One of her friends, a girl called Mavis, whom she had known ever since their junior school days, intended to go to college when she was eighteen and train to be a teacher. 'It's what me mum wants me to do really,' she told Eunice, 'and I don't mind. Mum wants me to have the chance she never had, y'see. She always wanted to be a teacher, but her parents couldn't afford to let her stay on at school. She left when she was about thirteen, and went to work in a shop. Why don't you go into the sixth as well, Eunice? I've heard it's quite good fun; better than ordinary school, anyway. And then perhaps we could go to the same college?'

But Eunice had no desire to be a teacher. Neither, she suspected, had Mavis. She was just doing what her mother wanted her to do. At least Mrs Foxton – Mavis's mother – had ambitions for her daughter, Eunice pondered, unlike her own mother. Edith Morton's idea was that Eunice should leave school and work in the boarding house, as she herself had been forced to do. But Eunice had other ideas. She did not mind leaving school – she was sick and tired of the place and the continual rules and regulations – but she wanted to go and work in the library. For once, she decided she must stand up to her mother.

'But I've got my School Certificate,' she argued. 'I can get a good job with that. Aren't you pleased I've passed my exam?'

'Of course I'm pleased, and your daddy is as well,' said her mother. She always referred to him as 'daddy', although Eunice never did. 'You've done very well, dear,' she added, a trifle grudgingly, 'but you know I've always wanted you to come and work here. It's a family business, and that was the idea.'

'Your idea, not mine,' said Eunice bravely.

'Don't be insolent, Eunice,' her mother snapped. 'I would never have dared to speak to my mother like that. Yes, I know you've got your School Certificate, so it proves you must be good at sums. So you can get your brain working on the boarding house accounts: the bills and all that sort of thing. I've never been any good with figures and money, and your daddy leaves it all to me, of course, like he does with everything. So that can be one of your jobs, if you're so keen on using this precious education you've got.'

Eunice was not very good at 'sums' either. She had managed to scrape through with a pass in her Mathematics paper, but the subject did not interest her. However, from what she could see, the boarding house accounts would be as easy as winking. The visitors paid cash at the end of the week and were given a receipt, so what was difficult about that? Then there was the gas and electricity and coal bills, and the grocery account to settle. Eunice was surprised her mother had even admitted that she found it a problem. Very rarely did Edith Morton confess to a failing in anything.

'Yes, all right, Mum, I don't mind doing that for you,' she agreed, and was gratified to see her mother's stern features relax a little. Now was her chance. 'I'll do the accounts for you, handling the money and giving the receipts and all that, if you can trust me.'

'Well, of course I can trust you, dear.' Her mother looked almost mollified.

'But that's as far as it goes. I'm not going to be an unpaid dogsbody like you were for me gran . . . Just listen a minute, Mum,' she added as Edith opened her mouth to protest. 'I don't want to spend all me life cooking and cleaning and washing pots. All right – I don't mind helping out a bit when you're busy, and serving at the tables, like I do now.' She had been pulling her weight, and more, considering she had also been studying for exams, ever since her gran had died three years previously. 'But I want to go out to work as well, like other girls do. I want to work in the library. You know I've always loved books.'

'Oh, you and your books!' Her mother's tone was a little disparaging, but not quite so much as it might have been. Often Eunice had been at the receiving end of her mother's sharp tongue for reading when she was supposed to be helping with some job or other. Her mother seemed to regard reading books as a waste of time; there were lots of other far more important things to do. She didn't understand how engrossed Eunice became in the lives of these fictional characters. To her, they became real and she found it hard to put a book down, especially at an exciting point in the story. But she thought her mother might actually be starting to listen now and to weigh up the pros and cons of her getting a job at the library. She seized her opportunity and pressed on.

'If I get a job – and earn some money,' she emphasised, 'then you could afford to pay somebody, couldn't you, to do some work for you?' She guessed her mother could afford it already if she wanted to, but she was inclined to be tight-fisted, like many northerners of her generation who could remember a time when they had 'not known where the next meal was coming from'. Her mother was frowning thoughtfully and pursing her lips. 'It makes sense, doesn't it, Mum?' she persisted.

'Yes, I suppose it does. We will have to see what your daddy thinks about it.' Eunice knew that 'Daddy' would think what he was told to think. The main thing was that her mother was relenting.

The upshot of it was that she had left school in the summer of 1939 and had gone to work in the lending library of Boots the Chemists on Bank Hey Street. It was the only time she remembered winning a battle with her mother. There had not been any vacancies at the Municipal Library, and so Eunice had been happy to work at Boots until such time as she could move to the 'proper' library. Then, in September, the war had started, and suddenly everyone had other, far more important, things on their minds. Were they all going to be bombed to bits in the opening days of the war? That was what many had anticipated; why else had they all been issued with gas masks?

But for several months it was very quiet: the phoney war – or the 'bore war', as they were calling it. Except that in

Blackpool there was a huge influx of RAF recruits filling the hotels and boarding houses. Edith Morton had other things to worry about as well as the fact that her daughter seemed, somehow, to have scored a point over her.

Eunice settled down at Boots' library and was very happy there. So much so that after a while she forgot all about applying for a post in the Municipal Library. But now, in the summer of 1941, she knew it was time she 'did her bit for her King and country'.

Chapter 3

oots, situated near the Town Hall and Talbot Square, was very pleasant store in which to work, both for the sales ssistants and the librarians. Although it was officially a hemist's shop, in reality the articles that could be bought nere were many and varied. As well as medicines and cures or all kinds of ailments there were make-up and toiletries, ancy goods and pictures, costume jewellery, toys and ames, kitchen utensils and gardening requisites.

Ever since she had started to work there Eunice had oved breathing in the aroma – a mixture of cough linctus, erfume, powder and scented soap – that pervaded the air. At first she had delighted in wandering around the well-tocked make-up and perfume counters, occasionally reating herself to a new lipstick, or a tiny blue bottle of Mischief scent. Now, however, those days had gone. Boots id its best, but there, as everywhere, there were restric-ions and shortages. Queues would form when word got ound that there had been an allocation of lipsticks or ace powder, or even such ordinary items as kirby-grips or favourite shampoo.

The lending library was at the rear of the shop and was

manned by Eunice, and Gwen, who was the same age as Eunice, and Olga, who was in her thirties and was in charge. The shelves were filled with a wide variety of fiction, ranging from crime to romance and historical novels, as well as the more serious classics and biographical works. It was mainly busy housewives or young women who frequented the library, so there was a preponderance of light romantic stories in gaily backed covers, it being assumed that this would be their choice of reading matter. It hardly seemed like work at all to Eunice, being surrounded by the things she loved so much: books, books and more books. And Gwen, who over the couple of years they had worked together had become her best friend as well as her colleague, shared her enthusiasm. If she were honest, Eunice knew she would be loath to leave the nice cosy environment, but what she had said to her mother was also true. She felt it was a waste of time stamping books and losing herself in a fictional world when many girls of her age were doing war work. Besides, she must not miss this opportunity to get away from home.

'Well, I've been and gone and done it,' she said to Gwen, when there was a lull in their activities in the middle of the morning. 'I've told them I'm going to join the Land Army.'

'Gosh! Have you? I thought you were never going to pluck up courage.' Gwen's brown eyes, which always reminded Eunice of aniseed balls, but with much more depth and warmth, shone with interest. 'Good for you. What did they say?'

'What you might expect,' replied Eunice. "We'll see about that" and, "You only want to get away from home." That's what my mother said. If only she knew how true that was! It'll be heaven to get away for a while, absolute heaven.'

'And I suppose your dad said nothing?'

'Funnily enough, he did,' said Eunice. 'He said it might not be such a bad idea. Honestly, you could have knocked me down with a feather. And, what's more, I think Mum will have to agree with him. Then she'll no doubt pretend it was her idea in the first place to let me go. Let me go, indeed! I don't think they could stop me if they tried – I am eighteen.'

'So am I – well, nearly,' said Gwen. She would be eighteen in August. 'You are lucky, Eunice. I wish I could go. I'd join the Land Army an' all if I could; then we could go together. But I know it's impossible. I can't leave Mum.'

'No, of course you can't,' said Eunice, smiling sympathetically. 'Never mind – there's one consolation. She's not such an old tartar as my ma, is she? You're not dying to leave home, like I am.'

'Honestly, Eunice – you're dreadful,' said Gwen, giggling a little. 'Your mum's not all that bad. She's always very nice with me.'

'That's because she likes you,' said Eunice. 'She thinks you're a nice girl – which you are, of course – just the right sort of friend for me. A good influence an' all that.'

'Oh . . . does she?' said Gwen, although she had heard Eunice say the same sort of thing before. 'We don't get much chance to be anything other than good, do we, either of us? I always have to get home to see Mum – not that I mind, of course – and your parents don't like you to be out late, do they?'

'No, not unless I'm with Ronnie,' Eunice sniggered. 'They think I'm safe with him, you see.'

'And . . . aren't you?'

'Of course I am,' she grinned. 'Ronnie's just a friend.'

Ronnie was the son of Mabel and Tom Iveson, who owned the grocery store round the corner from the boarding house. The couple were friends of her mother and father, although Eunice could not understand why: Mabel and Tom were a much jollier couple by far. The only thing they had in common, as far as she could see, was that they all attended the same church; Tom Iveson and her father were both sidesmen there. She knew her mother would have no objection – might welcome the prospect, in fact – if Ronnie were her steady boyfriend. But as far as Ronnie and Eunice were concerned there was no chance of that, no chance at all. She had known him ever since he was a small boy and with their parents being friends they were really more like brother and sister. They went out together sometimes, but only as friends. And if both their mothers wished it might be otherwise, well, Eunice thought that was a very funny idea, and so, she guessed, did Ronnie.

'He's down in the south of England, somewhere,' she said now. Preparing for the anticipated invasion of our shores by the enemy, she thought – only nobody dared to voice the words out loud.

'You write to him, though, don't you?'

'Yes, now and again. It's the RAF lads my mother's worried about, not Ronnie Iveson. She says she wouldn't trust any of "them Brylcreem boys" as far as she could throw them. I can't see why; they seem like very nice lads to me, most of 'em. She saw me talking to one of them the other day, that's billeted near us, and quick as a flash she was on the doorstep, shouting for me to come in. Honest, I was that embarrassed.'

Edith Morton had refused to have any of the RAF recruits billeted at her boarding house, but she could not stop her daughter coming into contact with them. The boys in airforce blue were all over the place in Blackpool; walking in pairs or small groups through the town, thronging the ballrooms and picture houses, drilling and doing manoeuvres on the promenade and sands. Eunice, and

Gwen too, had met several of them and danced with them at the Palace or Winter Gardens Ballroom, but that was as far as it had gone. Eunice would not have dared to let one of them walk her home or her mother would accuse her of 'making herself cheap'. She was supposed to be in by ten o'clock, although, since she had recently turned eighteen, a big concession might now be made to extend the deadline to ten thirty.

Gwen also had to be in by ten, as her mother was an invalid and needed more or less constant care. One blessing, however, was that her illness had not made her querulous and difficult as it might have done. She encouraged her only daughter to go out at least once a week, when a neighbour would come and sit with her. But Gwen was always anxious to get home by ten. The mother and daughter were devoted to one another, particularly as Gwen's father had died when she was only five years old.

Eunice had never really discovered just what was wrong with Mrs Singleton. Tuberculosis, she guessed; TB as it was always referred to. She was a gentle little person, and Gwen, small and delicately boned with baby-fine hair, was the image of her mother. But Gwen was quite tough, with a wiry strength beneath her seemingly fragile stature, whereas Ivy Singleton appeared to be growing more skeletal each time Eunice saw her. She was not confined to bed, although she rested for a large part of each day. She was able to slip out to the local shops, mainly to get a dose of fresh air, but the short journey was as much as she could manage without overtiring herself. Otherwise Gwen, with the help of willing neighbours, did the shopping and made sure there was always someone near to see to her mother's needs. Eunice had gathered they were not badly off, however, which was one consolation. Mrs Singleton paid a woman to clean their house in

Layton, and Gwen always seemed to be acquiring new clothes; at least she had done so until the wartime restrictions had begun to take effect.

Eunice was sorry for her friend. They never discussed just how poorly her mother was, or whether, in fact, she was ever likely to get better. Eunice doubted that she would, but Gwen usually appeared cheerful and optimistic. This, at times, made Eunice feel guilty at her own resentment and the way she grumbled at her home situation. They were both in the same boat, lacking the unlimited freedom to please themselves, but for different reasons. Eunice realised that her friend's predicament was far worse than her own. She might soon have the chance to break free from the restrictions she moaned about, whereas for Gwen there was no escape. Not unless 'something happened' to her mother, and that was too dreadful to contemplate.

Gwen's next remark surprised her. 'I know I can't leave home,' she said, 'and nor do I want to, not really. Well, it's something I never think about because I know it's no use. But there's no reason why I should stay here at Boots, is there? Actually, I'm thinking of applying to work at the aircraft factory.'

'At Squire's Gate?' asked Eunice. 'It's a long way, although I think there's a bus that goes there from where you live.'

'No, I'm hoping they'd take me at the bus station site,' replied Gwen. 'It would be a lot nearer.'

Vickers Armstrong had opened an aircraft assembly plant for the manufacture of Wellington bombers at Squire's Gate, on the airport site at the southern end of the town. But there was also a sub-factory on the upper floors of Talbot Road bus station, which had been camouflaged with black paint and now employed hundreds of men and women workers at the north end of the town.

'Good for you,' said Eunice. 'I think that's a great idea. What does your mum say? Have you told her?'

'Yes, I've mentioned it, and she's all for it. She's so unselfish, you know, Eunice. She makes me feel really guilty at times.'

'Me too,' said Eunice. Her friend was echoing the very thoughts that had just been passing through her mind. 'But what have you to feel guilty about, for goodness' sake? Nothing, as far as I can see. You're always there for your mum, aren't you?'

'Oh, I don't know . . . It gets me down at times; then I have a bit of a moan and a weep to myself. Anyway, I said to Mum that I might have to do a night shift now and then at the factory, and she said not to worry about it. Our neighbours are very good, and I think she feels she'll be doing her bit through me, even though she can't do anything definite herself. She can't take any of those Ministry of Pension people, like your mother's doing, although we've got room for some.'

'My mother had no choice, had she?' said Eunice. 'Not with all those bedrooms going spare. I'm hoping Mum won't kick up too much fuss about the Land Army. I shall go whether or not, but I'd rather she was agreeable about it.'

To her surprise her mother appeared to have changed her mind completely by the time Eunice got home that evening.

'Your daddy and I have been having a talk,' she said, 'and we've decided we'll let you join the Land Army – that is, if you still want to.'

'Of course I want to,' said Eunice. 'Thanks, Mum. Thanks . . . Dad.' She glanced across at her father, already ensconced in his fireside chair, waiting for his meal to appear on the table.

He nodded briefly at her. 'That's right,' he mumbled, returning to his evening paper.

Eunice doubted that her parents had discussed the matter at all; her father would have returned from work not all that long ago so there would hardly have been time. Still, there were to be no more arguments and objections, and for that Eunice was thankful.

She wasted no time in posting off her application to join the Women's Land Army – the WLA – and was very soon called for an interview at the town hall. This was merely a formality as they were only too willing to take healthy and eager young women such as Eunice. She was told that she would receive instructions about her training in due course, and that her uniform would be sent by post to her home address. She could hardly wait, rushing home at the end of each day to see if the parcel post had been. And then, one day in August, there it was in a huge brown paper parcel. In spite of her impatience she knew she must open the parcel carefully; brown paper and string were precious commodities in these wartime days, to be stored away and reused.

She drew out a pair of fawn corduroy breeches, two matching shirts, two pairs of thick woollen socks, one pair of shoes, one pair of very stiff boots, a pair of dungarees, a green jumper and a green tie striped with red and bearing the letters WLA in yellow. To complete the outfit there was a green felt armband with WLA embroidered in red and surmounted by a crown.

She couldn't wait to try it on although she knew she would have to curb her impatience until she had eaten the nourishing stew that her mother had cooked for their tea. She realised that one thing she would miss would be her mother's cooking. Edith always managed to eke out the rations and had become quite an expert at concocting economical but tasty dishes with the aid of the recipes brought out by the Ministry of Food. She listened eagerly to the five-minute programme *Kitchen Front*, which was broadcast each morning after the eight o'clock news. No, it was not all bad, living at home.

Eunice had seen the idealistic recruitment posters of land girls with rosy cheeks and dazzling smiles, carrying a sheaf of corn or holding a fluffy lamb in their arms. As she looked at herself now in her full-length wardrobe mirror she realised that the image that looked back at her might well have been one of those girls, but without the props. She knew she was good-looking, with her dark curly hair and bright blue eyes, and the uniform, though it had not been designed with the intention of flattering the female form, did, in fact, do that very thing. Women, as a rule, did not wear trousers, not even in the female branches of the armed forces, and these knee breeches appeared novel and quite arresting, showing off her slim waist and the curve of her hips to the best advantage. The green sweater was tightly fitting and accentuated her generous bust. Eunice, turning sideways to the mirror, was not displeased with what she saw. She wondered if she should have been sent the next size, but she smiled at her reflection and decided it would do very well.

She had the good sense to realise, however, that the uniform would not stay in pristine condition for very long. A great deal of hard and dirty work lay ahead for her, but she was not afraid of that. She sat on the bed and thumbed through the *Land Army Manual*, a booklet that had been included in the parcel. 'Farming work', it read, 'means hard physical strain, but any girl who endures it finds compensation in the knowledge that she is playing a very important part in National Service.'

There was a great deal more, written in somewhat

dictatorial prose, which warned the 'town girl' against adopting a superior attitude to country folk, regarding them as backwoodsmen or country bumpkins. Town girls were advised to tone down their make-up and nail varnish and not to appear at local dances in 'Bond Street' creations. Honestly! As if we could afford them, thought Eunice, or even get enough coupons for such things. It was suggested that the aspiring land girl should practise strengthening exercises before she actually joined up: carrying buckets full of water for half an hour or more at a time, for instance, or attempting to pitch earth on to a barrow to see whether she could bear the aches and pains entailed. There were remedies for roughened and chapped hands – olive oil and beeswax warmed in the oven and then applied as a paste – and chilblains, and a list of essential items to be taken, in addition to the uniform. Two complete sets, at the very least, of underwear and nightwear; house slippers; 'walking out' shoes; one or two frocks, for changing into in the evening; a woolly scarf and gloves; a bicycle – if you possess one; and toilet requisites.

It was all very fussy and bossy, Eunice thought, as though they were treating the new recruits like children. All the same, she began to feel a stirring of excitement at the thought of setting off on her journey in two weeks' time. She was to travel by train to Gloucester, and from there she would be driven, with a lot of other girls no doubt, to their training hostel in the Midlands.

'Hmm . . . that jumper's far too tight,' said her mother, when Eunice displayed her uniform to her parents. Her father, as usual, said nothing, but he nodded grimly; disapprovingly, she thought, as though he were agreeing with her mother. 'You'll have to ask for a bigger size. You can't go around showing all you've got, not in front of all them farm hands.'

'They'll have been called up, Mother,' said Eunice, 'all except the farmers. That's why they're employing land girls, because they're short of farm hands.'

'You always have to have the last word, don't you?' sighed Edith. 'Apart from that – that jumper – you look . . . very nice.'

Eunice was surprised to see her mother's lips curve into the semblance of a smile, and could that possibly be a tear glinting in the corner of her eye? She felt touched and so she answered quite calmly. 'Yes, I know it's a bit tight, Mum, but it's quite comfy. Perhaps it's meant to be like that – close-fitting, you know. Anyway, I can't very well start arguing about the uniform as soon as I get there, can I? Here – have a look at this.' She passed her mother the *Land Army Manual*. 'It's all the rules and regulations. They're going to make sure we behave ourselves, so you don't need to worry about me.'

'That's what I like to hear,' said Edith primly. 'I'll read it later . . . Come along now, Eunice. Get out of that uniform – you'll not be wanting that for another couple of weeks – then you can help me with the washing-up. Their ladyships seemed to have used a mountain of pots tonight. Mind you, I must be fair; they do take their turns at helping . . .'

Ever since she was a tiny girl, Iveson's Grocery Store had been one of Eunice's favourite places. It stood in the centre of a row of shops – including a chemist's, an ironmonger's, a greengrocer's, a fishmonger's and a draper's – just round the corner from their boarding house. She loved the pungent smell that assailed her nostrils as soon as she entered, that of cheese and bacon and coffee and freshly baked loaves. Ivesons did not bake their own bread, however, but had it delivered in the morning from a local bakery. She was fascinated by the large hams hanging from nails in the ceiling and the swish of the bacon slicer as it cut off the pink and white rashers. There were huge yellow slabs of cheese and butter, cut off as requested by the customers and wrapped in greaseproof paper; brown and white sugar, and tea in big barrels, scooped out and sold in paper bags of dark blue and brown; a row of biscuit boxes with glass tops along the front of the counter containing such favourites as custard creams, Nice – pronounced 'nees' – biscuits, chocolate fingers and shortbreads; and shelves and shelves of tinned and bottled goods – fruit, salmon, baked beans, pickles, jams and marmalades.

At least that had used to be the case until, in the early days of the war, rationing had come into force. Butter, sugar, tea, bacon, ham and cheese were now rationed and all other commodities were in very short supply. Nevertheless, Mabel and Tom Iveson managed to make a reasonable display in their shop window and on their shelves with such items as were available. Margarine was now being widely used instead of butter – although most housewives hated it – and there was a large stock of this piled in a pyramid shape in the window with a notice stating 'No Coupons Required'.

Every family was registered with a particular grocer and it was usually the job of the housewife, or the daughter of the house, to go each week to collect the rations, when the appropriate snippets of paper – the coupons – would be cut from the ration books. The Mortons, of course, were registered with their good friends the Ivesons. The order, sometimes, was quite a large one as the Civil Service women and any visitors who might be staying had also to produce their ration books, and if this was the case then Tom Iveson would deliver the goods in person, on his heavy black bicycle with the carrier on the front.

Until he had joined the army soon after the start of the

war, this had been the job of Ronald Iveson; since leaving school at fifteen he had worked alongside his parents in the family business. Eunice could not remember a time when she had not known Ronnie. They had been at the same infant and junior schools, although they had not had much to do with one another there as Ronnie was two years older than Eunice and was in a higher class. They had attended the same Sunday school too, at the church where their parents were members. Ronald, at eleven years of age, had gone on to the local secondary school, whereas Eunice, two years later, had passed the scholarship exam and gone to the Girls' Grammar School – something of a feather in her cap for Edith Morton and she had not been able to help herself boasting about it a little. Although, to give her her due, she had not gone on about it all that much to Mabel Iveson. Edith liked Ronald – as she always insisted on calling him – very much indeed. She considered him to be a respectful and well-mannered boy and she admired the way he had settled down to helping his parents in their business. 'Ronald's not got any fancy ideas, you see,' Eunice had been told. 'He knows where his loyalties lie.'

Ronnie was at home on a forty-eight-hour pass the weekend before Eunice was due to go to Gloucester, and she had agreed to go out with him on the Saturday night. She liked Ronnie very much indeed; there was nothing you could dislike about him and she enjoyed herself when she went out with him. Some girls she knew were already engaged to young men who were in the forces, but she had no thought, yet, of getting engaged to anyone. Ronnie was just the boy round the corner, and the few boys she had been out with, apart from him, were local lads she had known at church or, long ago, at Junior school. She hoped, one day, she might meet someone exciting and different. There had been precious little chance of that with her mother's eagle eye upon her all the time, but soon she would be far away from her mother's control.

One thought, however, had occurred to Eunice. If she were to marry Ronnie – however ridiculous the idea might be – she could not foresee any problems with her in-laws. She was very fond of Mabel and Tom Iveson and she knew they felt the same about her. One of her earliest memories was of Tom giving her a little bag of floral gums – tiny scented sweets in jewel-bright colours of red, purple, yellow, orange and green – every time she went in the shop. Tom was tall and thin with sparse ginger hair, whereas Mabel was short and plump with bubbly blonde curls and smiling grey eyes. They reminded Eunice of Jack Sprat and his wife in the nursery rhyme, and they were both jolly and friendly and comfortable to be with. Their friendship with her parents had long been a mystery to her, but it was said that opposites attracted one another.

Eunice was proud of her new land girl uniform. She would have liked to show it off to Mabel and Tom – and Ronnie, of course – but she didn't see how she could do so. The weather was warm and she would feel a fool walking along the street in thick corduroy trousers and a woolly jumper; it would be a different matter if this was the country and not the town. But she knew the real reason was because her mother would accuse her of flaunting herself. She did not think Mabel would remark on her figure-hugging jumper and neither, she guessed, would Ronnie. However, on the Saturday evening she put on a floral summery dress and a short jacket and walked the hundred yards or so round the corner to meet Ronnie. The Ivesons did not live over the shop, but in a smallish three-bedroomed house a few minutes' walk from it.

It would have been more usual, she knew, for Ronnie to have called for her, but she always took the opportunity to pop round to see Mabel and Tom Iveson – Aunty Mabel and Uncle Tom, as she had been encouraged to call them. She chatted with them for a few moments, while Ronnie was still upstairs 'getting himself all spruced up', as his mother put it. She found them far more interested in her Land Army venture than her own parents were. She remarked on the fact, though trying at the same time not to criticise them.

'I don't talk about it all that much to Mum and Dad,' she said, 'because they go all quiet. I don't suppose they want me to go really. In fact, I was surprised they didn't kick up more of a fuss, especially my father, you know what he's like about the war. But funnily enough it was Dad who said it might not be a bad idea, then Mum had to agree, I suppose.'

'They know they've no choice, Eunice,' remarked Mabel. 'You might be called up soon anyway, and the Land Army's the least of all the evils, as far as they're concerned. I dare say they're quiet because they don't want to admit that it's actually happening and that you'll be leaving them. You're very precious to them, you know, love, and they don't want to let you go. I know your mother's rather strict with you at times, but she thinks the world of you, and so does your father.'

Then they've got a strange way of showing it, thought Eunice, but all she said was, 'Yes, I suppose I know that really.'

'I've known your mother a long time,' Mabel went on, 'ever since we were girls. Then when Tom and I took over the shop from his father we found ourselves living round the corner. That was before you were born, of course, or our Ronnie. Our Chrissie was just about one year old when we started at the shop and your mum and dad hadn't been married very long. So we all got friendly, like, with us being just round the corner and going to the same church.'

Eunice gave a wry smile. 'Even though you're like chalk and cheese?' Mabel raised her eyebrows questioningly and Eunice, emboldened, went on, 'Well, what I mean is, my parents aren't exactly the life and soul of the party, are they, especially my father? And you and Uncle Tom, you're so lively and such good fun.'

'Thank you, dear,' said Mabel, but with a slight hint of reproach. 'But we're all different, aren't we? We are the way the Good Lord made us, and you must remember that your father had a rough time in the last lot; the war to end all wars, as they called it. And look at us now, at it again.'

'Yes, I know,' said Eunice, feeling a little chastened. 'I know he was gassed in the trenches and all that, but he doesn't talk about it much; neither of them does.'

'Aye, your dad had a bad time, right enough,' said Tom. 'I was one of the lucky ones. I escaped with nowt but a shoulder wound, but what your dad suffered . . . Well, it's made him rather bitter, and I can't say I blame him.' Eunice knew that her father had suffered from gas poisoning. He had been invalided out before the end of the war and had been left with a chronic chest complaint, which flared up from time to time. She knew also that his hatred of the Germans was intense and that no way would he have wanted her to join one of the fighting services, even though it was unlikely that women would be actively involved in combat.

'Your dad thinks you'll be safe down in the countryside,' Tom went on. 'That's what he said to me. As Mabel was saying, you're very precious to them, Eunice. That doesn't mean to say that our Chrissie and Ronnie aren't precious to us, but I think we're a bit more philosophical about things, aren't we, love?' He turned to his wife. 'We knew they'd ave to join up, and now – well – we're proud of them, ren't we?'

'I'll say we are,' agreed Mabel. 'Chrissie's like a dog with wo tails now she's been made up to corporal. She didn't ike her brother being one up on her.' The brother and ister each had two stripes now, Ronnie in the Lancashire usiliers and Chrissie in the WAAF.

'What exactly does Chrissie do?' asked Eunice.

'Oh, we're not allowed to ask,' replied Tom. 'It's all very ush-hush. Summat to do with navigation and plotting, we hink. All we know is that she's stationed in East Anglia vhere the bombers fly from. We're not sure what our onnie's doing, neither. They're just training and waiting or . . . well, whatever might happen, I suppose. Thank od he got through that Dunkirk débâcle, anyroad.' onnie had been a member of the British Expeditionary orce and it was after the retreat from Dunkirk that he had een awarded his stripes. He did not say why, but his arents guessed he was able to give, as well as to receive, rders and was able to remain calm in a crisis. 'Well, here's he man himself,' said Tom, smiling fondly at his son as he ntered the room.

Ronnie was a striking, if not particularly handsome, igure in his khaki uniform. He always wore it when he was ome on leave; young men in civvies tended to be looked at skance. His bright ginger hair, glossy and well groomed, vas his most arresting feature, above a homely-looking ace with thoughtful grey eyes and a mouth that could urve readily into a smile.

'Talking about me, are you?' he asked. 'Hi there, Eunice. Vhat have they been telling you?'

'Oh, wouldn't you like to know?' she teased. 'Nothing ad, though.'

'Well, that's OK then.' He grinned. 'Are you ready?

Right – off we go. Ta-ra, Mum; ta-ra, Dad.'

'Ta-ra, love. Nice to see you again, Eunice. Take care of her now, Ronnie. Have a good time . . .'

'Where are we going then?' asked Ronnie, tucking his arm companionably through hers as they walked down the street. 'Pictures? Dancing? A walk on the prom? What do you fancy?' Easy-going, Ronnie usually left the decision to Eunice.

'Oh, I don't know,' she said. 'What would you like to do?'

'I don't mind . . .'

'Well, I'm not really dressed for dancing,' Eunice replied. 'I've got ordinary sandals on. If you'd said that was what you wanted to do, then I'd have got dolled up a bit.'

'Why should you? You're fine just the way you are.'

'And the queues at the Odeon and the Princess will be enormous on a Saturday night,' she said. 'Let's go and see what's on at the Tivoli. You can usually get in there without any trouble.'

'OK; suits me fine.'

It was not all that far to walk along Dickson Road and Talbot Road to the small cinema in the arcade. There was a George Formby film showing. He was not really one of Eunice's favourites, but she knew that Ronnie liked him. She saw his face light up. 'Oh good,' she said. 'Your favourite, Ronnie. Isn't that lucky?'

As it turned out she enjoyed the film nearly as much as Ronnie did and found herself laughing out loud at the inane antics and the cheeky songs of the Lancashire lad with the wide grin. His humour really was quite infectious. Ronnie bought her a small tub of ice cream with a tiny wooden spoon at the interval.

It was dark when they left the cinema, but the absence of streetlamps was made up for by the light of the moon; and

Eunice had her pocket torch in her bag as she always did, just in case it was needed. They chatted easily as they walked the mile or so home, arm in arm. It was Eunice, however, who was doing most of the talking, about her forthcoming Land Army venture and her uniform and of how her friend Gwen wished she could go too, but had now gone to work at the aircraft factory.

'You'll write to me, won't you?' said Ronnie, 'like you do now. Let me have your address in Gloucestershire as soon as you can.'

'Yes, I will,' she replied. 'And of course I'll write to you – when I'm not too busy milking the cows or driving the tractor or . . . or doing whatever else they want us to do.'

'I don't think they'll expect you to drive a tractor just yet, will they?' he asked, looking rather worried.

'No; it was just a joke, Ronnie,' she laughed.

'You will take care of yourself, won't you, Eunice?' he asked. They had reached her gate now and he looked at her anxiously. 'You know I'm . . . well, I'm very fond of you.'

'I know, Ronnie,' she replied. 'And so am I. Fond of you, I mean. We've been friends for a long time, haven't we? . . . I'd better go in,' she added. 'My mother doesn't like me to be late.'

She knew she could have invited him into the house and her mother would not have objected – in fact, she would have been quite pleased – but Eunice did not want her to get the wrong idea. She and Ronnie would not be seeing one another for quite a while and it was better to leave things the way they were.

'I've had a lovely evening, Ronnie,' she said. 'Thanks ever so much. I've really enjoyed it.'

'We'll do it again? When we're both home on leave?'

'Yes . . . whenever that might be. Goodness knows when I'll be able to get home from Gloucestershire.'

'We'll have to try and get our leaves at the same time, shall we?'

'Yes . . . if we can.'

'You'll take care, Eunice, won't you?' he said again.

'Course I will.'

'And you'll send me a photo, will you, of you in your Land Army uniform?' he asked, laughing. 'I'm dying to see it.'

'Yes, in fact I'll put it on for you the next time we're both home.' She grinned at him. 'How about that?'

'Yes . . . great,' he said.

She reached up and kissed his cheek and he held her close, just for a moment. 'Goodbye, Eunice. Take care now . . .'

'Good night, Ronnie. You take care as well. I'll write, I promise. 'Bye for now.' She hurried up the path.

When she turned round on reaching her door to wave to him, he was still standing there. He had a strange look on his face that she had not seen there before: a look of concern and – if she had not known it to be ridiculous – of deep affection . . . love, almost? He waved to her now in a cheery manner, then walked away.

Could it be possible, she wondered, that he might feel more for her than just friendship? He had told her he was fond of her. But of course he was; she had already known that, but it was a fondness that came from a close friendship, that was all. She dismissed the idea as nonsense. Ronnie, no doubt, was apprehensive about returning to the war; anxious about what the future might hold and a little saddened at the thought of not seeing her or his parents for quite a long time. She was apprehensive too, as well as being excited at the prospect of leaving home. Who could tell what the future might hold for any of them?

Chapter 4

Eunice was surprised at how upset she felt at saying goodbye to her parents. She had looked forward for so long to her first real taste of freedom, but when the moment finally arrived to board the train she was aware of a sinking feeling deep inside her and, to her annoyance, she felt tears springing to her eyes. She tried to blink them away because her mother was looking tearful too, and the last thing she wanted was an emotional farewell with both of them weeping and wailing.

'Now, you've got everything you need, haven't you, love?' asked Edith, as she had done half a dozen times already. 'Your sandwiches and that little flask of tea?'

'Yes; they're in my shoulder bag. You put them there yourself, Mum.'

'And your gas mask? Yes, that's right . . . And you did remember to pack everything they said you'd need on that list, didn't you?'

Eunice nodded. Her mother knew perfectly well that all was in order; she had insisted on helping with the packing herself. Edith was just chattering to fill in the empty moments before the departure of the train, everything that needed to be said having been said over and over again. Her father was standing there silently, as was his wont, looking even more downhearted than usual.

'Oh, I've just remembered,' said Edith. 'Did you pack some . . .' She glanced uneasily at her husband, who didn't appear to be listening anyway, then moved closer to whisper in Eunice's ear, 'some . . . STs? You might be miles away from a chemist's shop.'

'Yes, Mother,' replied Eunice, a touch of exasperation returning now to temper the feeling of sadness. Yes, it would be good to get away. At least she would not have to put up with her mother's preoccupation regarding even her most personal affairs. Edith was the sort of mother who kept a close watch on her daughter's monthly event. Possibly there was some excuse for this because Eunice, since starting with her periods at fifteen – somewhat later than most girls – had been irregular. Her mother worried about the matter, even though the family doctor said it would right itself given time; but Eunice resented what she considered to be interference.

'Good heavens, Mother,' she said now. 'We won't be out in the wilds, you know. I don't suppose we'll lose contact with civilisation.'

'There's no need to be cheeky, Eunice,' said her mother automatically, but with less of her usual brusqueness. 'I'm concerned about you, that's all; and so is your daddy.'

'Aye, take care of yourself, love,' said Samuel, smiling weakly as Eunice glanced across at him. 'And don't forget to write. We'll be wanting to hear how you've settled down.' It was the longest utterance – it could hardly be called a speech – that she had heard her father make for ages. He reached into his back pocket and drew out his wallet from which he took a ten-shilling note. He pressed it into her hand. 'Here you are. You might need a few little extras. We don't want you to go short.'

Eunice was very touched and she leaned forward and kissed her father's cheek. 'Thanks . . . Dad,' she said. 'You take care as well; take care of that chest of yours.'

'Aye . . . I'll try.'

'Goodbye then, Eunice.' Edith put her arms around her daughter in a rare show of affection. The luggage had already been taken into the compartment and lifted up on to the luggage rack by a helpful young airman, and now the guard was preparing to wave his green flag. She kissed her daughter. 'Time to go,' she said with a forced brightness at the shrill blast of the guard's whistle. 'You'll write to us as soon as you've settled, won't you, dear? Take care of yourself and . . . be a good girl.'

Typical, thought Eunice, as the train slowly drew away. Her mother just couldn't resist a final admonition, probably because of that RAF lad who had been so helpful with the luggage. She leaned from the corridor window and waved, her parents waving back until the billowing smoke from the engine enveloped her and forced her back inside. Thankfully she entered the compartment and sat down on the only vacant seat where she had placed her shoulder bag.

'Goodbyes are hell, aren't they?' said the airman who had helped with the luggage. 'Especially with doting parents.'

'Yes . . .' she replied, a little feebly, unable to come up with a witticism. She was feeling all mixed up, sad and yet happy, looking forward to the adventure that lay ahead, and yet so terribly apprehensive.

'Joining up, are you?'

'Yes . . . well, sort of,' she said. 'Not the WAAFs, though. I'm joining the Land Army. I'm on my way to Gloucester.'

'Oh, jolly good show.' The lad, who looked even younger than herself, grinned at her, then turned to speak to the young man next to him, another RAF recruit. At least she guessed they were recruits, new to it all, as she was. They both looked so young and inexperienced, scarcely out of the schoolroom.

The two young men were soon deep in conversation and, not wanting to appear to be eavesdropping, Eunice turned to look out of the window. The Fylde countryside looked quiet and peaceful on this bright September day. Black and white cattle, and sheep grazing in the fields; barns stacked high with hay; smoke drifting from farmhouse chimneys. It was hard to imagine there was a war on at all, and Eunice guessed the countryside she was bound for would be equally peaceful. A little hillier though, maybe. She recalled from her school geography lessons that Gloucester was near the Cotswold hills, and there would be more wooded areas and forests. The Fylde landscape was comparatively treeless.

Eunice, in her eighteen years, had never travelled any further than the Manchester area: Rochdale, to be precise, which was her father's home town. It was there that she had spent the only holidays she had had, with her mother and father, at times when the boarding house was not too busy and Edith could be spared. Not the most exciting of places to spend a holiday, especially as her paternal grandparents had been a sanctimonious couple, steeped in the traditions of their Methodist chapel. It was little wonder that her father was so taciturn and morose, she had thought, with parents such as his. Her uncle Charlie, however, her father's brother – the only one of the family with any life about him – had owned a motor car and he had taken them out and about; into the Cheshire countryside and north to the moors and to Clitheroe castle. But the holidays, such as they were, had come to an end four years ago when the elderly couple had died within a few months of one another. Eunice guessed that the visits had been mainly duty visits anyway. Besides, her Grandma Gregson had died the previous year and Edith, now running the boarding house single-handedly, was finding it even more difficult to take time off. And so Eunice had learned to be content with Blackpool and had had little desire to go further afield.

The two airmen left the train at Preston with a cheery 'Ta-ra', humping their kitbags down from the rack and then bounding out on to the platform as though they hadn't a care in the world. The two seats they had vacated were soon occupied, this time by young men in khaki. The train became very crowded, mainly with servicemen, standing in the corridors as well as filling every available seat. Soon it became almost impossible to push your way along the corridor because of the suitcases and kitbags and folk blocking the way. Eunice, feeling unaccountably more nervous as the train rattled on its way, thought that a visit to the toilet might not be a bad idea, but she decided to wait until she got out at Crewe. She didn't want to lose her seat or to draw attention to herself.

The people in the compartment were by no means chatty or friendly; they were mostly middle-aged, apart from the soldiers and a young sailor in the far corner, and were all quietly minding their own business. A British trait, Eunice mused, unless a crisis should arise when everyone would suddenly become bosom pals. She read her *Woman's Own*, at least she kept her eyes glued to the page although the article she was trying to read, about 'Make Do and Mend', was not really impinging on her mind. She realised she was feeling a little hungry, having eaten only a slice of toast at seven thirty, despite her mother's entreaties that she should get a good cooked breakfast inside her. She toyed with the idea of getting her sandwiches and flask out of her bag, but decided against it. There was little enough room to juggle with a sandwich and a cup of hot tea; she would most likely end up scalding the elderly lady next to her. She would wait until they arrived at Crewe. There would be a good half-hour's wait there for the next train, plenty of time to eat and to do anything else that was required.

All the railway station signs, since the start of the war, had been removed or blotted out, so unless you had travelled along the same route before, it could be difficult to know when you had arrived at your destination. Eunice had studied the timetable. After Preston, the first big station on the line, there were Wigan, Warrington and then Crewe, as well as several little country stations. As it happened, it was obvious when they arrived at Crewe. By that time the silent occupants of the carriage had begun to communicate a little, telling one another, 'Yes that's right – Crewe next.' The majority of them were getting out there, this station being one of the main junctions in the country.

One of the soldiers helped Eunice with her case, even carrying it out on to the platform, for which she was extremely grateful. It felt as though it weighed a ton, thanks to the heavy boots and shoes; she hoped she would not have to carry it far here, or when she arrived at Gloucester. She staggered along the platform to the ladies' room, feeling as though her arm was being pulled from its socket, and made use of the facilities. The dingy waiting room, smelling of stale smoke and dust, was not an ideal place to eat her lunch, and the snack bar, serving hot drinks, sandwiches and rock buns, appeared so crowded that you could not even get in through the door; besides, she had her own flask of tea. Fortunately she could see an empty space, just one, on a form halfway down the platform and she made a beeline for it.

The corned beef sandwiches, with just a hint of pickle, were cut delicately into triangles, the way her mother always prepared them, and Eunice found them delicious; as was the slice of home-made fruit cake, wrapped in a separate piece of greaseproof paper. Dried fruit was scarce, almost impossible to come by now, but Edith still had a goodly supply of currants, raisins and sultanas in her store cupboard, saved since the start of the war and used only sparingly. Eunice found herself thinking fondly of her mother now, and it surprised her that she should feel that way so soon. Perhaps the saying was true, about absence making the heart grow fonder, or was it the home comforts, in particular the food, that she would miss?

The space next to her was vacant again now, but it was not likely to remain that way for long. As she put her flask back into her bag and brushed the crumbs from her skirt she saw a young woman heading towards her, carrying, or rather dragging, a huge suitcase and looking extremely worried.

'Is anybody sitting there?' she asked, in a breathless little voice. 'I mean . . . are you saving that space for somebody?'

'No . . . no, I'm not,' replied Eunice. 'It's all yours. Come and join me.'

'Oh, thank you,' said the girl, for that was all she seemed to be – younger than Eunice herself. 'I don't think I could have carried that suitcase another yard.' She flopped down in the vacant space and Eunice could tell from the tone of her voice that she was very near to tears. 'I hope the platform I want isn't far away, but I'll have to sit down for a few minutes.'

'I know the feeling,' said Eunice, smiling at her. 'My case weighs a ton as well. And I'm not sure which platform I want either. I was just having a bit of a breather before I find out.' A sudden thought struck her. 'Where are you going, if you don't mind me asking?'

'Gloucester.'

'Well, fancy that; so am I. You wouldn't be joining the Land Army, by any chance?'

'Yes . . . yes, I am.' The relief was apparent in the girl's grey eyes as she smiled nervously back at Eunice. 'Oh, isn't that marvellous? I can't believe it. I was feeling so lost and scared, and now I've found somebody else going to the same place. Isn't that a coincidence?'

'Yes, rather,' Eunice said, although she didn't think it was so very unusual. She had assumed that somewhere along the journey, particularly at Crewe station, she might meet other land girl recruits heading the same way. 'There might be some more of us, you never know, when we get on the next train.'

'Yes, but even if there aren't, you and I can travel together, can't we?'

'Sure,' said Eunice. She too was pleased to have discovered a fellow traveller. The girl seemed very nervous. Eunice decided that somebody had to take charge and her new companion looked pretty nearly exhausted already. How would she cope with life on a farm, she wondered. 'The first thing to do is to find out where the train goes from. I'll ask this man. Excuse me . . .' Eunice jumped up and approached a porter pushing a heavy truck.

He told her the train for Gloucester was due in fifteen minutes and would depart from the platform adjacent to the one where they were sitting. That was a relief. They needed to carry their cases only a few yards, then they stood and waited. They waited for longer than fifteen minutes, more like forty, but that was not unusual in these wartime days. Whilst they were waiting Eunice learned that her companion was called Olive Pritchard. She came from

Wigan – they must have travelled on the same train without seeing one another – and she was nineteen years old. Eunice was surprised at this; she had assumed that she herself was the elder of the two. Olive was small and slim with a pale complexion and wispy fair hair, which was cut very short. She had a nervous breathless way of speaking and blinked her eyes rapidly as she spoke. Eunice put it down to the fact that Olive too was leaving home for the first time and was more than normally apprehensive about what might lie ahead. Her parents had not wanted her to join one of the armed services either, so the Land Army had been the obvious choice.

The journey to Gloucester seemed to take for ever. The train stopped at each small – unnamed – country station and was, if possible, even more crowded than the first one had been. Fortunately there were, once again, a couple of willing servicemen to help the girls heave their luggage on to the train, but they were forced to sit on their suitcases as far as Birmingham, when they managed to find two vacant seats.

There were two young women in the compartment, and as one of them was already wearing Land Army uniform it was obvious where they were bound.

The uniformed girl grinned. 'Hi there. I bet you two are going to the same place as us, aren't you?'

'I rather think so,' said Eunice. 'We're joining the Land Army. I see you're all prepared. I didn't know whether we were supposed to wear uniform or not.'

'Just thought I'd break it in,' said the young woman. 'No time like the present. I'm Rose, by the way.'

'And I'm Dorothy,' said the other one.

They all introduced themselves and before long the four of them, even Olive, were chatting as though they had known one another for ages. Rose and Dorothy, both in their early twenties, were married, but as yet, childless. 'And we wanted to do our bit,' they said. They knew the route, having travelled along it many times, and were able to inform the other two when they finally arrived at their destination.

They waited on the forecourt outside Gloucester station, a tired and somewhat dispirited little bunch. There were seven of them by this time; Eunice and Olive, Rose and Dorothy, and three other girls, two of whom were wearing their uniform, who had come across and joined them.

'So – what do we do now?' said Rose.

'Someone's supposed to be meeting us, aren't they?' said Eunice.

'I hope they haven't forgotten,' said Olive. 'Oh dear! Whatever would we do?'

'Course they've not forgotten,' said Eunice more confidently than she was feeling. 'Our train was late, wasn't it?'

'All the more reason for them to be here.'

'They've probably gone back to . . . wherever it is and decided to come back later. There – what did I tell you?'

They all looked in the direction of a lorry, which screeched to a halt a few yards from them. A young woman, dressed in Land Army uniform that had clearly seen a good deal of wear, jumped down and greeted them.

'Hello, there – sorry you've been waiting. They told me the train was late – as usual – so I popped into town to do a couple of errands. I'm Sheila, by the way, and I'm your forewoman.' She tapped at the armband she was wearing, embroidered with a red letter F. 'And this is to prove it,' she laughed. 'Don't worry, though; I'm not going to boss you around like a school prefect. I'm just there to show you the ropes, sort out any problems, that sort of thing. Righty-oh, then. Sling your cases in the back. Gosh, that's a weight!

Hop in now – there's just about room for you all. OK then; hold tight. Off we go . . .'

It was a bumpy ride through the leafy country lanes. Eunice, peering out through the back of the lorry, found herself marvelling at the dense foliage. In places the overhanging trees, just beginning to turn from green to the rich hues of autumn, met overhead, forming a canopy through which the late afternoon sun shimmered in intermittent shafts of gold.

None of the new recruits knew exactly where they were bound, except that it was a training hostel. After about fifteen minutes the lorry swept through a gateway and up a long carriage drive, coming to a halt in front of a large manor house. The greyish-yellow stone had mellowed with age – it looked as though it had stood there for hundreds of years – and its mullioned windows glinted in the sunlight.

'Gosh!' breathed Eunice. 'Is this where we're going to live?'

Sheila jumped down and opened the tail board. 'Righty-oh, girls, here we are. Let's be having you. This is Stapleton Hall.' She laughed at their astonished faces. 'That's right – have a good gawp. It affects everybody like that. Quite something, isn't it? But believe it or not, this is going to be your home for the next couple of months. Make the most of it, that's what I say. Goodness knows where you might end up afterwards. We've no footmen, though, so you'll have to carry your own cases.'

She led them up a wide staircase leading from the spacious entrance hall, to a large room on the first floor, which contained four bunk beds. 'There we are. Sort yourselves out, who wants the tops and who wants the bottoms. But this one's mine.' She put her hand on one of the lower bunks. 'Apart from that it doesn't matter. I 'spect you'll all snore; they usually do.'

'You're here all the time then, are you?' asked Eunice.

'Well, for the time being at any rate,' Sheila replied. 'You never know when you might be moved. Like I was saying, I'm your forewoman. I've been in the WLA about a year and a half, and they asked me if I'd like to do this extra training. It's ten bob a week extra, so it's not to be sniffed at.'

'For looking after new recruits?'

'Yes, sort of. But I go out to farms every day, like you lot'll be doing. Anyway, I'll leave you to unpack now. There's plenty room for all your stuff.' She gestured towards the huge oak wardrobes and chests of drawers. There were two of each, old-fashioned and cumbersome, but very roomy. 'And the bathroom's just along the corridor. Cheerio, then. See you later. Dinner's at half-past six, in the dining room.'

'And where's that?' asked Rose.

'Ground floor. Go through the hall and follow the smell of cabbage. You can't miss it.'

'She's a good sort,' said Rose. 'I'm feeling more cheerful already. But I'll be better still when I've been to the lav and had a wash. I'll go and find the bathroom. Sorry, girls; I can't wait . . .'

They discovered there were, in fact, two bathrooms on that floor. Both held enormous panelled baths with claw feet, large washbasins of blue and white flowered porcelain, a little crazed with age, with lavatories to match, and – wonder of wonders – fluffy white towels, although each girl had brought her own.

'I think we've landed on our feet here, don't you?' Eunice remarked to Olive.

'I hope so,' replied Olive. 'Yes, it all seems . . . very nice. I've got a terrible headache, though. I'll have to take two aspirins before we go down for dinner. I hope it won't be cabbage. If there's one thing I can't stand it's soggy cabbage. From what that Sheila said it sounds as though it might be cabbage every night.'

Dorothy raised her eyebrows. 'You're jolly lucky to get cabbage, soggy or otherwise. Hasn't anybody told you there's a war on? Personally, I'm so hungry at the moment I could eat a horse, never mind cabbage.'

'We might be doing that before long,' laughed Rose.

'Oh, you don't really think so, do you?' asked Olive. 'I know I simply couldn't . . .'

'It's a joke,' said Rose. 'At least I think it is. Come on, you lot. It's nearly half-past six. Let's go and follow that cabbage smell. I wonder who does the cooking?'

The dining room was the most elegant room Eunice had ever seen and she gazed round in amazement. The walls were panelled in light oak wood and the deep red velvet curtains at the windows toned with the red of the patterned carpet. Admittedly, it was threadbare in places and the edges of the curtains were faded. The whole room, indeed, had an air of faded grandeur, but it was impressive for all that.

There were two long tables running parallel down the centre of the room, each covered with a white damask cloth and laid with silver cutlery. Sheila, who was already seated at the head of one of the tables, beckoned to her little lot, the seven new recruits, to come and join her. There were, in all, twenty-four young women in the hostel, one group having almost completed their training, one part-way through, and the other just beginning.

A distinguished-looking, middle-aged lady with silver-grey hair and wearing a pale blue twinset and pearls, was seated at the other end of the long table. When all the girls were sitting down she rose to her feet and tapped gently with a spoon on the rim of the water jug.

'Good evening, gels,' she said. From the way she addressed them it was obvious she was out of the top drawer.

There were murmurs of 'Good evening . . .' Some seemed to be addressing her as 'Matron' and others as 'Mrs', then a name that Eunice could not quite make out.

'And a special welcome to our new gels,' she went on. 'I will come and meet you all individually as soon as possible. I am Mrs Stapleton, and I am your warden – or Matron, if that's how you'd like to think of me.' She smiled graciously. 'At all events, I am here to look after you and to help you all I can. If you have any problems, just go to Sheila, or if she can't sort them out then I will try to do so. But she usually can, can't you, Sheila?' She looked enquiringly in the forewoman's direction, and Sheila smiled and nodded back at her. 'Now . . . we will say grace.'

Eunice, somewhat bemused, lowered her head as the woman intoned, 'For what we are about to receive . . .' She had not known what to expect, but it was certainly not this. It was for all the world like boarding school, something out of a book by her favourite writer, Angela Brazil. It all seemed very strange to Eunice that first night, as it did to the other new recruits, but the general consensus of opinion was that they had struck lucky in this, their first billet.

They learned that Stapleton Hall had been in the family for generations. They had been yeoman farmers in the beginning, tending their own small estate. Much of the land, however, had been sold off over the years to neighbouring farms. Mrs Stapleton, now a widow in her early sixties, had decided to offer the house to the Government as a training hostel, knowing that sooner or later the property was sure to be requisitioned. And she had offered her services as a warden, to which they had been pleased to agree. The wardens put in charge of young women were usually middle-aged; often spinsters or widows with no one dependent on them. Both of Mrs Stapleton's sons, in their early thirties, were serving in the war, one in the army and the other in the RAF. They had both left home on marrying, several years ago, to live and work in Gloucester, one as an accountant, the other as a surveyor. Neither of them, to their father's disappointment, had shown much interest in the land, which was the reason he had decided to sell.

Mrs Stapleton was helped in the house and garden by Joe and Elsie Makepeace. The couple were what might be termed old retainers, having been employed there since long before the last war. They were a few years older than their employer, but very fit and active. Elsie was the cook, assisted by a couple of kitchen maids; girls from the village who also helped with general duties about the house. The land girls, however, were expected to make their own beds and keep their rooms tidy. Joe looked after the garden and the small collection of livestock: hens, geese, rabbits and a couple of pigs. He was helped by two lads from the village who were not yet old enough for call-up. At one time, apparently, there had been an impressive garden, the pride of the Stapleton family, to which visitors had been invited at certain seasons. Now, however, the rose beds, herbaceous borders and smooth green lawn were planted with vegetables. There was still a lily pond, but the tennis courts were now a home for the livestock.

The new girls soon grew accustomed to the routine of the household. The meals, in large tureens or dishes, were placed on the table by the cook and her helpers, then it was the job of one girl at the end of each table to dish out the food to the others, passing it along the table until everyone was served. The food, on the whole, was nourishing and quite palatable. It was shepherd's pie that first night, with nicely browned potatoes and – yes – cabbage, but all the plates, including Olive's, were sent back clean. The girl, however, had asked for only a minuscule amount of the dreaded vegetable.

They were awakened each morning at five forty-five by the ringing of a bell. Then, after they had washed, dressed and made their beds, it was down for a cooked breakfast of porridge, bacon and fried bread, and thick slices of the greyish-white bread to which they were all becoming accustomed, spread with margarine and plum jam. Before they went off to their various farms they were expected to assist in making their own sandwiches for their lunchtime break. These usually consisted of one cheese sandwich and one beetroot, with, occasionally, bloater or some other hardly recognisable paste. Eunice had never experienced beetroot sandwiches before, and she soon began to wish she might never have to set eyes on them again, but she knew she must either eat them or go hungry. There was an abundance of beetroot growing in the fields, and the picking of it on a wet winter's day was one of the most unpleasant of the land girls' jobs.

Looking back on it afterwards, Eunice realised she had enjoyed her two months' training far more than she had expected she would. The comfortable billet, of course, was a bonus, although the girls had to do their share of household chores, just as did the ones in the less luxurious hostels. There was a roster for clearing away the tables after the evening meal, washing up, then resetting the tables ready for breakfast the following day. They were expected to be in by ten o'clock every evening, when the door would be locked, although they could, if they wished, ask for a pass till eleven on Wednesdays and Saturdays.

'Bloody hell! This lot's worse than flamin' boarding

school,' Rose was heard to remark to her friend, Dorothy, usually known as Dot.

'Not that you and me would know anything about that, kid,' her friend replied, chuckling. 'Them places is only for toffs, like old Ma Stapleton.'

As the new recruits got to know one another better Eunice began to realise that Rose and Dot, the young married women, were not as ladylike as they had seemed to be on a first acquaintance. They were, in fact, what her mother would have termed 'rather coarse'. Their language was colourful, but they were good-hearted lasses who, in spite of their grumbles, adapted to the routine of the hostel very quickly. They were always ready for a laugh and a joke, and Eunice enjoyed their company very much indeed. It took all sorts to make a world, as she remembered her dear old Grandma Gregson remarking, and you certainly came across all sorts in the WLA.

Olive Pritchard, the young woman from Wigan, was just about as far removed in personality from Rose and Dot as it was possible to be, although she did lose some of her timidity after the first few days, and began to look a little less anxious and unhappy. Eunice had heard her weeping quietly to herself on the first night and she had jumped down from her top bunk to ask her what was the matter.

'I'm homesick,' the girl had moaned, not too loudly, although there was a warning cry of, 'Shhh! We're trying to get to sleep,' from across the room, and a less polite 'Put a sock in it, can't you?' from another direction.

'I guess we're all homesick,' whispered Eunice, 'but there's nothing we can do about it. At least we've got decent digs.' Then, as another muffled sob escaped from Olive: 'Come on now. It won't seem so bad in the morning. And we're all in the same boat, aren't we?'

'You will be my friend, won't you?' asked Olive. She

looked pleadingly at Eunice, her grey tear-filled eyes blinking rapidly.

'Of course I will,' said Eunice. 'All of us'll be friends; Rose and Dorothy and the other three as well, you'll see.'

'But you and me,' whispered Olive. 'I hope we get sent to the same farm.'

'Yes . . . so do I,' replied Eunice, although she was not feeling too sure about that. 'Come along now.' She patted Olive's shoulder reassuringly. 'Hush now and go to sleep. We'll be disturbing the others.'

Olive snuffled quietly for a little while, then her rhythmic breathing told Eunice she had gone to sleep. The next night, when she heard her sniffing again, she decided it was best to be cruel to be kind. Poor Olive would need to get over her homesickness by herself. Eunice felt rather mean, but she was relieved when, the next night, Olive did not weep.

Each morning they were driven out to various farms in the area where they did their training and Eunice, as she had guessed might happen, was paired off with Olive. The seven new recruits got on quite well together in their bedroom, or dormitory, which was how Eunice thought of it, the image of boarding school never far from her mind, although there were no midnight feasts; they were all too exhausted. They found during the day, however, that they were divided into three little groups: Rose and Dot, Eunice and Olive, and a threesome consisting of Pauline, Babs and Kathy, the other new recruits. Those three girls were all from the same town, somewhere in Shropshire and, though they were not exactly cliquish, the fact that they had known one another before made them into a separate little entity.

Eunice tried hard to jolly Olive along a bit and even managed to make her laugh at herself and her mistakes, instead as regarding them as major catastrophes.

'Nay, lass, dunna take on so,' said a – fortunately – good-natured farmer when a cow kicked over a bucket of milk after Olive had laboured long and hard to extract each drop. 'You're not the first lass as it's happened to, not by a long chalk. There's no need to get upset now.' Olive had burst into tears.

'It's all right for you; you've got the knack of it and I haven't,' she had complained to Eunice who, as usual, happened to be nearby. 'I know the cow got fed up, 'cause it took me so long. Oh dear! I don't think I'm ever going to be able to do it.'

'I'm not all that good either,' replied Eunice casually. 'That Primrose kicked me last week and I've still got the bruise to prove it.' They had done their initial training in milking on mock cows with rubber udders, and these were their first attempts at the real thing. 'Come on, cheer up,' she added. 'It's the dance tomorrow night. You know you've been looking forward to it.' She was gratified to see Olive nod and even try to smile a little.

Dances were a rare occurrence in that particular neck of the woods. The girls spent most of their evenings in their rooms, lying on their beds chatting, reading, writing letters or darning endless pairs of socks. Eunice had learned, in their nightly chats, that Olive, like herself, was an only child. Her parents were elderly and seemed to be even more protective of their daughter than were her own parents. The difference was that Olive, very shy and lacking in self-confidence, did not find it easy to make friends, unlike Eunice; nor did she have the strength of purpose to stand up to her parents, if only a little. She had worked as a typist in a solicitor's office since leaving school, the only young woman in the very small practice, which consisted of two elderly brothers. It was a wonder her parents had allowed her to join the Land Army at all, but she was of call-up age, Eunice reminded herself, therefore they would have had no choice. She reminded Eunice quite a lot of her friend Gwen, back home in Blackpool, in looks at any rate, but without Gwen's toughness and cheerfulness.

She wrote to Gwen every week as well as to her parents, and she was pleased to hear that her friend now had a boyfriend. He was an RAF recruit – an AC2 – whom she had met in the Palace Ballroom on one of her rare visits there. He would be in Blackpool for only a few months, the length of his training, but Gwen seemed very smitten with him. Eunice felt happy for her, especially as Mrs Singleton, Gwen's mum, liked him too.

She wrote to Ronnie as well and his letters to her arrived regularly every week or so. He told her he hoped to have a forty-eight-hour pass or even a few days' leave over the Christmas period and hoped she would be able to do the same.

She did not know yet about her Christmas leave. By that time she would have moved to her first farm placement, wherever that might be. For the moment she was quite content at Stapleton Hall. There were, inevitably, many hours of boredom when the girls, after their daily stint at their farms, had to amuse themselves. Sometimes, when they were not resting on their beds they listened to records on an old wind-up gramophone, an ancient model that had belonged to Mrs Stapleton, or had a sing-song around the upright piano in the room that had been allotted to them as their common room. Maggie, one of the girls who would soon finish her training, was a good pianist who was able to play by ear, vamping out such tunes as 'Bless 'Em All', 'Run, Rabbit, Run' and 'We're Gonna Hang out the Washing on the Siegfried Line'. The girls' voices would almost raise the roof and for a while they would forget their homesickness and separation from loved ones, or their aching limbs.

Very occasionally a few of them would pay a visit to the small fleapit of a cinema in the nearest small town. This was quite a precarious undertaking, involving a walk or a bicycle ride of more than a mile along a dark country lane. The bicycles on loan to the land girls were heavy black cumbersome things, many of them with faulty brakes or without lights. Eunice had learned to ride on Chrissie Iveson's bike, although she had never had one of her own. She wondered if Aunty Mabel might lend her the bicycle to bring back with her when she had her first leave, or she might even be able to get round her mother to buy her one as a Christmas present. Edith Morton, though a strict parent, could be quite generous when it came to birthday and Christmas presents. Eunice had been invited to go with the other girls to the cinema. She had grave doubts about the bicycle ride, but she decided she would give it a try.

'It's all right for you. You can ride a bike, but I can't,' Olive told her. 'Not that it matters, 'cause you wouldn't catch me going along that lane in the dark, not for a hundred pounds. You don't know what might jump out at you.'

Eunice realised she half agreed with her friend. She hesitated a moment, then: 'It's OK, Olive, I won't go,' she said. She too had not yet become accustomed to the hoot of owls, or the flittering of bats, or the scuffle of small animals in the hedges and undergrowth. 'I'll stay and keep you company. I don't want to risk life and limb either, and certainly not for an old Charlie Chaplin film. There's a dance at the village hall, though, on Saturday night. Sheila says they'll arrange transport as there's quite a lot of us who want to go. You'll come, won't you?'

Eunice was rather surprised when Olive agreed that she

would. Moreover, her clear grey eyes, her best feature, lit up at the prospect. 'I've never been to a dance,' she said wistfully. 'At least, not without my parents, and then only to a church social. I've always wanted to, but I've never been brave enough to go on my own. But you'll be there this time, won't you?'

'Yes, we'll all be there, Olive.'

'Do you think . . . do you think anyone will dance with me?'

'Yes, of course they will,' said Eunice.

Dances were held infrequently so this would be a red-letter day in the land girls' social calendar. Rose and Dot washed their hair very early in the morning, before breakfast, putting in rows of Dinkie curlers, which would remain in all day, covered by a turban. And as they got ready in the early evening Eunice was amused to see the two of them rubbing gravy browning into their legs, as a substitute for silk stockings. Then each of them kept as still as possible whilst the other one drew a 'seam' down the back of the legs with an eyebrow pencil.

'Bloody hell!' cried Rose, as her friend giggled and wobbled. 'You've made it go all crooked, you silly cow!'

Some of the girls, including the trio from Shropshire, opted to wear their uniforms for the dance. This was encouraged by the WLA as a show of patriotism, but it was not obligatory. Eunice took the rare opportunity to dress up a little, wearing a favourite floral summer dress and court shoes. She was surprised, and pleased too to see how different Olive looked – quite attractive, in fact – out of her uniform. Her dress of pale green rayon crêpe was a little old-fashioned, the sort of thing her mother might have worn, but the colour enhanced her silvery-grey eyes. Eunice helped her to make the most of her sparse blonde hair, brushing it up around her face like a halo, then persuading her to add a dusting of powder to her cheeks and a touch of pink lipstick.

'There – you'll be the belle of the ball,' she remarked, as though to a much younger girl, forgetting, as she often did, that Olive was more than a year her senior.

None of the girls need have worried about the shortage of partners. There were servicemen there from the nearby RAF and army camps, making the numbers of men and women present about equal. Many of the dances, however, were included to ensure there were no wallflowers: the hokey cokey, the palais glide, and a progressive barn dance. It was a very innocent village hall affair, organised by the local church, with strict rules about no alcohol, and the whole thing was over by ten thirty. It was, no doubt, a little tame compared to what some of the girls were used to at home, but everyone seemed to enjoy it, and it was an opportunity for all of them, servicemen, land girls, and the local villagers, to fraternise and forget their worries. It was even possible at times, there in the heart of the Gloucestershire countryside, to forget there was a war on at all.

They danced to a wind-up gramophone to the music of Glenn Miller and Joe Loss, singing along as well to the records of Bing Crosby and Vera Lynn. Olive's cheeks were pink with excitement by the end of the evening and she proclaimed she had never enjoyed herself so much in all her life.

She was not always so carefree and happy, however. Neither were any of the other girls, for that matter. Inevitably, they grumbled amongst themselves about many of the awful jobs they were called upon to do; but most of them realised it was better to get on with the task in hand, whatever it might be, with a good grace and a cheerful smile, rather than allowing resentment and despondency to take control.

'It's all right for you. You're twice as big and heavy as I am, and stronger too,' moaned Olive, finding her thin arms aching and her once elegantly manicured hands chapped and bleeding, after humping heavy sacks of wheat or picking beetroot in a muddy field in the pouring rain.

'I'm not all that big and strong,' retorted Eunice. 'Give over, Olive. You make me sound like Pansy Potter, the Strong Man's Daughter.' This was a cartoon character, familiar to readers of the *Beano* comic, and Olive even smiled a little.

'Honestly, though,' she said. 'I never thought it'd be as bad as this, did you? And I thought beetroot picking must be the worst job ever, till they put us on Brussels sprouts.' This harvest, reaped in the couple of months before Christmas, made the job one of the coldest and most objectionable of all. Eunice had to agree that she hated it.

It had been pleasant enough in the mellow autumn days they had experienced when they first joined the WLA; walking with a herd of cows along a country lane, listening to the song of birds or seeing the white tails – or scuts, as they learned they were called – of rabbits as they lolloped across a meadow, and silvery spiders' webs, glistening with dew in the hedgerows. Learning to drive a tractor had been a memorable experience too, but not so pleasant were the routine jobs: muck spreading, cleaning out stalls and byres and pigsties, and hedging and ditching.

'Cheer up,' said Eunice to her friend, as she so often did, at the end of another gruelling day. 'It's not all bad. At least, we've got the best digs in the county; I'm sure they must be.'

'Not for much longer,' said Olive gloomily. 'We'll be hearing soon, won't we, about where they're sending us? It might be somewhere awful. Mavis and Joan, those girls that left a few weeks ago, they're in a terrible place. Rose said she'd seen them in Gloucester and they were going on about how dreadful it was.'

'Don't be such a Job's comforter,' said Eunice. 'You never know, we might be sent somewhere really nice. You know – a jolly farmer and a red-cheeked farmer's wife, like they were in those reading books we had at school. Did you have those, Olive? Old Lob was the farmer's name, and there was a cow called Mrs Cuddy and a horse called Dobbin. It all sounded so lovely.'

'I don't remember,' said Olive. 'It doesn't sound much like the real thing to me. I don't believe such places exist. Or if they do, then we won't get sent there,' she added gloomily. 'Anyway, wherever we go, let's hope they put you and me together. D'you think they will, Eunice?'

'Yes . . . probably,' replied Eunice, trying to smile. She guessed it was inevitable that she and Olive would be paired together. Still, it was sometimes better the devil you knew, she thought philosophically. And she could not but be flattered that Olive so obviously wanted to be with her. The girl had improved quite a lot in confidence since the early days, but the thought of their inevitable move seemed to be filling her with doubts. Eunice knew she must try to be the confident, optimistic one and give Olive all the help she needed.

Chapter 5

It turned out as Olive had hoped. She and Eunice would be together. Olive's delight in hearing they were to be partnered was transparent, and Eunice felt a pang of guilt that she was not similarly overjoyed. But she had made up her mind she would help Olive all she could and she was, in truth, looking forward to her first real war work. They learned that the farm was called Meadowlands and, like their present billet, it was in Gloucestershire, but much further south.

'I wonder if it's as picturesque as it sounds?' mused Eunice. 'Meadowlands . . .'

'I doubt it,' replied Olive, and even Eunice felt a little apprehensive, dubious that they could be so fortunate with their digs a second time.

They were both pleasantly surprised, however, when they arrived at their destination after a bumpy ride of over half an hour in an army lorry. Meadowlands was a stone-built, ochre-tinted farmhouse in an idyllic setting in the lee of the Cotswold hills. The farmer and his wife, not surprisingly, were called Mr and Mrs Meadows. What was amazing, though, was that the two of them seemed to be the couple from Eunice's childhood reading book come to life: the ruddy-faced farmer with a genial smile and his apple-cheeked wife in a blue dress and dazzling white apron.

Mrs Meadows took them up a narrow winding staircase to their room whilst her husband obligingly followed with their heavy cases. Eunice was not surprised that they were to share, but the attic room with a sloping roof, tucked away under the eaves, was spacious and looked comfortable. There were two single beds with colourful folkweave counterpanes, a large wardrobe and dressing table and a few empty shelves. The floor was uncarpeted, but a couple of boldly striped rugs relieved the spartan effect of the stained wooden boards.

The farmer's wife smiled at them. 'We hope you'll be nice and comfy here, the pair of you.'

'I'm sure we will; thank you,' replied Eunice, and, 'Yes . . . thank you very much,' Olive added in a timid little voice. She had complained of feeling sick on the journey and she still looked rather white and shaken.

'Nah then, lassie, there's no need to look so scared,' said Mrs Meadows. 'We want you to be happy here, me and Bert. I know it's not like your own home, but we'll do our best, won't we, Bert?' She turned to her husband, who had just entered to room, red-faced and almost bow-legged with the exertion of carrying the first case.

'Aye, we will that,' he replied. 'I don't know what you've got in yon case, though. The kitchen sink as well as everything else; that's what it feels like.'

'Oh, I'm sorry,' said Olive, whose case it was. 'It's the boots and shoes, you see, and—'

'It's OK, lass, I'm only joking.' He grinned at them both. 'You're the first two land girls we've had and, like Annie says, we want you to be happy here. You'll have to work hard, though, you mun be sure o' that. Two of our farm hands have been called up and we've no sons to help wi' t' work. Two lasses, that's been our lot. They're good girls, mind you, both of 'em.'

'Aye, that's right,' Mrs Meadows beamed. 'Two daughters we've got, both of 'em married now with kiddies of their own. It'll be nice to have a couple of lasses around the place again. Now, I'll leave you to settle in and Bert'll bring the other case up . . .'

'It looks as though we've landed on our feet again,' whispered Eunice when they had gone.

'Mmm . . . It seems too good to be true, though,' said Olive. 'There's got to be a snag. We couldn't be so lucky again.'

'The snag'll be the hard work,' said Eunice. 'It's for real now, Olive. We're not playing at it any more. We're being employed to do the work of two farm hands. You heard what Mr Meadows said.'

'It felt real enough to me before,' said Olive gloomily. 'Well, let's hope they don't grow Brussels sprouts here. I shall be sick, I'm sure, if there are any on my plate on Christmas Day.'

But they did grow Brussels sprouts at Meadowlands, of course, which had to be gathered and dispatched in the weeks leading up to Christmas; it was now nearing the end of November. There was sugar beet too, another bugbear for the girls to endure. The beet, slimy with mud, slipped through their icy fingers, their feet felt frozen in spite of their heavy boots, their wet breeches clung to their knees, and the only way to prevent the rain from running down their necks was to wear a piece of sacking as a shawl.

'What frights we must look,' said Eunice on one particularly rainy day when her hair was hanging down in rat's tails and she had a constant dewdrop on the end of her nose. 'If we stand still in the middle of the field, the birds'll think we're a couple of scarecrows.'

'I'm past caring,' moaned Olive. 'All I want is a hot bath. Oh dear, I don't know how much longer I can stand this.'

'Just be thankful you can have a bath,' Eunice reminded her. Although the farmhouse was over a hundred years old it had been modernised with both electricity and up-to-date plumbing. 'It's more than a lot of the girls can do.'

They had learned from some of the other land girls, whom they met from time to time at dances and get-togethers in the nearest small town, that there was a good deal of resentment amongst some of the farmers at being obliged to employ mere girls; and, more particularly, from the farmers' wives. They heard many horror stories – which, in all probability, did not lose anything in the telling – of inferior food, eaten in the kitchen whilst the farmer and his family dined elsewhere; of ancient farmhouses with no electricity and scarcely any plumbing; of bowls of ice-cold water in bedrooms for their ablutions, or, very occasionally, a tin bath in the kitchen filled with water heated in kettles, then used by each of the girls in turn – in the same water. Many were expected to do housework as well as their work on the farm, and to be in by nine o'clock at night. This last was no hardship, as there was usually nowhere much to go, especially on cold winter evenings.

Eunice and Olive found it hard to believe their good fortune. Even Olive complained less frequently now, and though she often looked exhausted, the country air had brought a rosy glow to her complexion, her cheeks had filled out and her arms and legs had become less scrawny. This was due to Mrs Meadows' appetising meals. The two girls dined with the farmer and his wife, sitting down each evening in the dining room to a substantial meal. It was usually a stew or a casserole dish made from cheaper cuts of meat – only on Sundays did they have a roast dinner – eked out with a wide variety of the nourishing vegetables that were grown on the farm. Eunice could not have imagined she would ever eat rabbit, having being reared on the tales of Peter Rabbit and the Flopsy Bunnies, but the first time she tasted the dish she had not realised what she was eating. She had believed it was chicken, it was so tender and tasty. She saw Olive turn a little green around the gills when Mrs Meadows told them – after the meal – what it was. Eunice decided that the best option was not to think about it, but to enjoy whatever was served to them. Neither had she eaten liver before, or kidneys, but she was often so hungry at the end of the day that she was grateful for anything.

Breakfast was taken at six o'clock in the kitchen. Even so, it was a cooked breakfast, Mrs Meadows being up and about before the land girls. It was not always bacon and egg – sometimes toast and fried tomatoes, a juicy kipper or bloater, or fried bread and dripping – but they were always given something substantial, 'to put a lining on your stomach' as she told them, before they started the day's work.

Eunice came to the conclusion that Mrs Meadows was just as good a cook as her own mother, although she was not so tactless as to say so to Edith in her letters home. She told her parents she was missing them. In a way, she supposed she was, that was when she thought about home at all. Most of the time she was too busy, too engrossed in her new life to give a thought to what was going on in Blackpool. It seemed like another world, light years away, both in time and space.

All the same, as the December days passed she began to look forward to going home for the Christmas holiday. Mr Meadows, with the permission of the WLA, had said that both the girls could go home for four days. Ted, his remaining farm hand, who lived in the nearby village, would come in as usual each day, and a couple of village lads would help out as well, although he intended to keep the work to a minimum.

Ronnie still continued to write to Eunice. As he had requested, she had sent him a photo of herself in her WLA uniform and one to her parents as well, of course. Whilst they were staying at Stapleton Hall a few of them had gone into Gloucester one Saturday afternoon and had their photographs taken by a professional photographer, one who did not charge too much. He had taken scores of land girls, he said, and servicemen and women too, and to prove it there was an array of them adorning the walls of his small studio. It was quite the done thing to send such mementoes home to families and sweethearts. Not that Ronnie was a sweetheart.

Eunice's photo showed her to her best advantage. Her eyes were sparkling and her dark curly hair billowed like a cloud around her head, thanks to the photographer's skilful lighting. Her sweater, about which her mother had complained, did, indeed, enhance her shapely figure, and her hat – the much-hated article of headgear that none of them liked wearing – was held lightly in her hands. Eunice couldn't help wondering what her mother's reaction might be!

Ronnie too had been granted leave for Christmas, a precious three days. She would see him some time, although Christmas Day, for each of them, would be spent in the bosoms of their own families. Chrissie Iveson would be home on leave as well.

Olive, also, was excited at the prospect of going home to see her parents. Mr Meadows drove the two girls into Gloucester in the farm wagon on the Saturday before their leave so that they could do their Christmas shopping. They had decided they must buy gifts for their kind-hearted hosts, the farmer and his wife, as well as for their family and friends at home. Most things were in short supply. It was no longer possible to buy fancy boxes of chocolates decorated with ribbons and pretty pictures, which had always been a good stand-by for Christmas gifts. Head-scarves, however, were all the rage; quite a fashionable article of headgear at the moment. Both girls bought some of these. Eunice chose a patriotic one adorned with Union Jacks and a red and blue border for her friend Gwen, and a rather less garish one for her mother, which depicted horses' heads and horseshoes, a reminder to Edith that her daughter was a land girl. Both girls chose sombrely striped ties for their fathers; Eunice guessed that Olive's father came out of the same mould as her own.

What could she buy for Ronnie? She knew he would have bought a present for her. Eventually she decided on a book. He did not read as much as she did, but she found a book about trains, with a few coloured plates and lots of black-and-white photos. Trains were a keen interest of Ronnie's. He had once told her he would have liked to be an engine driver if he had not gone into his parents' grocery business; and before he joined up he had been building a model railway in the loft.

It took the girls ages to decide on a gift for Mr and Mrs Meadows. They had agreed a joint present would be best. There was an antique shop just off the high street selling, it seemed, a lot of junk, but amongst the dross they caught sight of a small china figurine of two little girls holding hands. The farmer and his wife had two daughters – who would be visiting them on Christmas Day – and they had now acquired two more girls whom they treated almost as though they were their own.

The couple were delighted with the gift, Mrs Meadows even shedding a few tears as she opened it, which she insisted on doing the moment they presented it on the morning of their departure.

'You really shouldn't have. What dear girls you are,' she enthused, while her husband, looking rather embarrassed, added, 'Aye, you're a couple of grand lasses, but you shouldn't go spending yer money on us. Anyroad, ta very much. We'll treasure it, we will that.'

'You don't want to go lugging those great suitcases about,' Mrs Meadows had said to them the night before. 'See – I'll lend each of you a canvas bag. It'll be a lot lighter, and you won't need your uniforms, will you? Leave 'em here and I'll wash 'em. Try and forget you're land girls for a few days, eh?'

Now, the following morning, she gave each of them a carrier bag containing a few parcels, each wrapped in greaseproof paper. 'That's for yer mams – a bit of farm produce as I'm sure won't go amiss. There's butter, cheese, bacon, a nice bit o' pork, and some new-laid eggs. Keep it under yer hat – well, not literally,' she laughed. 'You know what I mean, although there'd be room for it, wouldn't there, in them monstrosities you wear? Watch them eggs now; don't go breaking 'em. And here's a little something for the pair of you. Open it on Christmas Day.' She gave each of them a tiny parcel wrapped in red paper, hugging them and kissing them on the cheek. 'God bless – look after yerselves now. Have a safe journey and a lovely Christmas. Ta-ra then; see you in a few days.'

Mr Meadows drove them to the station and they travelled together as far as Wigan where Olive left the train. Eunice had become quite fond of her, but all the same, it would be nice to have a few days without her. They had been together constantly ever since they had met up on

Crewe station more than three months ago. It would be good to have some different company, to see her old friend Gwen again and to catch up on all the news at home.

When she saw the distant silhouette of Blackpool Tower appearing on the horizon, soon after they had passed through Kirkham, Eunice knew she was well and truly home. It was Gloucestershire that began to feel like a distant memory now as she realised how much she was looking forward to seeing everyone again. She was surprised her father was waiting for her at the station barrier, a hunched-up figure in an overcoat and trilby hat. He looked distinctly fed up although he did manage a wave and a semblance of a smile as he caught sight of her coming towards him.

She put her bags down and kissed him on the cheek. 'Hello, Dad. It's good to see you, but I didn't expect you to meet me. I hope you haven't been waiting long.'

'Ages,' he replied. 'Your train's over half an hour late.' Eunice was on the verge of telling him that it was not her fault, when he added, a trifle grudgingly, 'Still, you can't help it, can you? I suppose it's all we can expect when there's a war on.' His eyes softened a little and his cautious smile could be glimpsed again as, at last, he returned her kiss.

'Anyroad, it's nice to see you, lass. You're looking well. Your mother insisted on me coming to meet you. She thought you'd be laden down with luggage, but I see you've not brought very much. Well, give it us here and we'll be making tracks. Your mother's making a special meal. We'd best not keep her waiting any longer.'

After that unusually lengthy discourse Samuel Morton fell silent again. They strode out together in the gathering dusk through the cluster of streets behind North Station. The boarding house was less than ten minutes' walk away, ideally situated, in peacetime, for visitors arriving and departing.

'I wondered what on earth had happened to you. Wherever have you been till now?' Edith's welcome was less than auspicious as she dashed down the hallway on hearing the key turn in the lock.

'Sorry, Mum. The train was late,' said Eunice. Surely her mother might have realised that.

'Well, yes, I suppose so,' said Edith, still rather ungraciously. 'Anyway, get yourselves inside and shut that door, or we'll be having the ARP warden after us.' Only then, when the door was firmly closed, did she look properly at her daughter. Eunice was glad to see, in spite of her off-hand greeting, that her mother was now smiling warmly.

'Let's have a look at you then.' She took hold of her daughter's arms, observing her closely. 'You look well, dear, very well indeed. Roses in your cheeks, and I do believe you've put on weight, our Eunice.' This was something that Eunice did not particularly want to hear. 'It's grand to see you. We've missed you, love.' She kissed her cheek and Eunice returned her kiss.

'It's good to see you as well, Mum.'

After her show of affection Edith quickly reverted to her normal brusque self. 'Well, now, you'd best get your coat off and get ready for tea, although it'll probably be burned to a cinder by now. Is that all the luggage you've got? Not very much, is it? Where's that big suitcase that belongs to me and your daddy?'

'I didn't need it, Mum, not for five days. Mrs Meadows lent me a bag. And she's sent you this.' She handed her mother the carrier bag. 'It's some stuff from the farm: cheese and bacon and eggs, and there's a piece of pork, I think.'

Edith peeked in the bag and sniffed. 'Aye, I can tell there's some cheese in there. I hope it hasn't gone off. Still, it's all very welcome. I'll write the lady a little thank-you note.' Eunice was relieved that her mother was receiving the gift with a good grace. She could just as easily have said that she didn't want to accept charity. 'Pork, you say? Mmm . . . that'll be a treat. We'll have it tomorrow, Christmas Eve. I've got a big chicken for Christmas Day, thanks to Tom Iveson. They're as hard to get hold of as bags of gold, but Tom managed to get us one, being in the trade, you know.'

'That's nice,' said Eunice, starting to head off up the stairs. 'I'll just go and get ready then.'

'It's your usual room, Eunice. Their ladyships,' she meant the Civil Service women, 'have all gone home for Christmas, but I thought I'd best leave their rooms as they are. So there's just your daddy and you and me at the moment. Just our little family . . . Don't be long now; I'll be putting the tea out in a few minutes.'

Everything in the house was familiar, and yet it looked strangely unfamiliar. The tick of the wooden clock on the mantelpiece seemed louder; Eunice had scarcely noticed it before, but she gave quite a start when it chimed five o'clock. Her mother had certainly gone to town with the 'welcome home' meal. Cottage pie with minced beef containing not a scrap of gristle, and rich gravy. It was not 'burned to a cinder', as her mother had gloomily prophesied. The potato topping was nice and brown and crispy – just the way she liked it. It was served with carrots and turnips mashed together with, if Eunice was not mistaken, some of their precious butter ration. To follow there was home-made apple pie with lashings of creamy custard.

'There now,' said Edith, a mite smugly. 'I don't suppose

you've been getting food like this on that there farm, have you?'

'No, Mum,' replied Eunice, knowing that that was what her mother would want to hear. A white lie was preferable to hurting her. 'It's the best meal I've had in ages.'

Edith gave a self-satisfied smile. 'I guessed as much, although I must admit you look well, doesn't she, Daddy?' Samuel nodded, but made no comment. 'I've got a surprise for you,' Edith went on. 'The Ivesons are coming here for Christmas tea, and then we're going to their house on Boxing Day. Mabel and I have arranged it.' She looked coyly at Eunice. 'We thought you and Ronald might like to have some time together.'

Eunice laughed. 'Honestly, Mum, how many times do I have to tell you that Ronnie and I are just friends, that's all. It's no use you and Aunty Mabel wishing it might be something else because it's not going to happen. We don't feel that way about one another. It'll be nice to see Ronnie again, of course; we've been writing to one another. But he may well have other plans; he might not want to spend all his time with his family, or with mine.'

'Well! So that's all the thanks I get,' said her mother, crossly. 'I was only trying to make a nice few days for you, and so was Mabel.'

'Yes, I know, Mum, but I've got other people to see as well. I must go round and see Gwen and her mother. And Mavis – you know, my friend from school. She's at college now and I want to know how she's getting on.'

'Oh well, you'll make your own arrangements, of course.' Edith bristled and stood up abruptly. 'If we've all finished we'll get this table cleared. Come along, Eunice. A little help's worth a lot of pity.'

Eunice did not dare to go out that evening; besides, she was tired. She sat by the fire with her parents and listened to the wireless: *Happidrome*, a programme of forces' favourites, and the nine o'clock news, read by Alvar Liddell. The news was a little more optimistic these days, despite the recent sinking by the Japanese of the great warships, the *Prince of Wales* and the *Repulse*. The German armies, which had seemed to be invincible, were at a standstill outside Moscow as the grim Russian winter descended. And the spirits of all had been lifted by the news that the USA had entered the war following the attack on Pearl Harbor. Winston Churchill, it was said, was to spend Christmas in Washington, cementing the new military alliance with his powerful ally.

Mavis was enjoying her course at a college in the Yorkshire countryside, she told Eunice when they met the next day. She would be exempt from call-up as she was training to become a teacher. The Yorkshire village where the college was situated was an oasis of calm, she said, although bombs had fallen on nearby Leeds and Bradford. It was hard to imagine there was a war on, and Eunice agreed that it was the same in Gloucestershire.

Gwen, however, was proud of the war work she was doing, helping to make Wellington bombers. Although she was only fastening rivets together which, in truth, was extremely boring, she was enjoying the camaraderie at the factory and was united with her colleagues in their resolve to 'blow Hitler to blazes'. A surprising statement for her once peace-loving, gentle friend to make, thought Eunice, but there was a new toughness about her. Gwen's mother insisted that she was keeping very well, but Eunice could see that the woman's health had deteriorated since she had last seen her. She admired Gwen even more for her ability to care for her and also to do her vital war work.

'I must admit I'm feeling a bit low at the moment,' she

told Eunice, although it was not apparent. 'Bill's gone home for Christmas, to his parents in Stoke-on-Trent. He's been made up to corporal now,' she added proudly.

'Jolly good,' said Eunice. 'It's still going strong then, with you and him?'

'Yes, very much so,' Gwen smiled and blushed a little. 'He wants us to get engaged, but I think it's rather too soon. It isn't that I'm not sure – I am – but I think we ought to wait a bit. They've asked him if he'd like to train as a flight engineer.'

'You mean he'd actually be flying?'

'Well, yes, eventually. At the moment he's ground crew, but he'll be leaving Blackpool soon anyway.'

'Oh dear; you'll miss him.'

'Yes, I will. He's the right one for me, Eunice. It's funny how you know, but you do. Mum thinks so too. She thinks the world of him.'

'Then why don't you go for it, if you're so sure? It's wartime and . . .' She did not like to add the words, 'and you never know what might happen', but Gwen said them for her.

'Yes, I know. We don't know what's going to happen tomorrow.' She paused, then: 'What about you?' she asked. 'Have you met anybody down in Gloucestershire?'

'By "anybody" I suppose you mean men?' Eunice grinned. 'Well – no – I haven't.'

'No handsome flying officers or whatever at the dances you go to?' asked Gwen. 'You do go to dances, don't you?'

'Yes, now and again, but I haven't met anyone that takes my fancy . . . or who fancies me. Give me a chance, though. I've only been away for three months.'

Eunice reflected that that was quite long enough to have met someone and fallen in love, but she had not done so. Gwen had known straight away that Bill was the one for her. Eunice was happy for her, but how could she be so sure she wondered. What was it all about, this falling in love, this certainty that you had met the person with whom you wanted to spend the rest of your life?

'I wish I could meet someone and feel the way you do,' she said, 'but it hasn't happened. I suppose I will know, will I . . . when it does?'

'I'm sure you will,' said Gwen, smiling.

'The Ivesons are coming for tea tomorrow,' said Eunice. 'Ronnie and all the family. It'll be good to see him again. My mother keeps hinting and hoping, you know, that he and I will fall madly in love – honestly! But I've told her she's barking up the wrong tree there.' She tried to ignore the amused and rather knowing gleam in her friend's eye.

'Nice lad, though, Ronnie, isn't he?' said Gwen.

'Oh yes, one of the best.' Eunice laughed. 'He'll make somebody a wonderful husband one day; I've always thought so . . . Oh, look, Gwen.' She suddenly remembered the photo she had been meaning to show to her friend and she delved into her shoulder bag. 'I had this photo taken a little while back: me in my uniform! Quite a lot of us had them done. You can keep it, if you like – that's if you really want a picture of me!'

'Of course I do,' said Gwen. 'Wow! You look smashing, kid. Are you sure you've not got a boyfriend tucked away down in Gloucestershire? I'm sure you must be turning a few heads.'

'No, not a one,' laughed Eunice. 'Thanks for the compliment, though. I must admit the photo is rather flattering. I think my mother thought it was – what shall I say? – a bit . . . brazen, tarty? You know what I mean.'

'What did she say?'

'Nothing really. It's more what she didn't say. She just sniffed and said, "Very nice, Eunice." ' They both laughed.

'Have you got a photo of your Bill?'

'Sure. You don't think I'm letting you get away without seeing a picture of Bill, do you? I've got some in my bedroom. Come on up and I'll show you . . . Shan't be long, Mum. Look, isn't this a lovely photo of Eunice?' Mrs Singleton smiled and agreed that it was.

Bill Collinson was a round-faced young man with a smiling mouth and sparkling humorous eyes. So much Eunice could see from the studio photograph of him in his uniform, a similar pose to the one of herself in her Land Army outfit. His corporal's stripes were prominently displayed and his forage cap was perched at a jaunty angle on what was obviously very fair hair.

'He looks very nice,' said Eunice. 'Really friendly and cheerful.'

'So he is,' said Gwen happily. 'And this is one of the two of us together that my mum took in the back garden.'

Bill was several inches taller than Gwen. He was standing with his arm thrown protectively round her shoulders and she was leaning close to him. They were the very picture of young love and happiness.

'Very nice,' said Eunice again. She was so pleased for her friend, but she could not help feeling a pang of – what? – envy, maybe. No, envy was too strong a word. She could not possibly be envious of Gwen. But, oh, she did so wish that the same thing might happen to her. Perhaps, one day it might happen. Like it was always doing in the books she read . . .

No one ate very much at teatime on Christmas Day, which was hardly surprising as they had all eaten a huge Christmas dinner only a few hours earlier. Edith Morton had opened a precious tin of red salmon, as well as using the remains of the chicken to make sandwiches. She had also made an enormous trifle; then there were the usual mince pies, and a Christmas cake topped with hard icing to resemble snow, with a tiny plaster snowman and a couple of fir trees stuck into it, which came out year after year.

'We'll be eating up till New Year,' she remarked, somewhat peeved that her lavish spread had gone largely unnoticed. 'It'll be sandwiches and trifle for lunch tomorrow whether you like it or not.' She cast a baleful glance at her husband and daughter. 'I'll wrap 'em in greaseproof paper and they'll keep fresh enough in the larder.'

'Yes, don't go eating too much at lunchtime,' chuckled Mabel. 'Don't forget you're all coming to us for tea.'

It had been quite a happy little gathering in the Mortons' dining room, normally used by visitors or, of late, by the Civil Service personnel. Paper streamers which, like the snowman on the cake, came out annually, were strung from wall to wall. They were more than a little tatty by now, as were the paper bells that opened out concertina fashion, and were pinned to each corner of the room. But it was all very festive and cheery as they toasted one another in sweet brown sherry and hoped that by the same time next year it would 'all be over'. A forlorn hope, as they all realised.

There were eight of them: Edith and Samuel; Mabel and Tom; Eunice; Ronnie; and Chrissie, accompanied by her friend Fiona, another corporal in the WAAF. Fiona's home was in the Scottish Highlands and she had considered it too far to travel for such a brief period of leave. The pair of them, jolly and light-hearted girls, certainly added to the gaiety of the mood.

'Do you feel like a walk on the prom?' Ronnie whispered to Eunice as the little company was getting ready to play a game of consequences, organised by Fiona.

'Yes, why not?' agreed Eunice. The family gathering was becoming claustrophobic and she always felt inhibited, somehow, when her parents were there. She was aware that her mother and Ronnie's mother exchanged knowing glances as the two of them departed, but she did not care. Let them think what they liked. What she wanted at the moment, more than anything else, was a bit of fresh air and freedom.

'Whew! What a relief,' she said as they walked off down the road, heading for the sea. 'It's a bit much when they're all together, isn't it – our mothers vying with one another? Well, it's my mother really, not yours, I must admit. Mum always has to have the last word.'

'Yeah, I know what you mean,' said Ronnie. 'Anyway, never mind them. I was dying to get away so you and I could have some time on our own. I've missed you, Eunice.' He squeezed her shoulder.

'Me too, Ronnie,' she answered.

They walked along the road arm in arm, their footsteps keeping time with one another's, chatting easily about this and that. They talked about their respective families and she told him about Gwen and how she seemed to have met the love of her life.

Ronnie was quiet for a moment before he answered, quite casually, 'Well, that's nice for her, isn't it? I like Gwen . . . What about you, eh? You've not got off with one of the farm hands or . . . anybody?'

'No, 'fraid not,' she laughed.

'You go to dances, don't you?' he asked.

'Yes, sometimes. We all do; it's something to look forward to and it makes a change to get dressed up now and again. The powers that be prefer us to wear our uniforms when we go to dances, but we don't always comply. It's not very easy trying to dance in clod-hopping boots.'

'That's what we fellows have to do,' smiled Ronnie.

'Well, that's different, isn't it? Do you go to dances, Ronnie?'

'Sometimes. They have them in the NAAFI. The local girls come and some of the lasses from the ATS camp nearby.'

'Sounds like good fun.'

'Yeah, it's OK, I suppose,' he replied. He didn't sound very enthusiastic.

They had reached the promenade now. They crossed the tramtrack to the sea side, then leaned against the railings, looking out across the vast expanse of sea, its blackness relieved here and there by the white cap of a wave.

'Eunice, I've got something for you,' Ronnie said suddenly. He reached into the pocket of his greatcoat and drew out a small box. 'Here you are. Happy Christmas.' He handed it to her, then leaned close and kissed her cheek.

'Thank you, Ronnie,' she said, very touched at his gesture. 'But . . . you've already given me a present, a lovely one.' Earlier in the day he had given her a leather-bound copy of *Emma*, her favourite Jane Austen novel. She had been pleased and rather surprised that he had remembered something she must have mentioned casually, although he knew, of course, of her love of books.

'Oh, this is just a little extra,' he said, 'but I didn't want to give it to you in front of all the others. I saw it in the window of a little jeweller's shop, and it reminded me of you, somehow. I hope you like it.'

Feeling quite mystified she opened the box, then she exclaimed with delight at the small cameo brooch on its bed of black velvet. It pictured the head and shoulders of a young woman, but of the eighteenth century, not of the present day; the era, in fact, of Jane Austen. 'It's beautiful, Ronnie,' she said, standing on her tiptoes and kissing his cheek. 'Thank you ever so much. Do you know, she's just like I've always imagined Emma to be; you know, the Jane Austen book you gave me?'

'Maybe . . .' Ronnie nodded. 'To be quite honest, she reminds me of you. Anyway, I hope you'll wear it.'

'Of course I will. Pin it on my coat, Ronnie, and I'll start wearing it straight away.'

As he did so she noticed that certain look in his eyes that she had seen there once before . . . or thought she had – a look of deep affection; but it had gone almost as soon as it had appeared.

'Come on,' he said. 'We'd best be getting back. We don't want your mother starting to panic.'

'Oh, don't worry,' said Eunice, laughing. 'I expect they'll still be playing consequences. She's a live wire, that Fiona, isn't she? She even managed to get my father laughing, and that takes some doing . . .'

They walked the mile or so back to Eunice's home in their usual companionable way. What a good friend he is, she reflected, and how much she would miss him when she returned to Gloucestershire. It was as though she had never realised until that moment just how much his friendship meant to her.

Chapter 6

The meal at the Ivesons' home on Boxing Day was more or less a repetition of the one at the Morton household the day before: the same kind of food, the same company. But they had all learned a lesson from the previous day; they had eaten sparingly at lunchtime and were, therefore, able to make short work of Mabel's abundant provision.

Ronnie set off on his lengthy journey back to his camp in the south of England soon after teatime. It was not far to the station and he insisted, at first, that he would walk there on his own. In the end, however, after loud protests from his parents, he agreed to his father accompanying him, although there was only his heavy kitbag to carry and he was well used to managing that by himself.

He had hoped that Eunice might be the one to go with him, but he had felt reluctant to suggest it. She had not suggested it either, and neither, to his surprise, had his mother. So he was obliged to say goodbye to her in front of everyone. He kissed her cheek, but that was no more than he did with his sister and her friend Fiona, and his mother and Aunty Edith. That was what he had always called Eunice's mother when he was a little boy, but he found it rather stuck in his throat these days to call her Aunty. She would certainly disapprove of him calling her Edith, so he usually ended up calling her nothing at all.

Eunice looked sad as he said his goodbye to her and he thought he could see the beginning of a tear shining in the corner of her eye. But he knew he might have been mistaken – wishful thinking, he supposed – because he had not noticed any other sign during the two days they had spent together that she regarded him as any other than a very good friend – which was how they had always been with each other.

'Take care, Ronnie,' she said, but that was what all the others had said too. 'And don't forget to write to me. I look forward to your letters.' Well, that was something, at any rate.

His father gave him a friendly hug as they said goodbye at the station and then set off back home before the train departed. Farewells were ghastly; all that waiting around and not really knowing what else to say, so Ronnie was relieved when he was on his own again and could settle back in his corner seat alone with his thoughts. Alone, that was, except for the other people in the compartment. A couple of RAF blokes were chatting together in the corner and the rest of the occupants seemed to be civilians, no doubt returning home from visiting relations. The populace was still being asked, disapprovingly, 'Is Your Journey Really Necessary?' but maybe Christmas was a time to relax the guidelines a little.

His thoughts as the train pulled away from the station, and for the greater part of the long journey, were of Eunice. What an idiot he had been, he pondered, not to have told her how he felt about her. He had wondered, when he had first joined the army, whether it might be a question of absence making the heart grow fonder, distance lending enchantment and all that. He was sure to miss Eunice after the close friendship they had enjoyed for so many years, but he had been surprised at just how much he had missed her. And he had realised, the last time he was home on leave – just before she left herself to join the Land Army – that he had fallen in love with her.

He could have told her then, but he had not done so. He had been half afraid that she might laugh at the idea – although Eunice was not a teasing, thoughtless sort of girl; not at all – but she might have been surprised, and he was fearful that it might damage their precious friendship. Besides, it would not be fair, he had told himself, to expect her to become his sweetheart or girlfriend or whatever, not when she was setting out on a new phase of her life. She had to be free to meet other people – other men, maybe – whilst she was in the Land Army, although the thought of that was agony to him. Just as he should be free, he supposed, to meet other girls. But he had decided that Eunice was the only one he wanted.

That was why he had asked her to send him a photograph, but he had made it only a casual request and she had not seemed to think it was strange at all. When the photo had arrived his feelings had grown stronger than ever. She was so beautiful . . . Of course, he had always known that, but the picture revealed other attributes as well. She appeared innocent and artless; a lovely young girl on the brink of womanhood, despite the fact that her sweater showed her gorgeous figure to the best advantage. He was aware of that too; he was only human after all!

'Gosh! She's a corker,' some of his messmates had said. And what harm had there been in letting them think she was his girlfriend? Maybe, with a bit of luck, she soon would be. 'You lucky old devil, Iveson!'

Well, he had gone and funked it again. He had really

meant to tell her this Christmas time. Just why he had not done so he could not say. The claustrophobia induced by their two families, maybe; and then Eunice had seemed so surprised when he gave her his special gift that he had not wanted to do anything to spoil the pleasure of the moment.

He wondered whether or not he should write and tell her how he felt. It might be easier in a letter. On the other hand, maybe not. No, he would wait until they were next on leave together; then he really would take the bull by the horns, so to speak. He smiled to himself, thinking of Eunice on the farm. He hoped she would not be, literally, taking a bull by its horns.

But Ronnie had no idea just how long it would be before he saw Eunice again, or what would have happened in the meantime.

Eunice was not due to return to Gloucestershire until the following day, and Chrissie and Fiona also had an extra day. Eunice wondered, in passing, why Fiona had not made the effort to travel up to Scotland to visit her family or whoever she might have up there. It was a long way, certainly, but worth the trouble, surely, at Christmastime? One never knew, though, what friction and animosity there might be in other people's families. Fiona certainly seemed contented enough – very happy, in fact – to be spending the leave with her friend.

Eunice left Blackpool more encumbered than when she had arrived. Her parents had taken heed of her hints and their Christmas present to her was a Raleigh bicycle. It was an austerity machine, as they all were now – a black upright model with no fancy attachments. But it was clean and bright, sparkling with newness, a far cry from the ancient machines loaned out from HQ, and Eunice was more than pleased.

Mrs Meadows' gift, though small, had delighted her too: two white cotton handkerchiefs each with an embroidered E, surrounded by tiny flowerets, in the corner, and finished off with a delicate crocheted border; Mrs Meadows' own handiwork, Eunice guessed. What a very kind and thoughtful person she was. She tucked them away carefully in her travel bag, together with Ronnie's book and the gifts of lavender bath cubes and Californian Poppy perfume from Mabel and Chrissie.

Fortunately she had to change trains only once, at Crewe, and, just as she had done before, she encountered Olive on the platform. To her surprise the other girl was wheeling a bicycle too, a black upright model that was almost a twin of her own; a Humber, though, not a Raleigh. She was wearing her usual tense expression, albeit not quite as anxious as the first time they had met. Her face brightened when she saw Eunice and she laughed.

'Well, fancy that! Great minds think alike, it seems. It's a present from my parents; is yours?' Eunice agreed that it was, then Olive went on to say, 'It's all right for you, though. You can ride a bicycle, can't you? It's more than I can do. Goodness knows how I'm going to learn.'

'It's as easy as winking,' said Eunice. 'Don't give up, Olive, before you've even started. We'll have you riding in no time, up and down those country lanes; it's a wizard place to learn. Come on now; the train's here. Let's see about getting these bikes in the guard's van . . .'

Mr Meadows met them at the station and, fortunately, there was just about room for the bicycles, as well as the girls and their luggage, in the back of the farm truck.

'It's grand to see you both again,' said Mrs Meadows, welcoming each of them with a hug and a kiss on the cheek. 'Eeh, we've missed you, haven't we, Bert? We've had a lovely Christmas, though, with our two lasses and their husbands, and the grandchildren. Such a crowd of us there was on Christmas Day. Come on, now; sit yerselves down. I've made a nice toad-in-the-hole, then there's plums and custard for afters . . .'

The weather turned very cold, as was only to be expected in January and February. Eunice had never seen so much snow. Snow did fall in Blackpool – the first winter of the war had been a particularly bitter one with snowdrifts of six feet and more – but it did not usually stay long, being quickly dispelled by the salt sea air. Here, however, it lingered, coating every field, tree, hedgerow and rooftop with its sparkling whiteness – a scene straight from Fairyland or from a Christmas card, but it was not so romantic when one had to work in it. Six o'clock in the morning, in the cowshed, became a time almost to look forward to instead of one to dread. At least it was warm and dry and the smell of the hay and the milk and the softly lowing animals was strangely comforting. Less pleasant was the white-washing of byres, barns and pigsties, a job that was undertaken when the weather was inclement and it was not possible to work in the fields.

Olive's bicycle-riding lessons had to be postponed until a thaw set in. She had seemed relieved, and Eunice guessed she was afraid of making a fool of herself and worried, also, in case she should never get the hang of it. As it turned out, though, she learned quite quickly in the end, surprising herself as well as Eunice. Inevitably, she had taken several tumbles into the ditch, but she was learning to put on a show of stoicism instead of dissolving into tears. Then, one day, Eunice let go of the saddle and, unaware at first that she was really doing it on her own, Olive rode off down the lane.

'Well done! I'm proud of you,' Eunice told her.

'Are you really?' said Olive, pink-cheeked with excitement. 'Do you know, my parents said I'd never learn. They were very loath to buy the bicycle at all. Just wait till I tell them.'

Eunice reflected, as she had done before, that Olive's problems stemmed mainly from having overprotective and anxious parents; as she had herself, but she felt she was beginning to break free of the shackles.

'That's right, you tell 'em,' she said now. 'You're not a little girl any more. Neither are we playing at farming any more. Do you remember those mock cows with rubber udders? What greenhorns we were! We've come on by leaps and bounds since those early days. I think we should feel very proud of ourselves. Oh, come on, Olive,' she went on as her friend did not answer. 'We're getting real good at it all. Milking cows – proper ones, and hedging and ditching, and whitewashing. We can even drive a tractor; well, after a fashion. There's no end to our talents, I tell you.'

'It's all right for you. It all comes dead easy to you,' said Olive, but not quite so plaintively as usual. 'It takes me ages to get the hang of things. I don't know what I'd do if you weren't there to help me.'

'I'm not the only one who helps you,' Eunice grinned knowingly at her. 'Well – am I?'

Olive gave a quiet smile and blushed a little. 'Oh, I suppose you mean . . .'

'Yes, I mean Ted. I've noticed how he's always near at hand when you want some help.'

'Not always . . .'

'Well, obviously not every time, not if he's working at the other end of the farm. But you must admit he's often around when you need him.'

'I expect it's because he knows I'm dead hopeless.'

'I expect it's because he likes you a lot. Oh, come on,

Olive; anyone can see that the two of you are getting friendly.'

'There's nothing in it,' Olive replied quickly. 'I mean, we're not – well – going out or anything.'

'You went to the pictures with him.'

'Only once.'

'Well, that's a start, isn't it? And you do like him, don't you?'

'Yes, I suppose I do. But . . . why on earth should he be interested in me? I mean to say, I'm not pretty, not like you. And I'm not all . . . lively and cheerful like you are. I sometimes feel all awkward and tongue-tied, and I don't know what to say to people.'

'Don't run yourself down, Olive. You are pretty, you know, especially now you've let your hair grow a bit longer. And I dare say the reason Ted likes you is *because* you're quiet. Ted's quiet as well; he's rather shy, isn't he? I think you'd make a lovely couple.'

'Oh, go on; what a thing to say!' Olive giggled, but she sounded rather pleased at the idea. She fell silent for a while as they walked back up the lane towards the farmhouse, wheeling her bicycle between them. She would not need any more riding lessons now. After a few moments: 'I've never had a boyfriend,' she said. 'When I went to the pictures with Ted it was the first time ever that I'd been out with a man. It felt ever so strange.'

'You'll get used to it.' Eunice grinned at her. 'Not that I'm all that used to going out with men myself.'

She reflected then that what she said was very true. No, she was not used to going out with men at all, no more than Olive was. She had had one or two 'dates' – if you could call them that – with local lads at home, and, of course, she had been out with Ronnie, but these outings were certainly not dates. She had never had a steady boyfriend and that, she supposed, at her age, was quite unusual. Her mother had always kept an eagle eye on her, so there had never been an opportunity for her to meet someone different. She had wondered if she might do so when she was away from home, but so far there had not been anyone in whom she could take more than a fleeting interest. Would she ever meet someone who was special to her, she wondered? It looked as though Olive had already done so and that was a little surprising: that her shy and insecure colleague should have a boyfriend whilst she, Eunice, was still on her own.

It had been heartwarming to watch the gradual awareness developing between Olive and Ted Adamson. Ted, the one remaining farm hand at Meadowlands, was twenty-four years old. At the present time, 1942, farm workers were exempt from call-up until they were twenty-five although it was rumoured that the age for conscription would soon be reduced to eighteen. Ted was a bachelor who lived with his parents in the nearby village. He was a quiet, homely and well-mannered man, with brownish hair and greyish eyes. Eunice hadn't been long on the farm before she discovered that he was kind and helpful and very likeable. An ideal friend for Olive, she now realised, and over the next few months, as winter gave way to spring, their friendship developed.

The war news was depressing. America was now an ally, and the morale of the nation had been boosted on hearing that. However, there was despondency on hearing, in February, that the island base of Singapore had surrendered to the Japanese. Malaya had already been abandoned and Burma was soon to follow. Sixty thousand British soldiers had been taken into captivity.

As if that was not enough, there were also heavy losses at sea: 275 merchant ships, en route for Britain, were sunk in what became known as the Battle of the Atlantic. Consequently there were even more food shortages on the Home Front. A visit to the cinema did little to cheer one up either, as the news reels showed the sinking of grain ships. The nation was encouraged to use more potatoes to save flour, which was now becoming a precious commodity, and there were numerous 'Food Flashes' at the cinema and on the radio proposing economy measures.

Eunice, together with her fellow land girls, was realising more and more the importance of her work. They had come in for a good deal of criticism in the early years of the war, but now it was a different story. Agriculture was fundamental to survival and the WLA was seen to be doing a vital job. A quote from a farmer in their own magazine, *Land Girl*, did a great deal to boost their flagging spirits. 'Girls like this cannot help but win the war,' he said, and Eunice, for one, set to her work with renewed vigour.

On the whole she was very contented. No one could say that a land girl's pay was good, but Eunice was quite satisfied. To be left with ten shillings a week to spend after the statutory deduction for her board and lodging, felt like riches indeed after what she'd had at home.

It was in the spring of 1942 that the land girls were issued with an officer-style greatcoat, and also a black oilskin mackintosh and sou'wester – ideal garments, they might have thought, for keeping out the rain, but, in reality, they were too stiff and heavy to work in, and only succeeded in making the girls even hotter and sweatier. The khaki greatcoat, however, was a stylish garment, very smart to wear, and Eunice was more than satisfied at how well she looked in it, especially as she was now entitled to wear the first red half-diamond stitched on to the sleeve. These were issued to denote the length of service and she had now been in the WLA for six months.

'Ted's joining up,' said Olive, in a tearful voice, one evening towards the end of March. They were taking a short rest in their bedroom after a hard day's work in the fields. Olive and Ted were no longer trying to disguise their feelings for one another. Olive had not confided overmuch in Eunice – that was not her way – but it was plain to see the way things were progressing.

'Well, I should think that's fair enough,' replied Eunice evenly. 'I expect he feels that he wants to do his bit, doesn't he, especially the way things are going at the moment? And men who are not in uniform do tend to get funny looks, don't they? Some chaps'll do all they can to steer clear of the army.'

'Ted's not like that,' retorted Olive. 'It was his mother who didn't want him to join up. His father had a dreadful time in the last war.'

'Yes, so did mine,' said Eunice.

'Anyway, Ted's decided to enlist now.'

'Jolly good for him, that's what I say.'

'You would, wouldn't you? It's all right for you. You haven't got a boyfriend to worry about, but . . . well, I'm getting very fond of Ted . . . and I thought he was of me.'

'I'm sure he is, Olive, but that doesn't mean that he can't do what he thinks is right.' Eunice tried not to care about the effect Olive's harsh words had on her.

'You have no idea, have you?' said Olive, a trifle petulantly. Eunice was determined not to be drawn into a quarrel.

'What's he going to join then?' she asked. 'The army or the RAF?' She took it for granted that the land-loving Ted would not want to be a sailor.

'I don't know,' said Olive. Her lips closed in a stubborn

line. Then, 'We haven't talked about it much,' she said, 'not since he first told me.'

'You must have some idea, though.'

'All right then; the army. He likes his feet firmly on the ground, does Ted.' Olive looked so down in the dumps and disillusioned that Eunice felt she must try to make her see reason.

'Oh, come on now,' she said. 'It won't be so bad. I know you'll miss him, but you'll have letters to look forward to, like lots of girls do. You'll be one of hundreds, just the same as you – thousands, even.'

'That doesn't make it any better. The thing is, he doesn't really need to go, not until he's twenty-five. That's next year, and it might all be over by then.'

'And it might not,' replied Eunice ominously. 'Anyway, they'll be calling up all the farm workers who are over eighteen before long, you'll see. Ted's just going a little bit earlier, that's all. Try to encourage him, Olive. It'll only make it worse for him if you're moping around like a wet weekend. Come on, cheer up.' She sniffed the air appreciatively. 'I think Mrs Meadows is cooking shepherd's pie, or hotpot. Whatever it is, it smells jolly good.'

Mr and Mrs Meadows were sorry to hear that their one remaining farm hand would soon be leaving, although they both gave him every encouragement, knowing he was following the dictates of his conscience. They decided to do what several other farmers in the vicinity had done: apply for a couple of German prisoners of war to help with the work.

This particular POW camp was right in the heartland of England and the prisoners were driven each day in army trucks to the outlying farms. Two men were quite quickly assigned to Meadowlands, which was only a few miles away, and they started to work there even before Ted Adamson left. One of them, a very young man who seemed to be little more than a schoolboy, was called Werner. The other one was Heinrich Muller, a navigator in the Luftwaffe who had been shot down during the Battle of Britain. He had already spent two years in prison camps when he was sent to work at Meadowlands.

The POWs came in for a good deal of resentment from some of the farm workers. It was the responsibility of the Government, who were bound by the Geneva Convention, to ensure that the prisoners received humane treatment. No one could object to that; it was only what the British would expect for their own lads held prisoner overseas. But these Germans, in the eyes of some, seemed to be treated as welcome guests instead of as the enemy. Their working hours were shorter than those of the average farm worker – nine o'clock in the morning till four in the afternoon; what was more, they were provided with transport there and back.

Some farmers made no secret of their animosity, having as few dealings as possible with their unwelcome employees, but Mr and Mrs Meadows treated their two POWs with kindness and consideration. It was Mrs Meadows' view that the poor lads were somebody's sons, even if they were on the opposite side in the conflict, and as such deserved to be treated with dignity and civility. There were, however, fairly strict rules about fraternising, which had to be passed on to Eunice and Olive.

'You can speak to them, of course,' said Mrs Meadows. 'I wouldn't want you to give them the cold shoulder like some folks round here are doing. But . . . well . . . don't let them get too friendly, like. You never know; they're not the same as us.' She laughed a little uneasily. 'That goes against what I was saying, doesn't it, about trying to be kind to them? It sounds as though I'm as prejudiced as the rest, but I'm not. Only . . . just be careful, girls, that's all.'

'She doesn't need to remind us,' Olive remarked later to Eunice. 'I shan't go near them if I can help it. It gives me the creeps, having the enemy working on the farm. Ugh!'

Eunice was trying to be tolerant, as Mrs Meadows had suggested, although she half agreed with what her friend was saying. 'I don't suppose we'll come into contact with them very much,' she said. 'I expect Mr Meadows will give them work well away from us. But we'll have to be polite, Olive. If Ted were taken prisoner, then he'd be the enemy, wouldn't he? And we wouldn't want anybody being nasty to him.'

'Ted's still here,' said Olive stubbornly, 'and I don't suppose he'll like working with the enemy, not when he's soon going to be fighting them. Well, not those two, of course – they're safe for the rest of the war, aren't they? – but he'll be fighting the rest of 'em.'

Eunice found herself thinking, suddenly, of her friend Ronnie, in his camp in the south of England. She supposed that he too was safe for the moment . . . but for how long?

'Ted won't actually be fighting, not just yet,' she told Olive, 'although I suppose they're all preparing for . . . something or other; but they're not allowed to talk about it. I've got a friend in the army as well. You've heard me mention Ronnie, haven't you?'

'Oh yes; the one who gave you that nice brooch.'

'Yes, that's right. Anyway, I get the impression from what he says that they're leading up to something. I suppose he could be sent abroad at any moment,' she added thoughtfully, knowing that that would concern her very much.

'And that's supposed to cheer me up, is it?' snapped Olive.

'No, I'm sorry; I was just thinking aloud. Try not to worry about Ted. He's doing the right thing, believe me. And it might all be over sooner than we think.'

'Huh! Pigs might fly,' said Olive, determined not to be comforted.

But Eunice's thoughts at that moment were with Ronnie. She had not heard from him just lately; perhaps it was she who owed him a letter; she had been so busy that there had not been much time for letter writing. But she still remembered to say a little prayer for him from time to time, that God would keep him safe.

Eunice's attitude towards the prisoners of war was coloured, almost without her being aware of it, by her father's prejudice. Samuel Morton's experiences in the trenches during 'the first lot' had left him with an abiding hatred of the Germans. He had suffered badly from the effects of mustard gas, barely escaping with his life, and this had damaged not only his health but his personality as well. To him, the only good German was a dead one; he could not – and would not even try to – forget.

As well as this bigotry, which Eunice had grown up with, she knew she must heed Mrs Meadows' warning not to be too friendly. Moreover, it was continually being drummed into the population, by means of posters and news flashes at the cinema that 'Careless Talk Costs Lives', and that you had to 'Be like Dad and Keep Mum'. Not that Eunice would have given away any secrets even if she had known any, but she had always been cautioned to look upon all Germans as untouchable.

Mrs Meadows had said, however, that they should not totally ignore the POWs or do anything to make them feel too unwelcome. If Olive wished to walk past them with her nose in the air, then that was her affair, but Eunice, in spite of her misgivings, knew she could not be so discourteous. She was a friendly girl and it was not in her nature to spurn anyone, even a German.

She was somewhat disconcerted at first by the frank stares of the elder of the two men whenever she passed by. She would smile politely and say 'Hello', and they did the same, but she could feel the fellow's eyes still on her as she walked away. She was aware that her close-fitting green jersey might be showing off her curves rather too much. It was the same garment that had made her mother tut disapprovingly when she had first tried it on. Eunice had never been dissatisfied with her figure, which sometimes caused a few wolf whistles when she went to a local dance in her uniform. She knew she was pretty and she enjoyed the admiration of the British lads, be they servicemen or locals.

But a German; that was something else altogether. The one called Heinrich was quite good-looking, with the blue eyes and heavy blond hair that so many of them had. But she knew she must not do anything – anything at all – to encourage him as she might have done with one of our own young men. She made up her mind that the next time he looked at her in that bold way she would return his stare with a frosty one of her own.

She found, however, that her best intentions, not to snub him but to put him firmly in his place, were scuppered one day in mid-April. She was passing close to the place where he and Werner were sitting by the hedge, eating their midday snack, when she was faced with a smile of such warmth and guilelessness – or so it seemed to her – that she could not help but smile back at him.

Chapter 7

Looking back on it all, much later, Eunice knew that that was what had started it all: a glance and a smile. Then another glance had passed between them, one in which they both acknowledged that they would like to know one another better. Not at that particular moment, however; Werner was there, and so was Olive.

'Cheeky devil!' Olive said as they walked across the field, on their way to the farmhouse for their midday snack. 'Did you see the way he smiled at us? He'll get no change out of me. I know his sort; thinks he's God's gift to women. Anyway, he's a German.'

Eunice did not answer at first. You don't know him, Olive, or his sort, she was thinking. 'Oh, I don't know,' she replied after a few seconds' pause. 'He seems quite nice really. They both do. It's better to smile than to make a rude gesture, isn't it?'

'They wouldn't dare!'

'No, maybe not; not to us. But you couldn't blame them. It's what I've seen some of the locals do to the POWs; stick two fingers up when they happen to see them.'

'So what? What do they expect when all our ships are being blown to bits?'

'It's hardly their fault, Heinrich and Werner's.'

'Oh, so we're on first-name terms now, are we?'

'Don't be silly, Olive. I just happen to know what they're called, that's all, and so do you. How does Ted get on with them?'

'I don't know. I've not asked him,' snapped Olive.

But Eunice knew from her own observations that Ted was getting on well enough with the Germans. She had seen him instructing them without any show of hostility, and they had been paying attention to him very politely. Ted would be leaving soon, in about ten days' time, to join a Gloucestershire regiment, which, no doubt, was why Olive was so ill tempered.

She cheered up, however, that evening, when Mrs Meadows reminded them that the Young Farmers' Ball, to which they had both been invited, was the following Wednesday. Not that they needed any reminding; they had both been looking forward to it.

The farmer's wife, to their great surprise, had asked both girls, several weeks ago, if they would like to go to the ball. 'Bert and I'll be going, like we always do,' she told them. 'I know we're not Young Farmers any more,' she chuckled, 'but it's tradition, like, and there'll be lots of young 'uns there. We've invited Ted an' all.' She smiled knowingly at Olive, obviously realising that the two of them were friendly. 'Our treat, of course, to all of you. I'm sorry we've no special partner for you, Eunice love, but I know you'll not be short of dancing partners once we get there, a pretty girl like you.'

Olive, for once, had seemed pleased and happy. 'Oh, how lovely,' she cried, a smile transforming her face, removing the petulant look she so often wore nowadays. 'Thank you ever so much, Mrs Meadows. Does Ted know? He hasn't said anything.'

'Yes, I asked him earlier today, but told him to keep quiet till I'd mentioned it to you. He's been before, of course. It's a chance for Young Farmers to get togged up for a change, out of their overalls and wellies; to say nothing of their wives and girlfriends. It's quite the highlight of the social calendar round here, isn't it, Bert?'

'The only one, I'd say,' he replied. 'I don't reckon much, meself, to getting all tarted up like a dog's dinner, but the womenfolk enjoy it.'

'Oh, don't be such an old spoilsport, Bert!' said his wife. 'You know we always have a good time.'

'Thank you very much, Mrs Meadows,' Eunice said. 'It's very kind of you to invite us. Don't worry about me not having a partner. I don't mind.' But secretly, she did, just a little.

'Never mind, lass,' chuckled Bert Meadows. 'You can dance with me, so long as you don't mind me trampling all over yer feet.'

Eunice laughed. 'No, of course I don't. What will we wear, though? It sounds as though it'll be quite a posh do. I'm sure I haven't got anything suitable, and I don't suppose Olive has either.'

Mrs Meadows beamed at them. 'Don't worry; I've thought of everything. Come along upstairs with me and I'll show you what I've found.'

Mystified, they followed her into the bedroom she and her husband shared. She opened the door of the large mahogany wardrobe and took out two dresses on hangers, enveloped in cotton covers. 'There now, what do you think about these?' she asked, taking away the wrappers. 'They belonged to our Connie and Phyllis. They wore 'em at the last farmers' ball they went to, afore they both got wed.

They won't wear 'em now, that's for sure.' She shook her head and laughed. 'They've both of 'em got a bit broad in the beam since they had the kiddies; they take after me. But they'll fit you two slim young lasses a treat, that is, if you don't mind wearing second-hand togs. We can freshen 'em up with a bit of trimming here and there. Make do and mend, you know, like the Government are always telling us to do.'

She was obviously so delighted with her idea that Eunice and Olive could not possibly have refused, even if they'd wanted to. But both dresses were beautiful – both ankle-length, one of a pale green silky rayon with cap sleeves, a sweetheart neckline and a beaded bodice; the other made of mid-blue silk-taffeta with wide shoulder straps and with bow trimming on the bodice top and at the waistline.

'They're lovely, Mrs Meadows,' said Eunice. 'Aren't they, Olive?' Olive agreed that they were, indeed, very nice. 'Are you sure your daughters won't mind us wearing them? After all, they don't know us.'

'No, but they've heard all about you and they'd be only too pleased to think that their old dresses were being used again. Well, not all that old,' she amended. 'These 'ere bows are a bit faded, and some of the beading's come loose here and there on this one, but I can soon have 'em looking as good as new. I'm quite good with a needle, though I say it myself. Now, which are you going to choose? Eunice? Olive? I bet I can guess.

'There, I was right,' she said delightedly as Olive opted for the demure pale green dress and Eunice for the more daring – inasmuch as she would be showing her bare arms and shoulders – and sophisticated blue one.

It was these renovated dresses that the two girls tried on in their bedroom several weeks later, with Mrs Meadows proudly watching them. The somewhat shabby bows on

Eunice's blue dress had been replaced with smart black velvet ones, and the skirt, which had been a little faded, was now covered with a layer of filmy black tulle. Olive's green dress now had an edging of silver braid to the sleeves and neckline and sparkling new silver beads decorated the bodice.

'There now, you'll be the belles of the ball, both of you,' said Mrs Meadows, clapping her hands. 'Just wait till Ted sees you,' she whispered to Olive. 'And there'll be crowds of young men queuing up to dance with you.' She nodded confidently at Eunice, not wanting her to feel left out.

'Thank you,' said Eunice, very pleased at the way the dress suited her, the blue matching her eyes and the fitted bodice showing off her figure to its best advantage. The trouble was, there would be no one there to take any notice – no one, that was, that she cared about. 'You've done a wizard job, Mrs Meadows.'

'Mmm . . . yes, thank you,' echoed Olive, preening herself in front of the mirror. 'I must admit we do look . . . very nice.' She smiled in a self-satisfied way, her earlier ill temper quite forgotten.

The following day Eunice and Heinrich found themselves working together, hoeing a field of cabbages. 'Your hands are sore,' he said to her, in careful English, after they had smiled at each other, then worked together in silence for several minutes. 'You do not usually work on the farm, I think . . . Eunice? That is your name, is it not?'

She smiled. 'No. I mean, yes . . . I'm called Eunice. But I've not worked on a farm before, not till I joined the Land Army. I worked in a library. You understand? You know . . . with books.'

'I think so.' He nodded.

She put down her hoe for a moment, easing her aching

back, then she looked ruefully at her reddened hands. 'Yes, they look a mess, don't they? Very ugly – that's with milking the cows.'

'No, not ugly,' he said. 'You are a very pretty girl . . . Eunice.'

She tried to ignore his last remark and quickly changed the subject. 'You speak very good English,' she told him.

'I learn it at school,' he replied. 'And also the farmer, Herr Meadows, he is very good to me. He lend me a dictionary with German and English so I understand better.'

They were quiet for a while after that. Eunice looked round anxiously for Olive, but the other girl was nowhere in sight. With Ted's departure only just over a week away the two of them were trying to work together as much as possible and the farmer did not seem to mind. A few moments later, however, when Mr Meadows walked across the field, she noticed that Heinrich moved a few yards further away from her.

'Is not good, I think, for us to talk too much,' he said later, when the farmer had gone. 'Not when people watch. Is wrong, they tell us, to talk to English girls. Is *verboten*.'

'Yes . . . *ja*,' she replied, smiling. 'I know what they say. They say it to us as well. But we're doing no harm, are we?' He seemed not to understand. 'I mean . . . it isn't wrong, is it, just to talk? It is . . . good?' she asked.

'*Ja*, very good.' His bright blue eyes twinkled as he smiled at her.

She did not see him again that day. He must have been instructed to work elsewhere, but later that week she learned more about him. He was twenty-one, two years older than she was, and his home was in Remagen, on the River Rhine. His father owned a chemist's shop there and Heinrich was training to become a pharmacist. The war had interrupted his studies, but he hoped to go back eventually and take over the family business.

No one, as yet, seemed to have paid much attention to the little chats they had together. Olive and Ted were too preoccupied with one another and Mr Meadows was always too busy to spare them a second glance. Werner, no doubt, was aware of the attraction between his fellow prisoner and the English girl, but she guessed he would keep his thoughts to himself. Eunice knew, though, that she must be careful, not only because people might notice, but because the more she saw of Heinrich, the more she was getting to like him. And that would not do. No, it would not do at all.

The Young Farmers' Ball turned out to be, as Mrs Meadows had intimated, quite a splendid occasion. It was one of the few highlights of the social life in the neighbourhood. It was held in the Assembly Hall of the nearest small town. Observing all the gaiety and glitter in the crowded room, to say nothing of the buffet table, practically groaning beneath the weight of the food, it was almost impossible to believe that these happy and carefree people were, in reality, in the middle of a brutal war. Moreover, at that moment, the news was grim and it seemed that the end was nowhere in sight.

All the women, without exception, wore long dresses. Some of the older women were wearing their fur capes or velvet jackets, dating from a couple of decades before. Although it was, supposedly, the Young Farmers' Ball, the majority of the gathering could not, in truth, be called young. This was especially true of the menfolk, many of whom were decidedly middle-aged. Most of the farm hands were in the forces and only a few young ones, like Ted, remained. These, also, were liable to be called up at any time. The agriculture of the country would then be entirely in the hands of the elderly farmers and their very young assistants, helped by the WLA and the prisoners of war.

It was the men who looked strange to Eunice, rather than the women. It seemed odd to see them wearing collars and ties, to say nothing of suits, or jackets and grey flannel trousers. Very few of them were wearing dinner suits, and the ones who did looked a little ill at ease, as though they were about to burst out of their stiff collars and tight jackets. All, however, had donned their best clothes: their pinstriped suits and crisp white shirts or more casual sports jackets and trousers.

'You look very smart,' Eunice remarked to Ted, who looked quite the dandy in a navy-blue suit and a most un-Ted-like boldly patterned red and blue tie.

He seemed pleased. 'You didn't recognise me, eh? Just got it out of moth balls, to tell the truth,' he laughed. 'I've got to try and keep up with you two beautiful girls. In fact there's a room full of beauty queens tonight, but you two cap the lot.' He looked admiringly, not only at Olive, but at Eunice as well. 'Very nice; very nice indeed.'

'Come on, Ted. Let's go and dance,' said Olive, pulling at his arm, and he went without demur. Eunice could see her friend was less than pleased that Ted was noticing how attractive some of the other women looked, when his eyes should have been only for her. But her ill temper was soon forgotten, as the two of them stumbled around the floor to the strains of 'It's Foolish but It's Fun'. Their attempt at a quickstep involved a good deal of falling over one another's feet and laughing. At least it was good to see Olive enjoying herself so much.

'May I have the pleasure?' asked Bert Meadows, standing in front of Eunice and grinning broadly. 'Come on, lass. I promised I'd dance with you, didn't I?'

'Promised? Don't you mean threatened?' said Eunice, laughing as he proceeded to tread on her toes.

'Now, now, don't be cheeky! The missus and I used to do a fair quickstep at one time. It's a while ago, mind you. She says she gets out of breath now.' Annie Meadows, very regal-looking in purple silk, was sitting in a corner of the room, happily chatting to a fellow farmer's wife. 'Are you enjoying yerself?' Bert asked Eunice, a little anxiously, ''cause that's what we want you to do.'

'Yes, I am, thank you – very much so,' she replied.

'Well, that's all right then; that's the spirit.'

It was no less than the truth. She was enjoying the evening very much indeed. It was such a change from the dreary monotony of the work on the farm. During the winter the days had seemed endless. It had been bitterly cold and when the snow had gone the rain had started. Now, spring had arrived and the lighter mornings and evenings were helping to make the work seem less arduous. As was the arrival of a new farm worker . . . Eunice tried to stifle such thoughts when they arose. A friendship such as that was strictly forbidden; even to think of it was dangerous.

She was not short of dancing partners. Several of the elderly farmers asked her for a dance, pleased to be seen with one of the prettiest girls in the room. Eunice realised she and Olive had been done a singular honour in being invited. There were very few of the other land girls present; just another two whom they remembered from their training course. The majority of the younger women were farmers' daughters. She danced with some of the younger men too – farm hands she knew from the neighbourhood – and there were several community dances, like the palais glide and a progressive barn dance. It was pleasant to dance to a real band – albeit a small one, consisting of a piano, percussion, saxophone and French horn – instead of a wind-up gramophone or tinny piano, which was the norm at the occasional dances at the mess or in the village hall.

She decided it would be best not to ask any questions about the buffet – who had provided it and how on earth had they managed to do so? – but just to eat and enjoy it and be thankful. The long trestle table, covered with dazzling white damask cloths, was laden with platters of home-cooked ham, chicken, beef, pork, salads and crisp rolls spread with butter, and to follow there was trifle with real cream and a mouth-watering selection of fancy cakes.

'Ask no questions and you'll be told no lies!' Mrs Meadows whispered. 'Actually, we've all been doing a bit of hoarding . . . and a bit of black market business. Strictly forbidden, of course, but it's only once a year. And it's been a grand do, hasn't it?'

Eunice agreed that it had. She had enjoyed herself immensely. Why then, should a pair of humorous blue eyes keep entering her mind, and the sound of a guttural, accented, though softly spoken, voice? 'You are a very pretty girl . . . Eunice.'

The thought of Heinrich was with her as she lay in bed that night, and this time she did not try to quell it.

Eunice was essentially a town girl. Before she joined the Land Army she had scarcely been able to distinguish one wild flower from another, apart from the obvious ones like the buttercup and daisy. Trees, more particularly, had been almost a foreign country to her. In Blackpool, and the Fylde countryside in general, there was a dearth of trees. In Stanley Park, of course, they grew in abundance around the lake, but that was a good bus ride out of Blackpool and was a place that Eunice had visited only rarely. Sycamore, oak, birch, beech – they had all been the same to her: just trees. Now she was able to distinguish them all by the shapes of their leaves, the texture of their bark, or their silhouette against the summer sky.

Even in winter, she had come to appreciate the beauty of trees, their filigree patterns of branches looking like lace against a grey sky. When they had first arrived at Meadowlands, in the late autumn, the long straight furrows of the ploughed fields had been deep brown, sometimes rimmed with frost. Eunice had been reminded of a hymn she had sung in the infants' school.

> See the farmer sow the seed, while the field is brown;
> See the furrows deep and straight, up the field and down.

Then, she had no idea what a furrow was and certainly had never seen one.

Then, as the spring arrived, the furrows had been speckled with green as the tiny shoots appeared. 'God will make the golden corn grow where all is brown,' the song had said, and as the year drew onwards that was what had taken place. Eunice found she was experiencing the satisfaction that came from working close to nature, as though she were a real country girl, and to marvel at the beauty of the changing seasons: the brown and grey and silvery white of winter, the fresh green of springtime, the blue of the summer sky and the gold of the corn. The hedgerows were scattered with delicate pink wild roses, and the scent of meadowsweet and honeysuckle lingered on the air. She knew the names of many wild flowers now: purple and white clover, coltsfoot, campion, vernal and vetch. And she was learning to recognise the song of the birds: the thrush, the blackbird, the twittering sparrows, and, for the first time in her life, she had heard a cuckoo.

Now, summer was giving way to early autumn, and Eunice was soon to discover which was the worst job of all on the farm – threshing corn. The dust got everywhere: in your eyes, mouth and ears, even finding its way through layers of clothing into your underwear. Her eyes were red with continual rubbing and there was always the fear that a mouse – or, even worse, a rat – might suddenly run across her feet. Eunice found it impossible to conquer her fear of these creatures, and it was no use her fellow workers telling her that the rodents were more frightened than she was. Olive, of course, was scared out of her wits as well, which was some consolation. The land girls took a turn at most things in the harvest field: pitching up, feeding the threshing machine, humping heavy sacks of grain, or carrying away the chaff in a large hessian sheet.

There were other tasks, however, which were much more congenial. One that Eunice enjoyed particularly was the harvesting of the apples in the farm orchard. One morning in early September, as she gathered a basket of windfalls from the dew-spangled grass, she felt that never in her life had she been more contented. The smell of the ripe apples was like wine; she felt heady with it. Later in the day she would climb a ladder to pick the fruit from the topmost branches, or someone else would do the climbing while she would receive the apples, handling them carefully and making sure they did not bruise. In her past life apples to Eunice had been just apples, either red or green. Now, she was proud that she knew the characteristics of each variety and she found unexpected beauty in the subtle variations of their colours, from palest pink and orange to deep crimson and glowing green. Worcesters were rich and red; Monarchs were veined in pink and green; Bramleys one could only describe as green; whereas Cox's Orange Pippins, to Eunice, were all the shades of autumn: red, orange, russet and gold, streaked like a sunset sky. These were her favourites, not only to look at and smell, but to taste; crisp and juicy with a tang that was neither sweet nor sour, but utterly mouth-watering.

But the reason for her contentment was not due entirely to her feeling of harmony with her surroundings, or the enjoyment of her work, but to anticipation of what the day might hold. She was hoping it might be Heinrich who would come to assist her with the apple gathering later in the day, even if it were only for a short time. They usually managed, for some period in each day, to work together for a little while, but they both knew they had to be very, very careful. They had known one another for several months now, and during that time their friendship, tentative at first, had grown deeper.

'You have a friend, perhaps, Eunice?' Heinrich had asked her a few weeks after they had first met. 'A man friend? A soldier who writes to you?'

'Yes,' said Eunice. 'I have, as a matter of fact. A young man who lives near me at home. We've been friends for years.'

'A soldier?' Heinrich asked again. 'He is in the British Army?'

'Yes, he's in the army,' Eunice replied, realising as she said it that Ronnie and this young man, hoeing the turnips alongside her, were deadly enemies. She had tried to close her mind to the fact then, and she had continued to do so as she and the young German realised they were becoming far more interested in one another than it was wise to be. They had been careful, extremely careful, not to be alone too much together, or at least not to be seen to be alone. They had not even touched, apart from a casual brushing together of hands as they worked, until the end of the summer. She had been aware a few times, however, of Olive's mistrustful eyes watching the two of them, but, so far, the girl had not voiced her suspicions, if, indeed, she had any.

As the summer drew to its close the two POWs, along with some helpers from the nearby village, stayed later than usual to help with the harvest. It was inevitable, when Eunice and Heinrich found themselves together behind the steadily growing strawstack, that he should steal a kiss, the very first one; just a gentle fleeting kiss on the corner of her mouth. Neither of them spoke, and they drew apart quickly before anyone should notice they were alone together, but his kiss left Eunice weak with longing for him.

The next night, though she knew it was dangerous, Eunice found they were again together, and alone, behind the same strawstack. His kiss that night was much more lingering. His arms went round her and she felt her mouth opening beneath the pressure of his lips. They were playing with fire; they both knew it, but it made no difference.

'Oh . . . Eunice,' he whispered. 'I have wanted you . . . for so long.'

'So have I,' she replied, before he kissed her again. She leaned back against the hay, but the sound of Olive's voice – 'Eunice, where are you? It's time we were going back' – made them spring apart. When the girl appeared round the side of the strawstack Heinrich was already several feet apart from Eunice, picking up his jacket and then making off across the field to where the army lorry would soon arrive to take him and Werner back to the camp.

'Good night, ladies,' he said in a faintly accented voice, nodding his head and clicking his heels together.

''Bye, Heinrich,' said Eunice casually, but Olive did not reply to him.

'You've got straw in your hair,' she said to Eunice. The look she gave her spoke volumes.

'Is it any wonder?' Eunice gave a careless laugh. 'Come on, let's get back to the farmhouse and have a good wash. I don't know about you, but I feel filthy. There's straw everywhere, not just in my hair.'

'I know what you're doing, you and that German fellow,' said Olive as they started to walk across the field.

'What do you mean? I suppose you're referring to . . . Heinrich?' Eunice forced her voice to sound innocent, even a little incredulous.

'Yes, your POW boyfriend. Don't try to pretend you don't know what I'm talking about, 'cause I've seen you together, and I've seen you jump apart when you thought somebody was coming.'

'You're being ridiculous, Olive,' Eunice replied easily. She knew she must deny that there was anything between them. Both she and Heinrich were aware of the consequences if it was ever to be discovered that they were too friendly. He could be in serious trouble for fraternising; she had heard that POWs could even be shot for such an offence, although she was not sure of the truth of that; and she would undoubtedly be disciplined and moved to another farm, probably one where the regime was much harsher. 'I admit I've talked to him,' she went on. 'Why shouldn't I? Mrs Meadows had told us we must be polite to them, and that's all I've done, just spoken to him now and again.'

'We're not even supposed to do that,' said Olive. 'I don't care what Mrs Meadows says. They are the enemy and that's how I regard them. Ted's fighting them, isn't he? At least he will be when things get moving. He wouldn't approve of what you're doing.'

Eunice sighed. 'You believe what you like; I don't really care. I know I'm not doing anything wrong.' She knew that

Olive was distinctly peeved because she had not had a letter from Ted for several weeks. She had been disgruntled ever since he'd joined up, but finding out he was not much of a letter writer had done nothing to improve her mood.

'Do you know what they used to do to girls who fraternised with the enemy, in the last war?' Olive continued.

'Yes, as a matter of fact I do,' Eunice replied, 'but go on, tell me, if it'll make you feel any better. I know you're dying to.'

'They used to cut all their hair off,' said Olive, in a self-satisfied voice, 'and sometimes, in the worst cases, they used to strip them and cover them with tar and feathers.'

Eunice felt herself go cold for a moment, but she managed to laugh. 'Oh, come on, Olive,' she said, sounding much more friendly. 'You're barking up the wrong tree, honestly you are.' She linked the other girl's arm in a companionable manner. 'I know you're upset about Ted, but you'll get a letter soon; I'm sure you will.'

'Why doesn't he write, Eunice?' asked Olive in a plaintive, quite different tone. 'He promised he would.'

'And so he does, but perhaps not quite as much as you'd hoped. Some men are not very good at writing letters. Perhaps Ted is one of them.' After all, thought Eunice, he had left school at fourteen to work on the land, but she did not say that. 'I expect your Ted is a man of action rather than words, isn't he?' She grinned slyly at the other girl and Olive blushed a little.

'Yes, I suppose he might be,' she said, giving a coy smile.

'Good, you're smiling again,' said Eunice as they reached the farmhouse. 'Now – a good wash, then one of Annie's tasty meals. Life isn't all bad, you know.' She breathed an inward sigh of relief. She had managed to steer Olive's thoughts away from Heinrich and herself, but for how long? She only hoped her colleague had not voiced her suspicions to Bert and Annie Meadows.

The next day a letter arrived from Ted, and Olive was in a much more cheerful and optimistic frame of mind. She made no further reference to her suspicions regarding Eunice and Heinrich. Had she really seen something, Eunice wondered, or was she only guessing? Whatever it was, she knew she must be extra careful for a while. For a few days she tried to avoid him, but she knew it was inevitable that, sooner or later, they would find themselves together again.

He caught up with her in the apple orchard late one afternoon. He was working extra hours at the farm again as the corn was threshed and the apples, pears and plums were harvested. Eunice was alone, as the village lad who had been assisting her had gone home for his tea.

'You avoid me, *ja*? There is . . . something wrong, Eunice?' He took hold of her arm, but she stepped back, looking around in a guilty manner.

'Yes . . . I mean, no . . . there's nothing wrong with me. With you and me.' She smiled at him a little shyly. 'But Olive – you know, the other girl – she's getting suspicious.' He looked perplexed, so she went on, 'I think she's guessed . . . about you and me, that we are . . . friendly.' And yet, what had it amounted to? A few stolen kisses, that was all.

'Ah yes . . . Olive. A sad girl, I think, that one. She never smiles. Do not worry, Eunice. We do nothing wrong.' He smiled at her so beguilingly that her heart turned a somersault. 'I see you tomorrow, *ja*?' He squeezed her hand, then, very quickly, he was gone.

But he was there again with her the next day. She was not sure how he had wangled it, but he came to assist her with the apples for some part of every day. She guessed he had swapped jobs with Charlie, the village lad. Heinrich was generally well liked on the farm, as was Werner, their status having undergone a subtle change to co-workers rather than POWs.

As autumn approached there was a sad sort of beauty in the turning of the year: the yellowing leaves, the misty haze that hung over the fields morning and evening, and the golden harvest moon hanging low in the darkening purplish sky. The moon, though, had ceased to be a thing of beauty in these wartime days. A 'bomber's moon' was what they called the full moon; ideal conditions for night flying.

Eunice again closed her mind to the fact that Heinrich was one of the enemy. She knew she had fallen in love with him, and, although he had not said so, she was sure he felt the same way about her. Surely, to feel like this about someone – even an enemy – could not be wrong? So far they had only kissed, but Eunice knew that very soon their feelings for one another would have to be expressed more fully.

'Eunice . . . could we meet somewhere else, somewhere secret,' he whispered, as they worked together late one afternoon in the orchard. 'Where we can be alone, without anyone seeing us.'

She nodded, a little unsurely. 'Tomorrow – it's my half-day,' she said, after a moment, 'just mine, not Olive's. I'll be cycling to the village. At least . . . that's what I'll say I'm doing. Perhaps we could meet . . . somewhere?'

He nodded. '*Ja*, I will do that. Where?'

'I'm not sure . . .' She thought for a moment. 'Maybe . . . the barn at the far end of the farm? Over there . . . Do you know the one I mean? It isn't used very much.'

'Yes – I know the one. I will wait there for you, Eunice.'

'Heinrich, do be careful. If anyone were to see us—'

'They will not see, do not worry.' He shook his head and smiled. 'Herr Meadows, he ask me to work at the hedge in the bottom field, the one near the barn. He trusts me now; he leaves me alone. And Werner, he always believes what I say. Werner is a good friend. Tomorrow . . . Eunice.' He kissed her cheek, then he had gone.

Chapter 8

She hadn't intended it to go so far. She had only wanted to be alone with Heinrich for a little while, so that they could embrace and he could tell her – maybe – that he loved her. But when his arms were around her and his lips were upon hers, and when he whispered, as he finally did, 'I love you, Eunice . . . *Ich liebe dich* . . .' then she was powerless to do anything but give herself to him completely.

It wasn't the wondrous earth-moving experience she had expected. The heaviness of his body and the fact that he seemed to know exactly what to do took her by surprise. She had assumed that it was the first time for him, as it was for her.

'I am sorry,' he said later. 'I did not know . . .' That she was a virgin, she supposed.

'It doesn't matter,' she told him, trying to smile, but she was sore and her thighs were aching and, for some inexplicable reason, she felt like bursting into tears.

'Eunice, remember, I love you,' he whispered, kissing her gently on her forehead. 'Come . . . we must go. No, you go first, I think then I will go.'

'Goodbye, Heinrich,' she said, a little embarrassedly,

brushing the straw from her khaki trousers and straightening her jersey. 'I will see you soon. Tomorrow . . .?'

'*Ja, ja*, I will see you, Eunice, tomorrow. Take care. Always you must take care.'

What Eunice did not know as, stiff and sore, she mounted her bicycle and rode away down the lane, was that she was never to see him again.

She was quiet that evening as they all sat around the dining table. She was trying to behave normally, but the enormity of what she had done, what she had allowed Heinrich to do, was pushing all other thoughts out of her mind. It will be all right when I see him again tomorrow, she told herself. He has told me he loves me . . . That was what she had been waiting to hear. So why was it that now, when he had finally spoken those three words, she should feel so let down, so disappointed, so . . . ashamed?

Olive, strangely enough, did not seem to notice her discomfiture. She had received another letter from Ted and her thoughts, quite naturally, were centred around herself and her boyfriend. She was chattering in an animated way, most unlike her usual withdrawn and taciturn manner. Ted, still stationed in the south of England, was due for a short period of leave and they were making tentative plans to travel up to Wigan for a day or two, so that he could meet her parents.

'That's if it's all right with you and Mrs Meadows?' Olive enquired of the farmer. 'Just a weekend, we had in mind.'

'Aye, that should be OK, lass,' said Bert Meadows. 'When are you thinking of going?'

'His leave starts in three weeks' time.'

Annie Meadows nodded. 'Yes, that will suit us fine, Olive. Eunice will be back from her leave by then, won't you, dear? . . . Eunice, are you listening? You're miles away. I dare say you're thinking about it already, aren't you, dear?'

'What's that, Mrs Meadows? Sorry; yes, I was miles away. I was thinking about Pauline, actually. I met her this afternoon in the village . . .' that part, at least, was true enough, '. . . and she says they're still not very happy at that awful farm. We're jolly lucky here, I can tell you.' She smiled apologetically at Annie Meadows. 'Sorry, what were you saying?'

'That you're on leave soon. Next week, isn't it? Olive was just telling us that she and Ted are going to have some time together very soon. That's good news, isn't it?'

'Yes . . . very good,' said Eunice. 'I did hear that bit, although I must admit I was wool-gathering. Jolly good, Olive.'

The thought of her leave had been pushed to the back of her mind, so involved had she been with her growing affection for Heinrich.

To her amazement Heinrich was not at the farm the next day, and neither was Werner. She did not dare to ask anyone where they were and she went through the day in a state of puzzlement, anguish . . . and fear. She did not learn the truth until dinner that evening, when Mr Meadows remarked, very matter-of-factly, that the harvest work at Meadowlands was practically finished and the two POWs were needed elsewhere. What was more, they would not be returning. They had been moved, at very short notice, to another farm.

Eunice took a deep breath and forced herself not to react, at least not in the way she was reacting in her mind. Thoughts and fears were spinning round and round in her head like a whirlpool. She was aware of Olive's eyes upon her and those of Mr and Mrs Meadows too, although that might have been just her imagination, the result of a guilty conscience.

'Well, that's a surprise,' she said, her voice sounding, to her own ears, a little false and strained and much louder than she had intended. 'They were good workers, weren't they?' She did not dare to ask where exactly they had gone or, indeed, anything at all.

'Yes, they were,' replied Bert Meadows briefly.

'Nice young men too,' Annie added. 'You could easily forget they were Germans.'

'I couldn't forget,' said Olive with a sideways glance at Eunice.

'Well, that's the way things are in wartime,' said Bert. 'Here today and gone tomorrow. I don't know what they expect us to do, though. I've just heard I've to plough up two more fields. I'll have to try and get some more help from the village.'

Eunice was stunned beyond belief, unable to comprehend what she was hearing. She tried to tell herself that Heinrich could not have known of this; it must have been as much of a shock to him as it was to her. He had said he loved her. He wouldn't have said that if he had known it was the last time he would see her . . . would he? But maybe that was why he had said it, because he knew it was the first and last – and only – time they could ever make love.

There was nowhere she could go to cry, to let her feelings out. At bedtime Olive was there with her, only a few feet away in the other single bed. Olive had said nothing more, but the thought of the POWs hung heavy between them. Eunice feared she had not heard the last of it, but fortunately, at the moment, her colleague was preoccupied with her own affairs. Her scalding hot tears oozed between her eyelids at night, soaking the pillow, but she did not dare let her sobs be heard.

During the day she tried to escape from Olive, making excuses to do her farm work on her own; then she would find some relief in fits of weeping. She loved Heinrich so much and she would not believe that he would leave her like this, without a word. She wondered, hopelessly, if she could get in touch with him. When she came to her senses, she was frightened, more frightened than she had ever been in her life.

She knew full well what might be the outcome of what she and Heinrich had done. Supposing she were pregnant? Supposing she was having a baby and the father of it was . . . a German! Her parents would never forgive her. Her father would throw her out of the house; he might even kill her. That was no exaggeration, considering the way he felt about the Germans. There was, of course, the possibility that nothing had happened. She had heard it said that you couldn't 'catch on' the first time you did it. But she had also heard that this was an old wives' tale, and she did know of a girl who had lived near to them to whom this had happened. She had only done it once – or so she said – and she was pregnant.

One of the main problems was that she might not know for ages whether she was or wasn't. She had only just had a period, a few days before 'it' happened and, always irregular, that had been the first one for more than two months. It was certainly a worry; in fact it was a catastrophe. If she had to wait two months, as she often did, by that time it would be . . . too late. Whatever would she do?

Her father met her at the station and carried her case home. His smile of greeting and his kiss on her cheek were as cautious as ever. 'Nice to see you, Eunice. You're looking a bit peaky, though; not as well as you did in the summer. Nowt wrong, is there, lass?'

'No, nothing at all, Dad. I'm just tired, I expect. The harvest work's been pretty exhausting; threshing and potato picking and . . . and working in the orchard.'

'Aye, you're getting to be a real country lass, aren't you?' His glance was kindly and sympathetic and she could see the affection in his eyes. Samuel Morton was not a man to show his feelings, but she realised at that moment that he really did care about her, in spite of his habitual reticence and his inability to form a close bond with her. She realised too that she was fond of him. He was her father and, although it might not always be apparent, she was sure he had a father's pride in her. She could not bear to let him down. She gave an inward shudder. Whatever had she done?

Her mother also remarked that she did not look as bright and healthy as she had in the summer. Eunice again denied that there was anything the matter.

'Well, perhaps the Blackpool breezes will put some roses back in your cheeks,' said her mother. 'You're here for quite a while, aren't you?'

'Yes . . . a week.'

'That's nice, dear. Ronald's at home as well, you know. Well, he's not actually here at the moment. I think Mabel said he was arriving tomorrow. It's embarkation leave, you know, so goodness knows where they'll be sending him, poor lad. So you and he will be able to spend some time together, won't you?' Her mother looked at her coyly.

'Yes, Mum,' said Eunice, smiling to herself. Her mother never gave up.

She reflected as she unpacked her case that it would be good to see Ronnie again. A day or two in his company might help her to forget her own worries for a while. And there was, of course, the possibility that her fears were groundless; that she might not be pregnant after all. But quickly on the heels of that thought there followed another. Whatever would Ronnie think of her if he knew what she had done? She could never, ever tell him. He would, she knew, be so disappointed in her. She began to feel guilty again and ashamed of herself. Even now, though, she was still convinced that Heinrich had loved her. He could not have known in advance that he was to be moved to another farm. And it was, after all, only a short while ago. Maybe he would try to get in touch with her? She tried not to think of the disappointment she had felt after they had made love in the barn. Maybe it was always difficult at first . . .?

She was feeling guilty too that she had not written to Ronnie just lately. Other matters had pushed the thought of him to the back of her mind. She remembered that he had mentioned he would be on leave soon, hopefully at the same time as herself. She had not realised, however, that it would be embarkation leave. His mother and father would be anxious about him, but she knew from her previous conversations with them that they would try to view it philosophically. She decided she would go round to see them that evening. Already her own problems were receding a little. It was good to be home.

'Why don't you go and meet our Ronnie at the station?' said Mabel when Eunice popped round to see them later that evening. 'He'll be ever so pleased to see you. He's been saying in his letters that it seems ages and ages since he saw us, and you, of course, with him not getting the leave he wanted earlier on this year. And how are you, dear? Still enjoying the Land Army?'

Eunice agreed that she was, but that she was glad of the week's rest and the chance to see Ronnie, especially as he would be on embarkation leave.

'Yes, I suppose it's only to be expected,' said Mabel, sounding very resigned to the fact that her son would soon be going overseas. 'Tom and I knew he'd be sent to the fray sooner or later. They've been kicking their heels long enough in the south of England. And it never happened, did it?' Eunice guessed that by 'it' she meant the expected German invasion; everyone knew about it and dreaded it, but it was a word that was seldom spoken out loud.

'Of course they're very cagey about where they're sending them,' she continued. 'It's all very hush-hush, but it's Tom's guess it'll be Egypt, what with all that trouncing we had at Tobruk. They've got a new commander though, now, the Eighth Army: that General Montgomery. Tom says he'll be the right chap to give the Germans what for. Yes, I expect it'll be Egypt, dear; where else?'

'Yes, I suppose so,' replied Eunice, thinking that Egypt sounded an awful long way away.

Ronnie could hardly believe his eyes when he saw Eunice waiting at the barrier at North Station. He had been feeling somewhat down in the dumps because he had not heard from her for what seemed like ages. It was probably only two or three weeks since he had last written to her, but she had not replied. He had mentioned, in previous letters, that he would try to make his leave coincide with hers. Unfortunately, the whole summer had gone by and he had not managed it. This leave – embarkation leave – had been sprung upon him suddenly and he had been hoping against hope that Eunice would be home as well. And there, by some miracle, she was. Thank you, God! he said in a silent but fervent prayer. He had made up his mind that it was now or never this time. He was going to tell Eunice exactly how he felt about her.

There was a spring in his step and he knew there must be

an unmistakable light in his eyes as he hurried towards her, but he must not make it too obvious, not just yet. But Eunice's eyes were shining too as she stepped forward to greet him.

'Hi there, Ronnie. Lovely to see you again.'

He kissed her cheek. 'Good to see you too, Eunice. It's been so long . . . far too long.' And then, because he could not help himself, he put his kitbag down and threw his arms around her in a bear hug. She laughed, not seeming to mind at all.

'Come on, then,' he said, shouldering his kitbag and offering his other arm for her to link. 'Home, James, and don't spare the horses!' An old adage of his father's which he frequently found himself using.

'Yes, indeed,' said Eunice. 'Your mum and dad will be pleased to see you. How long are you home for, Ronnie?'

'A full week, thank goodness.'

'Same here,' said Eunice, 'but I've already had a day of it. So . . . you're off overseas, then?'

''Fraid so. We knew it would come sooner or later.'

'North Africa?'

'Where else? It's supposed to be all very hush-hush, but that's the only place they're sending troops to at the moment. Let's not think about it yet, eh? What are you doing tonight? Do you think we might go out for a little while? A stroll on the pr[illegible] . . . whatever?'

'Yes, sure; if your pare[illegible]an spare you. That would be lovely.'

'Oh, Mam and Dad will be seeing quite a lot of me . . . See you later then, Eunice,' he said as he left her at her gate. 'Shall I come round and call for you?'

'Yes, why not? My parents will be pleased to see you as well. Seven o'clock, shall we say?'

'OK, that suits me fine.'

So far, so good, thought Ronnie. She seemed genuinely pleased to see him, and he fancied he saw something else there beneath her smiles and cheerful chatter. A touch of sadness, a hidden anxiety? Could it be because she was sad at the thought of him going so far away? He felt emboldened and he was determined he was not going to funk it this time. He had to tell Eunice that he loved her.

She had almost forgotten how much she enjoyed Ronnie's company. What a pleasure it was to be with him again. The light was fading as they walked towards the promenade. It was a still, clear night, and they leaned against the railings as she remembered they had done on their last leave together, looking out over the sea. It had been pitch-dark then, except for the faint light of the moon and stars. This evening there was a glorious sunset. They stood there silently for a few moments, watching the sun slowly sinking in the darkening sky – a sky shot with streaks of orange, pink and vermilion amidst the blue – causing millions of golden pennies to shimmer in the dark turquoise of the sea. It was to be an unforgettable moment for both of them. They turned and smiled at one another.

'There's no place like Blackpool, is there?' said Eunice, in a voice that was quite awestruck. 'These glorious sunsets . . .'

Ronnie nodded. Then: 'Eunice,' he said, almost in a whisper. 'There's something I want to say to you. I've been wanting to tell you for a long time.' He put his hand over hers where it lay on the iron railing. 'Goodness knows why I haven't said it before. God knows, I've wanted to.'

'What is it, Ronnie?' she asked softly.

'Eunice . . . I love you. I love you so very much.'

For a moment she couldn't speak. She just stared at him,

unbelievingly. Then: 'Oh, Ronnie . . .' she breathed. 'I . . . I don't know what to say.'

'I know you probably don't feel the same about me,' he went on, 'but I had to tell you, I just had to. It's been burning away inside me for so long. I know we've been friends for ages and you don't think of me in that way, but I had to take the chance . . . and find out . . . if you might . . .?'

She shook her head gently, but not as a sign of negation, just to stop his flow of words. 'Hush,' she said. 'There's no need to say any more; not now.' She smiled up at him, moving her face imperceptibly towards his. He lowered his face, and then his lips met hers in a tender kiss, the first real kiss they had ever exchanged. He drew back for a moment, gazing at her with wonderment in his eyes; then he kissed her again.

Eunice realised what a fool she must have been not to have guessed how Ronnie felt about her. She recalled seeing the same look in his eyes a couple of times before and how she had wondered, and had then dismissed the idea as ridiculous because he had not said anything. And what did she feel about Ronnie? Did she love him? Most certainly she did . . . as a very dear friend. But it was comforting now to be held in his arms and to know she was with someone who truly loved her and would never let her down; that much she knew already.

It was quite dark when they moved away from the spot and they walked home as though in a daze with their arms around each other. It felt strange, thought Eunice, after so many years of being Ronnie's friend – one of his best mates, in fact. Strange, but nice and warm and so reassuring.

They went to the cinema the next night as they had done so many times before, but this time, in the seclusion of the back row of the Odeon, Eunice felt Ronnie's arm steal around her and they kissed several times. They walked on the promenade afterwards and in a solitary corner of the colonnades Ronnie stopped and put his arms round her. 'Eunice, I love you so much,' he told her again.

'I know you do, Ronnie,' she replied, 'and I'm so glad.' She knew she could not, in complete honesty, reply that she loved him too. She did love him, but maybe not in quite the same way that he loved her . . . not yet. But she knew as she succumbed to his ever more passionate embraces that this felt so right and she was so very contented and unafraid with Ronnie.

'No, Eunice . . . darling,' he said – it was the first time he had used the endearment – after a few moments of unrestrained kisses. 'Not here . . . not now. It wouldn't be right, not for you and me. It has to be . . . just right.' She knew exactly what he meant. He thought too much about her, as she did of him, to make love on the promenade.

They walked home and she went into his house for a cup of tea with his parents. They behaved towards one another as they had always done, as close friends who exchanged cheerful banter and laughed together at private jokes. But Eunice noticed a knowing gleam in Mabel's eye and a tiny smile playing around her lips as she watched them.

The next night they went dancing at the Empress Ballroom in the Winter Gardens. Eunice leaned her head against the rough serge of Ronnie's battledress. She felt proud of him in his uniform and was pleased he had chosen to wear it instead of civvies. She felt his lips brush the top of her head, her forehead, her temple, as he drew her closer to him. They belonged together, she and Ronnie. She realised it now. How could it be otherwise when they had been such good friends for so long . . . and how foolish she must have been not to have known before.

They did not stay very long at the Empress Ballroom and when they returned to Ronnie's home she found they had the house to themselves; something that she was sure her own strait-laced parents would never have allowed. She wondered if this was what Ronnie had planned. He told her his father was out fire watching and his mother had said she was going round the corner to visit a neighbour and would not be back until after eleven o'clock. Eunice remembered the understanding gleam in Mabel's eye and she guessed that Ronnie's mother had decided to let them have some time on their own.

They sat on the settee; the room was only dimly illuminated by a table lamp and the glow from the embers of the fire. She had noticed that Ronnie had bolted the door when they came in, but she had made no comment; in case his mother should return unexpectedly, she surmised, but the chances were she would not do so.

He drew her into his arms and kissed her, gently at first and so lovingly. 'I love you, Eunice,' he whispered. 'You have no idea how much.'

'I love you too, Ronnie,' she replied now, knowing that she did, without a doubt, love him. It could well be, at the moment, that it was the love that had stemmed from a deep friendship, but she was beginning to discover things about Ronnie that she had been unaware of before – passion and desire and longing. She found now that her desire to be near him, to be a part of him, was as keen as his.

It was all so simple and so natural; the coming together of two people who, she now believed – and Ronnie certainly believed – belonged together. She found his lovemaking to be a wonderful experience. He was tender and gentle, inexperienced maybe, but she was comforted by his nearness and his quiet words of love to her. There was none of the furtiveness and the feeling of shame she had felt after her encounter with Heinrich in the barn at Meadowlands. She pushed away the thought that had suddenly come into her mind. It was no time to be thinking of that with Ronnie's arms around her and his voice whispering in her ear.

'Eunice . . . will you marry me?' he asked afterwards as they sat quietly together holding hands. 'Not just because of that – I don't want you to think I've trapped you – but because I love you so very much. And . . . I believe you love me?'

'Yes, I do, Ronnie,' she replied, 'and . . . of course I will marry you.'

'We'll get engaged straight away,' he said. 'We'll choose a ring tomorrow. OK, darling?'

'Yes . . . Very OK, Ronnie,' she smiled. 'And just think how pleased our parents will be. I'm afraid they'll say, "We told you so".'

'Well, let them,' laughed Ronnie. 'It may have taken us a while, but we got there in the end. We know now, don't we, darling?'

Eunice nodded happily. 'Listen, Ronnie,' she said. 'I'm going now before your mother comes back.' Somehow she did not feel like confronting Mabel just at that moment. She felt no guilt, but she guessed that Ronnie's mother would know intuitively what had happened. 'I'll see you tomorrow . . . darling,' she added. The word felt a little strange, but she would get used to it, she was sure. She and Ronnie would have lots of things to find out about one another, but as lovers now as well as friends.

It occurred to Eunice that night as she lay wide awake in her bed – sleep was such a long time in coming – that if by some chance she should happen to be pregnant following her encounter with Heinrich, then this would have solved all her problems. She immediately felt a sharp stab of guilt

– how dreadful of her to be thinking like that – but she knew, nevertheless, that it was true. She had promised Ronnie she would marry him and the relief that she felt – along with the guilt – was indescribable.

She started to think, in fact, that this might be an answer to her problems, even to her prayers. Maybe Heinrich did not love her after all; maybe he never had, but had just been amusing himself with a gullible English girl. It hurt to think that way, but perhaps it had been nothing more than a casual fling to him. And now Fate had, miraculously, given her a second chance with her old friend Ronnie. She made up her mind there and then that she would do everything she could to be the best wife Ronnie could wish for, and she would forget all about Heinrich. At last, in the early hours of the next morning, she fell asleep.

He bought her an engagement ring the next day, a small solitaire diamond, which they chose together at Samuel's jewellers. Their parents seemed surprised at the suddenness of the engagement but, nevertheless, delighted at the news. It was what they had always hoped for, especially Edith and Mabel. There were no arguments about them being too young. Ronnie, after all, was twenty-one, and in these fraught wartime days lots of couples were getting engaged and married at a very early age.

'We must have a party,' said Edith at the breakfast table the following morning. 'After all, it isn't every day that your only daughter gets engaged, is it, Samuel? And to such a nice young man as well.'

'No,' replied Samuel. 'I mean . . . yes, have a party if you want to. But there's no need for a lot of fuss, is there? It'll only be us and the Ivesons, won't it? Anyway, you please yourself; I'm off to work now.'

Her father had received the news of her engagement in

his usual phlegmatic manner, although Eunice thought he was quite pleased. He had always liked Ronnie, and as her mother was obviously delighted at the news her father would raise no objections. Eunice had suggested to Ronnie that they should get the ring first and then make the announcement to their parents as a *fait accompli*. It might have been more proper, she knew, for Ronnie to have gone to her father to ask for her hand in marriage, but she assured him that her father would only be embarrassed and that it was her mother who ruled the roost anyway.

She was surprised at how pleased her mother was at their news. But Eunice suspected that one of the main reasons was that Edith felt her daughter would be safe with an engagement ring on her finger – safe from the lecherous advances of servicemen or farm hands or any other undesirable characters she might meet whilst working as a land girl. If she only knew . . .

'We're not bothered about a party, Ronnie and me,' she said now. That was what they had decided. It was sufficient for the two of them to be together. These family get-togethers were a bit wearing at times. 'Dad's right. What's the point in making a lot of fuss? It's only extra work for you, Mum. There would only be us there, and Aunty Mabel and Uncle Tom. Chrissie can't get home and there's nobody else to invite, is there?'

'Of course we're having a party,' retorted Edith. 'Don't be such a spoilsport, our Eunice. And whatever would the Ivesons think if I didn't put on a bit of a do? I've got a tin of red salmon I've been keeping for a special occasion and a tin of peaches, and I expect Mabel will want to contribute something, although I don't want charity, I'm sure. What's the matter with you, anyway? I thought you'd have been over the moon, getting engaged to a lovely young man like Ronald. You are sure, aren't you? I mean . . . it is what you want, isn't it? To be engaged to Ronald?'

'Of course it is, Mother,' replied Eunice. 'We don't want a fuss, that's all. Anyway, you can't expect me to be "over the moon", as you say, when Ronnie's going overseas next week, and for goodness knows how long.' She looked plaintively at her mother. 'I shall miss him, Mum. That's why I'm a bit quiet, maybe.'

'Hmm . . .' Her mother gave her a shrewd glance. 'It didn't seem to worry you at one time, being parted from Ronald.'

'Well, it does now,' said Eunice, knowing that it would worry her very much indeed.

'All right, dear.' Edith's glance softened a little. 'If you've decided that you're fond of Ronald, fond enough to think of marrying him, then that's . . . very nice. Cheer up, now. You've still a few days left to be together. And we won't take up too much of your precious time with this party. Why don't you invite your friend Gwen to come along? She's a nice lass, is Gwen, and it's ages since we saw her.'

'OK, Mum, I might. Yes, I think I will. I don't know which shift she's on at the factory, but I'll call round later today.'

Gwen and her mother, Ivy, were dining when Eunice called round that same evening.

'Don't worry,' said Gwen, when Eunice began to apologise for disturbing their meal. 'I'm only too pleased to see you. I'm on late shift this week, so we have our meal as late as possible before I set off. I'd no idea you were home. Why didn't you let me know you were coming on leave? I haven't heard from you for ages.'

'No, I'm sorry,' replied Eunice. It was true that she hadn't written to Gwen for quite some time. Her involvement with Heinrich had affected her concentration. She had spent much of her spare time day dreaming and her letter writing had suffered in consequence. She had written duty letters to her parents, knowing they would panic if she did not do so, and also, infrequently, to Ronnie. 'Autumn's a very busy time on the farm, but I know it's no excuse really. I'm sorry I didn't write to tell you, Gwen. Actually, I came home on leave because Ronnie's here as well and . . . we've just got engaged.'

She held out her left hand with a broad smile on her face. But there could be no mistaking Gwen's delight and surprise as well.

'Oh, that's wonderful. Congratulations!' she cried. 'Isn't it wonderful, Mum? I'm so pleased for you, Eunice. But you and Ronnie? I'd no idea it was . . . like that. You always said you were just good friends.'

'Ah well, it seems that we're a bit more than that now,' laughed Eunice.

'Yes, that's very good news, dear,' said Ivy faintly. Her voice – her whole being, in fact – seemed to be gradually fading away. Eunice was amazed that the frail little woman was still hanging on to life, but there was obviously a fighting spirit there. 'Aren't you going to tell Eunice your own news, Gwennie?' she asked, smiling proudly at her daughter.

'Oh, all right then,' said Gwen, laughing. 'I didn't want to upstage her, that's all.' She too held out her left hand, displaying a small crossover diamond ring. 'Snap! We've got engaged too, Bill and me.'

It was Eunice's turn now to say how pleased she was, and from the rapturous expression on her friend's face she could see that this was, indeed, an occasion for rejoicing. 'Well, fancy that!' she said. 'Congratulations to you too. When did this happen? And why didn't you tell me?'

'It was only last weekend,' replied Gwen, 'when Bill was

on leave. We got the ring, then went down to Stoke to see his parents. There hasn't been a chance to tell anyone really . . . Come on, Eunice, you can help me to clear these pots away, if you don't mind. I'm due at the factory in less than an hour and I like to leave everything shipshape before I go.'

She settled her mother in an armchair by the fire with a rug over her knees, then the two young women cleared the table and washed the pots.

'So it all happened quite suddenly,' Gwen continued. 'Bill persuaded me that it was time we were engaged – not that I needed any persuading, really – but I always have to consider Mum, you know. Bill's flying now. He's been made up to sergeant and he's a flight engineer. He's with Bomber Command in East Anglia.'

'Gosh! You must be frantic with worry,' said Eunice. 'I know I would be if it was Ronnie.'

'I just hope and pray all the time that he'll be safe,' said Gwen. 'I really do pray, every night. But I've learned that you can't spend your life in a state of continual terror. You've just got to get on with things and hope for the best. And I've got a gut feeling that he's going to be OK, that he'll come through it all.'

'I hope so, Gwen,' said Eunice, very sincerely. 'When are you getting married? Have you made any plans?'

'No, not definite plans, but next spring, we hope.'

'Why not now, if you're so sure of one another?'

'Well, it's Mum, you see. I've got to stay with her, and if Bill and I were married I'd want to be near him. By next spring she may be well enough . . .'

Or she may not be here at all, thought Eunice. A look at her friend's momentarily stricken face told her that this was something that Gwen knew only too well. 'Anyway, that's enough about me,' said Gwen brightly. 'What about you and Ronnie, eh? That's a surprise if ever there was one. What's brought this about? I thought you weren't all that keen.'

'I was always very fond of him, you know,' said Eunice. 'And now . . . well . . . he's going overseas – he's on embarkation leave, you see – and things have moved on between us, quite a lot actually, and so . . . we got engaged. Our parents are thrilled to bits, especially our mothers – and we've known one another such a long time.'

'You haven't got engaged because your mother wants you to, have you?' said Gwen, giving her a teasing look. 'What about you? You love Ronnie, don't you?'

'Yes . . . of course I do. Why do you ask?'

'Because you look a wee bit strained, that's all.'

Eunice sighed. 'I suppose I'm worried about Ronnie going away – to the desert campaign, you know. I've only just realised . . . that I love him.'

'When are you thinking of getting married?'

'Oh, we haven't talked about that yet. We can't, with Ronnie going to Egypt. When the war's over, I guess . . .' For a brief moment Eunice had been tempted to confide in Gwen, to tell her about Heinrich, and her fears about what might have happened, but she decided against it. Her friend would be shocked and rightly so. Eunice herself was the only one person in the world who knew what she had done, and that was the way it must stay.

'What I really came for, Gwen, was to ask you to come to our engagement party. On Friday it is, Friday teatime. There'll only be us there, and our parents, but I know my mum would like to see you again.'

'Thank you; I'd like to,' said Gwen. She hung the damp tea towel over the back of a kitchen chair and closed the cupboard door. 'There – that's all done and dusted . . . Yes, I'll come for an hour or two, Eunice. It'll be nice to see your folks again, and Ronnie, of course. I'll bring my overalls to change into, if you don't mind, then I can go straight to the factory. Mrs Taylor – that's the lady next door – won't mind seeing to Mum. She's a widow as well and they spend a lot of time together. I don't know what I'd do without her, to be quite honest. She gets Mum into bed when I'm on nights, and Mum knows she can knock on the wall if she's in any trouble. Although she's been OK so far, touch wood, and I'm home again at eight o'clock in the morning.'

Gwen was tying a turban round her short fair hair as she spoke, adjusting it in the kitchen mirror. She was already wearing a grey boiler suit, the uniform of the factory workers. Eunice was filled with admiration for her friend's ability to hold down a tiring wartime occupation and look after a sick mother, and all with such cheerful optimism. She must be worried sick about her fiancé, Bill, engaged in bombing raids over Germany.

Her thoughts turned to Ronnie. She, Eunice, would be anxious about him, fighting in the Desert War. He did mean a great deal to her. It would be dreadful if anything were to happen to him. It didn't bear thinking about.

'Hey, you're not listening.' Gwen's voice interrupted her rambling thoughts. She waved a hand in front of Eunice's face. 'Hello, there . . . I was just saying that it's time I was going.'

'Oh, sorry, Gwen. Woolgathering again, I'm afraid.' She smiled reassuringly. 'I'll stay and chat to your mum for a little while, shall I?'

'Yes thanks. I was going to suggest it, if you're not too busy. You're not dashing off to meet Ronnie?'

'Not tonight. He thought he'd better have a night in with his parents. With them working at the shop all day they haven't had much chance to have a real good chat. I've seen him every other night, though.'

'Good – you make the most of it. And I'm really pleased at your news.'

Eunice nodded. 'I thought you would be. See you on Friday, then?'

'Yes – Friday.'

'Our Gwennie's such a good lass,' said Ivy, when her daughter had departed. She had kissed her mother affectionately, but without making too much fuss, Eunice noticed. She did not ask her if she'd be all right on her own, or to make sure she knocked for Mrs Taylor if she needed any help. These things went unsaid. Mrs Singleton and her daughter quite clearly understood that the older woman's health was failing rapidly, but Eunice guessed that Ivy would be irritated by too much fussing. There was a wealth of love there, however, between the mother and daughter.

Eunice thought about her own mother, brusque and domineering, and always determined to have the last word, and she wondered if her feelings for her mother, and for her father too, ran as deeply as did Gwen's. She felt a bit regretful and a tiny bit envious, but she told herself that all families were different. Her parents cared about her; of course they did, as she did about them. One thing was certain, though: she could never, never have confided in them about Heinrich.

Eunice drew her chair close to Mrs Singleton. It was not easy to catch every word she spoke. 'And I'm glad she's got such a lovely young man,' Ivy went on. 'I don't think you've met Bill, have you, Eunice?' She replied that she hadn't. 'Well, he's just the right one for her. I don't know why I'm so sure, but I am. And it makes me happy to know that she'll be all right when I've gone.' She held up her hand as Eunice frowned a little and opened her mouth as if to protest.

'Oh no, dear, it's no use me pretending any different. I know, and our Gwennie knows as well. But I'm not complaining. I've had a good life: a loving and caring husband and a daughter who's just the same. She was a precious gift to us, you know, dear. I was turned forty when she was born and we'd given up hope of ever having any children. And I've lots of good friends who pop in to see me . . . Now, I've done enough talking.' Her voice had become even fainter and huskier. 'Tell me about the Land Army. I was brought up in the country, you know, just over the Pennines in the West Riding. I only moved here when I married Alec. And I still miss the country . . .'

Eunice talked to her about her experiences on the land, trying to make them as amusing as she could; her early trials with milking the cows, how they all hated the tasks involved in threshing, and how lucky she had been in her placement compared with some of her colleagues. Ivy's eyes closed and her head began to nod as Eunice talked.

She was wondering what to do when she heard the back door opening. 'Cooee, it's only me, Ivy . . . Oh, hello, who are you?'

Eunice explained that she was Gwen's friend, and Mrs Taylor, the woman from next door, introduced herself.

'This often happens now,' she said. 'She's sleeping a lot more than she used to, bless her. Off you go, dear, and thanks for looking after her. I'll take over now.'

Eunice felt strangely sad as she walked home through the dark streets. Poor Ivy, and poor Gwen . . .

Chapter 9

At the Tower Ballroom the girls stood two and three deep at the edge of the dance floor, waiting to be asked to dance by one of the myriad servicemen who frequented the place. The RAF were in the majority, as Blackpool was one of the chief training areas for the boys in blue, but there were also British Tommies in their khaki battledress, and a handful of sailors, as well as Polish, free French and Australian servicemen. But they had all been overshadowed, at least in the eyes of many of the girls, by the advent of the Yanks.

The immaculately dressed GIs had started to appear in their hundreds in the Tower, Empress and Palace Ballrooms in the summer of 1942, and the whole concept of ballroom dancing had begun to change. Now, thousands of feet danced to the strains of 'Deep in the Heart of Texas', 'American Patrol' and the 'Woodchoppers' Ball'. The girls could not resist these bright and breezy young men from across the Atlantic, always seeming so good-humoured and full of life and vigour. What was more, they were so very smart; the fine material of their stylish dark green uniforms was a stark contract to the rough serge of the RAF and army outfits of the British troops.

With the American GIs had come the jitterbug, a style of dancing which, at first, was frowned on by the authorities as it required far too much space on the ballroom floor and was dangerous to other, more conventional, dancers. There were plenty of places, however, just off the actual ballroom where the GIs and their partners could indulge in this acrobatic cavorting.

Earlier in the year the Empress Ballroom had suffered a minor disaster. The boots of the various servicemen had taken their toll on the dance floor and the hall had been closed for repairs. This happened again in the autumn, and so, on the last night of his leave, Ronnie and Eunice found themselves at the Tower Ballroom.

Eunice had not visited this particular dance hall very much, as her mother had always declared it was 'common' to go there. It was where girls went if they wanted a 'pick-up', she maintained. The Winter Gardens, however, she considered to be not quite as bad, but the Palace, in Edith's view, was the only one that could be considered wholly respectable as it was there that they included a lot of the nice old-time dances as well as the modern ones. But Eunice was an engaged woman now and she considered she had the right to please herself. Besides, Ronnie was with her, and Edith trusted Ronnie implicitly.

The Tower Ballroom was famous for its Wurlitzer organ and the outstanding playing of Reginald Dixon. Mr Dixon, however, was now serving in the RAF and his place had been taken, very ably, by a lady named Ena Baga. She was already very popular in the town and her signature tune, 'Smoke Gets in Your Eyes', was becoming almost as popular as Reginald Dixon's 'Oh, I Do Like to be Beside the Seaside'.

Eunice and Ronnie were quickstepping round the floor

to the strains of 'Don't Sit Under the Apple Tree'. Eunice felt very happy as she snuggled closer to Ronnie. They had had a lovely few days together and she had enjoyed his company as always, now of course, there was the added delight of their new-found love.

She was glad they had come to the Tower. Her mother was wrong to say that the place was common and vulgar. There was rowdiness in some corners, where the Yanks and their partners were jitterbugging, but the whole scene seemed, to Eunice, to be straight out of a Hollywood musical and she and Ronnie like the leading actors. It was not quite real and she felt as though she might, all of a sudden, wake up. She was mesmerised by all the gold and glitter, the shimmering crystal and red velvet, and by the melodic and haunting music of the organ. The floor itself was a work of art: over thirty thousand blocks of wood, so Ronnie told her, oak, mahogany and walnut, laid in an intricate design; not that you could see much of it beneath the hundreds of dancing feet. And the ceiling, which she had not noticed before, was another masterpiece, consisting of delicately painted frescos of flowery bowers and woodland scenes and maidens dancing with their swains.

'Happy, darling?' Ronnie asked, and she smiled up at him, nodding contentedly.

He was quietly singing to himself the words of the song Ena Baga was playing. Suddenly he tightened his hold of her. 'You won't, will you?' he asked.

'What?' She looked at him with a puzzled frown. 'I won't do what, Ronnie?'

'Sit under the apple tree with anyone else but me,' he said, laughing a little, but his eyes were wary. 'Like it says in the song. You won't, will you, Eunice?'

'Of course not, Ronnie,' she replied. 'Don't be silly. Whatever gave you that idea?'

She felt at that moment a chill of fear run through her. Don't sit under the apple tree . . . She recalled the apple orchard at Meadowlands: the ripe fruit heavy on the branches, the windfalls in the dewy grass, the early morning mist. Then, swiftly came the memory of Heinrich's hand caressing her arm, his lips brushing gently against hers. She stiffened involuntarily, but Ronnie did not seem to notice, or, if he did, maybe he took it as a sign that she was indignant that he should doubt her.

'Of course I won't, Ronnie,' she said again. 'Honestly, what a thing to say! As if I would . . .'

Mr and Mrs Meadows were delighted to hear of Eunice's engagement, as she had thought they would be.

'Well, that's wonderful news,' said Annie, 'although I can't say I'm all that surprised. You've had that look in your eyes for quite some time, as though you were off in some little world of your own. Now we know why, don't we?' She beamed knowingly. 'But you won't be leaving us yet awhile, will you? We don't want to lose you, but of course if you're thinking of getting wed . . .'

'Leave the lass alone, Annie,' said her husband. 'That's none of our business, is it?' He grinned at Eunice. 'She's a real nosy parker, my missus. But I agree with what she says, mind, about not wanting you to leave. You're a grand little worker.' His glance moved from Eunice, across the dining table to Olive, who was looking rather put out at all the fuss being made over her colleague. 'Both of you are,' he added. 'I must admit I was dubious when they suggested I should have a couple of land girls, but you've been worth your weight in gold, the pair of you.'

Olive smiled, looking somewhat mollified. 'Thank you,' she murmured. 'That's nice to hear.'

'Isn't it just?' said Eunice, smiling at the other girl as

though she hadn't noticed her peevish expression. 'Don't worry, Mr Meadows. I won't be leaving you. Ronnie and I have no immediate plans for getting married, not for a while, at any rate. He's on his way to North Africa, so it looks as though I won't be seeing him for quite a while . . . That's why we decided to get engaged.' She cast a fleeting glance at Olive, who was staring at her fixedly, an unfathomable expression on her face.

'What's up?' asked Eunice later that evening, as the two young women were getting ready to go to bed. 'Have I done something to upset you? Come on, Olive,' she added, because her colleague was sitting on the edge of the bed, staring down at the floor, the very picture of despair.

'It's all right for you,' muttered Olive. 'Everything goes just right for you. You get everything you want. No sooner have you lost one boyfriend than you've got another, and I don't think you want him really, do you, that Ronnie? Five minutes ago you were just friends. And then when that German fellow does a bunk you're suddenly flashing an engagement ring.'

Eunice felt worried. If the worst came to the worst she feared that Olive would very quickly put two and two together. She decided the best thing to do was to pretend that she regarded Olive's remarks as being too silly for words. 'Have you quite finished?' she asked, forcing herself to laugh. 'Honestly, Olive, you're being ridiculous, and, what's more, I think you know you are.'

'I don't know any such thing. You were potty about that POW, and don't try to deny it. I noticed the look on your face when you found out he'd gone. Goodness knows what the pair of you had been up to, but I can guess.'

'Just you take that back, Olive Pritchard! How dare you suggest that Heinrich and I . . . You've gone too far this time, and you'd better admit it, right now or . . . or I'll never speak to you again. I'll get a transfer. I'm not going to work with somebody who's making vile accusations.' Eunice felt awful about telling lies but her front of righteous indignation did seem to be having some effect, which was what she was aiming for.

'All right then, I'm sorry,' said Olive sullenly, although she was obviously determined not to back down completely. 'But I know you were friendly with him and that you liked him.'

Eunice shrugged nonchalantly, breathing an inward sigh of relief. 'Yes, I liked him. I liked both of them. I felt sorry for them actually, although maybe we were not supposed to. We did work together sometimes and I talked to him, perhaps more than I should have done. But you've got it all wrong, honestly you have.'

'If you say so . . .' Olive cast her a furtive, not too certain, glance.

'I do say so. There's something else the matter, though, isn't there, Olive? I can tell.' She sat down beside her. 'Come on; we've got to work together, so we may as well try to be friendly. I thought we were friends. We always used to be.' They had, however, drifted apart of late, and Eunice knew it had been happening gradually since the arrival of the POWs. Olive had set herself against them from the start.

'I thought you would have been on top of the world,' Eunice went on, still being met with silence. 'You're going off on leave in a few days' time, aren't you, when Ted comes home?' She stopped, wondering if there was something she, Eunice, did not know about. Maybe it was all over between Olive and Ted, but surely, if that were the case, Mrs Meadows would have warned her.

'Yes . . . I'm going on leave,' replied Olive. The face she

turned towards Eunice was no longer angry or petulant, just worried. 'I'm taking Ted home to meet my parents. At least, that was the idea, but now, the more I think about it the more scared I get. I've got a real attack of the colly-wobbles, Eunice. I don't know whether I can go through with it.'

Olive's thoughts were turned once more upon herself, and Eunice was glad about that. 'Why not?' she asked. 'What's the matter?'

'Oh, it's my parents,' said Eunice. 'I keep wondering what they'll think about Ted and what they'll say to him.'

'But they know about him, don't they? They know you met him at the farm?'

'Yes, but they don't really approve. My mother never shut up about it the last time I was home, about how he wasn't good enough for me – a farm labourer! – and how they'd always hoped I'd meet somebody suitable. Somebody "nice and refined", that's what my mother said, who had a respectable office job. A solicitor, that's what they really wanted for me. And then I go and fall in love with a farm hand. I really do love him, Eunice. I know I've never had a boyfriend before and you might think I'm just clutching at straws, but I'm not. I do love him.'

'I know you do,' said Eunice, feeling a good deal of sympathy for her. Olive was still very insecure, which was the reason, no doubt, she lashed out with her tongue on occasions. 'And Ted loves you too. Anybody can see that he does. Never mind what your parents say. You're nearly twenty-one now, aren't you? You can please yourself who you get engaged to and who you marry. Your parents are just being downright snobbish. But I'm sure they'll change their minds when they meet Ted. He's a lovely young man.'

'Oh . . . do you really think so?'

'Yes, of course I do. And Ted's parents like you, don't

they? You've said how well you get on with them.'

'Yes, I do, although I was ever so scared about meeting them at first. They're nice ordinary people, like Ted. But my mother and father . . . well, they try to act as though they're something they're not. Dad's not all that bad. He works in the office at the coal mine, and Mother doesn't half put on airs and graces because he's not one of the miners. He's got quite a lot of friends who are, though, and she doesn't like it. It's always her friends who come to the house, not his: posh ladies – at least, she thinks they are – that she's met at church or at the whist club. She'll look down her nose at Ted; I know she will.'

Eunice gave a wry smile. 'Hmm, it sounds as though your mother and mine are two of a kind – in some ways, that is. My father is never given much of a say in things either. All parents have their faults, Olive. I was never allowed much freedom, you know – I've told you this before – until I joined the Land Army.'

'Your parents aren't snobbish, though, are they?'

'No, I must admit that's not one of their faults. Mum was brought up to "know her place" and she's always tried to make sure I know mine. She doesn't like me getting "big ideas".'

'And they approve of Ronnie, don't they? Even though he's a shop assistant?'

'Well, it's his parents' business, so I suppose it will be his one day.' Eunice did not want to get on to the subject of Ronnie again. 'Look at the time, Olive,' she said. 'Nearly eleven o'clock. Come on – hurry up and get your curlers in . . .' This was a nighttime ritual with Olive. Dinky curlers all over her head, which must have been murder to sleep in. '. . . Then we can both get our beauty sleep. Don't worry about Ted. I know he's quiet, but I don't think he'll let your mother intimidate him. It'll be OK, you'll see.'

'Oh dear – I do hope you're right.'

Olive's preoccupation with her problems, and her hair full of ironmongery, did not stop her from sleeping. In a few moments her gentle snores told Eunice she was well away. But sleep did not come quickly to Eunice. Her mind was filled with thoughts of Ronnie on his way to Egypt, and of what might happen to him, fighting in the desert. She tried to visualise the miles and miles of sand, the scorching heat, the advancing tanks and the gunfire, and she felt afraid. Did she love Ronnie as much as he loved her? She had told him so, and she knew that she did, indeed, care for him very deeply. Enough to marry him? She had thought so when they had got engaged. She had been determined to put all thoughts of Heinrich behind her, but now, returning to the farm, the spectre of him was there again. Had she, in fact, promised to marry Ronnie on the rebound? She had told Olive not to worry, but her own problems at that moment seemed insurmountable.

Olive came back from her few days in Wigan sporting an engagement ring. She told Eunice that the meeting between Ted and her parents had not been nearly as bad as she had feared. She gathered they had talked things over and had decided to welcome their daughter's young man, if not with open arms, then at least civilly.

'I told you so,' said Eunice. 'Things are never as bad as they seem.'

'My goodness! This engagement lark's catching on,' laughed Annie Meadows. 'Both of 'em now, Bill. A double wedding, eh, girls?'

'Mind your own business, Annie,' replied Bill.

Both girls smiled politely. Neither of them was giving anything away.

★ ★ ★

Eunice was beginning to feel sickly in the mornings. It was what she had dreaded, but had also half expected. She wondered at first if it might be just her imagination. The time for her next monthly period had come and gone, but that was nothing unusual. When the second one did not arrive she knew she was not imagining things. She had actually been sick now, although her stomach was almost empty and there was nothing much to bring up, only bile. She had shut the bathroom door tightly, hoping that Olive would not hear her retching, but luckily her colleague was not the easiest person to wake up in the morning.

She knew she must keep her knowledge of her condition to herself as long as she could, but there would come a time when everyone would have to know: Ronnie, his parents, her parents . . . She felt herself quail at the thought.

She decided that Mr and Mrs Meadows, and Olive, of course – Olive more than anyone – did not need to know. She would go home at Christmas and break the news to her parents, then she would not need to return. Some plausible reason could be given, she was sure. But she knew the first thing she must do was write and tell Ronnie. It was only fair that he should know first.

The battle of El Alamein was being waged in the Egyptian desert, and Eunice's concern for Ronnie's safety was just as real as that for her own condition. She had received only one letter from him since he went overseas. On the fourth of November there came a jubilant bulletin from the BBC that the Germans were in full retreat. But there had still been no word from Ronnie.

'What the hell are we doing here in this bloody awful place anyway?' moaned Jack, one of Ronnie's mates. It was a question they had all asked one another countless times. 'A bloody desert! I ask you, how the flamin' hell can that be worth fighting for?'

They all knew the answer, of course, as to why anyone should want to defend the Western Desert. Beyond lay Egypt, the Suez Canal and the Middle East. Germany was short of oil, but if the Germans managed to conquer the Middle East and all its oil fields, then they could have all the oil they needed. This particular war had been waging since 1940. At first the British had had only the Italians to fight. The Italians had suffered heavy losses, having incompetent generals and insufficient equipment. But things had changed drastically when General Rommel had arrived with the German Afrika Corps. He quickly drove the British troops back five hundred miles, almost to the River Nile.

The appointment of General Montgomery had been the turning point for the British Army. He began to inspire his troops with his own boundless self-confidence and give them back their faith in themselves. The three hundred Sherman tanks that the Americans had sent, as well as the 140,000 troops under the command of General Eisenhower had arrived at just the same time, and the victory in the desert that the British soldiers had longed for was now within their grasp.

They still grumbled, however. Maybe it was part of the British psyche to complain, Ronnie thought. He was not altogether unhappy. Scared out of his wits sometimes and missing his family and his lovely Eunice, by some miracle now his fiancée. But he had some good mates and, for the first time since he joined up, he was feeling that he really might be helping to win the war.

The desert was truly a dreadful godforsaken place, far worse than he had ever imagined. He had thought of it as being miles and miles of sand, like Blackpool beach, but on a much bigger scale – and without the people, of course. Ronnie found that the desert was, more than anything, a vast area of dust rather than sand. There was sand, and rocks too, but it was the pervasive dust, working its way into everything – your clothing and hair, even your food – that you noticed above all. From time to time the wind blew it into great billowing clouds, obscuring the whole of the landscape, such as it was, for the desert, in places, was just a vast expanse of nothing. The maps of many parts, hundreds of square miles, were just blank sheets of paper as there was nothing to plot; no landmarks, no features, no sign of habitation. One striking peculiarity of the desert was the depressions, huge pits in the ground with sides like towering cliffs, of which the tank drivers always needed to be aware. Vehicles on the move created their own little sandstorms, making visibility almost nil.

After a week or two Ronnie had grown accustomed to the heat. It was a question of having to get used to it; you had no choice – although, being ginger-haired and with the fair skin that went with such colouring, he was more prone to its effects than some of his colleagues. The early mornings were not too bad, but by midday the heat would have become overpowering, so hot that you could fry an egg on the tank, which they sometimes did. Towards sunset there was often a sandstorm, followed by a night that could be surprisingly cold; but that was a blessed relief.

Although he got used to the heat, and to the dust, Ronnie felt he would never be able to stand the flies. Like the dust, they were everywhere: all over the food, round your mouth, up your nostrils and into your eyes, constantly seeking moisture. He had seen marching soldiers black with flies, drinking the sweat off their backs. God help you if you were wounded in the desert, he often thought, especially if you were left on your own. This was one of his worst nightmares, as the flies swarmed around even the slightest cut, liking more than anything the smell and taste of fresh blood.

It was best not to think of such things. Better to concentrate, whenever possible, on the camaraderie of one's mates. Fellow soldiers, however different they might be from yourself in background or education, soon became bosom pals in circumstances such as these. Such a mate was Jack Sadler, a fellow tank driver who had already been in the desert for more than a year. He was twenty-one, the same age as Ronnie, and in peacetime he had worked in a woollen mill in Bradford. Ronnie gathered he had been glad to join up to escape from his overcrowded, possibly not-too-clean living conditions; from his parents who were constantly fighting and who, in spite of this, had managed to produce a child every couple of years. Jack was the eldest of eight, something Ronnie found hard to imagine. He was what might be termed 'rough and ready', his language was the most colourful Ronnie had ever heard, but when he was not moaning – as they all did, as a matter of course – he could be amusing and amazingly cheerful. He was looking forward to getting home, when it was all over, and marrying Trixie, the mill girl for whom he had bought a ring just before he joined the army. As soon as they had become friendly they had compared photos of their girlfriends. Trixie was a pert little blonde, nothing like Eunice, but very pretty all the same.

They sat together one evening in early November, in the comparative coolness of their tent, looking at their latest photos. Letters, more precious than ever out there in the desert, took quite a while to arrive. Ronnie wondered if Eunice was receiving his. She was so far away and the memory of those magical days they had spent together now seemed like a distant dream. Her last letter had contained a snapshot of the two of them that his mother had taken on the last day of his leave, with her box Brownie camera.

'She's a bit of all right, that Eunice of yours,' said Jack. 'How come an ugly bastard like you has managed to get a smashing bird like that, eh?'

Ronnie gave him a swipe, but only in jest. The two of them were constantly sparring in fun, and he knew that the remark had been meant as a joke. 'Hey, speak for yourself, mate. You want to take a look in the mirror at your own ugly mug. Your Trixie's a smasher an' all. Beauty and the beast, what?'

Jack laughed. 'Aye, summat like that. God knows what she sees in me. I know I weren't on t' bloody front row when looks were given out, but she seems well suited with me.'

'Same here,' replied Ronnie. 'I don't know what the hell Eunice sees in me either. But she loves me. I can hardly believe my luck . . . I didn't mean it, you know. You're not ugly, not at all. I suppose girls might think you were the rugged type. You know, dark and beefy and—'

'Hey, watch it! Bloody hell! I'll be thinking you fancy me yerself.'

'Not on your life! I can imagine you with Trixie, though. She's small and fair, isn't she, and you're . . . well, you're quite hefty and dark. Opposites, but complementary, you might say.'

'Never mind yer bloody big words. You're making me feel all horny, and it's no bloody use, is it? Trixie and I – you're right; we get on very well. I can't wait, I can tell you. Just thinking about her gets me going.'

Ronnie sighed. 'I know what you mean, mate.' He had already decided that on his next leave, whenever that might be, he would insist that he and Eunice should get married.

Now he had her, he wasn't letting her go again. 'I'm going to marry Eunice as soon as I can,' he said now. 'Listen, Jack . . . if we manage to get leave at the same time – God knows when, but we might – would you . . . would you be my best man?'

'Bloody hell, Ronnie! I've never been asked to be a best man before. Aw, come on. Your Eunice, she looks like a real posh bird. She wouldn't want the likes of me. Neither would yer ma and pa.'

'Yes, they would. My parents aren't snobbish and neither is Eunice. Anyway, what's important is that I want you to be there.'

'Yeah . . . well, thanks, mate. Aw, shucks – I'm lost for words.' Jack, for once, did seem to be just that. 'You know you might have to wait a bloody long time, don't you?'

'Yes, I know,' said Ronnie. 'We'll just have to do that . . . Now what do you fancy for supper this evening? What about a nice piece of grilled steak, or fish and chips and mushy peas, not forgetting the salt and vinegar?'

'I should cocoa!' Jack sniggered. 'Come on, let's get out the bully beef and biscuits.'

That was their standard fare, day after day, although there was also a limited supply of tinned goods. Jack had told Ronnie that it had been better when they were 'chasing the bloody Eyeties'. The Italians, as well as having copious supplies of tinned tomatoes and vegetables, had plenty of wine as well, which the British Tommies had put to good use when their enemies were captured. Now, one of their biggest problems was water, or rather, the lack of it. Sometimes they were down to half a gallon a day, which had to do for drinking, washing, and filling the radiator on the tank. But they had learned to look on the bright side; there might be an oasis around the next corner.

It was halfway through November, a couple of days

after he and Jack had had their little chat about wedding plans, that Ronnie received the letter from Eunice. The news that she was pregnant filled him, at first, with trepidation; although it was only to be expected, he told himself, after what they had got up to. Only the once, though. There had been no further opportunity, after that one and only time. Whatever would his parents say? Even worse, what would be the reaction of Eunice's parents? Edith Morton would be shocked to the core. Ah well, what was done was done and there was no going back. And then he began to feel quite pleased and proud of himself. He and Eunice were going to have a baby. He was going to be a father. They would be able to get married and . . . well, he hoped they would live happily ever after.

He reread Eunice's letter. It didn't read as though she was upset or worried; she seemed quite matter-of-fact about it all. She had decided she would not say anything to anyone until she must. She would go home at Christmas and break the news to her parents and, in all likelihood, not return to the farm in Gloucestershire. Ronnie counted on his fingers. By his reckoning – although he knew very little about such things – the baby would be born at the end of June or the beginning of July. Eunice wrote that she hoped Ronnie might be able to get leave at Christmastime as well. A forlorn hope, he mused. Surely she must realise that. He had been out here for less than two months, although it seemed like for ever. He hoped he might manage to get some leave before the summer . . . before the baby arrived. Compassionate leave, maybe? His spirits lifted when he read, once more, the ending of the letter.

She said she loved him and she couldn't wait to see him again. He had waited a long time for her to say she loved him. She had spoken those words during the wonderful week they had shared. Now, reading them again, he felt he could face anything just so long as Eunice loved him and was waiting for him.

He shoved the letter away in his tin box with his other few treasures, letters and photos. He decided he would not say anything about his impending fatherhood to anyone, not even to Jack; at least, not just yet.

Ronnie had imagined, naively, that one might be safe in a tank, especially in one of the Sherman models that the Americans had supplied. That was until his first sight of a burning body hanging out of a tank in front of him. It was a sight he knew he would never forget. That was their greatest fear: being hit in the petrol tank or the ammunition locker. If that were to happen the tank would be a blazing inferno within seconds and there would be little hope of getting out alive.

Another thing they feared were the 'devil's eggs', a nasty new weapon that Rommel had introduced. These were mines buried in the desert sand, and the only way to locate them was to send infantry ahead to prod the ground with bayonets. Ronnie – selfishly, he knew – was glad of the comparative shelter of his Sherman Mark 2.

It all seemed quiet on that November day. They had been lulled into a feeling of false security that the worst was over; after all, the Germans were supposed to be in full retreat, weren't they? Ronnie poked his head out of the tank turret, then his shoulders, and looked around. Tanks were not invincible, only against rifle shots, and then only if you kept your head down. He had momentarily forgotten this warning, his mind still preoccupied with Eunice's startling news.

The shot, seemingly, came from nowhere. He felt a short sharp pain in his shoulder and when he put his hand there in an instinctive movement it came away covered with blood. He was staring at it unbelievingly when he heard the shout, 'Ronnie, for God's sake get yer head down, you bloody fool!' The next minute the whole world exploded around him.

He was not aware of the tank bursting into flames, nor of his mate, Jack, with his own clothes on fire, dragging him to safety.

Chapter 10

Eunice was worried after a few weeks had gone by and she had had no answer from Ronnie following her letter telling him of her pregnancy. Was he so worried by the news that he didn't know what to say? No, that was not possible. He might well be worried, but she felt sure he would have written to set her fears at rest. No, the letter had been delayed. That was the only explanation, she told herself.

When, at the beginning of December, she did, at last, receive a letter, it was from Mabel Iveson, not from Ronnie. Eunice read the news that he had been wounded with feelings of shock and alarm, and with the realisation too, that she cared for him very deeply. She knew now that she loved him in the way a girl should love the man she was going to marry. Her only thought, at that moment, was for Ronnie; a heartfelt hope and prayer that his injuries were not too serious. His mother wrote that he had suffered a bullet wound in his right shoulder, which was affecting, for the moment, his ability to write. He had also been burned, but they were only surface burns, which would soon heal, on his legs and feet. At the moment he was being cared for in a field hospital, but would be sent back to England as soon as he was well enough to travel.

Eunice burst into tears at the breakfast table as she read and reread the letter. Annie Meadows was at her side in an instant with her arms around her. 'What is it, lovey? Your young man? He's not . . .?'

'No . . . no, he's not been killed.' She found herself sobbing uncontrollably. 'He's OK, I think . . . He's been wounded, that's all. That's why . . . why I'm crying . . . the relief.' She felt her tension draining away as Mrs Meadows held her close. 'I'm sorry . . .' Eunice blinked and tried to brush her tears away. 'Silly of me. There's not really anything to cry about, is there?'

'Of course there is. You're not silly at all. Your nice young man's been injured. That's enough to make anybody cry. But he's going to be all right, isn't he?'

Eunice nodded. 'Yes, I think so.'

'Well, that's good news anyway. Maybe he won't have to go back, you never know. Try and look on the bright side, lovey . . . Now, you just sit there nice and quiet and have another cup of tea, and then you can join Bert and Olive out there when you're feeling a bit better. That's OK, isn't it, Bert?'

'Aye, that suits me fine,' replied Bert, standing up and reaching for his working jacket from the back door. 'Take it easy, lass, for ten minutes or so. There's nowt as can't wait. I know you've not been yourself, just lately. Worrying about your lad, I dare say. Well, he'll be fine, I'm sure. Don't you fret now.'

Olive had remained silent during these interchanges, but that was nothing unusual. The two girls worked together amicably enough, at least to all outward appearances, but there was no longer the friendly comradeship there had been between them when they had first met.

'I'm sorry about Ronnie,' Olive said now, as she followed

Bert from the kitchen. 'I know you've been worried about him . . . haven't you?' She raised her eyebrows.

'Of course I have,' said Eunice, looking steadily back at her.

It was as they were getting ready to go to bed that night that Olive tackled her. 'You're pregnant, aren't you?' she said; not spitefully, Eunice noted, or gloatingly, but just as though she were stating an undeniable fact.

Eunice made a snap decision that it would be best not to prevaricate. She had tried to keep her morning sickness a secret, but obviously this had not worked. Olive was no longer the naive, overprotected young woman she had been when she joined the Land Army, and, living in such close proximity with her colleague, it was hardly surprising that she had guessed. Bert Meadows, also, had made the remark that morning that Eunice was not herself. How long would it be before the farmer and his wife put two and two together, if they had not already done so?

'I guess so,' Eunice replied, smiling weakly.

Olive did not say anything; she merely nodded.

'I've told Ronnie,' Eunice went on quickly. 'I wrote to tell him. I suppose he got the letter, but I don't know because he didn't reply. Now I know why; it's because he's been wounded.'

'So . . . what are you going to do?'

'We'll get married as soon as we can. I don't know when, because he's in hospital, isn't he? But we are engaged, after all.'

'Yes, it's just as well that you and Ronnie are engaged, isn't it?' Olive's eyes were unsympathetic and her face expressionless.

'What's that supposed to mean?'

'Nothing . . . nothing at all. Only that . . . he'll have to marry you now, won't he?'

Eunice felt the panic building up inside her. She wanted to shout at Olive, but knew she must keep her temper. It was only too obvious what she was hinting at. Eunice guessed that if it hadn't been for the fact that Ronnie had been wounded, Olive would have said a good deal more about her suspicions, that the child that her colleague was carrying was really the child of the German POW.

'There's no "have to" about it,' replied Eunice evenly. 'We were going to get married anyway. That's what you do when you've been engaged. It'll just be a bit sooner than we intended, that's all.' Eunice's main feeling was one of fear. Olive knew too much, or thought she did.

'What did your parents say?' asked Olive.

Eunice sighed and sat down heavily on the bed. 'I haven't told them yet. Goodness knows what they'll say.' She was speaking quite candidly now. 'I'm dreading telling them. They're so old fashioned about such things. But Ronnie and me . . . well, it happened when he was on embarkation leave. We . . . well, we just got carried away, you know how it is.'

'Maybe I do.' But Olive's enigmatic half-smile was giving nothing away. She's a sly one, thought Eunice, wondering in passing, about her and Ted.

'I'm hoping my parents won't say too much, with Ronnie being wounded. Well, my mother, I mean; my father will probably say very little, like he usually does. Mum likes Ronnie,' she went on, 'so that's all to the good.'

'Hmm . . . all very convenient,' said Olive.

She knows, thought Eunice. I'm sure she knows, but she won't dare say anything, surely; not to me or to anyone else. What did it matter anyway? When she, Eunice, left the farm in a few weeks' time she would not be coming back. She would never need to see Olive Pritchard again. The thought brought immense relief.

'What about Mr and Mrs Meadows?' asked Olive. 'Are you going to tell them?'

'I suppose so,' said Eunice. 'It's the least I can do. They've been very good to me; to both of us, you and me. It's only fair to tell them the truth.'

'So . . . you won't be coming back here?'

'No, I don't see how I can, do you?'

'Not really,' said Olive. She turned her back on Eunice, starting with the nightly ritual of the Dinky curlers. The conversation was at an end and the subject of the pregnancy was not mentioned again, not only that night, but for the rest of Eunice's time at the farm. But there remained a feeling of unease between them, and Eunice knew she would be relieved when it was time for her and Olive to say goodbye.

It would not be so, however, on saying farewell to Meadowlands and to the farmer and his wife. Bert and Annie Meadows, more especially Annie, had been kindness itself to the two young women, more like an affectionate aunt or grandma than a landlady. She greeted Eunice's news with concern, but without a great deal of surprise. She did not say she had guessed, but Eunice got the impression that she might well have done so.

'Oh dear, we will be sorry to lose you,' she said. 'We will that!' There were only the two of them in the sitting room late one evening, a couple of weeks before Christmas. Olive had gone to bed and Bert was out making a final check on the barns and cowsheds. 'I don't suppose you'll be coming back, will you? You'll get married, will you, as soon as you can?'

Eunice nodded. 'Yes, of course. We hope so.' She still had not heard from Ronnie, but she knew that, at the moment, he was unable to write.

'Well, at least you're engaged to be married, so that's a good thing, isn't it?'

Eunice nodded again, but feeling a little shamefaced.

'Don't look so worried, lass. I'm not condemning you.' Annie shook her head, smiling sympathetically. 'These things happen, don't they, especially in wartime? Young people falling in love and making the most of their time together. And you're a good girl, I know you are. Not like some of the flibberty-gibberty land girls I've heard about.' Annie leaned forward in her chair, and Eunice knew she was about to impart a juicy bit of scandal. Annie, for all her kindness and concern, was an inveterate gossip.

'I've heard tell of a lass on the Summerfields' farm who's in the family way. She won't let on who the father is, and Mrs Summerfield reckons she's no idea. She's been carrying on something shameful. Anyroad, she's off to a hostel now that takes care of such things. She'll have the baby adopted, then she'll be back at work again.'

'What – on the same farm?' asked Eunice.

'Yes, love, that's right. Betty Summerfield says she's a grand little worker, as good as any man, and she doesn't want to lose her. To be quite honest, she feels sorry for the lass. She's not got much of a home life and her parents don't seem to care about her. Not like you, Eunice. You've got loving parents, haven't you? I can tell you're a well-brought-up girl and they'll stand by you.'

'I haven't told them yet,' said Eunice, in a frightened little voice. 'Yes, I know they love me, but I'm terrified of what they're going to say.'

'They might surprise you,' said Annie. 'I'm a mother myself, don't forget, so I should know. To tell you the truth,' she lowered her voice, 'the same thing happened to our Connie. Five months gone, she was, when she got wed. She'd been plucking up the courage to tell me and her dad. Well, I was that shocked at first I didn't know what to say, and so angry with her. To think that a girl of mine should behave like that! Whatever would folks say? That's what I was thinking. Then I realised I was wrong. It doesn't matter two hoots what other folks say. They should mind their own bloomin' business.' Eunice had to suppress a smile. That was a good one, coming from Annie, who loved a good old tittle-tattle as much as anyone.

'I realised it was Connie I should be thinking about. So me and her dad, we rallied round her. It's what all parents worth their salt do, believe me, lass. And our Terence, our first grandchild, he's a grand little lad, and Les has been a wonderful husband. It'll all work out, don't worry, Eunice. They might be a bit . . . surprised, like, at first, but they'll soon get used to the idea.'

'I hope so,' said Eunice.

She received a letter from Ronnie the week before Christmas, just before she was due to leave the farm for the last time. Strictly speaking, the letter was not from Ronnie, but from a nurse who was writing on his behalf. The words were his, but in strange handwriting, but stilted because he was unable, she realised, to express exactly what he was feeling through another person. He said he was surprised at her news, but what did it matter? They were engaged and they would get married as soon as he was allowed to come home. He did not know when that would be. He would probably be sent back to England for a further period of rest and recuperation early in the new year. His burns, though superficial, had taken longer to heal than had been expected. Eunice guessed, also, from the tone of the letter that he was in a depressed state of mind. He mentioned that his best mate, Jack – he had written of him before – had been very badly burned in the tank explosion and was undergoing a series of operations.

'And to think I owe my life to him,' he wrote, or rather, the nurse in charge of him wrote. 'I am sorry you have to face the music alone,' said the letter, 'but I will help you a little by letting my parents know. I love you, Eunice, and I always will. All my love, Ronnie.'

Her feelings of guilt resurfaced as they had done quite often since her talk with Olive. The best thing she could do, of course, was to push all thoughts of Heinrich Muller to the back of her mind. But that was easier said than done. She doubted she would ever be able to forget or to forgive herself. Perhaps the baby was Ronnie's. She must hold on to that thought. There was no place now for any alternative.

Bert Meadows drove the young women to the station after a tearful farewell on the part of Annie and Eunice. Olive was very quiet. She would be returning after Christmas, when they hoped they would be sent another land girl to take Eunice's place.

Olive travelled with her as far as Wigan, where she left the train. It was a somewhat silent journey with both girls burying their heads in magazines, ostensibly reading. The trains were crowded, especially so as it would be Christmas in a few days' time, so there was little opportunity for chatter, even if they had felt like talking. When they did speak to one another they kept to safe inconsequential topics, reminiscing about their early days in the Land Army, especially at the training hostel, Stapleton Hall. They wondered how their former colleagues were faring, Sheila, Rose and Dot and the three friends from Shropshire. They had lost touch with all of them of late.

We are all 'ships that pass in the night', Eunice mused, as the conversation petered out once more. She doubted she would ever see any of them again. It was doubtful she would see Olive again either, she thought, as the train approached Wigan and her companion started to gather

her things together. Eunice found herself remembering the good times they had shared in the beginning; how she had helped Olive to settle into a life that was strange and bewildering and how they had worked and spent much of their free time together in an amiable, though never very close, friendship, until the appearance of the German POWs. She regretted that their relationship had turned sour. All the same she felt a surge of heartfelt relief when Olive stepped off the train, waving a last goodbye from the platform as she humped her bulging haversack on to her back.

'You'll keep in touch, won't you?' Olive had said in those last few minutes.

'Yes . . . sure,' replied Eunice.

'You'll write to me, won't you? Let me know how Ronnie is and when you're getting married.'

'Yes . . . yes, I will.' After her previous suspicions and animosity it was somehow comforting to hear Olive's friendly interest. 'Goodbye, Olive. It's been . . . nice knowing you.' She held out her hand, but, to her surprise, Olive leaned down and kissed her cheek.

'Goodbye, Eunice. Thank you for looking after me. You helped me to get used to it all and . . . well, I remember that and I'm grateful. I would never have settled down if it hadn't been for you. And you'll let me know, won't you . . .' she whispered in her ear after glancing round uneasily at the other occupants of the carriage, '. . . whether you have a boy or a girl?'

'Yes, sure,' she said again. 'I'll keep in touch.' Probably both of them guessed that she would not do so.

Eunice reflected as she watched Olive walk away that her own life as a land girl was well and truly over. She had started out with such high hopes. It was going to be a grand and glorious adventure, and now, a little more than a year later, she was going home again for good. All the new friends she had made she would never see again; and Olive, she realised, had been a friend of sorts, certainly the one she had come to know better than any of the others.

And there had been Heinrich . . . but what an utter fool she had been to believe in him. She was convinced now – she had managed to talk herself into it – that he had let her down, that he had never loved her. If it had not been for Heinrich and her foolish dalliance with him she would not be returning home now, pregnant and with her wartime career ended so abruptly.

Or . . . would she? That was something she truly did not know. Whose child was she carrying? It could very well be Ronnie's, and most of the time she convinced herself that it was; it must be. That was the only glimmer of hope she could see on the horizon. What a miracle it had been when Ronnie had told her that he loved her, and even more so when she had realised that she loved him. But Ronnie was far away at the moment, wounded and depressed. No doubt he was very lonely and longing to be home. But she too was more than a little frightened. How she wished that Ronnie was there with her at that moment.

She experienced a sense of *déjà vu* on arriving at North Station in the gathering dusk. Her father was there to meet her as he had done each time before, a shadowy uncommunicative figure in his dark raincoat and trilby hat. He pecked her cheek and the slight glint of affection in his eyes indicated that he might be pleased to see her, although he did not say so. She wondered if he and her mother already knew the news she was about to impart. Tom and Mabel Iveson would know, if they had received Ronnie's letter. Would they have told her parents? Eunice doubted that Mabel would have said anything. She was the sort of woman who could keep her own counsel.

'You've got a lot of luggage, lass,' Samuel Morton grunted, taking hold of her large suitcase, while Eunice humped her haversack on to her back and picked up another smaller bag. 'How long are you staying? A month?' His lips moved slightly in a rare attempt at humour.

'Oh . . . er . . . well, my uniform needs cleaning,' said Eunice, panicking a little. She had been forced to bring all her belongings as she would not be returning and Mrs Meadows had promised to send her bicycle on, by rail, in a few days' time. Eunice realised as soon as she had said it that it was unlikely she would be able to get her uniform cleaned during the Christmas period, but her father made no comment. 'And there's Christmas presents and all that . . .' she went on. 'Sorry if it's a bit heavy.'

'Ne'er mind. Let's be making tracks then. Your mother's cooking a nice meal . . .

'Bad do about Ronald,' he remarked a moment or two later.

'Yes, it is,' replied Eunice. 'But I think he's getting better.'

'Hmm . . . That's all right then.'

They did not speak again during their five-minute walk home. It was usually Eunice who instigated any conversation and she could not think of anything else to say.

Her mother too commented on the vast amount of luggage after kissing her quite fondly and saying it was good to see her. Always, though, with her mother, there had to follow a slight criticism or complaint.

'You're looking a bit untidy, Eunice,' she said, 'and your hair needs washing.' She eyed her rather shabby jumper and skirt. 'And I do believe you're putting weight on. You'll have to watch it or you'll be as big as a house side.'

Eunice frantically tried to pull in her stomach muscles. She didn't think she was 'showing' yet – her mother's turn of phrase – although it was true her already ample bust had increased in size. However, it was clear that her mother did not yet know the reason or she would have said so, unless she was being deliberately devious. It was typical of her, though, to mar what should be a happy homecoming with a disparaging remark.

'It's all that farm food, Mother,' she replied. 'And I know I may look a bit shabby,' she went on with as much resentment as she dared to voice. 'I can't afford new clothes and all my things need washing or sprucing up a bit. That's why I've brought them all home, to do some "make do and mend".'

'You don't need to shout,' said Edith, automatically. 'I was only saying . . . Anyway, come along now. Have a quick wash, then your tea will be on the table. I've managed to get a nice piece of fish – only cod, but it's nice and fresh – and I'm making some chips. Hurry up now. We don't want it going cold.'

Yes, I'm well and truly home, thought Eunice as she climbed the stairs to her bedroom. And for good this time. She was already wondering how she would stand the claustrophobic atmosphere of the house, especially with Ronnie still away. She was on her own, and she had yet to tell them the news that she knew, in spite of Annie Meadows' reassurances, would shock them rigid.

The conversation during the meal, quite understandably, centred around Ronnie and his injuries.

'Poor Ronald,' said Edith. 'He was always a nice boy and he's grown up into a grand young man. I'm glad you've seen sense at last, Eunice, and realised he's the right one for you. We must be thankful it's just a shoulder wound, although that's bad enough. Another few inches and it might well have been . . . Well, we mustn't think about that. He's alive and that's all that matters.'

'He suffered some burns as well, Mum.'

'Well, of course I know that, dear . . .'

'That's why he's not been sent back home yet – to England, I mean. They're waiting for them to heal. I had a letter from him; well, from his nurse, really. I think he's rather depressed.'

'Well, he would be, wouldn't he, after all that? I know Mabel and Tom are worried about him, all that way away, but naturally they're relieved it wasn't any worse. They'll be glad when he's home again.'

'Have you seen them lately?' asked Eunice.

'Mabel and Tom? Well, of course we have. We see them at church, don't we, and I see them most days in the shop?'

'What did they say – about Ronnie?'

'I've just told you. They're looking forward to him coming home. And they'll be glad to see you as well, Eunice. You must pop round and see them as soon as you can. Change out of that awful jumper and skirt, though . . . Whatever's the matter with you, girl?' said her mother, when Eunice did not reply.

'Nothing. I'm just thinking about Ronnie,' she answered.

She forced herself to eat every mouthful of the cod and chips, which were really delicious, then just a small helping of apple crumble and custard, before she faced her parents with her news.

'We'll clear these away, then I'll make a pot of tea,' said Edith, who was never inclined to linger after a meal was finished. 'Come along, Eunice . . .'

'Wait a minute, Mother,' she said as Edith made to stand up. 'Sit down, and you too, Dad. I've got something to tell you.' She knew it was now or never.

'What?' said her mother, looking at her suspiciously. Her

eyes narrowed. 'I know what it is. I can guess. You've been acting strangely ever since you came home. You're going to tell us it's all over between you and Ronald, aren't you? That you're going to ditch him, never mind that he's been wounded fighting for his King and country. I knew there was something, lady. I could tell as soon as you walked through the door.'

'Mother, stop it!' cried Eunice. She could have laughed out loud at what her mother was saying. 'It's nothing like that, honest. Do you really think I would do that to Ronnie? Actually, it's just the opposite.' She stared down at the tablecloth whilst her mother, for once, was silent. 'I'm . . . I'm having a baby,' she said in a quiet voice. Then, as her mother still did not answer she looked up, meeting her shocked disbelieving eyes, noting the expression of dismay, almost of horror, on her face. Yes, she had guessed it would be like this. 'Did you hear what I said? I'm having a baby. That's what I wanted to tell you. That's why I've come home and why I've brought all my things. Because . . .'

'Because . . . you're having a baby?' said her mother in a bewildered voice. She shook her head confusedly. 'No, surely not . . . surely not that, not after the way you've been brought up. After all I've said to you about . . . about making yourself cheap.' She sounded incredulous at first; then, as she continued to stare at her daughter – who was sitting there so complacently, as if she had not just uttered the words destined to bring a chill to the heart of any mother – her voice rose in volume.

'Well, you've done it now, haven't you? You've made yourself look cheap, right enough, to say nothing of what you've gone and done to your daddy and me. I shall never be able to hold up my head again, not in church or . . . or anywhere. To think that a daughter of mine should behave like that. It's disgraceful! You're . . . despicable! You're nothing but a common little trollop—'

'Hey, steady on, Edith.' Eunice was surprised to hear the much calmer voice of her father. 'There's no need to carry on like that at the lass. She didn't do it on her own, you know. It takes two—'

'Be quiet, Samuel!' snapped Edith. 'Don't start sticking up for her. She's been a downright naughty girl and I'm thoroughly ashamed of her. I was coming to that, though. Yes, lady . . .' She cast a venomous look at her daughter. 'You and Ronald. I'm not surprised you were in such a hurry to get engaged. I'm disgusted with Ronald, I really am. Just wait till I see him. He's let us down badly, and I thought he was such a trustworthy young man. It just shows how mistaken you can be—'

'You're not mistaken, Mother,' said Eunice, interrupting her mother's didactic flow. But it was only what, she, Eunice, might have expected. The chances were that she would calm down in a while when she had had her say. 'Five minutes ago you were saying that Ronnie was a grand young man. Well, so he is,' she said stoutly. 'I wouldn't have got engaged to him if he wasn't, so there's no need to go running him down now. Anyway, like Dad says . . .' she looked apprehensively at her father, 'it takes two. It's my fault, just as much as Ronnie's. But we are engaged, you know, and I can't see that we've committed any crime.' She was almost shouting now, without realising it. 'We're going to get married, as soon as we can.'

'Don't use that tone of voice with me, Eunice,' said her mother. 'Yes, I don't doubt it was your fault as much as his. No doubt you led him on, didn't you, and the poor lad wouldn't know whether he was on his head or his heels?' Eunice almost laughed. You just couldn't win with her mother. Then she felt a twinge of remorse. At least her parents had assumed that the baby was Ronnie's. They hadn't even stopped to consider that it might be someone else's.

'Edith, I think you've said quite enough.' Samuel's impassive voice broke once again into his wife's tirade. 'Just leave it, love. It won't do any good.' Eunice was startled to hear an endearment come from her father's lips; it was so very rare. 'Yes, I know it's come as a bit of a shock,' he continued, 'but it's not the end of the world, is it? She's not the first girl to get into this condition, and she certainly won't be the last.' She was touched to see a glimpse of sympathy and understanding in her father's eyes.

'Anyroad, we like Ronald, don't we? And Tom and Mabel are friends of ours. Happen the young 'uns have made a mistake, but it'll all work out. I reckon we'll have to just make the best of it.' Samuel smiled, a little self-consciously after the longest speech Eunice had ever heard him make in his life.

She was overwhelmingly grateful to him and felt like going across and hugging him, but she did not do so. Old habits died hard, and he was not that sort of a father. How different it might have been, though, if Samuel had known about Heinrich. She would have been flung out on to the street and never allowed to darken the door again. Her father was showing a forcefulness she had not known before in trying to defend her. She could well imagine that his new-found boldness could have revealed itself in attack, rather than defence, of her if he had known what she'd done.

'Stop making excuses,' snapped Edith, peeved because she was not getting the support she expected from her husband. 'I wonder what Mabel and Tom will have to say about this?' She nodded at her daughter, almost as though she were taking a malicious delight in her predicament.

'You'll have to go round and tell them tonight . . . after you've tidied yourself up a bit.' She looked pointedly at Eunice's far from new clothing. 'Let's see what they have to say about you leading their beloved son astray.'

'They already know,' Eunice said, waiting for the inevitable explosion.

'What!' said her mother. Her voice rose in a shrill crescendo. 'What did you say? What do you mean?'

'Ronnie's parents already know that . . . that we're going to have a baby. He's written to tell them. At least, the nurse who's looking after him has written. He thought it would be best if they knew before—'

'Before us?' screamed her mother. 'Mabel and Tom had to know, had they, before your daddy and me? And who else knows, for goodness' sake? That busybody nurse – no doubt she's spread it all round the hospital. And your friends in the Land Army, and that Mr and Mrs Meadows that you're always on about. Oh yes, they all knew before us, didn't they?'

'Before I came home for Christmas,' said Eunice. 'That's what I was going to say, Mother, if you'd let me get a word in. Ronnie wanted to let his parents know before I went round to see them – which I fully intend to do tonight. There's been no conspiracy to keep you in the dark. Mabel could have told you if she'd wanted to.'

'Yes, she could. And I shall be wanting to know why she didn't.' Edith was still determined to play the part of a hard-done-by martyr.

'She probably thought it would be better if the news came from me,' said Eunice evenly. 'Anyway, you know now, so that's that. And nobody else knows except my friend Olive who . . . well she guessed, actually. And I had to tell Mr and Mrs Meadows because they needed to know why I wouldn't be going back.'

'Hmm . . . so you're here for good now, are you?' Edith's face was devoid of expression. It was impossible to tell whether or not she was pleased at the prospect.

'Afraid so,' replied Eunice. 'That is, until Ronnie and I get married.' It all sounded so very unreal, especially as everything was being talked about in Ronnie's absence. No real plans could be made until he was home; and no one knew when that was likely to be or for how long. If he was fit enough he would eventually have to return to the conflict, she supposed.

'Hmm . . .' said her mother again. 'Well, you'll have to help me in the boarding house. I've still got my hands full with their ladyships from London, although they're all off home at the moment. And I'm hoping we might have a few visitors come the spring. Blackpool's one of the few places it's safe to visit. There'll be no question of you going out to work, not in your condition, although you're not showing yet . . . When are you due?'

'End of June or the beginning of July, as far as I know,' said Eunice. 'I'm not quite sure with me being . . . you know . . . irregular.' She glanced uneasily at her father. It was unheard of to discuss such things as periods in front of him. Samuel took the hint and left the table. He picked up the evening paper and sat down in his favourite chair.

'Yes, of course,' said her mother. She looked searchingly at her. 'You are sure, are you, that you're really having a baby? I know you've often been late; you've sometimes gone a couple of months. You've not just imagined it, have you, because you know you've . . . well, done something you shouldn't have done?'

Eunice gave a wry smile. 'I'm afraid not.' As she had thought might happen, her mother was calming down considerably now after her initial outburst. 'I've been very sick, especially in the mornings, although I'm getting over that now. And I am putting weight on, as you've already noticed, Mother.'

'Yes, morning sickness can be dreadful,' said Edith, sounding almost sympathetic. She quickly recovered herself. 'Anyway, come along, Eunice. It's no good sitting here talking when there's all these pots to be washed.' She rose abruptly and started clattering the plates together. 'We haven't even had our cup of tea with all this . . . er . . . excitement.' Eunice noted the last word and wondered if her mother could possibly, deep down, be rather pleased? 'Your daddy and I will have a cup later after you've gone round to see Mabel and Tom. Come on now – give me a hand with this lot, then you'd better get yourself changed and get round there . . .'

As Eunice had anticipated, Mabel and Tom Iveson had accepted the news of her pregnancy far more calmly than had her own parents; her mother, that was, because she still continued to be amazed at her father's sympathetic reaction.

Mabel flung her arms round her as soon as she came through the door. 'Eunice, lovey, how nice to see you. We had our Ronnie's letter – well, the letter his nurse wrote; you know what I mean – and we're not going to say one word of reproach, Tom and me, about what has happened. Come on in, love. We're that pleased to see you, aren't we, Tom? Sit yerself down and I'll make us a nice cup of tea. We were just going to have one ourselves, and I thought you might be paying us a visit. Your mum said it was today you were coming home. I didn't say anything to her about . . . you know. I thought it would be better coming from you, love. Was she . . . were they . . . very upset?'

'Mum was,' said Eunice. 'She went mad at me when I told her. And she was annoyed that she didn't know first. She thought you might have told her.'

'I didn't rightly know what to do,' said Mabel, 'knowing your mother. She's come round now, though, has she?'

'Sort of,' said Eunice. 'Yes, I think she's getting used to the idea. My father's been great, actually sticking up for me. I couldn't believe it.'

'Aye, well, that doesn't really surprise me. Your father's able to make up his own mind when he wants to . . . Now, you have a chat to Tom and I'll go and see to that cuppa.'

Conversation with Tom was a little more stilted. He asked, somewhat embarrassedly, how she was keeping. Was she feeling any ill effects, and she assured him that she wasn't, not any more. Then they talked about Ronnie and his narrow escape in the desert and that was much easier than discussing her own condition.

'Aye, the only thing we're bothered about now is getting our Ronnie home safely,' said Mabel, returning with the tea. 'Nothing else matters a twopenny damn, excuse my French! He's been very lucky, all things considered, and I thank God every night that he's been spared. His shoulder will heal, and his burns an' all; I hope they're not too bad, though. That friend of his came off much worse, poor soul, but he's alive, thank the Lord. Eh dear, this war's a terrible thing, isn't it, Eunice love? And to think it's the second one we've lived through, me and Tom and yer mum and dad.'

'Ne'er mind, it'll come to an end before long,' said Tom hopefully. 'And in the meantime we've quite a lot to look forward to, haven't we?' He beamed at Eunice.

By the time she left them an hour or so later she felt almost excited at the thought of the new baby. If only she could be sure that the child she was expecting was Ronnie's. Mabel and Tom seemed quite delighted at the prospect of having a grandchild, even though the circumstances were not ideal. And when she arrived home she found that her mother appeared to have had a complete change of heart.

'Come and sit down by the fire, dear,' she said, 'and I'll make you a nice cup of Bournvita.

'Your daddy and I have been having a chat,' she said, as Eunice sipped the bedtime drink that had been a favourite ever since she was a child. 'We're going to make sure that you have a lovely wedding, you and Ronald. It won't be a white one, of course,' she added, a little piously, 'but we'll make it as nice as we possibly can . . . under the circumstances. It'll be at our church – we don't want any hole-and-corner register office do – and we'll have a reception for family and a few friends. It will have to be here, I think. I'll see about that . . .' She pondered for a moment. 'And I'll make a proper cake, not one of those cardboard things, and perhaps you could ask Gwen to be your bridesmaid? Now, what do you think of that, eh?'

'Thank you, Mother,' said Eunice weakly. 'It all sounds . . . very nice.' It seemed as though her mother was already taking the matter into her own hands.

Chapter 11

Ronnie was sent back to Britain early in the new year, 1943, for a period of convalescence at a hospital in the south of England. He was to stay there for a few weeks, after which he would be allowed to return home to Blackpool for rest and recuperation. It would then be up to his own family doctor to make the decision as to when – and if – he was fit to return to his regiment. As it was a long journey to the north of England it was decided that his father would go to collect him and make sure he arrived home safely.

Eunice, at first, had very mixed feelings at the prospect of meeting Ronnie again. She wondered how it would be when they saw one another after a separation of several months, especially after what had happened to him. Would there be a restraint between them? Would he still feel the same about marrying her? His shoulder and arm had healed sufficiently for him to be able to write to her, but his letters sounded stilted and unnatural, as though he was no longer sure how to express himself in writing. He mentioned very little about their wedding plans, which were going on apace in his absence. Eunice wrote and told him, trying to make her letters as amusing as she could – how her mother was bent on organising everything, although a definite date would not be fixed until Ronnie was home and it could be seen how well he was recovering. The vicar at their parish church assured Edith that he would be able to arrange a ceremony with just a few weeks' notice, giving time in which to read the banns.

But what Edith could sort out ahead of time she was making it her business to do. She had already made the cake by the first week in January, using some of her precious store of dried fruit that had been hidden away in her cupboard since the start of the war. Tom and Mabel had helped out with the sugar and butter – best butter, not margarine, for an occasion such as this – and hoped to be able to supply her with sufficient ground almonds for the covering, if they were granted an allocation of this precious commodity. If not, then she would have to make do with that mixed nut substitute flavoured with almond essence; not the same thing at all, but as they were still being reminded, 'Don't you know there's a war on?'

By 1943 food rationing had become even more stringent. People now spoke of 'eggs-in-shell', which were a luxury, very hard to come by (although many folk knew of black-market farms out in the Fylde countryside that were willing to bend the rules). In 1942 shell eggs had been supplemented by dried egg powder from the United States. A good cook, which Edith considered herself to be, could do a lot with dried egg. She often used it in her cooking for her family and guests, but for Eunice's wedding cake only the shelled variety would do. Here again, Mabel and Tom had come to the rescue and, in this instance, Edith was not averse to dealing in a bit of 'under-the-counter' business. With her saved-up points she had acquired a variety of tinned goods: Spam, corned beef and pilchards, as well as a precious tin of red salmon, all of which, with a bit of ingenuity, could be dressed up to make appetising sandwich fillings; and tinned peaches and pears, two packets of jelly and a tin of Bird's custard powder, with which she intended to make an enormous trifle. The cream would have to be 'mock', to be sure, but she was determined that her daughter's wedding buffet would lack for nothing.

And their wedding outfits, she insisted, for herself and the bride, would be the best she could afford. She would have none of that Utility rubbish, she declared, not for a wedding. The Utility label had been introduced the previous year in an attempt to save material and cut out little luxury touches such as fancy trimmings and extra buttons; and, in truth, the garments were very well designed and of a price many women could afford. But Eunice was happy to go along with what her mother decreed.

Edith was in a much better frame of mind these days, set on planning the wedding with a zeal that was totally unexpected. Her earlier anxiety about what people might say seemed to have almost vanished, although she would occasionally remind Eunice, with the prim set of her lips or a slightly caustic remark, that this was not entirely the way she might have wished it to be.

At Sally Mae's, the popular dress shop in Abingdon Street, both women found the outfits they were looking for. Eunice, prompted by her mother and the shop assistant, chose a pink silky crêpe dress with a wrapover skirt.

'You might be showing a bit more by the time you wear it,' Edith whispered as Eunice tried the dress on in the cubicle, out of hearing of the inquisitive assistant. 'This wrapover will disguise your . . . er . . . figure well enough. We don't want folk talking any more than they need to,' she added, unable to resist giving her daughter a reproachful glance.

'Is it for a wedding, modom?' the saleswoman, in the severe black dress, had asked, smiling ingratiatingly; to be told, curtly, that it was, but that it was to be only a quiet occasion.

'Then I would suggest this pretty pink bridal dress,' she had replied, 'that is, if you don't require white? Very suitable, I might say, for a quiet wedding, and it will suit the young lady's colouring very well.'

Indeed, the dress, with its knee-length flared skirt and three-quarter-length sleeves set off Eunice's dark hair and blue eyes to perfection, and, as her mother had said, her thickening figure would be well hidden by the folds of the skirt. Edith chose, for herself, a turquoise blue costume in lightweight wool, one she would be able to wear for best afterwards, and a pink silky blouse to wear underneath it. They parted with their precious clothing coupons – it had taken nearly all their allowance for these extravagances – before going to visit the hat stall in the nearby market for complementary headgear. They chose a wide-brimmed cream straw hat with a pink flower trimming for Eunice, and a small blue straw with an eye-veil for her mother.

This shopping expedition, for Eunice, was a bright interval in what was, on the whole, a humdrum sort of existence. After the freedom of working in the open air for over a year – although she had not regarded it as freedom at the time – she found the work in the boarding house irksome and boring. She had not been well off in the Land Army, not by any means, but now she was dependent on her mother, once again, for her bed and board and such meagre wages as Edith felt inclined to allow her. This was her mother's way, Eunice guessed, of getting back at her for the disgrace she had brought to the family, although it was never admitted openly. She found she was missing the comradeship she had known on the farm – even that of

Olive – as well as the fresh country air, the beauty of the countryside and the animals she had grown to love.

She seldom went out here in Blackpool, except for shopping trips to town, where there was little enough to buy even if she had had the money. (Her wedding outfit had been paid for by her mother, a fact she would not be allowed to overlook.) In the evenings she sometimes went round to see Mabel and Tom, but, apart from that, she either stayed in and read a book or listened to the radio with her parents, or – very occasionally – visited the cinema on her own. Her one-time school friend, Mavis, was away at teacher training college and her best friend, Gwen, did not go out at all on pleasure trips now. She had even taken leave of absence from her job at the aircraft factory as her mother was seriously ill.

Ivy Singleton died at the beginning of February, and it was during the same week that Ronnie arrived back in Blackpool. It was a day of mixed emotions for Eunice, attending the funeral of her friend's mother in the morning, then, in the evening, going round to the Ivesons' home to see her fiancé again after a separation of four months. They had had longer separations, to be sure, at the beginning of the war, but this one seemed, to both of them, to have been like an eternity, with all that had happened.

Mabel and Tom, tactfully, left them alone for a while, and Eunice soon found that she need not have feared there would be any uneasiness between the two of them. The warmth of Ronnie's smile told her clearly that he was delighted to see her again. She could do no other than tell him how much she had missed him, falling willingly into his arms and succumbing to his passionate kisses the moment his parents left the room.

He was pale, which was only to be expected. The desert

sunburn had faded, he told her, during his stay in hospital, leaving his skin with a yellowy tinge that would soon vanish, he hoped, when he was able to go out and enjoy the bracing Blackpool breezes. His shoulder wound had healed, and so had the burns on his legs and feet, or almost so. They had been more severe, however, than was at first thought, leaving him not so agile as he had been before. A certain modesty and consideration for her sensitivity prevented him from showing her his injuries. She was thankful that his dear face, miraculously, had not been burned.

'My poor mate, Jack, copped it badly,' he told her, something she had already learned from his letters, but Ronnie seemed unable to come to terms with it. 'Rescuing me an' all; that's what makes it worse, to me anyroad. He's a friend in a million, is Jack.'

'He's recovering, though, isn't he?' she asked. 'They've been able to do something about the burns on his face?'

'Yes, he's had a couple of ops. He's still in the hospital near Portsmouth. I had to leave him there, poor devil. He was heavily bandaged when I last saw him, but they're letting him go back to Bradford soon. He's determined to come to our wedding; I've asked him to be my best man. Actually, I'd asked him before I knew about the . . . er . . . baby. Were your parents very annoyed? I've been real worried about you having to face them on your own. Is your mum still angry with me? I must admit, I'm dead scared of meeting her.'

Eunice laughed. 'Honestly, Ronnie, after all you've been through! No, she's OK about it now; you don't need to worry. I was worried, though,' she went on. 'Your letters . . . you didn't seem interested. I didn't know how you felt about the baby. I realise it must have been rather a shock when I wrote to tell you about it.'

'Not all that much,' he said, drawing her closer and

tickling her a little beneath her ribs. 'Not after what we'd been doing.' He grinned at her. 'And now, I'm thrilled to bits. Just think, Eunice, you and me . . . we're going to have a baby.'

'Yes, Ronnie; so we are,' she answered quietly.

'So when is it going to be, this wedding of ours? The sooner the better, I'd say, wouldn't you? Why didn't you arrange a date? You seem to have sorted everything else out: your dress, the food, your bridesmaid. And I've got my best man, touch wood.' He tapped his fingers jokingly on his forehead. 'And God willing . . .' he breathed, his tone suddenly turning solemn.

'We couldn't fix the date,' she told him, 'not until you came home. We wanted to see how well you were.'

'So now you know,' he said. 'Here I am, fit as a flea and raring to go.'

'You're sure?' She doubted he was as fit as he was making out.

'Sure I'm sure. I've to see my own doctor, and no doubt he'll grant me a few weeks' convalescence before I go back. We'll be able to get married . . . Soon Eunice, please.'

'As soon as we can, Ronnie,' she assured him. She wanted their marriage just as much as he did. She loved him; she was sure of that. 'I was real worried, though, when you hardly mentioned it in your letters. I kept telling myself we were engaged,' she glanced down at the small diamond sparkling on her left hand, 'but you seemed . . . I don't know . . . half-hearted about it all.'

'I was depressed, darling,' he sighed, 'for a long time. After I came round, after the explosion, there was this awful . . . emptiness. I knew I should be glad to be alive, and so I was. It wasn't so much the physical pain – my injuries are nothing compared with those of other blokes I met in hospital – but I was thousands of miles from home.

There had been no letters for ages, or so it seemed. And I knew my best mate had nearly been killed saving me. I was in the depths of despair for a while.' He lowered his head, staring down at the floor.

'Poor Ronnie,' she said, reaching out and gently touching his arm. 'But you're home now. It's all over.'

'Yes, I'm home now.' He looked up, smiling at her. But she could see the strain and anxiety still there in his eyes. 'And everything is going to be just . . . wonderful. I know it is. How soon can the vicar fit us in, do you think? Next week?'

'It'll take a bit longer than that, won't it; for the banns and everything?'

'Next month then? The first week in March? How about that, eh?'

'That sounds OK to me, Ronnie.' She grinned at him. They would be happy together – she knew that for sure.

She was concerned, however, that he was not completely over the depression he had been suffering. And if he should have to return to the conflict . . . She hoped, deep down, that he would not go back, not yet, not ever . . .

Gwen and her fiancé, Bill, had also been planning to marry in the spring of 1943, but Ivy's worsening condition and subsequent death had, as might be expected, forced them to put their plans on hold for a while.

Eunice went to see her friend the day after the funeral. Gwen was sorrowfully, but quite composedly and with dry eyes, sorting out her mother's possessions. Her good-quality clothing and footwear – Ivy Singleton had always been able to afford the best – were being stacked in cardboard boxes for the women from the WVS to collect. They would be put to good use in heavily bombed areas where unfortunate women had lost all their worldly goods.

'Our wedding is to be in four weeks' time,' Eunice told her. 'You're still able to be my bridesmaid, aren't you? I know you're in mourning for your mum and all that, but I'm not bothered what you wear.'

'I shan't be wearing black, if that's what you're afraid of,' said Gwen, with a ghost of a smile. She was clothed in the deepest black that afternoon, as she had been at the funeral the previous day. 'I don't think people stick to it as much nowadays, especially with clothing being rationed, but I like to show respect. I shall wear these clothes for a week or so. Then I'll be going back to work, so I'll be wearing my overalls again and trying to get used to life without Mum.'

'You'll miss her. She was a lovely lady, your mum.'

'Yes, I know,' said Gwen. 'Do you know, I can't remember ever having a wrong word with her, and that's quite something, isn't it?'

'It certainly is,' said Eunice, recalling the many irate words she and her mother had exchanged over the years. There could well have been many more, but she had always been afraid of overstepping the mark. Even now her mother was ruling the roost with regard to their wedding plans, and Eunice had decided it was easier to let her get on with it than argue about it. At least it was keeping Edith happy, and now Ronnie was home again she had someone to confide in and to laugh with about her mother's interfering ways. She was careful now, however, not to criticise her to Gwen, who, having just lost her own mother, would no doubt consider that Eunice was fortunate to still have both her parents. And so she was, she realised. They had been upset, understandably, about her pregnancy, but they had both supported her.

'It's a pity she didn't live long enough to see you and Bill get married,' she went on. 'She told me how much she liked him. It would have made her happy, but it all happened sooner than you expected in the end, didn't it?'

'So it did. I knew she wouldn't get better, of course, though I tried to kid myself otherwise. It was no good trying to pull the wool over Mum's eyes, though. She knew . . . and she was so peaceful and contented, Eunice. She kept telling me she'd had a good life and that I must be happy. So . . . I've got to try, haven't I? To be happy, I mean, and to go ahead with my plans. It's what she would have wanted.' There were tears glinting in the corners of her eyes now, although she was still trying to smile bravely. She picked up a favourite blouse of her mother's, a pretty blue one that Eunice had often seen Ivy wearing, gently stroking the fabric before placing it reverently on top of the pile in the cardboard box.

'So you and Bill will be getting married soon, will you?' asked Eunice, when she could see her friend was a little more composed again.

'Yes, we hope so. If Mother had still been here we would have got married in Blackpool. But we've changed our plans now. Bill's applying for a few days' leave, and as soon as we know when it is, we'll arrange to get married in Stoke-on-Trent, where his parents live. We'll get a special licence and get married in the register office. Then I shall go down to East Anglia with Bill and find digs as near to him as possible. I'll get a job in a munitions factory, pretty much like I've been doing here, I suppose.'

'Gosh!' exclaimed Eunice, very impressed at the competent way in which her friend was planning her future. She had always known, though, that Gwen had a quiet strength beneath her apparent reserve and frailty. 'Where will you live? Do you know?'

'I think Ipswich is the nearest big town,' said Gwen, 'although I know nothing about the place. I'll probably get rooms there, if I can, and a job.'

'You are brave,' said Eunice admiringly, 'moving to somewhere strange, where you don't know anybody.'

'No braver than you were, joining the Land Army,' replied Gwen. 'That took some courage.'

'Yeah, I suppose so . . . But there were lots of other girls with me at first.'

'And I'll have my husband with me, won't I?' said Gwen brightly. 'Or as often as we can manage. We'll keep in touch, Eunice, you and me, don't worry.'

'I was hoping I might be able to come to your wedding. Do you suppose it might even be before mine, with you getting a special licence?'

'Oh no, it won't be as soon as that. I shall have to stay here for several weeks until Mother's affairs are sorted out. And there's the house to be put up for sale. I dare say it'll be April at least before we get things organised. Never mind, though. I shall be at your wedding, sure thing. I wouldn't miss it for anything. Now, are you going to tell me about your dress, or is it a secret?'

Eunice told her friend about her wedding dress and also that she and Ronnie hoped to go away for a few days for a short honeymoon. Not very far because trains were hopelessly crowded and the propaganda posters were still asking travellers 'Is your journey really necessary?' Possibly they might go to Morecambe, the rival seaside resort to the north of Blackpool. Gwen knew the reason for the hasty marriage and had smiled knowingly when Eunice first told her.

'So that's why you got engaged all in a hurry, is it?' she had said. 'Never mind; you and Ronnie make a lovely couple, I've always thought so. And take no notice of what other folks say. Actually, I don't think anybody'll say anything. Well, it's wartime, isn't it? That's what they usually say. And that baby of yours – it'll be a very lucky little boy or girl with two smashing parents like you.'

Eunice had felt tempted to confide in her – she felt dreadful when anyone made a remark such as that – but she had decided not to do so. The fewer people who knew her guilty secret the better.

One of the biggest drawbacks to their marriage, in Eunice's opinion, was that after the honeymoon they would come back home to live with her parents. That was to say, Eunice would be living with her parents whilst Ronnie, after a few weeks' extended leave, would return to an army camp to serve out the rest of the war. The doctor had decided he was not fit enough to return to Africa and it was doubtful that he would be sent overseas again. It was a relief to Eunice to know he would spend the rest of the war in England, but she did not relish the idea of remaining under her parents' roof after she was married. However, it seemed she had no choice. She would not be able to afford digs even though she would, as a married woman, have an allowance. Besides, in a few months' time she would have a baby to look after as well. Her mother had said, magnanimously, that she and Ronald – and the baby, when it arrived – could have one of the larger first-floor rooms. Two of the civil servants had gone back to London, which was fortuitous.

At the moment she had the room to herself, sleeping in the double bed that the two women had shared; the bed that she would, eventually, share with Ronnie. That was another thing about which she felt apprehensive: sharing a bed with him under her parents' roof. Now, during the times they were left on their own, either in his parents' house or – very rarely – in hers, they behaved circumspectly, fearful that they might be disturbed. They had arranged a three-day honeymoon in Morecambe, where a friend of a friend of Mabel's had a boarding house. They would be a married couple by then, Eunice reminded herself, and no one would be able to say they were behaving improperly. Neither could her mother say anything, once she had a wedding ring on her finger; nevertheless, she wished it could be different, that she and Ronnie could have a place of their own away from prying eyes and listening ears.

It wasn't until the night before her wedding that the full impact of what she was doing came home to Eunice. She was marrying Ronnie, the man she loved and she knew it was right to do so. Her childhood friend had, miraculously, become her fiancé and everyone – their parents and all their friends – were delighted at this development. So was Eunice; there was no doubt about her love for him. But the fact – a fact she had found herself increasingly overlooking in all the excitement of the wedding plans – was that she was pregnant with what could turn out to be another man's child. This was not what she had planned. She had never meant to deceive Ronnie, but if her worst fears were to be realised and the baby should turn out to be Heinrich's, then she could be sentencing Ronnie – and herself as well – to a marriage based on cheating and lies.

She had even wondered at times if she should come clean with Ronnie and tell him what she had done. After all, it was not as if she had been unfaithful to him. It had happened before Ronnie had declared his love for her. But she knew she was deluding herself. She could never tell him. She felt at times that his tendency towards depression was balanced on a knife edge. It would not take much for him to retreat back into himself and to feel that life was unbearable, as he had confessed he had felt after his injuries. For most of the time, fortunately, he was cheerful;

almost the old Ronnie she had known for so long, and she knew she had to do all she could to keep him that way.

And so she had tried to keep her doubts and fears to the back of her mind. It was not always so easy, though, and her friend, who knew her very well, had guessed there was something amiss.

Gwen found her in the bedroom, sitting on the blue sateen eiderdown in a very downcast state of mind, when she called to see her the evening before the wedding.

'What's the matter?' she asked her friend, because Eunice looked for all the world as though it were to be a funeral the next day, not a wedding. 'Come on, cheer up; it's your big day tomorrow . . . What's the matter?' she asked again, sitting down beside her on the bed and putting an arm round her shoulders. 'Come on, you can tell me, whatever it is. You're not having second thoughts, are you?'

'No . . . no, I'm not,' said Eunice, because she wasn't, not about marrying Ronnie. 'It's just . . . everything. Mum and I are getting on one another's nerves.'

Gwen smiled a little. 'Well, that's nothing very unusual, is it?' she said, hoping that would suffice.

'No, I suppose not.'

'What have you fallen out about?'

'I can't really say we've fallen out about anything in particular. She's just so . . . oh, I don't know, so bossy and . . . organisy, if that's a word. Anybody would think it was her wedding, not mine.'

'Perhaps you should try to be pleased she's taking an interest, even if it's rather too much? She might, quite easily, have wanted nothing to do with it. You said she was shocked at first, didn't you, when you told her about the baby?'

Eunice nodded. 'Yes . . .' she said in a small voice.

'You're right. I shouldn't go on about her. I'm sorry, Gwen. I didn't mean to, especially as you've lost your own mum not long ago. I'm really sorry.' There were tears in her eyes as she looked at her friend. 'That's the one thing I didn't intend to do, in front of you.'

'Hey, come on,' said Gwen. 'No tears; it doesn't matter, honestly. I know your mother can be a bit of a pain, whereas mine . . . well, she was a real gem. I know I was very lucky. Anyway, it won't be for much longer, will it? You and Ronnie are getting married tomorrow, then you'll be getting away from your mother, and your father.'

'Only for a few days. We've got to come back, you know, and live here.'

'So? You'll have a husband then, won't you? I'm sure your mother won't try to boss you around when Ronnie's here.'

'He'll be going back to camp, won't he?'

'Oh dear! This doesn't sound like you at all,' said Gwen concernedly. 'You used to be so forceful, not afraid of sticking up for yourself. What's happened to you, Eunice? You seem cowed, somehow, as though you've lost your fighting spirit. I know it must have been a shock to you, finding out you were pregnant, but it doesn't matter all that much, does it, about having a baby? You would have married Ronnie in any case . . .'

To Gwen's astonishment – and somewhat to her own as well – Eunice burst into tears. 'The baby!' she cried. 'The baby; I wish folks would stop saying that word. Oh, Gwen, I've done something dreadful.'

'What?' said Gwen, aghast. 'What have you done?'

Eunice took hold of her friend's hands, gripping them tightly. 'I'll have to tell you,' she said, on an impulse. 'I haven't told anyone else, not a single person, but I can't keep it to myself any longer.' Her voice was the merest whisper. 'The baby . . . it might not be Ronnie's.'

'What!' Gwen looked even more shocked and dismayed. 'Eunice, what on earth are you saying? If it isn't Ronnie's, then who . . .?'

Eunice released her hands, moving a little away from her friend. She did not look at her as, falteringly, she told her about Heinrich and their developing friendship, and how he had vanished from the scene the day after they had made love.

'But you couldn't possibly have known you were pregnant,' Gwen interposed. 'You might not have been.'

'No, I realise that. But you know what I've always been like with my periods. It could have been ages before I knew for certain. Anyway, I came home on leave soon afterwards and Ronnie was here. You can't imagine how glad I was, Gwen; it was such a comfort. I didn't tell him about Heinrich, of course, but when I was with him – with Ronnie, I mean – I started to feel much better. I even began to forget my worries, it was so lovely for us to be together. And then . . . well, you know what happened. Ronnie told me he loved me, and things started to get very passionate all of a sudden. And . . . and we made love. And Ronnie asked me to marry him. And I said yes . . . I was so happy, Gwen.'

'You didn't try to . . . to trick him into asking you, did you?'

'No, of course I didn't. It never even occurred to me. It was only later that I realised that if I actually was pregnant, then this was an answer to my problem . . . wasn't it?'

'Yes, I suppose so,' said Gwen, a little unsurely. 'Yes . . . it must have seemed like that. And then you discovered you really were pregnant?'

'Yes, that's right.'

'So . . . you're not sure whose baby it is?'

'No, I'm afraid not. I'm hoping and praying it's Ronnie's. Most of the time I can convince myself it is, but . . . I can't be sure. You think I'm dreadful, don't you? You must do.'

'No, I don't,' replied Gwen. 'I'm trying hard to understand. Nobody else knows about this, do they?'

'That the baby might not be Ronnie's? No, of course not.' She hesitated, then: 'Only Olive,' she added. 'She was always going on at me about being friendly with a German POW, and then when she knew I was pregnant she started insinuating things. We had quite a row about it. I told her she was being ridiculous and that Heinrich and I had never . . . you know. I hated lying, Gwen, but she was such a nosy girl and I was frightened she might say something to the farmer and his wife. But I don't have any contact with Olive now. We sort of half promised to keep in touch, but we haven't done.'

'Well, you don't need to worry about her then. The chances are you'll never see her again anyway. I can understand that you feel guilty, keeping your secret from Ronnie. But it would only make things worse to tell him. You love him, don't you?' Eunice nodded. 'I guess you always did, deep down, even when you insisted you were just friends. Now it'll be up to you to make amends by showing him you love him. He deserves that, you know.'

'Yes, I know,' said Eunice in a tiny voice. 'And I do love him, so very much. Thanks for listening to me, Gwen. I feel tons better already.'

'That's what friends are for,' said Gwen. 'Now, dry your eyes and dab some powder on, and we'll go and have a cup of tea with your mum and dad. Then you'd best have an early night. You want to look beautiful for Ronnie in the morning, don't you?'

Chapter 12

'Nobody would think there was a war on. You've put on a lovely spread, Edith,' Eunice overheard a guest, one of her mother's friends from church, remark. She watched her mother preen herself and smile, a trifle smugly.

'Well, I've done my best and I can't do any more than that. It isn't every day that your only daughter gets married, is it?'

Eunice had recovered from what she now regarded as a crisis of nerves the previous day. She was determined to put the past behind her, as much as she could, and look to the future: her and Ronnie's future. She appreciated that her mother, indeed, had done well to make such an attractive buffet meal. There were open sandwiches of various kinds, decorated with pieces of tomato and sprigs of parsley, to make them look as tempting as pilchards, Spam and corned beef could possibly look; the red salmon needed no titivating, and those sandwiches very quickly disappeared. There were home-made sausage rolls too, and a variety of fancy cakes, some baked by Edith and some by Mabel; a large trifle and a separate fruit jelly decorated with mock cream; and the *pièce de résistance*, the wedding cake.

Many brides were having to make do with what were sometimes termed 'whited sepulchres', a cardboard structure, sometimes decorated with satin bows and trimmings, inside which lurked a tiny wedding cake. This was usually made with dried egg, and gravy browning and rum essence did their best to conceal the sparse amount of dried fruit. There were oohs and aahs of admiration at the cake, which was not a large one, but was covered with real icing over a layer of real almond paste. Edith was heard to remark, 'There's six eggs in it an' all, proper ones in shells, not your dried rubbish.' No one asked how she had come by them. All her friends knew they would do the same, if they could, for their own daughters' weddings.

Apart from the immediate families a few friends had been invited: four of Edith and Mabel's friends with their husbands, all members of the church where the wedding had taken place; the vicar had been asked to come along too, out of courtesy; and the four remaining civil servants from London who had been very kind to Eunice and Ronnie and had given them a nice EPNS teapot and hot-water jug. Then there were the Mortons and the Ivesons, including Chrissie and her friend Fiona, who had managed to wangle a weekend pass; Gwen, the bridesmaid and her fiancé, Bill; Jack, the best man and his fiancée, Trixie; and, of course, the bride and groom. Twenty-five people in all, a goodly crowd for what was intended to be a quiet wedding, chatting happily together and making short work of Edith's lunchtime buffet. It had been a morning wedding to allow the 'happy couple' to catch the train to Lancaster and then to Morecambe.

Eunice found, after her collywobbles of the previous night, that she was enjoying it all. It was her wedding day, despite all the complications and traumas, and she was so very happy to be marrying Ronnie. It was nice to be the centre of attention too, to be congratulated and made a fuss of, something which happened only once in a while. The next time she would be fussed over would be when the baby arrived. That was almost four months off and at the moment she was hardly 'showing'. The well-cut pink dress cleverly concealed the slight bulge, and no one would have guessed if they didn't already know. Eunice suspected that everyone did know, or had wondered, but of course no one referred to it.

The vicar, whom Eunice had known for most of her life, had conducted a simple and moving service. The hymns – 'O perfect Love' and 'Lead us, heavenly Father, lead us' – which everyone knew, had been chosen by Edith as being very suitable and traditional.

> Saviour, breathe forgiveness o'er us,
> All our weakness Thou dost know;

Eunice had sung, as well as she was able for the lump in her throat. She felt the words to be poignant and very appropriate. Had her mother had the same thought, she pondered, and included the hymn as another subtle hint that she had done wrong? No, she did not really think so, but she wondered if she, Eunice, would ever be able to forget the weakness she had shown that long ago day last September. There came into her mind, unbidden and with great clarity, the thought of the mellow sunshine, the apple orchard, the barn and Heinrich . . . She dismissed it at once. What a time to be thinking of such things, in the middle of her wedding service. She had turned to smile at Ronnie, and he had smiled, so lovingly, back at her.

The vicar had been invited along to the party not just out of politeness, but because Edith wanted him to perform a certain task, that of proposing a toast to the bride and groom. This was usually done by the bride's father, but Samuel could not be persuaded, even on such an auspicious occasion, to conquer the reticence of a lifetime. Eunice was not surprised at this. She had remarked to Ronnie that her father would sooner face life in the trenches again than make a speech in public. No, she admitted; that was an exaggeration, but she knew that nothing or nobody would be able to coax him and so they did not try. She was rather surprised that her mother had not chosen to undertake the task herself, but maybe she considered it would not be 'proper'.

At all events, the Reverend John Hunter made a very acceptable speech, saying what an admirable couple of young people they were, and that he hoped, God willing, that this wretched war would soon be over, then they could spend the rest of their lives in peace and happiness. There were murmurs of 'Hear, hear' from the guests, then everyone drank the health of the bride and groom in rich brown sherry, from a bottle that had lain unopened in Mabel's sideboard since Christmas. Ronnie thanked everyone 'on behalf of my wife and myself' for coming to the wedding and for all the lovely presents, and both sets of parents for making the occasion such a joyful one.

One speech that was missing, and no one bothered because this was such an informal occasion, was that of the best man. Traditionally, as they all knew, he should propose a toast to the bridesmaid, but no one would have expected Jack Sadler to do so. It was sufficient that he was there, as he had promised Ronnie he would be, before the terrible incident that had left both of them maimed. Jack had travelled across to Blackpool from his home in Bradford two days before the wedding, accompanied by his pretty little fiancée, Trixie. Eunice was filled with admiration that he had had the courage to do so.

She had gone round to Ronnie's home the evening after the couple had arrived, and she saw straight away why Ronnie thought so much of Jack.

'So this is Eunice?' he said, smiling as broadly as he was able, as one side of his face was very disfigured; though nothing like as badly as it had been at first, Ronnie was to tell her later. He did not attempt to kiss her or to throw his arms around her, although she guessed that at one time Jack would not have hesitated to do so, even at their first meeting. Instead he took her outstretched hand and squeezed it warmly. 'I've waited ages to meet you, luv, and it's worth the wait an' all, I can tell yer. Ronnie here wasn't fibbin' when he said you were a real corker.'

She laughed, looking straight into his eyes. 'And I've heard a lot about you too, Jack,' she said. 'I'm very pleased to meet you at last . . . and Trixie.' She turned to smile at the little blonde girl by his side. 'It's very good of you to come. I know Ronnie appreciates it, and so do I.'

'We wouldn't have missed it for t' world,' said Trixie, grinning at Eunice and then up at her fiancé. She was a very small girl, reaching only to his shoulder, very pretty in a childish sort of way, with bubbly blonde curls, reminiscent of Shirley Temple. Her rosebud mouth was scarlet and the circlets of rouge on her cheeks gave her the appearance of a china doll. 'It'll be our turn soon, won't it, Jack?' She stood on tiptoe and kissed his cheek. 'By the end o' t' summer we'll be wed. Jack has to 'ave another op, then there'll be nowt to stop us, will there, luv?'

'That's right, sweet'eart,' he replied. 'Nowt at all. And we hope you two'll be there. 'Appen Ronnie'll do the honours for me, same as I'm doing for 'im; 'ow about it, mate?'

'Sure,' replied Ronnie, 'provided I can get leave. I'll be back in the fray by then, you know.'

'Oh aye – I were forgetting,' said Jack. Eunice guessed he

would probably not be going back at all and she felt glad about that. She noticed he had a limp as well as his facial injuries. It appeared to be mainly one side that was affected. The skin on his left cheek and forehead was shiny and of a dark pink hue, stretched tightly so that it pulled his mouth out of shape, causing him to smile in a lopsided manner. It did not stop him from smiling, however. Jack had been noted for his laughing and joking, verging on the ribald – or sometimes downright rude, as Ronnie had said. He had been fortunate not to lose the sight of his left eye; the skin around it was taut, pulling the eyelid down so that one eye was almost closed in a permanent wink.

Eunice had warmed to them both at once, although she wondered at the close bond there seemed to be between Ronnie and Jack. They were so dissimilar, Ronnie being of a much quieter and gentler nature than his ebullient friend. Although Jack was nothing like as jovial and boisterous as he used to be, Ronnie told her. He was putting on a brave face, but he had been adamant that he could not make a speech at the wedding, not in front of all those people; something the old Jack would not have hesitated to do. Ronnie had assured him that it did not matter at all; his presence and continuing friendship was all that Ronnie cared about. Eunice knew that the friends you made in wartime could be vastly different from yourself and from those friends at home. Ronnie and Jack had found themselves together, far from home, in dangerous and unfamiliar circumstances, and so they had bonded in a way they might never have done in peacetime.

'Where will you and Jack live when you get married?' Eunice asked Trixie, when the two men were laughing together about comrades they had known. 'Will you be able to get a house – to rent, I mean?'

'Shouldn't think so,' said Trixie. 'Not till t' war's over,

anyroad; then happen they'll start building again. There's eight of 'em at Jack's 'ouse, not counting his mam and dad, when they're all there, although two more of 'em are in t' forces, same as Jack. And our 'ouse is bursting at t' seams an' all. I'm the eldest of six, so we can't live at home like what you're goin' to do. Happen we'll get digs near to t' mill. I reckon Jack'll be going back there when things is sorted out. We'd move in together now if we could, but we daresn't. You know how folks 'ud talk,' she winked at Eunice, 'and me mam'd have a pink fit. So would Jack's.'

'Are you still working at the mill?' Eunice asked. 'Didn't you have to enlist when you were twenty?'

'Oh no; it's a reserved occupation, see, working in t' woollen mill. We're on a contract job for t' Government, mekin' khaki cloth an' all that. I'll be glad to get back to summat a bit more colourful, like, but I'm doin' me bit, as they say, for t' King and country. I wish they'd get a bloody move on, though, and get it over with.'

'Don't we all,' said Eunice. 'I'm dreading Ronnie going back, although the doctor has said he's not fit to go overseas again, thank God.'

'Aye, you must be glad about that, and my Jack won't be going back at all. I used to say to meself that I wouldn't care if he ended up a prisoner. At least then I'd know he were safe for t' rest o' t' war. Of course, knowing Jack, he'd've tried to escape, wouldn't he, and got hisself shot? But what's 'appened to 'im's a lot worse than being captured, poor devil. He's ever so brave though, and cheerful, though he has his moments, believe me. Aye, he has his moments . . .' Trixie nodded meaningfully, staring into space. 'Them bloody Germans've got a lot to answer for, if you ask me. If I could get me 'ands on t' German swine who planted that bloody land mine I'd wring 'is rotten neck, I would an' all.'

'Mm . . . yes; can't say I blame you,' murmured Eunice, disconcerted for the moment at the mention of prisoners of war and of the one German who was responsible for Ronnie's and Jack's, much worse, injuries. She found it difficult to think of Germans in isolation. They were usually lumped together and thought of as 'the enemy', although she was sure there must be thousands of individual German servicemen who had got caught up in this conflict against their better judgement. Men who were decent, probably very nice amiable people. Men like Heinrich; she would never believe he had been a wicked man. Men like Hitler, though, and Himmler, Goering and Goebbels; they were downright evil, or so the British populace were always being informed. She wondered whether the great Allied leaders, such as Winston Churchill, Eisenhower and Montgomery were regarded in a similar light by the German people. Surely not; it must be obvious to all that those men were high-principled and honest, aiming only towards what was right; freedom for all nations.

'I don't suppose they're all bad, though,' she continued carefully, 'all the Germans, I mean. Some of them are probably just ordinary lads like Ronnie and Jack, wishing it was all over and they could go home.'

'Huh! You can think what you like. As far as I'm concerned they're all filthy rotten bastards,' said Trixie. Eunice could well understand her vehemence and she decided it might be better to get away from the explosive subject. She might well have felt the same way herself if she had not met Heinrich.

'It'll be nice for you and Jack to start your married life on your own,' she said, 'away from your families. I only wish we could do the same.'

'Why can't you then?' asked Trixie.

'Because . . . well, it makes more sense for me to stay at my parents' place for a while. They've loads of room and when Ronnie goes back I would be on my own if I was in digs somewhere.' That sounds pathetic, thought Eunice, as soon as she had uttered the words. But it would sound even more pathetic to say that her mother would throw a fit at the idea of her leaving home. 'My mother thinks it won't be so lonely for me if I stay with them,' she added. 'We'll get our own place as soon as we can, though.'

'Ne'er mind. I 'spect it'll be all for t' best,' said Trixie cheerfully. 'Yer mam'll be able to give you an 'and wi' t' baby, won't she? I know you're in t' puddin' club; Jack told me. Hey, you're not offended, like, are yer? It's me and me big mouth. I never know when to shurrup. We call a spade a spade, us Yorkshire folk; sometimes a bloody big shovel, ne'er mind a spade.'

Eunice realised she must have looked a little taken aback. She laughed.

'No, of course I'm not offended,' she answered. 'I guessed you would know about the baby. I dare say everybody knows.'

'What the heck! Folks should mind their own bloody business. It's a miracle Jack and me aren't in t' same boat.' Trixie gave a sly wink. 'We try to be careful, like, but it wouldn't matter much now. We'll be wed in a couple of months, I 'ope.'

'Good,' replied Eunice, a little embarrassed at such plain speaking from a girl who, until an hour ago, had been a stranger. You could not help but like Trixie, though; she was so honest and straightforward. 'You're right about my mother,' Eunice went on. 'She'll be able to give me a hand with the baby. I expect she's looking forward to it, although she wouldn't dare admit it. She was very upset at first, you see, about me getting . . . pregnant.'

'She'll soon gerrover it when she's got a new grandchild to swank about. I wouldn't get any help from my mam, that's for sure. She says she's cleaned enough dirty bums to last her a lifetime.'

'Mm . . . yes,' said Eunice. What she dreaded from her own mother was not too little help, but too much. Edith would interfere and try to take charge, as she did with everything.

'I'm reight glad I've met yer,' said Trixie at the end of the evening. 'You and me'll be good mates, I know we will. Good luck for the day after tomorrer. Jack and me's tickled pink to be going to a posh wedding.'

'Not all that posh,' replied Eunice. 'Don't expect too much.'

'Gerraway! It'll be posh to us. It'll be like one o' them big swanky dos what yer see in *Picture Post*. I've gorra new frock an' all. Pink, to make the boys wink!'

When the reception was over, Eunice was relieved to escape, from what seemed an endless afternoon, to North Station, to board the train to Preston, and from there to Lancaster and Morecambe. Gwen and Bill, and Jack and Trixie accompanied them to help to carry the luggage. Eunice was glad, for once, that her mother had had the good sense to keep away. When the guests had departed she would, of course, be up to her arms in soapsuds, washing the mountain of pots; grumbling, no doubt, but happy all the same. Edith, for most of the day, had looked as proud as a dog with two tails.

'Bye . . . Cheerio . . . Have a lovely time . . .'

'Don't do anything I wouldn't do . . .!'

Their four friends waved and shouted as the train drew out of the station, and Eunice and Ronnie waved back until a cloud of acrid grey steam billowed out, obscuring their view and forcing them to retreat back to their carriage.

'Chalk and cheese, those two couples,' Ronnie remarked.

'Aren't they just?' replied Eunice. 'They seem to be getting on well together, though, don't they? I noticed Bill and Jack were chatting away, so were Gwen and Trixie.' It was the first time Eunice had met Bill and she had known at once he was just right for her friend: sensible, quiet and thoughtful, and obviously very much in love with Gwen.

'They're made for one another an' all,' said Ronnie. 'Jack and Trixie, Bill and Gwen; anybody with half an eye can see that. Those two'll be happy marriages all right . . . Same as ours, darling.' He put his arm round her, and Eunice snuggled up to him. Everyone had grown used to courting couples behaving demonstratively in public now, and the other occupants of the carriage, a middle-aged couple and three servicemen, did not appear to be taking any notice. She turned to smile at her husband.

'Of course,' she replied. 'I'm very happy already, Ronnie.' And she was. It had been a lovely day.

'So am I,' he said. 'Happier than I've been in all my life. Eunice . . .' He lowered his voice, almost whispering in her ear. 'We would have got married anyway, you know. It's not just because of . . . the baby.'

She shook her head. 'I don't think that at all. Of course we'd have got married; not quite so soon, maybe, but we would.' The shake turned into a definite nod. 'Yes . . . we would.'

Eunice remembered the conversation she had had with Gwen only the previous evening. Now, once again, at Ronnie's reassuring words that they would have got married in any case, baby or not, she felt a stab of remorse. The child she was carrying might not be Ronnie's at all! The thought came home to her all at once with tremendous force, so much so that she almost gasped aloud. In the excitement leading up to their wedding day Heinrich had seemed a distant memory. He had come into her mind, briefly, at the very moment of her marriage, but she had managed to dismiss all thoughts of him, or had believed she had done so. The spectre of him was still there, however, and always would be, she supposed, until she knew for sure about the baby. But would she ever know for certain? She was haunted by the knowledge that she had done a dreadful thing to the man who was now her husband, the man she truly loved.

She took a deep breath and turned towards him. 'I love you, Ronnie,' she whispered, the words coming from the bottom of her heart.

'And I love you,' he replied.

They stayed in Morecambe for three nights. The boarding house was very similar to the one where Eunice lived, in a side street leading away from the promenade. The food was as good as could be expected for wartime, but Eunice and Ronnie were so hungry most of the time that they would have eaten anything that was put in front of them.

The March wind was cold, though not quite so blustery as in Blackpool; it was certainly not the weather for sitting around on the beach or promenade. They took long walks, north to West Bank and south to the ancient village of Heysham, striding out rapidly and working up an appetite for the next meal. And on the last day they took a bus ride to Lancaster to view the Norman castle, then climbed up to the high-domed Ashton memorial, which dominated the skyline and could be seen from miles away. There was a magnificent view from up there. Looking westwards was Morecambe Bay and the grey expanse of the Irish Sea; to the east the Forest of Bowland; and northwards the hills of the Lake District.

These could be seen also from the promenade at

Morecambe; they were at their most spectacular when viewed in the glow of the setting sun, standing out stark and black against the crimson and orange of the sky. The sun did shine sometimes despite the chill in the air and Eunice said she had never seen a more beautiful sight.

'Not even in Gloucestershire?' asked Ronnie.

'No,' she answered quickly, pushing her thoughts away from any memories of that place. 'We didn't have time to stand gawping at the sunset, anyway. I don't want to think about the Land Army now, Ronnie; I'm here with you.'

There were not many holidaymakers in the seaside resort, although in the summer it might be almost as busy as its rival, Blackpool. There was another young couple staying at the boarding house, honeymooners like themselves, Eunice guessed. They said 'Good morning' or 'Good evening' and exchanged a few polite words and a smile whenever they met, usually in the dining room, but they seemed to want to keep themselves to themselves, and that suited Eunice and Ronnie. The young man was wearing airforce blue and Ronnie, though he was on extended sick leave at the moment, had chosen to wear his khaki uniform. Young men in civvies tended to be looked at askance, even though there might be a very good reason for it.

It was even colder at night and the unheated bedroom felt slightly damp. Mrs Davis, the landlady, put a hot-water bottle in their bed each night, which took the chill off the crisp white sheets that covered the flock mattress. They pushed the bottle to the bottom of the bed then snuggled together for warmth. They were getting to know one another in every way, something they had had little opportunity to do so far. They had known one another for ages, to be sure, but their courtship had not been all that long and most of it they had spent apart. They had made love, in the fullest sense, only once. Now that they were able to give full rein to their emotions she found Ronnie to be gentle and thoughtful, considering her feelings just as much as his own needs. They learned from one another and were perfectly compatible.

In other ways too they found they got on well together. They were good friends as well as being husband and wife, and Eunice thought that boded well for the future. She hoped she would soon be able to put the past behind her completely, and prayed that it was Ronnie's child she was carrying.

Ronnie returned to a camp in the south of England in mid-May. Eunice was sad to see him leave, not only because she knew she would miss him, but because, when he had gone, she would be on her own again with her mother and father – a little girl again, in her mother's eyes, she feared, unless she had the courage to stand up for herself. It was a difficult situation. She was doing various jobs in the boarding house for a pittance: cleaning, assisting with the cooking, and dealing with the bookings – there were quite a few more this season – and the finance, a job her mother had always hated, but which Eunice could manage easily. As time went on, however, Edith refused to let her serve in the dining room; because of her 'condition' she had to be kept out of the public eye. Admittedly, she was given her bed and board. Even when Ronnie had been staying there Edith had taken only a token sum from him for their keep. Eunice supposed that, in her own way, her mother thought she was being generous, but she still felt as though she were under her mother's thumb and likely to remain so.

With Ronnie there Edith had not been so overbearing. She had treated her new son-in-law with the utmost respect and consideration. Eunice had felt at times that they were more like lodgers than members of the family. They had settled into a sort of routine during the couple of months they had spent there. Ronnie had sometimes gone to help in his parents' shop, otherwise time would have hung heavy for him. Eunice had done her chores in the boarding house, then they had all sat down together to share an evening meal – Edith and Samuel, Eunice and Ronnie. They had spent most of the evenings together too, listening to the radio, except for the times when they had escaped – Eunice always looked upon it as an escape – to the Ivesons' home or, occasionally, to the cinema.

They had not managed to recapture the delight they had discovered in getting to know one another during their brief honeymoon period. With her parents just across the corridor from their bedroom, Eunice had felt somewhat inhibited. Ronnie had said he understood, although she sensed he was a little impatient at her restraint, something she had certainly not shown during the few days they had spent in Morecambe. Anyway, it was not really advisable to make love now. In her eighth month Eunice was very large and extremely conscious of her bulk.

She was keeping well and there had been no complications, but she would be glad when it was all over. When Ronnie had gone she found she was growing more cumbersome than ever. She hated her appearance. Some days she felt too tired to do anything but sit in a chair and read or knit. Knitting had never been her strong point, but she had felt she ought to show willing, especially as her mother and Mabel's needles were clicking away madly making miniature garments. And she, Eunice, to her surprise, had managed to produce quite presentable little matinée jackets and bootees.

She had chosen white and lemon wool. This commodity

was very scarce, but Edith had managed to procure some precious skeins through 'a friend of a friend'. When anyone asked her, as they invariably did, whether she wanted a boy or a girl, she gave the expected answer that she didn't mind so long as it was all right. Secretly, though, she wanted a little girl; a girl who, later, would be a friend to her as well as a daughter. They would have a much closer relationship than she and Edith had ever had; she had made up her mind about that already. But if the baby was a boy . . . then he would be just as welcome. And they could always try again.

Chapter 13

Eunice was listening to *ITMA* when she became aware of the pain starting in her back. She tried to ignore it at first. She had been having vague pains on and off for the past week, but they had proved to be false alarms, receding after a few moments. She shifted around in the armchair, trying to get comfortable. Her father was snoozing on the sofa – he was not much interested in comedy programmes – whilst her mother, who was, surprisingly, quite a devotee of *It's That Man Again*, smiled and occasionally laughed out loud at the familiar catchphrases of Tommy Handley and company.

ITMA had become a treasured national institution since its advent in September 1939, very soon after the start of the war. Every age group, every social class in the country was united in common laughter at the antics of the well-loved and familiar characters: Mona Lott, Colonel Chinstrap, Claude and Cecil, the broker's men, Fumf, the German spy, and Mrs Mopp, the charwoman. Her catchphrase, 'Can I do yer now, sir?' with its double meaning, always caused Edith to purse her lips and frown a little, but she seemed genuinely amused and an altogether different person during the half-hour when *ITMA* was on the air.

It had been a contented, family sort of evening, typical of the ones that Eunice and her parents had spent together recently. She had held a skein of pale lemon wool on her outstretched hands whilst her mother wound it into a ball, ready to begin the next matinée jacket, then they had listened to the radio, as they did every evening. It had not been half as bad as she had feared with Ronnie back at the camp. He wrote regularly, as she did, and she was relieved that he was no longer in any danger. She almost believed that her mother was mellowing. She was certainly not so critical of her daughter, nor so overbearing as she had used to be. At times, indeed, she was quite kind, showing more concern for her comfort and wellbeing than she had ever done in the past. Eunice might have expected her to be impatient. Edith was of the school that believed that being ill was largely a question of mind over matter. Only in the direst emergency would Edith stay in bed and she had brought her daughter up to the same belief. Childbirth, Eunice had thought, might have been regarded in the same way, but her mother had been very sympathetic when she had seen the difficulty she was having in even moving about.

Gwen had got married the previous week in Ipswich, but it had been out of the question for Eunice to attend. She had been bitterly disappointed, but had realised she could never have made it there and back. All she wanted now was to give birth to the baby and to have her normal shape back again. It was the beginning of July, almost into the second week now, and she had been expecting things to happen since the end of June.

By the time *ITMA* had finished Eunice was in no doubt that things were on the way. 'Mum,' she said. 'I think it's started – the baby. And I'm sure this time; it's not a false alarm. Oh . . . oh help!' she cried as a sudden pain made her double up, and at the same time she felt a flow of water gushing from inside her. Looking down she could see the water trickling down her legs and on to the carpet. 'Oh dear! I'm sorry; I couldn't help it,' she said, collapsing back as the pain subsided, the apology coming automatically.

'Of course you couldn't help it, you silly girl,' said her mother. 'There's no need to apologise.' She looked warily at her husband, who had opened his eyes and was staring dazedly around, then she looked back at Eunice. 'Your waters have broken,' she mouthed. 'It's nothing to worry about,' she added. 'Sometimes it doesn't happen till much later; perhaps it means you won't be long. Come on now, love. Let's be having you. We'll get you upstairs and into bed, then I'll give Mrs Wilshaw a ring.' She was the midwife who had attended Eunice during her pregnancy.

'Samuel – she's started. Come on now, look sharp. Go and put the kettle on and try to make yourself useful. Don't look so worried. She'll be perfectly all right; she's only having a baby.'

Everyone told her she was very lucky to have been in labour only eight hours. 'With a first baby,' they always added, giving the impression that it would get easier with each successive child. But to Eunice the night seemed endless and at the height of her pain she vowed she would never, ever go through this again. This baby would be an only child, as she had been. The doctor, who had been summoned as a precaution as well as the midwife – Edith was taking no chances – gave her a little anaesthetic to help with the pain.

It was at six o'clock in the morning of the ninth of July that she was told, 'Push! Push as hard as you can – now!' She felt as though she was being ripped apart, but the sensation lasted only a few seconds, and then she knew that at last it was all over; she had had her baby. A child's cry, louder than she would have thought possible, echoed around the room.

'Well done, Eunice,' cried the midwife. 'And what a clever girl. You've managed that without needing any stitches. It's a wonder, though, it is that, 'cause he's a whopper!'

'He . . .?' said Eunice dazedly.

'Yes, you've got a baby boy,' said the doctor.

'And grand little chap he is an' all,' said the midwife. 'I'll just wipe some of this mess off him, then you can hold him.'

The doctor dealt swiftly with the afterbirth, and a few moments later Eunice was looking down at the baby that Mrs Wilshaw had placed in her arms. He was wrapped in a white blanket, one that had been knitted by her mother-in-law, Mabel.

A boy, thought Eunice. She did not feel at all disappointed that it was not the girl she had secretly hoped for. It sounded as if he was healthy if his lungs were anything to go by, and she could see he was not a tiny baby, not by any means. She gazed down at him, then she gave a gasp of astonishment. There could be no doubt at all whose child this was. It was uncanny. Although he was so small, the mouth, the nose and the chin were identical to his father's, and if that were not enough the bright ginger hair was the deciding factor. This was Ronnie's child. She felt the relief spreading all through her. If the child had been born with flaxen hair people might have wondered why, although a baby's hair was often fair at birth. Dark hair, on the other hand, would have been regarded as a legacy of his mother. But this ginger crop; there seemed to be masses of the bright auburn hair, clinging in tight curls to his scalp. He was the very image of Ronnie.

Eunice burst into tears; tears of happiness and of blessed relief. She had carried this burden for nine months – a burden of what might well have been deceit and shame – and now, in just a few seconds, all her worries had disappeared. It was all right. This was Ronnie's child. She would not need to deceive him after all. She could face the future with her husband knowing that they were a real family now with a lovely little son.

Mrs Wilshaw looked at her and smiled. 'That's right, love. You have a good cry if you want to; you deserve it. They're happy tears, though, aren't they? I can tell.'

Eunice nodded as she smiled at the midwife through a mist of tears.

The cries of the child had brought Edith and Samuel to the bedroom. 'Hello, there . . .' Eunice could hear Edith knocking at the door. Fancy her mother having the courtesy to knock – in her own house – and not barge straight in. 'Can we come in?'

'Of course you can,' said the doctor, motioning to the midwife to move some stained cloths out of sight. 'Congratulations, Mr and Mrs Morton. You have a fine grandson.' He shook hands with Edith, then with Samuel, who was following close behind his wife. 'I'll go now and leave Eunice in Mrs Wilshaw's capable hands. Goodbye, Eunice. Well done! I'll come and see you in a day or two.'

'Goodbye, doctor,' said Eunice, 'and . . . thank you.'

'Yes, indeed. Thank you very much, Dr Everett,' said Edith. 'Everything's all right, is it? No . . . complications?'

'I should say not,' replied the doctor. 'Quite an easy birth, although I don't suppose Eunice would agree with me. And he's a grand little lad, all eight pounds of him.'

'Eight pounds! Well, I never!' said Edith in an awesome voice. 'That's a good weight, isn't it?'

'Come and look at him, Mum,' said Eunice, 'and you too . . . Dad.'

Eunice kissed her daughter's cheek and gave her a brief hug before looking down at the baby. 'Well I never!' she exclaimed for the second time. 'Come and have a look at him, Samuel. I would never have believed it. It's like looking at Ronald all over again. He's the spitting image of him.'

'Well, bless me,' said Samuel, bending down to peer at the baby. 'So he is; and what a fine little chap he is, to be sure.'

'What did you expect?' asked Eunice. 'He's sure to be like his father, isn't he? And if he turns out to be as good as his daddy, then that will be . . . wonderful.' She could feel tears springing to her eyes again. What a lucky girl she was!

'He will be like both of you. He's sure to be,' said her mother. 'I expect he'll have your nice blue eyes; they run in our family. It's just that he looks more like Ronald at the moment, but he might change as he gets older.'

'No, he doesn't look much like me, does he?' said Eunice, 'and his eyes aren't blue. They're a sort of muddy grey.'

'All babies' eyes are that colour at first,' said Edith. 'Aren't they, Mrs Wilshaw?' The midwife, busy in a corner of the room, nodded her agreement. 'But they change after a while. They can't focus properly at first, you see. Can they, Mrs Wilshaw?'

That lady nodded again, rather impatiently, Eunice thought. She probably wanted the grandparents out of the way so that she could get on with things. Eunice looked down again at the baby wonderingly. He was staring up at her, unfocusedly, as her mother had said, then he closed his eyes, giving a tiny little sigh.

'We'd best be going,' said Edith, becoming aware that the midwife was looking at them pointedly. 'We'll let Mrs

Wilshaw get on with her job. I expect you're both ready for a cup of tea, aren't you? And how about some toast and a slice of bacon? As it's a special occasion, like.' Eunice and the midwife both agreed that that would be very acceptable.

'Righty-oh then, I'll go and see to it. I'll have to be getting their ladyships' breakfasts an' all before long. Come along, Samuel. You can see him again later.' Eunice's father was still staring, as if mesmerised, at the baby.

'I do believe he's got a look of our Eunice an' all,' he said, smiling diffidently at her as he followed his wife out of the room.

'Thank you, Dad,' said Eunice, smiling back at him. She put out a finger and gently stroked the little hand that lay stretched out like a tiny starfish on the blanket. She placed her finger beneath it and she felt the minute fingers curl around her own, grasping tightly. She smiled to herself. How strange it all felt but how wonderful too. He was a little stranger at the moment, but she would get to know him, as he would get to know her. She had not seen such a tiny newborn baby before and it seemed unreal to be holding one now. It was a miracle, she mused, that he should arrive so perfectly formed. Each little pink nail on his hands, and on his feet too – she lifted the blanket carefully to look at them now – was like a miniature pink seashell, no more than a fraction of an inch in length. His feet looked big, though, for the size of his body. Another resemblance to his father. She gave a slight giggle and Mrs Wilshaw came over to her.

'Yes, he's got legs an' all, bless him,' she chuckled. 'Making sure he's all there, are you, luv? Cover him up now and I'll put him down for a while.' The cot, which had belonged to Eunice as a baby, was already prepared at the side of the room. 'Your mam'll be back soon with our breakfast, and I'm ready for it, I can tell you. And after that we'd best see about you starting to feed him . . . Don't worry, lass,' she said, as Eunice began to feel – and look – rather apprehensive. 'I'll show you what to do. It'll come as natural as falling off a cliff. And here's your mam with our breakfast. Now, that's a sight for sore eyes; I could murder a cup of tea. Thanks ever so much, Mrs Morton.'

Edith beamed. 'Don't mention it; it's the least I can do.' She tiptoed over to the cot in an exaggerated manner. 'Let's just have another peep at him . . . Ah, bless him! Dead to the world, he is.' She leaned closer, gently stroking his cheek. 'What a lovely lad you are, aren't you? The image of your daddy.'

'Don't wake him up, Mum,' said Eunice feeling a surge of protectiveness towards her newborn child.

'All right, dear. I won't, but it's a pity if I can't take a look at my own grandson.' Edith reluctantly straightened up and made for the door. 'Let me know if there's anything else you want.'

'Thanks, Mum,' said Eunice, suddenly finding herself unable to suppress a yawn.

'You're sure to be tired, love,' said Edith kindly, 'after what you've been through, isn't she, Mrs Wilshaw? Now, eat your breakfast, there's a good girl. There's some nice crispy bacon, just the way you like it. I'll come and see you later. I'd have a sleep if I were you, when you've had something to eat.'

She was obviously thrilled to bits with her grandson. All the previous shame and dismay at her daughter's pregnancy had disappeared. Edith, in fact, seemed to think that she, Eunice, had done something wonderful, not given birth to a baby that had been the result of a moment of illicit passion.

'Now, first things first,' said Mrs Wilshaw. 'My! That looks good.' Between them they made short work of the bacon, toast spread with real butter, and the hot strong tea. By the time they had finished the baby was making little mewling sounds and they could see his tiny arms flailing in the air.

'Hello, he's awake,' said the midwife, 'and if I'm not mistaken he'll be ready for a bit of nourishment an' all.' Eunice was looking forward to a nice sleep; she could feel her eyelids beginning to droop already. But she knew the baby's needs had to come first – her own little son.

'Come along now, Eunice. Let's get you started on this feeding business.' Mrs Wilshaw marched briskly over to the cot, picked up the baby, still wrapped in his shawl, and deposited him in Eunice's arms. 'There we are, Mummy. Isn't he a lovely boy? Yes, I know you're tired, dear,' she added, noticing the look of weariness on her patient's face. 'You can have a nice long sleep afterwards, but this little lad wants seeing to first. And I'll need to get home and have a bit of shut-eye an' all. Come on now; undo your nightie, there's a good girl. What's up? You're not shy, are you?'

Eunice shook her head, although she wasn't quite sure how she was feeling. She hadn't given much thought to the idea of breast-feeding. Maybe she had imagined that the baby would have a bottle? 'Can't he have a bottle instead?' she asked tentatively.

'A bottle? Indeed he can't!' Mrs Wilshaw sounded most indignant. 'This is nature's way, and you're sure to have loads of milk, a big girl like you.' Yes, I know I've got a big bust, thought Eunice – she had been quite proud of the fact at one time – but there was no need to draw attention to it.

'Come along, dear,' the midwife went on, more gently. 'I know it seems strange, but you'll get used to it. I'll help you.' She pushed the baby's mouth towards Eunice's right breast and the child, instinctively, began to suck.

Eunice gave a start at the strange sensation. It was not exactly a pain, but a very odd feeling that was surging right through her, even down into the place which she guessed was her womb.

'He won't get very much at first,' said Mrs Wilshaw, 'but he has to suck hard to get the milk flowing, see? It'll get easier in time.'

Eunice didn't answer. She just sat there passively whilst the child sucked away at her breast. It was amazing how strong his little lips were and how he knew, automatically, what he had to do. But so did all newborn creatures, she supposed; kittens, puppies, calves, lambs – she was suddenly reminded of her days on the farm – they all fed from their mothers' breasts. Mrs Wilshaw was right: it was nature's way, and although it seemed strange, she would get used to it. Gently she stroked the baby's head, feeling the strong pulse beneath the fontanelle. Her own little baby; hers and Ronnie's.

'That's enough now,' said Mrs Wilshaw after about two or three minutes. 'Let's try him at the other side.' Eunice obediently moved the baby over to her other breast, and it all began again; that strange feeling racing through her body like an electric shock. 'There, I said it would get easier, didn't I? You're doing very well, Eunice. It looks as though he's going to be a greedy little lad, but you'll have no trouble feeding him. Some poor lasses find their milk dries up after a few weeks, but I can't see that happening to you.

'That'll do now,' said the midwife after a few moments. 'You're nearly falling asleep, aren't you, love? And I think his lordship's had enough for now.' She took the baby, whose eyes, like his mother's, were closing, and put him back in his cot. Eunice buttoned up her nightdress. 'What are you going to call him, Eunice? We can't keep on calling him baby, can we? Have you got a name for him?'

'No, not yet,' replied Eunice. It was something she and Ronnie had not discussed very much. If she was truthful, she'd avoided the subject because she couldn't face talking to Ronnie about the name of a baby that may well not be his.

'I'll wait and see what Ronnie wants to call him . . . seeing that he looks so much like his father,' she added with a smile.

'That's what folk always say about a little boy,' said Mrs Wilshaw. ' "Oh, isn't he the image of his daddy?" they say. It's better than saying he looks like the milkman, isn't it?' She laughed heartily and Eunice smiled. Or like a certain German POW, she reminded herself, with a sudden stab of guilt.

'Yes, it certainly is,' she replied.

'It gets you a bit cross, though, doesn't it, when folks don't say he looks like you, especially after you've done all the hard work? Never mind; he'll happen change as he grows up. Our Len used to be the spitting image of my hubby, and now he favours me; same big nose and big mouth, poor lad.'

And a big heart too, thought Eunice, with a sudden unexpected surge of gratitude towards the well-built middle-aged woman who was looking after her. She might be brusque and a trifle outspoken, but underneath the stiff white apron and the equally stiff manner she was a very kind and warm-hearted person. And an excellent midwife too. Eunice knew that it was Mrs Wilshaw's skilful handling of things at the moment of birth that had prevented her from needing stitches, something she had been dreading. Dr Everett, although he had been called at Edith's insistence, had not really been needed.

'Thank you,' Eunice said now, reaching out and grabbing hold of the woman's hand. 'I'm ever so grateful to you, Mrs Wilshaw; I really am. You've been wonderful.'

'Now then; don't start getting all silly and sentimental. It's me job, isn't it, and I like to think I do a good one.' The midwife patted her hand. 'I know you're a bit tearful, like. It's a normal enough reaction and you're ready for sleep now. I dare say you need the lav an' all, don't you? Come on then, carefully now; put your feet on the floor and I'll help you along the passage. You're sure to feel a bit wonky . . .'

It was surprising how weak she did feel, and Eunice was glad when, at last, she could settle down in the comfort of her bed. Mrs Wilshaw had gone, saying that the baby would sleep for a few hours now, all being well. She was too tired even to think any more. She closed her eyes and in less than a minute she was fast asleep. The child, as predicted, did not stir during her lengthy sleep. When she awoke, feeling instantly alert, she could hear the sound of voices and footsteps coming up the stairs.

'I'll just see if she's awake . . . Eunice, Eunice love, you've got visitors.' Her mother, after knocking gently, poked her head round the door. 'Ah, there you are. I thought I could hear you stirring. Here are the other proud grandparents, see. Look Mabel; look, Tom, isn't he a grand little lad?' Her mother tiptoed over to the cot in the overdone manner she had before. 'Let's see if he's awake. Oh, so he is, the little love; he's just opening his eyes.' Eunice's father too, in her mother's wake, was silently gazing into the cot.

But Mabel and Tom, before looking at the baby, went across to Eunice, who had hastily sat up and was leaning back against the pillows. Mabel stooped and kissed her cheek. 'Well done, dear,' she said. 'What wonderful news!

Our first grandchild. How are you feeling?'

'Oh, not so bad, thanks,' said Eunice. 'Better now I've had a sleep.'

'Aye; well done, lass,' repeated Tom, pecking her cheek a little embarrassedly.

'Well, aren't you going to have a look at him then?' said Edith, a little impatiently.

'Of course we are,' said Mabel, 'but first things first. We mustn't forget the baby's mummy. Here you are, dear.' She reached into the shopping bag she was carrying and brought out a half-pound box of Cadbury's Milk Tray chocolates. A rarity, indeed, and so were the next items she produced: two large Jaffa oranges, as precious as diamonds in these days of stringent rationing. 'We've just had an allocation this morning, would you believe?'

'Oh . . . that's ever so kind of you,' said Eunice, feeling quite overwhelmed. 'I haven't had an orange for ages. And my favourite chocolates too. Thank you so much.'

'It's no more than you deserve, dear.' Mabel smiled warmly at her. 'Now, let's have a look at this here baby.'

Their reaction was one of utter delight. 'Just look at all that ginger hair! And the same nose and mouth. Well, would you believe it? He's the image of our Ronnie. And what a sturdy little lad. Eight pounds, did you say? My word, that's a good weight . . .'

They could have sung his praises for hours, had the baby not started crying; whimpering at first, then crying in earnest. They knew it was time for them to go and let his mother feed him. Mabel told Eunice that they had sent a telegram to Ronald and that, hopefully, he would be granted compassionate leave and would be home as soon as possible.

The thought cheered her as she struggled, again, to feed the now hungry baby. Her father had disappeared very quickly when her mother had picked up the baby and placed him into Eunice's arms, as had Mabel and Tom. Edith lingered for a little while, but she did not try to interfere as Eunice, rather self-consciously, settled the baby at her breast.

'He seems contented enough now,' Edith said, nodding wisely. 'You may find that breast-feeding is not all that pleasant, Eunice – at least, I never found it to be so – but it's the best for the baby, or so they say. It's cheaper, too. I had no choice, though, when you were a baby. My milk dried up after a few weeks and you had to go on a bottle. Anyroad, I'll leave you to it for a while. I'll bring you some dinner up when Mabel and Tom have gone.'

Eunice was surprised at her mother's comments. So this feeding business did not come naturally to all women? It may have been that Edith was not one who took readily to motherhood. She had certainly never been overdemonstrative or affectionate. She had always been there, however, when she was needed, Eunice reminded herself; just as she would be for this little baby in her arms. She smiled down contentedly; he was already not the unfamiliar stranger he had been at first. And when Ronnie came home, perhaps tomorrow, then they could start to be a real family. The thought thrilled her immensely.

The civil servants, when they arrived home from work, came to see the new baby and the 'proud mother', as they insisted on calling her. They too commented that he had his daddy's ginger hair, but did not go on too much about it as they did not know Ronnie very well. Phyllis, Eunice's favourite of the four remaining women, even remarked that he had a definite look of his mother as well, which pleased her no end. She, Eunice, was so pleased he looked like Ronnie, but she wanted to feel he resembled her a little as well, especially – as Mrs Wilshaw had remarked – when she had done all the hard work! And she was delighted with the gifts of scented soap for herself, and the hand-knitted bootees and mittens for the baby.

Everyone was being very kind. Their next-door neighbours, from both sides, popped in during the evening for a few moments. One of them brought a tiny knitted cardigan in pale blue, and a cute little matching hat with a bobble, very suitable for a boy. The other neighbour had made two pairs of mittens and two pairs of bootees in lemon and white. Eunice laughed when they had gone and remarked to her mother that she would be able to set up a shop with bootees and mittens, not to mention matinée jackets and cardigans.

'Don't turn your nose up at them, Eunice,' her mother rebuked her. 'It's very kind of people to bother . . .' She did not add 'under the circumstances', but Eunice felt, for a moment, a hint of the former disapproval. 'And it's surprising how many you will need. Babies have a habit of being sick when you put them into nice clean clothes, and you used to chew your mittens into holes. Of course, I never allowed you to have a dummy. Nasty unhygienic things, they are. The little lad will never have one if it's anything to do with me.'

Eunice managed to bite back the retort that no, it was nothing to do with her mother at all. Instead, she assured her that she was not being ungrateful for the gifts. People, indeed, were being very kind and generous.

'I'm glad you appreciate it,' said Edith, sounding somewhat appeased. 'And don't forget that your daddy and I have promised to buy you a pram. As soon as you get on your feet we'll go down to the Co-op and see what they've got. I had a lovely Silver Cross pram for you when you were a baby, a navy-blue one it was. Like a little princess you were, sitting up in it.' Edith smiled reminiscently, to

Eunice's amazement, but just as quickly reverted back to her usual matter-of-fact tone.

'Anyway, we'll have to see what they've got in stock. I know I could have ordered one, but I didn't like to tempt fate . . . Just watch baby's head, Eunice. Don't let him loll sideways like that. You must support his head all the time. A baby's neck isn't very strong. There we are; that's better.' Edith deftly adjusted the child's position so that his head was nestling against his mother's upper arm. She had just finished feeding him for what seemed the umpteenth time that day, although she knew it was only the third.

'OK, Mum, I'll remember,' said Eunice, suppressing a sigh. 'Now, if you don't mind I'm going to try and get to sleep. And he's nodding off, see. I'll put him down again.'

'What about changing his nappy? He's sure to be wet again.'

'No, he's not at the moment,' replied Eunice. 'Mrs Wilshaw helped me to change him earlier so he'll be OK for a while.'

'Very well then, if you say so.' Edith bristled a little. 'Shall I put him in his cot?'

'No, it's all right. I'll do it. Here, can you hold him while I get out of bed?'

'Now watch what you're doing. You're still not too steady on your feet, Eunice.'

'I'm fine, Mother . . .' She placed her baby son in the cot, covering him over with the white flannelette sheet and the fleecy blue blanket with the appliquéd motifs of white bunny rabbits that Mabel had brought round earlier that evening. Eunice guessed she had been waiting to find out the sex of the child before buying the gift.

'Good night . . . baby,' she whispered. 'Sleep tight.'

'It's time he had a name,' said her mother. 'If I had had a

boy I would have called him John. That's a lovely name; so strong and purposeful.'

'It's up to me and Ronnie,' said Eunice. 'I like Timothy myself.'

'Timothy!' Her mother grimaced. 'Oh no, I don't like that at all. That's a silly-sounding name. But of course it's up to you and Ronald, as you say. Now, get back into bed and I'll put the light out for you.'

'No . . . thanks, Mum. I'm just going to the bathroom. I'll see to myself; I'm finding my feet again.'

'All right then, if you're sure . . .' Edith hesitated a moment, then leaned forward and kissed her daughter's cheek. 'Good night, love. Let me know if you want anything in the night. Don't be afraid to wake me up . . . We're very pleased, you know, your daddy and I,' she added before disappearing quickly through the door.

Her parents had been most generous, and kind too, Eunice thought as she settled herself for sleep. Her mother couldn't help her overbearing manner; it was unlikely she would ever change now. They had bought her two dozen terry-towelling nappies, by purchasing a couple in every draper's shop in town – they were in short supply as was everything else – and her mother had made several more from her boarding house stock of fluffy white towelling. Flannelette nightdresses, too, for the baby – that was what he would wear for the first few weeks, she had been told – and cot sheets and baby blankets.

Eunice's mind was full to overflowing with the events of the day. Yesterday she had been on her own. Now there was another little person in the cot beside her, one who depended upon her completely. She hoped so much that she would be able to cope with the responsibility; that she would never let him down.

Chapter 14

Eunice woke, she could not tell how long afterwards, to the sound of snuffling and a soft mewling. She was surprised at how instantly alert she felt; one moment she had been fast asleep, now she was wide awake. She switched on the bedside light and looked at the clock. One o'clock; goodness, was that all it was? The middle of the night and already the baby wanted feeding, and changing too, no doubt. The midwife had said he would need a feed every four hours at first, and the baby book Eunice had been given to read said the same. His last feed had been at nine o'clock and it was now four hours later. It was almost as though he could tell the time. She sighed as she put her feet out of the bed and on to the sheepskin rug at the side. He was yelling in earnest now and she didn't want her mother to wake up and come in making a fuss. This was a job she had to tackle on her own.

'Come on, baby,' she whispered, leaning over the cot and picking up the now screaming infant. She laid him across her shoulder as she had seen the midwife do – already it was instinctive to do so – then she felt the dampness of his nightgown against her hand. No wonder he was yelling; the poor child was sodden. Even though he was wearing a large nappy and a pair of rubberised pants, the urine had managed to seep through everything. She put her hand into the cot and felt at the sheet. Damn it! That was damp as well. The whole lot would need changing; his cot sheet and nightie as well as the nappy, and she had better see to his clothing before she fed him or she would be soaked as well.

She laid him on the bed, whereupon, leaving the security of her arms, he began to scream even louder. 'Hush! Hush!' she admonished him. 'You'll have the whole house awake. Oh . . . do shut up, baby!' Frantically she opened the drawer where the baby requisites were stored, pulling out a nappy, vest, nightdress and cot sheet, at the same time keeping an eye on him lest he rolled off the bed.

Oh dear! There was a damp patch on her counterpane now, where he had been lying; she should have remembered to put a towel down. Never mind; that would soon dry. She peeled off his soaking garments – his nightie and the tiny vest – then undid the giant-sized safety pins securing his nappy. Pooh! She wrinkled her nose in distaste. No wonder he was crying. The nappy was soiled too, with an excrement that was greenish in colour. She reached for the box of tissues which, fortunately, was to hand on the dressing-table top, wiping his little bottom and, at the same time, dragging the soiled nappy from under him.

'Oh damn! Oh, damn and blast!' she said, not bothering to whisper now. There was a smear of mess on the counterpane now, and still the child would not stop crying. Eunice found that she was starting to cry, too. What a mess she was making of everything. She so badly wanted to help the poor little baby, but all she was doing was making things worse.

Right on cue, there was a tap at the door and her mother entered the room. 'Oh dear! Having a bit of trouble, are we?' she asked. 'Well, it's only to be expected at first. Don't worry, love; I'll give you a hand with him.'

Eunice knew that never in her life had she been more pleased to see her mother, and it came automatically at that moment to tell her so. 'Oh, Mum, thank goodness you're here. Just hold him a minute, will you, while I clear this lot away. I wouldn't have believed a tiny baby could make such a mess . . . or such a noise.'

'Well, there you are,' said Edith. 'You live and learn. No, I'll see to the mess. You put a clean nappy on him, there's a good girl, and then get him fed, for goodness' sake, before he brings the house down.'

Eunice was very grateful to her mother, but she could tell that, secretly, she was enjoying the situation. Edith, with an enigmatic little smile on her face, gathered up the damp clothes and deposited them in a nappy bucket, then quickly replaced the wet cot sheet with a dry one. 'I did tell you, didn't I, that you should have changed him last night, before you put him down? But you thought you knew best. Well, never mind; like I say, you live and learn. Now, how are you managing with that nappy? Yes, you've made quite a good job of that. Here; wrap this blanket round him while you feed him, then he won't get cold. You can put his little vest and nightie on him later. There, there now . . .' She stroked the baby's cheek. 'Is your naughty mummy taking a long time? You're hungry, aren't you? Yes, you are . . . Here, give him to me, Eunice, while you get into bed.'

'Thank you, Mother,' said Eunice. 'You've been . . . a great help.' But she hoped that Edith would depart now and let her feed the baby in peace.

'That's all right, dear.' Her mother smiled knowingly. 'A little help is worth a lot of pity, and I knew you'd need some help, just at first. Now, I don't know about you, but

I'm dying for a cup of tea. I'll pop down and make us one, shall I? How about you?'

'Yes, thank you. That would be very welcome.' Anything to get her mother out of the room so that she could get on with the feeding on her own. Her breasts were feeling tight and her milk had already seeped on to the piece of towelling that the midwife had advised her to wrap around herself. The baby had stopped crying now as though he knew his nourishment was on its way. He fastened his hungry little mouth tightly around her nipple the second she put him to her breast.

Eunice lay back against the pillows holding the baby closely to her. He was happy now, safe and warm against her breast. Suddenly, she felt a surge of love for him, more than she had felt before. She found herself saying a silent prayer of thanks and a prayer too, that she would be a good mother to him. Her mother was back in a few moments with the cups of tea.

'I'll stay here while I drink this, if you don't mind, Eunice,' she said. 'I don't want to disturb your daddy.' She sat down in the Lloyd Loom chair at the side of the bed, staring intently at her daughter and the child at her breast. 'Don't mind me, love. There's no need to be embarrassed; I'm your mum, aren't I? Just get on with feeding him, there's a good girl.'

'All right,' said Eunice, sighing a little. 'But . . . I'd rather you didn't watch me. OK, maybe I shouldn't feel embarrassed, but actually I do. I'll have to change him to the other side now.' She looked appealingly at her mother who, behaving tactfully for once, smiled and looked away. Eunice quickly transferred the baby to the other breast, and instantly he was guzzling away with a very audible sucking noise.

Edith was still smiling. 'I'm sorry if I seemed to be

staring, Eunice love,' she said. 'I didn't mean to, but it was seeing you there with your baby, my own little grandson.' Eunice realised, to her astonishment, that her mother's eyes were damp with emotion. 'He's going to be a real blessing, that little boy; I know he is. I was cross with you at first, of course, when you told me. I thought you'd been a very silly girl . . . but that's all behind us now. It's all turned out very well, and this little lad is going to bring a lot of joy to us all. And you know I always liked Ronald. He'll make you a very good husband, Eunice.'

'Yes, I know that, Mum,' said Eunice quietly. 'It still feels . . . not quite real, though, having a baby of my own.' She looked down at the child, suckling contently in the comfort of her arms. 'I can't really believe it's happened.'

'That's the result, though, isn't it, when you let your feelings get out of control. Before you know it, there's a baby on the way.' Edith could not resist a curt little nod of disapproval. 'Anyway, enough said about that. He's not an unwanted child like some poor little mites are. Now . . . shall I leave you to it, Eunice? Can you manage?' Her mother stood up, then, a little tentatively, reached out and stroked her daughter's hair.

'Yes, I'll be OK now, Mum. Thanks for helping me.'

'That's all right. He should sleep till about six o'clock after this, so you'll be able to get some rest. Listen, love, you might not enjoy this breast-feeding very much. It doesn't always come naturally, like they say it does. But that doesn't mean that you love the baby any the less.'

'No, of course not,' said Eunice. 'I admit it feels strange, but I'm going to persevere. I must . . . for the baby's sake.'

'It will perhaps get easier in a day or two. Anyway, I'll get back to bed now. Good night, love; God bless.' She stooped down and kissed her daughter's cheek, then the top of the baby's head. 'Good night, baby . . . You'll have to give him a name soon, Eunice.'

The baby's eyes were closing now and his lips were relaxing their tight hold. She eased him away, feeling the soreness and tenderness of her nipples. She was surprised that her mother had said what she did about breast-feeding. At the moment she was certainly finding it an unusual experience. She pulled her nightdress up to cover her breasts, then looked down at the tiny head peeping out from the blanket, bright ginger curls against the blue. Ronnie's baby . . .

Ronnie . . . Her thoughts turned to her husband, who would be home tomorrow. No: today. It was already the early hours of the morning and he would soon be with her and his new baby son. How thrilled he would be. She must try to be a good wife to him and a good mother to their baby.

She could scarcely believe that things had turned out so well for her; it was really much more than she deserved, considering what might have been . . . Just when she had been so badly in need of comfort and guidance Ronnie had come along, showing her how much he loved her and giving her hope for the future. Now the future had become the present, hers and Ronnie's . . . and that of their baby son. If she had never done so before, Eunice now began to count her blessings.

Ronnie's delight in his baby son was transparent and Eunice felt her heart surge with love as she watched him.

'Oh, isn't he wonderful? I can't believe it! My ginger hair an' all,' Ronnie exclaimed, the moment he leaned over the cot and set eyes on the baby. 'And what a clever girl you are, darling.' He left the cot side for a moment to give his wife another hug and kiss. 'Thank you ever so much. Our own baby son . . .' He returned to the cot, gazing down longingly. 'Can I . . . do you think I could pick him up?'

'I don't see why not,' laughed Eunice. 'I don't want him to wake up, though, not just yet. I fed him not long ago and he usually sleeps for an hour or two after a feed. Go on, though. It's OK . . . Hold him firmly; he won't break; he's a sturdy little lad,' she added as her husband gingerly picked up the little bundle in the blue blanket, holding him as though he were made of spun glass.

Eunice, to her annoyance, was still in bed. She had argued with Mrs Wilshaw that she felt fine and she wanted to be up and about to greet her husband when he arrived. But the midwife ruled that she had to keep her feet up for a few days, 'to let things settle down'. As a great concession she could sit in the chair, if she wished, for an hour or so in the afternoon, but apart from that, bed rest was essential for new nursing mothers. So when Ronnie had arrived in the early evening after a long journey from the south of England she was sitting up in bed, still in her nightdress and fluffy bedjacket.

Ronnie sat down on the basket chair holding the baby a little awkwardly in the crook of his arm. 'Support his head, Ronnie,' she told him. 'Move your arm up a bit . . . that's better . . . or else his head lolls to one side. That's one of the things my mother told me. She's full of titbits of advice, you might know. Although I was surprised she knew so much about babies.'

'Well, she's had one herself, hasn't she?'

'Only one, though.'

'She's not being too domineering, is she?' asked Ronnie, lowering his voice.

'No more than usual,' replied Eunice, grinning. 'No, actually she's been a great help to me. She can't help being bossy, but I don't know what I'd have done without her; or your mum. All our parents have been great, in spite of . . .'

'In spite of us jumping the gun, you mean?' Ronnie laughed. 'Well, I'm glad we did, or we wouldn't have had this lovely little lad, would we?'

'I still can't quite get used to him being here,' Eunice said, smiling.

'Well, he's here all right,' said Ronnie. 'There's no doubt about that, all eight pounds of him. I don't know anything about it, but my mother says that's a very good weight for a baby.'

Eunice grimaced. 'I should say so! You didn't have to give birth to him!'

'Oh . . . darling!' Ronnie looked at her anxiously. 'I don't like to think of you suffering like that. Oh dear! Was it very bad?'

'No, I suppose not,' she replied. 'I thought it was at the time, but the midwife said you soon forget labour pains, and it's true; so you do. There's so much to think about afterwards – like being woken up in the middle of the night to feed him.'

'Oh dear!' said Ronnie again. 'Never mind; I'm home for a few days so I'll be able to give you a hand with him.'

'Not with feeding him, you won't.'

'Oh, no . . . I suppose not. I can hold him though, to stop him crying. And you can show me how to change his nappy . . . I say, have you realised? We keep saying "him" or "the baby". What are you going to call him?'

'You mean what are *we* going to call him,' said Eunice. 'I can't decide without you, Ronnie.'

'No, but I thought you might have some ideas.'

'Well, I haven't; not really. I like Timothy, but my mother thought it was a silly name.'

'It's nothing to do with your mother . . . I quite like it too, as a matter of fact. But I was wondering . . . You might not like the idea, though . . .'

'What idea? I can't say whether I like it or not if you don't tell me.'

'Well, you say our parents have been very good to us, and I agree that they have, so I wondered if we could call him Samuel . . . or Thomas . . . or both, after our fathers?'

'Mmm . . .' mused Eunice. 'Thomas Samuel . . . Samuel Thomas . . . Yes, I think it sounds better that way round; Samuel Thomas. We could call him Sam or Sammy; what do you think? Samuel doesn't sound quite right, somehow, for a baby or a little boy.' She was imagining a miniature version of her father. 'Yes, that's a good idea, Ronnie. And our parents will be pleased, you can be sure.'

'That's settled then,' Ronnie grinned broadly. 'I like the idea of a little boy called Sammy.'

'It's a good job we didn't have a girl!' said Eunice, laughing.

'Why?'

'Well, can you imagine a baby called Edith Mabel? Or Mabel Edith?'

'Yes, I see what you mean. A bit old fashioned, eh? Still, what's in a name? As they say. They're the names their parents gave them when they were born, Mabel and Edith, but I suppose fashions change in names as in everything else.'

'Yes. I never knew where my name came from,' said Eunice thoughtfully. 'I don't like it particularly, but I suppose my mother must have done. They only gave me one name, worse luck, so I can't call myself anything else. My mother says it's ostentatious to have two names; it's all right for the "upper crust", but not for ordinary folk like us.'

Ronnie laughed. 'Honestly, your mother! She's the limit sometimes. What would you like to have been called, then?'

'Oh, I don't know. I've never really thought about it. I'm

stuck with Eunice, aren't I?' But she did know. She had always wanted to be called Francesca. Such a pretty, romantic name, she thought. When she was a little girl she had read a story in one of her fairytale books about a girl called Francesca and the name had stayed in her memory. She had come across it again several years later in one of the romances she had read and she had made up her mind there and then that if ever she had a little girl, Francesca would be her name. She had already forgotten that at the height of her labour pains she had vowed she would never have another child.

At the moment, however, little Samuel Thomas – Sammy – now stirring slightly in his father's arms, was quite enough to cope with.

Chapter 15

'Oh . . . he's absolutely gorgeous!' cooed Gwen, leaning over the pram and gently stroking the baby's cheek. 'You must be thrilled to bits with him, aren't you, Eunice? And I bet Ronnie was tickled pink with his little son. He's the spitting image of his daddy . . . aren't you, Sammy? I would never have believed a baby could look so much like one of his parents. I always thought all babies looked alike.'

Eunice listened quietly to her friend's eulogy of praise about her baby, thinking again what a blessing it *was* that Ronnie's son looked so much like him.

Ronnie had returned to his camp now, but had been a marvellous help when he was home. Not that he had been able to help with the feeding, of course, but he had become quite adept at changing nappies and bringing up the baby's wind. Ten days had passed since the birth of little Samuel Thomas and Eunice was now on her feet again, pottering around the house, but under strict instructions from the midwife not to overdo things. There was little likelihood of that, because her mother, for once in her life, was waiting on both Eunice and the baby hand and foot. This was surprising, as in the past Edith had always been impatient with illness and had deplored staying in bed any longer than was absolutely necessary. It was her opinion that you died in bed and that you had to get up and pull yourself together. She was, of course, over the moon about her little grandson; hence the softening in her attitude towards her daughter. Eunice wondered how long it would last. She was beginning to feel rather like a patient in a nursing home, although she was not ill. She longed, at times, to have a place of her own, at the same time wondering how she would manage without the bolstering support of her mother.

It was good to see Gwen again. She had been bitterly disappointed not to attend Gwen and Bill's wedding, but her friend had brought some snapshots to show her, taken by one of Bill's airforce mates as they stood on the steps of the register office. Gwen looked radiant, and very smart too, in her neat little costume and tiny tip-tilted hat perched to one side of her blonde curls. Bill was grinning like the Cheshire cat, and Eunice knew that this was a match 'made in heaven' as one might say. Bill was back on his flying ops now, whilst Gwen was living in digs in Ipswich and working at a local munitions factory. She was on a flying visit to Blackpool, not only to see her friend, but to attend to some business matters. She had decided, after all, not to sell her mother's house, but to let it for the duration of the war. There was a family from Liverpool living there now, who had moved to the seaside to escape the bombing, and Gwen was making sure that all was running smoothly.

She looked curiously at her friend now. 'You're very quiet, Eunice. Are you still not feeling very well? I know it must be quite an ordeal, having a baby. I still have that torture to come.' She laughed, as though she didn't really mind very much.

'You're not . . .? You don't mean you're expecting a baby already?' asked Eunice.

'No, no, I'm not. We thought we'd wait until this lot's over and we're settled in our own home. It's something to look forward to. You never know, of course. There's many a slip . . . but we don't intend to start a family just yet. It was you I was asking about, though. I hope you don't mind me saying this, Eunice, but you seem – how can I put it? – a bit . . . deflated, somehow.'

Eunice sighed. 'Yes, I suppose I am. Ronnie's gone back, and I'm missing him.'

'Well, you're sure to be, aren't you?'

'And my mother won't stop fussing over me and the baby. Especially Sammy. Sometimes I feel as though he doesn't really belong to me.'

'It's because she's so thrilled with him,' replied Gwen. 'It stands out a mile; there's such a change in your mother I can scarcely believe it. It's obvious she loves him to bits.'

'Hmm . . . But I can't remember her lavishing so much affection on me when I was a kid.'

'Of course she did. She must have done, when you were a baby. You can't remember so far back, nobody can.'

'I mean when I was a little girl. She always seemed so harsh and critical. I'm not saying she didn't love me – I'm sure she did – but she wasn't very good at showing it. It was my gran who used to cuddle me and make a fuss of me and then my mother would say she was spoiling me.'

'Well, there you are then. That's what your mother's doing now: making a fuss of her grandchild. Perhaps grandmothers realise what they might have missed with their own children and are glad of a second chance, do you think?'

'Perhaps so,' replied Eunice. 'She's certainly a good help to me. You may think Sammy's good and placid now, but he screams blue murder in the middle of the night until he gets his feed.'

'And your mother wakes up, does she, and comes to help you?'

'Yes . . . sometimes. She changes his nappy and helps me to settle him down again.'

'Then I think you should be very thankful,' said Gwen, nodding her head assertively. 'Not all grandmothers would do that. Some of them just like to hand the baby back when it starts crying. I think that this could be the start of something good between you and your mother. I know you've had your differences in the past, but maybe that's all behind you now.'

'Yes . . . I hope so,' replied Eunice.

'And she's obviously forgiven you for – you know – having to get married in a hurry.'

'Yes, so she has . . .'

'Well, I think you've got a lovely baby and you've very lucky,' said Gwen. 'You must have been very relieved when he was so obviously Ronnie's.' She lowered her voice, although there were only the two of them and the baby in the house, Samuel being at work and Edith out shopping. 'I remember you telling me the night before you got married that you were scared that the baby might be – what was he called? Heinrich's? I've not said a word to anyone and I never will, but there was no need for you to worry at all, was there? It was Ronnie's baby all the time.'

Eunice smiled a little wistfully at her friend and then in the direction of the pram and the sleeping baby. 'Yes, you're right. I'm very fortunate. But it's all so strange and new, Gwen. Sometimes I can't quite believe it; that I've got a baby son, and that things have turned out so well for me. I know I shouldn't feel low, but it's because Ronnie's gone back, that's all.'

Gwen smiled reassuringly. 'And there's such a thing as post-natal depression, or so I've heard; I don't know very much about these things. Apparently it takes a while for your hormones to settle down when you've had a baby.'

'OK, we'll blame it on the hormones then, shall we?' Eunice grinned. 'But I am missing Ronnie.'

'Well, that's only to be expected. Like I'm missing Bill. It's all meetings and partings in wartime, isn't it? Oh God, Eunice! I wish it was all over.'

'Don't we all,' said Eunice feelingly.

There was a sound of snuffling and mewling coming from the pram. 'Oh dear; I do believe he's waking up and it's not time for his next feed yet.'

'Oh, good.' Gwen jumped to her feet. 'I'm dying to see him with his eyes open.' She leaned over the pram again. 'Yes, you've got your daddy's eyes too, haven't you, Sammy? Ronnie's got grey eyes, hasn't he, Eunice?'

'Yes, but all babies' eyes are that colour at first,' said Eunice, trying to sound knowledgeable, 'a sort of bluey grey. They may well change as he gets older. They might turn out to be bright blue, like mine.

'Listen, Gwen; I don't want him to start crying, and he may well do if I leave him lying there. It's not time for his feed, so what do you think about taking him for a walk? We could go down to the prom. It's a lovely afternoon and the fresh air will do him good; me as well.'

'Yes; a good idea, if you're sure you feel up to it.'

'Good heavens, I'm not an invalid. I've only had a baby. I'd better put Sammy's bonnet on, though, and his mittens.'

'Sounds like a good idea to me,' said Gwen. 'The Blackpool breeze can be chilly.' She watched interestedly as her friend very gently and lovingly tied the tiny blue pixie bonnet under the baby's chin, then placed the minutest woollen mittens on his little starfish hands.

They walked along Pleasant Street, past the boarding houses which, in peacetime, would be bursting at the seams with holidaymakers. Now they were filled with RAF recruits, one batch following on another as they did their basic training and then were sent on to other parts of the country for flying duties, or as ground crew. Gwen had first met her husband, Bill, when he was an AC1 training in Blackpool. The July afternoon was warm and sunny, but with a creeping little breeze nearly always present in the seaside resort, fluttering the cotton skirts and the headscarves of the girls walking on the promenade. One might be tempted to think there was not a war on there in Blackpool, so determined was the resort to keep a smile on its face and to go on entertaining the visitors who still flocked to the town. Not in such large numbers as before, to be sure, but weary workers from the factories, mills and mines of the Lancashire inland towns still sought respite from the war and renewal of their spirits in the bright and breezy town they had always loved. One local woman, indeed, had written an angry letter to the local *Gazette*, saying that Blackpool's atmosphere was just like one big party and people seemed to have forgotten there was a war on and men and women were dying out there.

This was not strictly true. The crowds might forget their troubles, temporarily, in the great ballrooms of the Tower and Winter Gardens, but the battle was still raging, its heartbreak being felt in some measure by every town and street in the land, despite the assumed gaiety and bravado. How could one forget, even in Blackpool? Amidst the holidaymakers RAF recruits were to be seen, strolling around the town when off duty. Otherwise, they marched through the streets, their loud-voiced sergeant at their side, or drilled and took part in bayonet practice on the miles of golden sand.

Now, however, it seemed as though that fear had passed. People were even daring to talk of ultimate victory, although it might be a long way ahead. There was good news in the air and at sea. On 17 May nineteen Lancaster bombers, with their 'bouncing bombs', had breached the two largest dams in the great manufacturing district of the Ruhr, and in the Battle of the Atlantic forty U-boats had been destroyed. And there was now talk of a 'second front'; a cross-channel assault on Europe by the Allied Expeditionary Force.

Baby Samuel gurgled and murmured softly, lulled by the swaying motion of the pram. 'I'm so glad you came to see me today,' Eunice told her friend. 'You've done me a world of good; you can't imagine how much I miss our chats.'

They had almost reached the North Pier, where crowds of holidaymakers could be seen walking along the wooden boards. Another woman had written to the local paper complaining about the 'disgusting behaviour' taking place on the sands below the piers, and sometimes in broad daylight too! It was agreed, philosophically, by the more broad-minded, that there was, admittedly, more activity under the piers than up on the boardwalk; but after all, 'There is a war on.'

But there was nothing of the sort going on that day. The tide was in, the white-capped waves lapping briskly against the supports of the pier and the sea wall.

'Me too. But hopefully it won't be for ever. Maybe me and Bill will move back here after the war,' said Gwen. 'D'you think we'd better turn round now and go back? It sounds as though that little lad is getting hungry – am I right? And I promised Mrs Taylor I'd be back in time for tea.' She was staying overnight with her former next-door neighbour before travelling back to Ipswich the following day.

'Yes, you're right; he's hungry,' said Eunice. The whimpering was getting louder and Sammy was now waving his arms around although he was not actually crying. 'We'd best be making tracks homewards. You can catch a bus at Talbot Square, can't you, Gwen, to take you to Layton? There's no need to come all the way back with me.'

'All right, if you're sure? I don't want you to have a funny turn on the way back. You know you've been told not to overdo things.'

'I'm as fit as a fiddle,' said Eunice. 'Stop fussing. It's been great to see you, Gwen. Do you think you'll be able to get over for Sammy's christening? I'm not sure when it will be, but I'll let you know as soon as I can.' She had already asked Gwen to be godmother to the baby. 'And Bill as well if he can manage it.'

'Sure thing,' said Gwen. 'I'll be there, no doubt about that, and Bill too . . . all being well. You know how it is. You can't take anything for granted these days. 'Bye, Eunice.' She kissed her friend's cheek. 'Take care of yourself, love, and look after this little one an' all. Bye-bye, Sammy.' She peeped into the pram again, tickling him under the chin. 'Be a good boy for your mummy . . . Oh look, there's a bus coming.' She sprinted the few yards from the corner of Talbot Square to the bus stop outside Jenkinson's café, waving vigorously as she boarded the bus.

Gwen thought about how much they'd both changed in the last month. Today they had laughed and joked together just as they had done in those long-ago days – at least they seemed long ago, although it was only a couple of years – when they had worked at Boots Lending Library. But things were very different now. They were both married women. Eunice was already a mother . . . Gwen wondered if Eunice felt for Ronnie what she herself felt for her beloved Bill, who was probably, even at this moment, preparing for another bombing raid over Germany. She said a quick prayer, as she did whenever the thought of him was uppermost in her mind, that he would return safely once again.

Eunice hurried home as quickly as she could after leaving Gwen. The baby was whimpering in earnest now and shuffling around as though he was uncomfortable. No doubt he was; his nappy would need changing yet again. He went through about a dozen a day and her mother's boiler was continually on the go. Edith insisted that the nappies must be whiter than white. Whatever would the neighbours think if they saw grubby nappies hanging on the line?

But Eunice was uncomfortable too, hence her hurry to get home. One thing she had not confided to Gwen was this whole messy business of breast-feeding; the reason, she suspected, that she felt so out of sorts. She would not admit to anyone that she did not enjoy the experience. It would make her sound so pathetic and inadequate and she knew she had to persevere for little Sammy's sake. She had always had a generous bust and guessed that that was the reason she had loads of milk; enough to feed triplets, she was sure. Her mother had informed her, however, that her size had little to do with it; that she, Edith, had always been slim, with no bust to speak of, yet she too had been awash with what seemed like gallons of milk. At least Eunice had her mother's sympathy over this: it was one matter about which they were in total agreement. Edith was the only person to whom she had confided her misgivings. Even Ronnie did not know.

She was continually damp and she felt that she was

smelly too. The odour of sour milk seemed to cling to her continually, although she knew she was probably much more aware of it than other people. In addition to a nursing brassiere, a great cumbersome thing, which she loathed, she wrapped round herself a thick wad of towelling; and even so the milk seeped through, leaving damp patches on her blouse.

Once at home she stripped off her uncomfortable clothing and the sodden nappy from the baby. She put a dressing gown around her shoulders and sat down on the bedroom chair with Sammy, now screaming loudly, in her arms. Instinctively his head turned towards her, nuzzling into her breast. The moment his lips found and closed round her nipple he gave such a sigh – of relief and satisfaction – that she was forced to smile. He guzzled and guzzled, making loud sucking noises and for several moments there was peace. She held him close to her, kissing the top of his downy head. She loved him so much.

Sammy had almost finished his feed when Edith knocked, then poked her head round the door. 'Have you been out, Eunice? Because you've left the pram in the hall, right behind the front door. I nearly fell over it when I came in. There's plenty of room in the dining room when you're not using it. I've told you that before.'

'Sorry, Mum,' said Eunice. 'Yes, Gwen and I went for a walk with Sammy, on the prom. He was screaming so loudly when I got back that I just abandoned everything and fled upstairs. I'll go and move the pram in a minute.'

'There's no need; I've already done it.' Edith gave a self-satisfied smile. 'And what about this little laddie? He's had his fill, has he?' Baby Sammy had now closed his eyes, but his mouth was still making tiny popping noises as he lay in the crook of his mother's arm, the very picture of health and innocence. Eunice saw her mother's eyes soften as she regarded him. 'Bless him . . .' Edith murmured.

'I should jolly well think he's had his fill,' replied Eunice. 'I feel as though he's drained me dry.'

'Here, give him to me,' said her mother, 'and I'll put a dry nappy on him while you tidy yourself up. Maybe you should think about putting him on a bottle, Eunice. I know you're not very happy about all this.'

'I wish I could, Mum, but Mrs Wilshaw says I shouldn't, not for a while yet. She says this is best for the baby.' Eunice knew that this was true and she felt guilty that she was not enjoying the experience as much as she should.

'Midwives don't know everything,' replied Edith tartly. 'Whose baby is it anyway? It's ours, not hers. It's up to us to decide what's best for him. You leave it to me.'

Eunice was tempted to tell her mother that Sammy was not 'ours' but 'mine'; that he belonged to her, Eunice, alone, and to Ronnie, of course, when he was there, but she lacked the courage to do so. She knew her mother meant well.

As she sat in the bath, something she was doing continually in an endeavour to keep herself clean and fragrant, she saw the milk dripping from her breasts like two leaking taps. She feared it would never go away. She persevered for the next few weeks, but eventually the midwife agreed to help her, albeit reluctantly and after consultation with the family doctor. She gave Eunice some tablets that she promised should do the trick. She felt ill for a few days, hot and feverish and light-headed, with pains in her breasts, but the milk gradually ceased to flow.

Eunice bought big red tins of Cow and Gate milk, with a picture of a bonny laughing baby on the front. Sammy adjusted very well to the change, and as she sat with him in her arms, watching the milk rapidly disappearing from the curved bottle, Eunice felt she had done the right thing. She was happy and her happiness affected her baby. As the weeks passed he put weight on, growing chubby and rosy-cheeked and chuckling a little just like the baby on the Cow and Gate tin. She was very proud of him.

Bottle-feeding had the added advantage that others were now able to help. Her mother, of course, insisted on giving Sammy his bottle from time to time and her father was persuaded to hold his grandson on his knee occasionally. But Eunice tried, continually, to keep the upper hand, to let it be known that Sammy was her responsibility and hers alone, and that she would welcome help, but not interference. It was difficult, though, when she was living in someone else's house. It was her childhood home, the place where she had always lived apart from the brief spell in the Land Army, but it did not belong to her. How she longed at times for a place of her own – hers and Ronnie's – where she could do exactly as she wished with no interference from others. By others, of course, she meant her mother, because Edith seemed unable to stop herself from taking charge.

One of Eunice's jobs was to collect the groceries, the weekly rations, from the shop belonging to her parents-in-law. Sometimes she took Sammy with her in his pram. His paternal grandparents were always delighted to see him and would spare a few minutes from their shop to fuss over him. If there were customers in the shop he would be passed round from arm to arm, loving the attention of the nice friendly housewives and he would coo and gurgle to his heart's content.

On this particular September morning, however, it was raining so Eunice left the pram and the baby at home. She collected the essential items – the two ounces of butter per person per week; the sugar, bacon and tea – and put them in her large basket, leaving the order, or at least the items of it which might or might not be available, to be delivered later by her father-in-law. Edith had been giving Sammy his bottle when she left, and when she returned she found to her surprise that he was still sitting on her mother's lap. He seemed uncomfortable, however, and was squirming and wriggling.

Eunice took a closer look, then she cried, 'Mother, what on earth do you think you're doing? Sammy's too young to sit on a potty. Just look at him, for heaven's sake! He doesn't like it.'

Edith was holding the child on to a tiny blue potty, and from his red scowling face it was obvious that he was none too keen on the idea and, what was more, that he would not oblige and do what was required of him. Unable to contain herself Eunice dashed across the room and made a grab for her baby, sending the pot, fortunately empty, rolling away across the carpet.

'Come along, Sammy; come to Mummy then. Whatever is your silly old grandma doing?' She cradled him in her arms. 'Never mind then. Hush, don't cry.' The child had started to whimper and she stroked his ginger curls and kissed his cheek. 'It's all right now; Mummy's here. Hush now . . .'

'Well, I like that!' Edith jumped to her feet, almost exploding with rage. 'Silly old Grandma, indeed! I was doing you a favour, if you did but realise it. Trying to save you the trouble of all those dirty nappies.' Or save herself the trouble, thought Eunice, because she had to admit that her mother did more than her fair share of the washing. 'I don't know why I bother sometimes, Eunice; you're so ungrateful.'

'I'm not,' cried Eunice. 'But he's far too young for all that. Little babies haven't got control over their bladders, or their . . . their bowels until they're much older; about two years old. That's what it says in all the baby books, and I bet if you asked Mrs Wilshaw she would tell you the same.'

'Baby books!' scoffed Edith. 'I brought you up all right without resorting to any baby books. And you were clean and dry by the time you were a year old – apart from the nighttime, of course. I wouldn't stand for any nonsense, I can tell you.' No, I bet you wouldn't, thought Eunice. 'And neither will you with Sammy if you've any sense. They're never too young to learn what you expect of them.'

'Well, I don't expect him to perform to order like a performing monkey, not to please me or to please you,' retorted Eunice. 'He's all right now, see, aren't you, Sammy? You didn't like that nasty cold potty, did you?' As if in reply the child smiled at her; he was just beginning to focus with his eyes and to smile in recognition of people he knew. 'I'm going to put a nice dry nappy on you now,' she went on, ignoring her mother. 'And if you wet it straight away it doesn't matter, does it? No it doesn't matter a bit.' Again, as if in reply, the baby responded by doing what his gran had been wanting him to do in his potty. An arc of liquid shot up into the air, wetting Eunice's arm and then her skirt, before cascading on to the carpet.

Edith tutted loudly. 'There you are, you see, you silly girl! If you'd not been so impatient you could have avoided that. He'd have done it in the proper place if you'd waited. But of course you know best, don't you? You always do.' She stormed off into the kitchen to get a cloth, whilst Eunice, smiling to herself, put a clean nappy on the baby, followed by his rubberised pants.

'There now,' she whispered, sitting down with him on her lap. 'All nice and dry again. We'll have to see if we can pacify Grandma, won't we? Oh dear, oh dear, whatever have we done, Sammy? I'm sorry, Mum,' she said as her mother re-entered the room. 'You've got your ideas and I've got mine. But I really don't want to start with toilet training just yet. OK?'

Edith shrugged. 'If you say so. But I think you're making a rod for your own back. He's your child, though, so I suppose you'll go your own way. You want my help when it suits you, though, don't you? I hope you've not forgotten it's the christening on Sunday. And who's making the party for all them folk, godparents and God knows who else?'

'Yes . . . I know, Mum,' said Eunice. 'And I'm very grateful, really I am. Ronnie's mother's helping out as well though, isn't she?'

'Yes, I suppose so. But it's at my house, isn't it, as usual. It's me that has all the clearing away and washing up to do.'

'We'll all help,' said Eunice quietly. 'You know we will.' But her mother was determined to be a martyr and Eunice knew she would have to leave her to it for as long as it lasted. She sighed inwardly, then cheered up almost immediately at the thought that Ronnie was coming home for the christening. Her husband would be home tomorrow.

Chapter 16

Ronnie laughed out loud when Eunice told him the tale about her mother and Sammy and the unsuccessful potty training. 'What a storm in a teacup! Honestly, Eunice, our troops are still going through hell and high water out there, and all you have to worry about is a piddling little row with your mother.'

Eunice grinned. 'I like your choice of adjective, Ronnie. Very apt, or was it unintentional?'

'What? Oh yes, I see what you mean.' They both collapsed into giggles, holding on to one another in their merriment. Eunice still held her husband close when their laughter had subsided.

'Oh, Ronnie, it's so good to have you home again,' she sighed, leaning her head against his shoulder, feeling him stroke her hair and kiss her forehead. 'I've missed you so much.'

'So have I; so very much,' he murmured before he kissed her again, properly this time and lingeringly. 'What about your mother then?' he asked as they gradually drew apart and sat down together at the side of the bed. 'Is she still feeling a bit peeved, or has she forgiven you? She seemed

OK to me when I came in; at least I didn't notice anything.'

'Yes, we're OK again now, Mum and me,' said Eunice. 'I could hardly believe it really, Ronnie. She actually came and apologised to me, last night when I was putting Sammy to bed.'

Eunice had, indeed, been very surprised when her mother had entered the room looking a little sheepish and – if it were possible – repentant.

'I'm sorry, Eunice.' She started to speak at once, very quickly. 'That incident with the potty this morning. I shouldn't have done it; I know that now. Sammy's your baby and it was nothing to do with me. It's up to you to decide about things like that.'

'It's OK, Mum; forget it,' said Eunice. 'It doesn't matter, honestly.' To her amazement she could see tears in her mother's eyes.

'I've been so happy since you had this baby, Eunice,' she went on, 'and I do so want to help with him, if you'll let me.'

'Well, of course I will, Mum. I do let you already, don't I? You've been a great help.'

'It's like a second chance to me, you see, love . . .' Eunice remembered her friend Gwen saying something of the sort; that grandparents saw their grandchildren as a chance to put right some of the mistakes they might have made the first time round. 'When you were a baby I was so busy . . . so very busy helping my mother and I feel that I might have . . . well . . . neglected you.'

'I'm sure you didn't, Mum.' Eunice had, truthfully, never felt that. 'And Gran was always there.'

Edith sighed. 'Yes, your gran. My mother . . . God rest her soul,' she added in an undertone. 'But she wasn't always easy to get on with, you know. And she had me right there, under her thumb.' She demonstrated, sticking her thumb out at right angles. 'She took you over, almost completely at times, and I was too scared to say anything. And you thought the world of her; I used to feel quite jealous sometimes.'

'Yes, I know she was very fond of me,' replied Eunice. 'I used to think—'

'What? That she loved you more than I did?'

'No; that wasn't what I was going to say. I felt that she was much kinder to me than she was to you.' Eunice remembered, suddenly, that she had said the selfsame thing to Gwen about her mother, herself and Sammy; a different threesome, but the same situation repeating itself.

Edith seemed to know what she was thinking. 'Yes, that was true. She doted on you whilst I used to get the rough edge of her tongue. My mistake was that I didn't stick up for myself as much as I should have done. And then, after she'd gone . . . well, it was too late. You and me, Eunice, I felt we'd drifted apart. We'd missed out on such a lot. And then I could see myself getting like my own mother: bossy and interfering . . . Oh, dear! I'm so sorry, love; I can't seem to help myself at times, but I do love you. And little Sammy . . . well, that baby's turned out to be such a blessing.' She leaned over the cot, smiling at the child who was staring up, wide-eyed, at them both.

'Come on, Mum. Don't upset yourself.' Eunice put an arm round her, something she could hardly ever remember doing in the past. 'It's never too late, is it? And I've always known that you loved me. So does my dad, though I know he finds it hard to say so.'

'Your daddy . . . Oh well, that's another story,' said Edith, sniffing back her tears. 'It was the war that changed your daddy; the last one; the war to end all wars, so they said. Huh! How little they knew . . . Let's hope that Ronald comes through this one without any such repercussions.

Anyway, love, what I was saying about Sammy and that there potty – I was only trying to help, in my own way, and to save us some dirty nappies. You took to it like a duck to water, Eunice, when you were a baby. You were always such a good little thing.'

'Oh well, I'm glad about that,' said Eunice, laughing. 'Come on, Mum, cheer up and let's forget all about it. It's the christening on Sunday.'

'Yes, and I'll still some baking to do.' Edith was her old self again almost immediately. 'And your husband will be home tomorrow. I think I'll make one of his favourite apple pies . . .'

Ronnie had arrived in Blackpool in the late afternoon, after travelling for the best part of the day. Eunice had gone to North Station to meet him, taking Sammy with her in his pram. The train had been about half an hour late, which was nothing unusual. When she saw him coming along the platform, waving and smiling cheerily, with his kitbag humped over his shoulder, she realised just how much she had missed him.

'Oh, you can do no wrong, as far as my mother's concerned,' she told him now. 'You're a hero; so are all the lads who are fighting for King and country. I'll give her her due: my mother's certainly patriotic. No, it's me she was mad at, but she's come round now, as I've just told you. But I get so tired sometimes of her fussing and trying to take over, I must admit.'

'She's a good help to you, though? I know you said when Sammy was born that she wouldn't let you lift a finger.'

'No, she wouldn't, not at first. And she certainly seems ready to make amends now. Until the next time . . . No doubt she'll be her old bossy self again before long. I don't think she can help it. But I do try to stick up for myself, like I did over that blasted potty. Oh, Ronnie, it was so funny, really it was. And then he went and weed all over the place. You should have seen her face.'

'I can imagine,' grinned Ronnie. 'Your mother is not overendowed with a sense of humour, is she? Come on, love, we'd best tidy ourselves up and go downstairs. She's already told me she's making a slap-up meal, so we mustn't go and spoil it for her. I'd rather stay here, though, I must admit,' he said ruefully, patting the silken eiderdown on which they were sitting. 'But we haven't time . . . have we?' He looked at her mischievously.

Eunice jumped to her feet. 'No, we certainly haven't. Don't start getting ideas.' She smiled coyly. 'There's tonight though . . . and tomorrow night.' She realised she was looking forward to their intimate moments just as much as Ronnie was.

But before that they must go round and pay a visit to Ronnie's parents. After they had finished Edith's welcome home meal of steak and kidney pie, followed by the special apple pie – and had duly complimented her on her, once again, excellent cooking – they settled baby Sammy in his pram for the trip to his paternal grandparents.

'Be careful with him in the night air,' Edith warned. 'Make sure he's warmly wrapped up.' She could not resist making a point, however slight, but Eunice knew even her mother would not dare to say, as she so obviously thought, that they were upsetting the baby's routine. He was usually being prepared for bed at this time, but this was a special occasion. Ronnie's parents would want to see their grandson as well as their son.

'It seems strange, visiting my parents,' he said as they walked the short distance to his former home. 'Having lived there, I mean, and now I'm just a visitor. My place is with you, though, of course,' he added, putting an arm round her and drawing her close, 'and I wouldn't have it any other way.'

'I wish we could have our own place, Ronnie,' said Eunice pensively. 'We will, one day, won't we?'

'So do I, darling,' he replied. 'Just wait till this lot's over, and then we will, I promise. It can't be long now . . .' She knew he would not say very much; it was still all very hush-hush. 'Plans are going ahead. Perhaps by this time next year; who knows?'

Mabel and Tom were delighted to see their son and baby grandson, but they welcomed Eunice just as enthusiastically. She was always sure of a welcome there and she felt just as much at home, if not more so, than she did in her parents' house. Sammy, who was certainly breaking with his routine tonight, was passed to his grandma then to his granddad. He smiled and chortled at both of them.

'Here, go to your daddy then,' said Tom, passing him over to Ronnie. He sat down in the armchair, holding his baby son rather tentatively in his arms. 'Hello there,' he said, sounding a mite embarrassed. 'I'm your daddy.' The child stared at him uncomprehendingly. His eyes were turning a brighter blue now, like his mother's, but there was no spark of animation there.

Ronnie turned to Eunice. 'He's not smiling at me. Why is that? He smiled for you and for Mum and Dad. What have I done wrong, eh?' He spoke jokingly, but Eunice knew he was a little upset.

'He doesn't know you yet, Ronnie,' she said gently. 'He doesn't recognise you. But he will do. I bet by the end of this weekend he'll be smiling away at you like he does at the rest of us. He's only just started smiling,' she added.

'And then he'll go and forget me again,' said Ronnie gloomily. 'Oh, this blasted war! I wish it would come to an end.'

'Don't we all, son?' said his father. 'Aye, it's been a long time, but we're getting the upper hand now, aren't we? They don't tell us much.'

'I hope so, Dad,' said Ronnie.

'Now, now; never mind all this war talk,' said Mabel. 'You're home, aren't you, and our Chrissie and Fiona will be here tomorrow.' She turned to Eunice. 'I hope you don't mind me mentioning it, dear, but I think Chrissie was rather disappointed she hadn't been asked to be godmother to Sammy. She hasn't said very much – it's not her way to make a fuss – but I think she wondered why.' It was not Mabel's way, either, to make too much of things or to take offence, but Eunice did, in fact, feel rather guilty.

'I know,' she said. 'I'm really sorry, but I didn't know what to do. I did think about Chrissie, with her being Ronnie's sister, but I did so want Gwen to be godmother. We've been friends for a long time and . . . and she's been such a good friend to me. And Ronnie said it was OK; he didn't mind who I asked.'

'That's right,' said Ronnie casually. 'What does it matter? It's only a formality, isn't it? But I felt I had to ask Jack. He was my best man and he's thrilled to bits to be asked again for this. And Bill, Gwen's husband, is going to be the other godfather. He's managed to get leave, so he's coming up with Gwen.'

'It's not just a formality, Ronnie,' said Mabel. 'You shouldn't dismiss it so lightly. I happen to think it's rather important. You're asking people to make promises on behalf of that baby; making sure he's brought up in a Christian home and all that.'

'Surely that's up to Eunice and me, isn't it?' said Ronnie. 'We'll do all that's needed there, won't we, love? We'll make sure he goes to Sunday school and everything, like you did, and Eunice's mam and dad did. I don't see the need for godparents meself, but that's what they want in the Church of England, don't they? Two godfathers and a godmother for a boy, and two godmothers and a godfather for a girl. Trixie's coming with Jack an' all, so she might feel she's had her nose pushed out.'

'We don't know Trixie all that well, though, do we?' said Eunice. 'Goodness me!' She laughed. 'I didn't realise it was going to cause all this palaver. Perhaps we should ask them all, like royalty do. They have umpteen godparents, don't they?'

'Never mind,' said Ronnie. 'Happen the next one will be a girl, eh, love? And our Chrissie will be first choice. How about that?'

Mabel nodded. 'That would be lovely, dear.'

Some of the same people were gathered in the Mortons' dining room for the christening as had been there for the wedding earlier that year. The civil servants from London were there, but this time there were no friends from the church. Eunice and Ronnie had wanted it to be a quiet affair with just their immediate family and friends.

Jack and Trixie had travelled from Bradford the previous day and were staying with Ronnie's parents. It made a full house as Chrissie and her good friend Fiona were there as well, on a forty-eight-hour pass from their camp in East Anglia. But Mabel had welcomed them all cheerfully. The more the merrier was her belief and there was plenty of room. She was determined to observe the proprieties, however. Whatever Jack and his pert little fiancée got up to at home was their own business, but under her roof she would make sure that all was respectable and above board. She put up a camp bed for Jack in the living room – he agreed laughingly that that was 'just the ticket' – whilst Trixie slept in the room that had once been occupied by

Ronnie. Chrissie and Fiona seemed quite content to share the double bed in Chrissie's room as they had done on a previous visit.

It did not occur to Mabel that a certain amount of 'hanky-panky', as she termed it, had happened under her roof on at least one occasion. That behaviour, indeed, had led to the event for which they were all gathered that weekend, the christening of baby Samuel Thomas. But so well loved was he now that the circumstances of his conception had been forgotten.

The Reverend John Hunter conducted the simple baptism service on Sunday afternoon. They all gathered round the font whilst the vicar made the sign of the cross on the baby's forehead, and the godparents, Gwen, Bill and Jack, promised on his behalf to 'renounce the devil and all his works'. Archaic words, and Ronnie had feared that Jack might smirk or make a joke of it. But no; he had misjudged him. His oftentimes skittish mate was on his best behaviour and showed no sign of irreverence. Gwen was proudly holding the baby whilst the other two looked on solemnly. Sammy, as they might have guessed, yelled vigorously when he felt the cold water on his face.

'Crying the devil out, that's what they say,' whispered Edith, standing next to her daughter.

'Hush, Mother!' hissed Eunice. That was a silly old wives' tale. Besides, she refused to believe there was anything of the devil in her lovely little son, despite the words of the baptism service, which implied that all babies come into the world tainted by 'original sin'. She would be glad when she was able to hold her own baby again. It seemed strange to have someone else taking charge of him this afternoon, although she had to admit that Gwen was coping very well with him.

Gwen was wearing the neat little suit she had worn for

her wedding, with the tiny tip-tilted hat. Eunice had not known from the black and white photos Gwen had shown her what colour the suit was. It was a pale turquoise blue, the hat a shade darker, and it contrasted well with the outfits that Eunice and Trixie were wearing. They, too, had opted to wear the clothes they had worn for Eunice's spring wedding. Eunice had no coupons to spare – or money either, for that matter – to buy anything new. Besides, she had not yet got her wear out of the wedding suit and she guessed she would never be likely to do so. Occasions such as this were few and far between. Probably it was the same for Trixie, although she could imagine the young woman turning up anywhere in the shiny cerise-pink dress, regardless of the occasion.

The other young people at the christening – Ronnie, Bill, Chrissie and Fiona – were proudly wearing their uniforms, of the army, RAF and WAAF respectively. They all bore sergeants' stripes on their sleeves, and Bill his wings, denoting that he was a flier. The exception was Jack. He had been invalided out of the army, due to his severe burns. He had had another operation since they had last seen him and the skin on his face was no longer so shiny and bright pink and his eye was now open. He was hoping to return to his job in the woollen mill before very long.

The spread that Edith put on afterwards did not vary much either from the one she had prepared for the wedding: sandwiches of various kinds, eked out with the inevitable pilchards, Spam and corned beef; jelly and trifle; fancy cakes; and, again, a fruit cake – the christening cake – baked by Edith with the precious ingredients supplied by herself and Mabel. Not quite as rich in fruit this time, but it was iced, with 'Samuel Thomas' piped on in blue. Mabel had even managed to unearth from the shop storeroom a sugar cradle with a tiny baby inside. It was not quite pristine white, but as no one would eat it, it did not really matter.

'It was a lovely day, wasn't it?' said Eunice, lying contentedly in Ronnie's arms much later that same evening. It was, in fact, well turned midnight, so it was already the next day, Monday, the day that Ronnie was due to return to his camp. Jack and Trixie, Bill and Gwen, and Chrissie and Fiona would also be returning to their various homes or duties at the same time. The eight young people had had an impromptu party earlier in the evening at Mabel and Tom's home, Eunice and Ronnie joining the others when they had put Sammy to bed. Edith had very graciously offered to look after him, and they had both enjoyed the jovial company of their friends, something which Eunice realised she'd missed greatly in the last few months. The beer, watered down with lemonade, flowed freely and they ate the leftovers from the christening party which Edith had insisted they should make use of.

'And that party tonight was just what we needed,' Eunice went on. 'It does you good to let your hair down now and again and forget about the war.'

'Yes, it was terrific,' agreed Ronnie. 'I've not enjoyed meself so much for ages. No . . . that's not quite true,' he added, giving her a quick kiss. 'I enjoy being with you, on our own – that's the best of all – but the company, I mean, us all being together. It was great.'

'I was surprised to hear that Jack and Trixie have delayed their wedding plans,' said Eunice. 'She told me, when we got married, that it was going to be this summer.'

'Yes, they've put it off till early next year,' said Ronnie. 'There's no rush really. They know they won't have to be parted, with him having left the army, and Trixie has decided she wants a big do; white dress and bridesmaids and all the works, if they can manage it. They're saving up, 'cause neither of their parents can afford very much.'

'Yes, she was telling me about it, but I should have thought the most important thing was to be married and to be together all the time,' said Eunice, snuggling closer to her husband.

'Oh well, I shouldn't think it makes much difference,' laughed Ronnie. 'I don't suppose they're exactly "saving themselves for marriage", do you?'

'Ronnie, what a thing to say! Trixie wants to wear a white dress.'

'So what? That won't worry Trixie. She's a very determined young woman.'

'Yes, maybe you're right,' Eunice mused. 'Why shouldn't she have her fairy-tale wedding if that's what she wants? She's every right to look like a princess for once in her life. From what she says, she had a pretty hard time when she was a kid, looking after her little brothers and sisters. Although I must admit she wasn't grumbling about it.'

'So did Jack, from all accounts. It makes you and me look quite unique; privileged, you might say, you being an only one and me with just one sister.'

'It all depends on how you look at it,' said Eunice. 'Being an only one has its drawbacks. I always wanted a brother or sister, but it never happened.'

'Yes, maybe there's something to be said for being one of a large family. It hasn't done Jack or Trixie any harm. I dare say they're so used to it that they'll go on to have dozens of their own kids.'

'Dozens?'

'Well, four or five at least, I should think. Jack told me once that Trixie couldn't wait to have kids of her own, even though she's done more than her share with her mother's brood.'

'Mmm . . . We're ahead of them though, aren't we?'

laughed Eunice. 'Speaking of brothers and sisters; your sister and that friend of hers, Fiona, they get on awfully well together, don't they? I think they're such a nice pair of girls – well, women I should say; they're not really girls any more. I've always liked your Chrissie.'

'Yes, they certainly get on well together,' replied Ronnie. There was something in his tone of voice that made Eunice glance at him sharply.

The penny suddenly dropped. 'Do you mean that your Chrissie and Fiona, that they . . .'

'Well, yes,' said Ronnie. 'That's what I suspect. Our Chrissie was never very interested in boyfriends, but perhaps she didn't know why . . . until she met Fiona. You've got to admit they look very happy together.'

'Gosh!' exclaimed Eunice. 'What about your mother and father? Do you think they know?'

'I shouldn't think so. I certainly won't tell them. They might be suspicious if Chrissie never gets married – and there won't be any more grandchildren, of course, not if it depends on my sister.'

'If you're right . . .'

'Yes, if I'm right. Don't worry your head about it, darling. Promise me you won't.'

'No, I won't. I'll be too busy worrying about you. It'll be up to us to provide the grandchildren then?'

'Yes . . . Do you feel like starting now?' He drew her closer to him, his hands straying the length of her body.

'Yes, of course I do,' she murmured, responding to him. 'What do you think?'

'When it's all over we'll have our own little house, I promise you, darling,' said Ronnie. 'Just you and me and Sammy, and then . . . as many more babies as you want.'

'Just another one would do – a little girl – or two more at the most,' she replied dreamily. 'But for now . . . Oh, just make love to me, Ronnie! I'm going to miss you so much . . .'

But there was a long way to go before it was, finally, 'all over'. When 1944 dawned everyone knew that this would be the year of what had become known as D-Day. It was hoped too that it might be the year of victory.

Preparations for D-Day had become impossible to conceal. Ronnie reported to Eunice that signs of it were to be seen everywhere in the south of England. A ten-mile-deep stretch of coast from the Wash to Land's End was closed to visitors. If that was not indication enough, there were tanks and armoured vehicles and heaps of shells piled up by the sides of the roads. The ports and rivers were crammed with vessels and there were more American GIs around than ever before.

And then, on the morning of Tuesday, 6 June, the authoritative voice of John Snagge broadcast to the nation, 'D-Day has come. Early this morning the Allies began the assault on the north-western face of Hitler's European fortress.'

There were, inevitably, heavy losses, particularly amongst the airborne forces. Eunice was anxious about Bill, Gwen's husband, until she heard from her friend that he had come safely through the initial assault at least. Her own husband, still not agile enough after his injuries, was not involved in the actual invasion. He felt guilty not to be taking an active part in it, but Eunice could only be thankful that he was safe, or comparatively so; for the war was still waging in insidious ways that no one had ever imagined.

'Hitler's secret weapon' had been a national joke ever since it had been first mentioned in 1939. Now it was here: the V1, the flying bomb, quickly nicknamed the doodlebug, descending on London and the southern counties, and it soon became clear that it was no joking matter. A new wave of evacuees arrived in Blackpool, this time from London's East End. The V1s were followed by the V2s, and the year that had begun with such high hopes in Britain ended in gloom and despondency, not helped by the snow and fog.

It was a miserable winter; not quite as severe as the one of '39, the first winter of the war, but by now everyone was weary of the conflict and dispirited by recent setbacks. But the tide was turning. British troops had occupied the Ruhr valley and were on the march through Germany. When the news broke that Hitler had committed suicide it seemed that it really was, at last, all over.

But it was only when the nation heard Winston Churchill broadcast on the afternoon of 8 May that everyone knew for certain that the war had ended. The Allies had been victorious. This was Victory in Europe Day; time for the parties and bonfires and celebrations to begin.

Chapter 17

Victory parties were held in the streets of Blackpool, as they were in towns, cities and villages all over Britain. Some were organised almost as soon as victory in Europe had been declared, others later in the summer. Although it was all over in Europe the war in the Far East was still continuing and many British servicemen were still involved.

Winston Churchill was determined that British troops and ships should take part in the invasion of Japan. Tokyo and other major Japanese cities were devastated by the attacks of the avenging American and British planes. But the Japanese put up a ferocious resistance, any attempts to land on Japanese soil being thwarted by suicide bombers, known as the kamikaze. It was not until 6 August that the war in the Far East was brought to a dramatic conclusion by the dropping of the first atomic bomb on the city of Hiroshima, followed by one on 9 August on Nagasaki. Japan was forced to surrender and accept the demands of the Allies.

But the dreadful destruction of the cities and the deaths of thousands of people brought a chill to the hearts of the celebrating millions in Britain. The event was not discussed overmuch, or if it was talked about it was in hushed, almost unbelieving voices, lest it should mar the jollifications.

The street party that was to be held in Eunice's neighbourhood was planned for the middle of August. It had been decided by the organising committee, of which both Edith and Mabel were members, that this was a suitable time. The school children would be on holiday and many of the servicemen, including Ronnie, would have returned home. The civil servants, billeted with Edith for the duration of the war, had now gone back to London, and the house was returning to its former status as a boarding house. There were not many visitors booked in, however, for the summer of 1945; it would take a while for the war-weary Britons to get into the habit of holidaymaking again. So Edith had plenty of time, and a new-found energy, it seemed, to throw herself into the preparations for a slap-up Victory party.

The ladies of the committee went round to each house in the neighbourhood, requesting donations for the occasion. Nearly everyone responded enthusiastically. There were promises of cakes, scones, sausage rolls, sandwiches, jellies and trifles, and those who did not wish to bake usually donated a small gift of money. Others promised to lend tablecloths, a great many of which would be needed to cover the trestle tables borrowed from the local church. And there were many offers of help, from the men as well as the women, to decorate the street where the party was to be held with flags and streamers and bunting. Many of the houses, indeed, had been sporting Union Jacks in their windows since 8 May, along with pictures of the King and Queen and the two princesses, Elizabeth and Margaret Rose, and Winston Churchill with his now famous cigar and V for Victory sign.

So when Ronnie arrived home in the middle of August it was to a neighbourhood bedecked in red, white and blue. Streamers and flags fluttered from lampposts and windows, and bunting stretched in a zigzag line along the street where the party would take place in two days' time. Eunice and Sammy had been waiting to greet him when he embarked from the train at North Station, wearing, for the last time, his khaki uniform. The sight of his wife and child brought tears of joy to his eyes. He had been more fortunate than some of his colleagues – if you could call being wounded a stroke of fortune – because he had spent the last two years of the war on home ground and had been able to see his little son growing up. Every time he went home on leave he had seen a difference in him. Sammy was always puzzled for the first day or so, wondering who this stranger was that his mummy was calling 'Daddy'. And then, when the child was beginning to recognise him and go to him willingly, the leave would be over and Ronnie would have to say goodbye again.

Now the goodbyes were over. He was home for good and at last they could start their family life in earnest. He hoped it would not be too long before they had a place of their own, as he had promised Eunice. As he walked towards her, watching her lovely blue eyes light up with pleasure at seeing him again, his heart nearly burst with love for her. And for Sammy, too. The little boy was two years old now and had long since finished with his large pram. He sometimes rode in a pushchair, which Eunice had brought with her now, but he was an independent child and insisted on walking whenever he could. He was jumping up and down excitedly now, holding on to his mother's hand and waving frantically with the other. His bright auburn hair glowed like a beacon and his eyes were as bright a blue as his mother's. Ronnie hoped that the light in them was one of recognition.

He dashed through the barrier, flung his kitbag down and hugged and kissed his wife. Then he turned to the little boy and swept him up in his arms. Sammy did not struggle to get down as he sometimes did. He looked at him, a mite curiously, and then, after a pause, he said, 'Daddy'. Ronnie realised he might have been instructed to say it; nevertheless it warmed his heart, thrilling him beyond measure.

'Hello there, Sammy,' he said. 'Yes, I'm your daddy and I've come home, to stay this time. Isn't that nice?' The child nodded, although it was doubtful whether he understood. 'Now, you get into your pushchair and we'll all go home. What about that, eh?'

'No . . . walk, walk,' said Sammy as Ronnie tried to lift him into the small pram.

'He's getting rather wilful,' said Eunice. 'I can't always give in to him, especially when I'm in a hurry, but he's a good little walker, aren't you, Sammy? I tell you what; we'll let Daddy's kitbag have a ride in your pushchair, and you can help me to push it. How about that?'

Sammy thought that was a great idea and the three of them made their way home, taking rather longer than they should have done. But it didn't matter; they had all the time to get to know one another again, thought Ronnie, with his arm around his wife's shoulders and his eyes upon the sturdy little figure trotting along beside her, who was, by some miracle, his son.

'Oh, my goodness, Ronnie, whatever is that?' Eunice exclaimed, laughing when she saw him in his demob suit. 'It makes you look like a spiv.'

'Yes, I'm inclined to agree with you, my love,' replied Ronnie. The suit was dark grey, almost black, with a white pinstripe, made of a material that was obviously Utility.

'But it was either this or an awful brown one, and I've never liked brown suits. It's good to get into civvies, though, I've got to admit. That khaki cloth's like sand-paper next to your skin. I used to itch like mad at first, but you get used to anything after a while.'

'I'll never get used to you in that,' giggled Eunice. 'You've still got some nice clothes you used to wear before the war, haven't you? What about your sports jackets and flannels? And that yellow pullover?'

'No; I'm wearing my demob suit to go round to my parents. I want to see the look on their faces,' Ronnie smiled mischievously.

Eunice and Ronnie were getting ready, on the evening of his arrival, to go to see Tom and Mabel. It had taken longer than it should have done; it was the first time they had been alone together since arriving home in the middle of the afternoon, and one thing had led to another. 'Come on, we'd best get a move on,' she said now, pink-cheeked and bright-eyed, 'or my mother will be wondering what we're up to.'

'Don't you think she can guess?'

'Mmm . . . probably. But it's very good of her to give Sammy his bath while we . . . er . . . get ready. Come on, Ronnie, let's get him into bed and say good night to him . . . together.'

'Together – that's what I like to hear,' smiled Ronnie, unable to resist kissing her again. 'We're a real family now, darling.'

Ronnie and Tom, inevitably, talked politics whilst Eunice and Mabel discussed the plans for the forthcoming party, which was much more important and interesting, at the moment, than who had won the recent election.

'Well, that was a turn-up for the book and no mistake,'

said Tom, 'the Labour Party coming to power. Don't you think so, Ronnie?'

'I'm not so sure,' replied Ronnie. 'There have been definite signs of a move to the left; I've seen a lot of it in the army.'

'Aye, I dare say it was the forces' vote that swayed things,' said Tom. The election had been held on 5 July, but it was not until the twenty-sixth of that month, when the votes of the servicemen had arrived from overseas, that the result had been announced: a landslide victory for the Labour Party. 'It surprised me, though. You'd think the lads would have supported the fellow that led them to victory.'

'Oh, I don't know so much about that,' said Ronnie. 'There were a lot that didn't agree with everything he did. And it was the opinion of most of us that it was time for a change.'

'Yes, mebbe,' said Tom thoughtfully. 'You said "most of us". Are you telling me that you voted them in, then?'

'I'm telling you nothing, Dad,' said Ronnie, laughing and touching his nose. 'It's a secret vote, isn't it? Well, it's supposed to be.'

'I've made no secret of the fact that I'm a Conservative,' replied Tom. 'Always have been and always will be. That's right, isn't it, Mabel? We've always been true blue Tories, haven't we?'

'Oh, for goodness' sake, give it a rest, will you, Tom?' said Mabel. 'Honestly, he's never shut up about it since that lot were voted in. We've got to make the best of it, that's what I say. I've got to admit that I thought old Winnie would get back. It seems a shame, folks turning their backs on him after all he's done. But we must give 'em a chance, this new lot.'

'Don't forget we've got our own business,' said Tom,

'and a grand little shop it is an' all. We don't want them taking it off us, do we?'

'Don't talk rubbish, Tom! That's not going to happen,' retorted Mabel. 'What about Eunice's mam and dad? They've got their own business too; the boarding house. Well, Edith has, at any rate; I know Samuel's never had much to do with it. How's it doing, Eunice? Are there a lot of visitors in this week?'

'Not as many as my mother would like,' replied Eunice. 'But it's early days, isn't it? Folks are still a bit hard up. Maybe by next year they'll all be thinking about holidays again.'

'Yes, we all deserve a holiday,' said Mabel, giving a little sigh. 'Do you know, I've always had a fancy to go to Torquay? I've seen pictures of it. It looks lovely; all them hills and palm trees and gardens; "the English Riviera", they call it. But I've never been. I'm trying to persuade your dad to take me sometime, perhaps next year.'

'Yes, why not, Mother?' agreed Ronnie. 'Why not go this year, as soon as you can? Like you say, you do deserve a holiday, and so does Dad. I'll be starting back at the shop next week; that's what we've agreed, haven't we? And happen Eunice could come in and help me out now and again. Her mother'll look after Sammy, won't she, Eunice?'

'Here, steady on, lad,' interrupted Tom. 'I've not said as how we're going. Come to think of it, though, it's not a bad idea. Aye, we'll write off for one of them holiday guides, shall we, Mabel? Then . . . we'll see.'

'Do you really mean it, Tom?' said Mabel, looking flushed and happy, but rather unbelieving.

'Yes, of course I do, lass,' he replied, smiling affectionately at her. He still loves her a lot, after all this time, thought Eunice, seeing the light of devotion in his eyes. 'Besides, if our Chrissie can go away on holiday,' he continued, 'then I don't see why we shouldn't.'

'Chrissie?' said Eunice. 'Why; where has she gone? I knew she'd been demobbed, but I haven't seen much of her.'

'No, neither have we,' replied Mabel, sounding a little indignant. 'She came home about three weeks ago. That would be when you saw her, but she only stayed here a week. Then she went up to Scotland to see Fiona; way up in the Highlands she lives, near Inverness. Then the next we heard, the two of 'em are having a holiday together, if you please, in Edinburgh. They're supposed to be coming back here when they've finished their gadding about.'

'You don't sound very happy about it, Mother,' said Ronnie. He gave Eunice a knowing glance as if to say, What did I tell you? 'Don't you like Fiona?'

'Yes, I like her very much,' said Mabel. 'She and our Chrissie, they seem like . . . well, like soul mates, if you know what I mean. They're very good friends, I know that, and I suppose they'll find it hard to go their separate ways after being so long together in the WAAFs. But we've all got to get back to normal, and I thought Chrissie might have wanted to spend a bit more time with us, her mam and dad . . . that's all.'

'What about her job?' asked Ronnie. Chrissie had worked as a shorthand typist in a local government office ever since she had left school at sixteen. 'Isn't she going back to the town hall?'

'That was the idea,' replied Mabel. 'At least, I thought it was. Her job's still there for her if she wants it. But she was doing a lot of hemming and hawing when she was home; said she felt like a change. I told her she should be thankful she's got a good job to go back to, but there's no talking to our Chrissie when she's in one of her stubborn moods. Anyroad, I reckon she'll do as she likes. She's over twenty-one; I can't tell her what to do any more.'

'I expect she's just restless,' said Eunice, 'with being in the WAAFs for so long. I'm sure she'll settle down.'

'But where?' said Mabel. 'That's the question. I've a feeling she's not going to settle down here. Don't ask me how I know, but I think she's up to summat. Very secretive she's become, just lately.'

'Well, I've been in the army for ages,' broke in Ronnie, 'and I'll tell you what. I'm more than ready to settle down; in my old job as well. I'm not wanting anything any different.'

'You've got a wife and child, Ronnie,' said his mother. 'Our Chrissie hasn't – got a husband, I mean. And that's another thing . . .' She stopped talking suddenly. 'Oh well, never mind, eh? I expect it'll all sort itself out in time. The war's over and that's the important thing when all's said and done. We're at peace again, and that takes some believing . . .'

'Now, Eunice; this Victory party. You've said you'll help, won't you? Serving the teas and then helping to organise the games?'

'What about me?' asked Ronnie. 'Can I help?'

'Of course you can,' said his mother. 'But you'll have your hands full looking after Sammy, won't you, while his mummy's busy?'

'Yes,' said Ronnie, grinning proudly. 'I will that. Getting to be a proper little handful, isn't he, Eunice? Do you know, Mam, he walked all the way home from the station this afternoon . . .'

'Seems as though you were right about Chrissie,' said Eunice to Ronnie later that night. 'Your poor mum; she was quite upset. Do you think she suspects anything?'

'No, I don't think so,' said Ronnie. 'Or if she does, then

she doesn't understand it. She can't quite work it all out in her mind.'

'Do you think Chrissie and Fiona are planning to stay together?' asked Eunice.

'I wouldn't be at all surprised,' said Ronnie. 'Maybe they'll get a flat together somewhere; after all, there's nothing unusual in that, is there – two young women sharing a flat?'

'Where? In Blackpool, or up in Scotland?'

'Goodness me, I don't know, Eunice. No . . . somehow I don't think Chrissie will come back to Blackpool.'

'What about us trying to get a place of our own?' said Eunice. 'We can't go on living with my parents for ever, can we?'

'We're OK for the moment,' said Ronnie. 'It's handy living near the shop. I'm starting work again next week. And if you come and help out there while my parents are on holiday, then we'll need your mother, won't we, to look after Sammy? We've got a roof over our heads and a lot to be thankful for. Come here now . . .' He drew her into his arms. 'We've done quite enough talking. Let me show you how pleased I am to be home . . .'

The Victory party was a resounding success. The day was warm and sunny with only the gentlest breeze to flutter the flags and buntings. Trestle tables were set up in the middle of the road from which, of course, all traffic was banned for the afternoon. Each child had to bring his or her own chair and crockery: a plate, cup and bowl. One advantage of this was that each mother would do her own washing up after the party was over.

There were few colours to be seen in the street that afternoon apart from red, white and blue. The girls wore cotton frocks, many of them in blue or red checked gingham, and had red, white and blue ribbons tying up their plaits or curls. The boys were not quite so colourful. White shirts seemed to be the order of the day and a few red or blue pullovers. Many of the children wore home-made paper hats. There was still a shortage of paper – it was a commodity not to be wasted – but some had been spared for this special occasion and cut into zigzag shapes to represent crowns. And many children waved Union Jacks, although these had to be put to one side when the eating commenced.

Eunice, Edith and Mabel were among the dozen or so women who served the excited children, going along the length of the table offering, first of all, the sandwiches. Edith had decreed that the bread and butter stuff – or, more correctly, bread and margarine – must be offered first, otherwise, given a choice between that and cakes, the sandwiches would be left.

There was a huge variety of sandwiches, as they had been made by many different people: salmon paste, bloater paste, Spam, corned beef, pilchards, banana. This fruit, absent from the shops for so long – indeed, many children had never set eyes on a banana before – was now available again in short supply. It made a novel sandwich if mashed up finely and spread over the bread, although it was turning a little brown by now. There were jam sandwiches too, made by those frugal housewives who could not spare anything else, but they were always popular with the children who did not mind the jam oozing from the sides in a gooey mess and getting all over their fingers. They did not seem to care overmuch what they were eating; they were all so wild with excitement at being together in such novel surroundings. There were gallons of orange squash, poured into cups and beakers, not without the occasional spill on the tablecloth or party dress, but there were no cross words that afternoon.

There were piles of sandwiches left, however, to be eaten for supper later in the evening in many of the helpers' homes. But short work was made of the cakes – mainly jam tarts and buns iced in red, white and blue – the jellies and the trifles, covered with mock cream and hundreds and thousands.

Then the crockery was cleared away, the tables and chairs moved to one side and it was time for the games to begin. One might have wondered how the children could jump about after consuming all that food, but, needless to say, they did, and without anyone being sick, which was quite a miracle. There were children of all ages, ranging from toddlers of Sammy's age to eleven- and twelve-year-olds. The older boys and girls, those who were already at senior school, considered themselves too old for childish games. They had not been unwilling to join in the eating, but when it came to the time for the games and races they stood to one side or, in some cases, offered to help. Eunice and the two other young women who had been delegated as games organisers were only too glad of assistance. There were sixty or so excitable youngsters who required a good deal of calming down and sorting out into circles and lines. Fortunately, however, there were no rebellious children, just an overflowing of high spirits, and they all joined in willingly with the time-honoured games they had grown up with: 'The Farmer wants a Wife'; 'A-Hunting We Will Go'; 'B-I-N-G-O'; 'The Big Ship sails through the Alley-alley-o'; and the hokey cokey.

Eunice, as well as doing her share of organising, was keeping her eye on her own little boy. His daddy was holding him by the hand, as did the mums or dads of other toddlers, letting them join in the less boisterous of the games. He was dressed in patriotic colour too: a blue romper suit made by Edith, and a red cardigan his other gran had knitted for him. His face was beaming with delight and he waved his little flag triumphantly although he could not have understood what it was all about.

At the end of the festivities he took part in the toddlers' race. Eunice was apprehensive lest he should fall and her heart was in her mouth as she watched him trot gamely towards the finishing line without stumbling once. He did not win, but he was delighted with the bag of jelly sweets that the little ones were all given. Ronnie ran to pick him up and he stared round, looking for Eunice in the crowd of grown-ups.

'Mummy, Mummy,' he yelled when he spotted her. 'Look, look . . .' He waved his bag of sweeties and his flag, nearly poking his daddy's eye out in the process.

Eunice's heart nearly burst with pride and joy as she waved back to him. Her very own little son, and her husband. She was fortunate, indeed, and she resolved again, as she had done before, to put the past behind her and to count her blessings.

Mabel and Tom wasted no time in arranging their holiday. As she had told Eunice and Ronnie, Mabel intended to 'strike while the iron was hot' and make a booking before Tom changed his mind. Not that she thought he would, but there was no harm in making sure. It was mid-September when they set off from North Station, early one Saturday morning. It was a long journey to Torquay, but they were as excited as a couple of youngsters as they waved goodbye to Eunice and to little Sammy. The child, for once, had condescended to ride in his pushchair. He had been told that his mummy was in a hurry to get back to Gran and Granddad's shop because she was going to help his daddy while they were away. And he had to be a good boy for

Grandma Edith, who was going to look after him.

'He's always a good boy, aren't you, Sammy?' said his doting grandmother. 'We're going to have some fun together, you and me, aren't we? It's just for this week, mind, while Mabel and Tom are away. I don't really approve of working mothers.'

'Yes, just for this week, Mum,' said Eunice. 'That's all . . .'

She enjoyed her week at the grocery store even more than she had anticipated. Ronnie had been back working there for three weeks and at his departure each morning she had started to feel rather lonesome again. She had seized eagerly on his suggestion that she should help out at the shop. It would be wonderful to get out of the house each day and to meet and talk with people, even though they might only be neighbours and acquaintances, many of whom she had known for most of her life.

She wore the white overall, like Ronnie's, which Mabel usually wore, but gathered in at the waist with a broad belt; she was several sizes smaller than her mother-in-law. The staple foodstuffs were still rationed, and it was forecast that this would continue for several years, and the points system still operated for tinned goods. Items that had been in short supply, however, were beginning to find their way back into the shops: eggs, oranges and bananas, and there was a plenitude of apples and pears from the local farms, as it was now harvest-time. Tinned fruit too, and tinned meat and salmon, and jam and marmalade. The jam was still mainly of the plum variety, and the marmalade was rather lacking in peel, but the jars were colourful and made an attractive display on the shelves.

It was the week for harvest festival services and celebrations to be held in the local churches and schools, and children would be reminding their mothers that they must take a basket of fruit. Eunice hit on the idea of making up baskets – or, rather, cardboard shoe boxes covered with crepe paper – herself, and these proved to be very popular. One precious banana, one orange, plus a few rosy apples and mellow plums and pears made an attractive little gift to lay on a table or near an altar.

As she handled the fruit, especially the rich red Worcesters and the Cox's Orange Pippins, streaked with russet and gold, she found herself thinking of the orchard at Meadowlands; the autumn sunshine glinting through the leaves of the apple trees, the branches laden with fruit and the windfalls lying on the grass, and, inevitably, of the young man who had worked along with her gathering the harvest. Then, as if from nowhere, a tune popped into her head.

'Don't Sit Under the Apple Tree . . .' She remembered dancing with Ronnie at the Tower Ballroom to the tune, and, as clearly as anything, she could hear the voice of the young woman vocalist, and then Ronnie saying to her, 'You won't, will you? You won't sit under the apple tree with anyone else but me?' She had said that of course she wouldn't. She was engaged to him; of course she would not be unfaithful. But it was too late; she had already betrayed him . . .

'Penny for them,' said Ronnie, stealing up behind her as she stood in the storeroom at the back of the shop, an apple in each hand. He put his arms round her waist. 'You looked as though you were miles away, darling.'

'You made me jump,' she said, laughing. 'Yes . . . actually I was miles away. The apples made me think of Meadowlands, of Mr and Mrs Meadows and . . . and Olive. I was wondering how they were all getting on.' Well, it was partly the truth.

'Oh, yes; Olive,' said Ronnie. 'I remember you telling me about her. Rather a clinging vine, wasn't she? I got the impression you didn't get on awfully well with her.'

'She was OK,' said Eunice dismissively. 'She was insecure and homesick, but then so were we all at first, though some didn't admit it.'

'Happy days, eh?' said Ronnie.

'Some of them were. You tend to forget the bad times, don't you?' she went on. 'I was just remembering the sunny days in the orchard . . . not the freezing cold mornings in the cowshed, or the rain trickling down your neck when you were picking sugar beet. I expect Olive'll be married to Ted now; you know, the farm hand she got friendly with. I wonder . . .'

'Why don't you get in touch with her?' asked Ronnie. 'For old times' sake and all that.'

'No; I don't know her address,' said Eunice hurriedly, although it would probably be easy enough to find out. Eunice still sent a Christmas card to Mr and Mrs Meadows and probably Olive did the same. 'Anyway, we weren't bosom pals; not like you and Jack, or Chrissie and Fiona . . . I didn't really make any close friends in the Land Army.'

'No, you weren't in it all that long, were you?' Ronnie grinned broadly. 'Thanks to our little . . . er . . . indiscretion.'

'Yes, that's true,' said Eunice thoughtfully.

'Don't you miss him?' asked Ronnie. 'Our little Sammy.'

'Of course I do. But he's OK with my mother this week. I sometimes think he's hardly missed me,' she added, rather regretfully.

Chapter 18

Eunice realised there was a big wide world out there that she knew very little about. She had been living a sheltered, provincial sort of life with only her small son and her immediate family for company. Working in the shop for a week had opened her eyes. Admittedly, she had not moved out of the area. The people she had met were neighbours, plus the occasional visitors taking a late-season holiday and a couple of travelling salesmen. But it has been refreshing to see different faces and to chat with people she had only been on nodding terms with beforehand.

Moreover, she realised that being away from Sammy had not done him – or her – any harm. He was used to her mother who loved the child very much, and he had accepted the fact that he would not be seeing his mummy until she came back from the shop at teatime. Sometimes she had gone home at dinnertime whilst the shop was closed from one until two o'clock, but her mother, oddly, had seemed to resent this. Edith had made it clear that she was the one in charge of Sammy that week although, perversely, she had also made it clear to Eunice that this 'going out to work lark' was only to be a temporary measure. Mother and daughter were getting along well enough now, but old habits died hard and Edith could not help her bossiness coming to the fore now and again.

Times were changing, if only a little at the moment, and some women were beginning to question their role as housewives or, in many cases, as skivvies for ungrateful husbands. Women had been employed in all sorts of work during the war, which had hitherto been only the province of men – as bus conductresses, or even as drivers, as railway guards or in heavy industry – and many of them resented handing their jobs back to the menfolk when they returned from the war. There was a feeling in some quarters that anything a man could do a woman could do just as well.

Eunice looked back to the time when she had been a working girl. Before she had given it up to join the Land Army she had been a librarian, and what happy days they had been, she reminisced now. She had been surrounded by books, which she had always loved, and she had had ambitions, then, to leave the small Boots library and apply for a position in one of the Blackpool branch libraries, or even the main one in Queen Street. And then the war had put paid to her plans. Indeed, it had seemed more tempting, then, to join up and get away from home for a spell.

But things were different now. People were settling down again to life in a peaceful Britain, albeit a largely austerity one, and looking to the future.

Eunice knew that her future, for the present, lay solely with her husband and child. Some day, maybe, she might resume her career as a librarian, but for the moment she was contented. Sammy was nearly two and a half. She and Ronnie had talked about having another child, but so far nothing had happened. And it was not for the want of trying, she thought mischievously. She would love to have another baby; the little girl she had always dreamed about, she pondered . . . but she reminded herself that another boy would be just as welcome.

The only – very slight – worry on an otherwise cloudless horizon was her concern for Ronnie. He did not admit there was anything wrong, but he was not always the bright and cheerful person he had been before the war started and for quite a while afterwards . . . in fact, until he had received his war injuries.

She had known he had suffered from depression, but at the time of their marriage he had seemed to have recovered from it, and he had been thrilled at the birth of Sammy. But she had noticed, since he had returned to work at the shop, that he had become, from time to time, a little moody and withdrawn; not very often, but often enough for her to notice. He seemed less tolerant of Sammy too, frowning or occasionally tutting when the little boy made what Ronnie obviously thought was too much noise or too much of a mess.

Eunice tried to understand. She knew that depression stemming from war injuries could recur for quite a while afterwards. Her own father was a case in point. She recalled that her mother had said how the war had changed him. Eunice had never known him to be any other than a very taciturn, sometimes moody, man, although he could, on rare occasions, speak his mind. Oh dear! She did so hope that Ronnie would not turn into that sort of person; she had believed him to be so very different from her father.

During the week his parents had been in Torquay, however, Ronnie had seemed much improved. She wondered if, maybe, he would prefer to work on his own, away from his parents? There was little chance of that, though. They depended on Ronnie as he, indeed, depended on them.

Mabel and Tom had come back from their holiday in Torquay in high spirits. They called round to see Ronnie and Eunice and little Sammy – plus Edith and Samuel, of course – on the Saturday evening. They both went into raptures about the Devon resort, Mabel more so than Tom, who usually left most of the talking to his wife.

'You should see all the palm trees and the yachts in the harbour and the blue sky,' she enthused. 'You'd think you were in the south of France, honestly you would.'

'Hmm . . . I dare say it rains, though, sometimes, doesn't it,' remarked Edith, 'same as it does here?'

'Not while we were there, it didn't,' countered Mabel. 'We had an Indian summer, didn't we, Tom? The sun shone all the time, and the sea was that calm, just like a mill pond. We had a sail in a little boat across to Brixham, and another day we went out to Cockington Forge; real oldy worldy, wasn't it, Tom?'

'Aye, but it's back to reality now, lass,' he said. 'You'd best start coming down to earth. We've a shop to run.'

'Oh, I know that, Tom, and I'm ready an' all. But the rest has done me good, it has that. You and Samuel should try and get away for a break,' Mabel said, turning to Edith. 'You'd love Torquay. Of course I know it's a bit late now for this year, but perhaps next spring . . . I should think about it if I were you.'

'Don't forget we've a boarding house to run, at least I have,' said Edith. 'I can't go taking time off whenever I feel like it.'

Mabel and Tom had gone back home soon afterwards, making the excuse that they had a lot of unpacking to do, but Eunice knew there had been something of an atmosphere and it was her mother who had caused it. Edith had even more to say when they had gone.

'How does she think we can afford a holiday in a posh

place like that? We're not made of money.' Eunice did not answer that remark; even if they were not made of money she knew her parents could well afford to go away if they wished. 'Anyroad, what have I been doing while they've been gadding about? I've been left holding the baby, that's what I've been doing. Not that I minded having Sammy, don't get me wrong, Eunice, but some of us have been working jolly hard while they've been living it up.'

Eunice held her tongue. She could see her mother was somewhat overwrought. Maybe she could do with a holiday, as Mabel had suggested. So could most people after six years of war, but Eunice could not remember the last time, even before the war started, that her parents had taken a holiday.

'I think Mabel's right,' she said. 'You could do with a holiday, you and Dad. Why don't you think about it?'

'Don't talk daft, Eunice. We've got visitors in, and then it'll be winter.'

'It won't be winter just yet. Next spring then, before the visitors start coming.'

'Oh, I don't know. We'll have to see about it . . .'

Eunice certainly hoped her mother would 'see about it'. Apart from the fact that it might do her a lot of good, it would be wonderful to have the house to themselves for a while, just her and Ronnie and Sammy. She wondered sometimes if that was what was wrong with Ronnie: that he was, in truth, fed up living with in-laws.

'I'm sorry about Mother,' she said to Mabel the next week when she took Sammy to see his daddy and his grandparents in the shop. 'She was so offhand with you. I was quite embarrassed.'

'Oh, don't you worry about that,' laughed Mabel. 'I know your mother only too well; I should do by now, and I'm not easily offended . . . To be quite honest,' she added confidingly, 'I get the impression she would really like a holiday, but I think it's your dad. He's . . . well, he's a bit of a stick-in-the-mud, isn't he, dear? If she could persuade him that she needs a break, then he might listen. Or perhaps you might have a word with him?'

'Yes, I might,' said Eunice, a little unsurely; she had never been given to tête-à-têtes with her father. 'My mother certainly needs a break . . . perhaps from me as much as from everything else,' she added.

'Oh dear!' said Mabel. 'I thought you were getting on well now?'

'Well, so we are, up to a point, but Ronnie and I wish we could get our own place. There doesn't seem to be much of a chance of that at the moment though.'

There was a housing shortage in Blackpool, as in other towns, although council houses were starting to be built on the outskirts of the town and there were pre-fabs going up on some spare land in Bispham. Ronnie had put their names on the housing list. But he was talking also about saving up enough to put a deposit down and buy a little house of their own.

Eunice's friends were all settled in their own homes. Jack and Trixie had now been married for two years and already had two children, a boy of eighteen months and a three-month-old baby girl. They had been granted a council flat on the outskirts of Bradford, having had their names on the housing list from the day of their marriage. They had moved in only a couple of months ago and Trixie had enthused wildly about it in one of her – very occasional – letters; about the view over the hills from their sixth-storey window and her shiny new kitchen. In the early days of their marriage they had lived in furnished rooms, as there was no space for them at either of their parents' homes.

Eunice had suspected when she and Ronnie, with little

Sammy, had gone to the wedding that Trixie was already pregnant; and that had soon proved to be the case. They had had their posh fairy-tale wedding, however, which was what Trixie had so much wanted, and now they had settled down cheerfully and happily to what must be a life, if not of hardship, then certainly not one of plenty. Eunice did not doubt that they would have a child each year until they had the five or six they were aiming for.

She often looked back to that day, recalling how radiant Trixie had looked in her billowing dress of parachute silk, with her two bridesmaids, one of her own and one of Jack's sisters, dressed in vivid pink, Trixie's favourite colour. Their dresses had been made from the same length of parachute silk, dyed by her mother; a little streakily, but it was very effective. No one ever enquired where the silk came from, but many brides of that era managed to acquire some. Then there had been the rowdy reception in the church hall with relatives and friends in abundance from both sides of the family. Eunice guessed that Ronnie had been a little disappointed not to be asked to act as best man as Jack had originally suggested, but Jack had explained that he was obliged to ask one of his several brothers. Ronnie and Jack were still best mates. Jack and a heavily pregnant Trixie had spent a week at Edith's boarding house earlier that year. Edith had magnanimously lowered the charges, which Jack had appreciated without being the least bit offended. Edith could be very sympathetic when it suited her. Eunice was pleased for them that they were so happy. They seemed to radiate contentment and joy.

It was the same with Gwen and Bill, although their circumstances were vastly different. They had moved back to Blackpool a few months ago, at the end of the war when Bill was demobbed. The house that Gwen had been left by her mother had been sold, and with the proceeds they had bought – outright – a small house on the outskirts of the town in North Shore. Bill had found employment as a garage mechanic, the job he had done before the war, and he hoped one day to have his own business. Eunice guessed it would be sooner rather than later. He was a very go-ahead young man. Gwen had lost her beloved mother, and that, of course, had distressed her greatly, but since then life had been quite pleasant. They had a delightful little daughter, Belinda, aged nine months – she had arrived sooner than they both had planned, but she was very welcome for all that – and Gwen, like Trixie, was the very personification of contented motherhood.

Eunice met her old friend, Mavis Foxton in town, quite by chance, one Saturday afternoon just before Christmas, and it was obvious that Mavis was now wildly enthusiastic about her career as a junior school teacher. She had been fortunate to be given a post in Blackpool, not far from where she lived.

'Hello there; how lovely to see you again.' Mavis greeted Eunice warmly and Eunice agreed that it was, indeed, good to see her. She felt sorry, and a little guilty too, that she had not kept in touch with her. They had been quite close friends at school and then life had taken them in entirely different directions.

'So this is your little boy, then?' said Mavis after various pleasantries had been exchanged. 'He's a grand young fellow, isn't he?'

'Well, yes; I think so,' smiled Eunice.

'You called him Samuel, didn't you? I remember that was your father's name, wasn't it?'

'Yes, but we call him Sammy.'

'Hello, Sammy.' Mavis beamed at the child, who was tugging at his mother's hand, none too keen at waiting whilst she chatted on the street corner.

'Say hello to Mavis,' prompted Eunice, but he scowled and hid behind her coat, quite surprisingly, as he was usually a friendly little boy. She felt rather annoyed with him. Children always seemed to let you down when you most wanted to show them off and she wanted her friend to see what a grand little lad he was. But she supposed he was tired. They had been in town for a couple of hours and he had insisted on walking most of the time.

'He's tired,' she explained. 'Into your pushchair then, young man, if you're not going to talk to us.' She lifted him into the pram and he didn't protest. A yawn showed her that he probably was getting weary of town and the child's-eye view of little else but the pavement and grown-ups' legs.

'How old is he now?' asked Mavis.

'Nearly two and a half.'

'He's like his daddy, isn't he? What I remember of Ronnie, that is. I didn't know him very well.'

'Yes, the image of him.' Eunice smiled.

'I've heard news of you from time to time,' said Mavis, 'even though I haven't seen you. It's funny, isn't it, that we haven't bumped into one another before, with us both still living in Blackpool? But then you're at the north end of the town and I'm in South Shore. I was really lucky to get a teaching post so near to my home. Not quite on the doorstep, though; it doesn't do to live on top of the kids you teach, but it's near enough to make travelling quite easy. There's a handy bus from the end of the road.'

'You're still living with your parents then?'

'Oh no; didn't I say? No, I moved out about six months ago. I share a flat – well, furnished rooms, really – with a teacher friend. A female friend, I hasten to add,' she laughed. 'Teachers are not exactly overpaid, but the rent's not all that high, and it beats living at home, I can tell you! You need a bit of independence, don't you?'

'Er, yes . . . I suppose you do.'

'What about you and Ronnie? You've got your own place, I expect?'

'No, as a matter of fact we haven't; not yet. We're still at my mother's – at the boarding house, you know. There's plenty of room and it makes sense to stay there for the moment. We've got our own rooms, of course. It's like a flat, really . . .' This was not strictly true. They had their own bedroom and a very small adjoining room, now, for Sammy to sleep in, but they all dined together and, for the most part, spent the evening together as well. 'But we're hoping to move out before very long,' she added. 'Ronnie is talking about putting a deposit down and buying our own house.'

'Very nice,' said Mavis. 'You must be doing well.'

'Yes, not so badly. Ronnie works in his parents' business. You remember, the grocery shop? Yes, they're doing very nicely. There's not much competition round there.'

'And it will be yours one day, I suppose; yours and Ronnie's?'

'I suppose so; I've never really thought about it,' said Eunice. 'I worked there for a while in the autumn while Ronnie's parents were on holiday, but I wouldn't like to do it as a regular job. What about you, Mavis? You're quite a career girl now, aren't you? There's no . . . boyfriend in the picture?'

'Not at the moment,' replied Mavis – a trifle edgily, Eunice thought. 'There have been one or two. There was a nice RAF lad that I met at the Winter Gardens – he was training to be a pilot, actually – but . . . well, I don't know what happened to him. And there's a young man I work with who seems quite interested; very interested, in fact . . .

But yes, you're right; my career is important to me. I really enjoy it. We're up to our eyes at the moment, of course, with Christmas; carols and cards and Nativity plays; never a spare moment. I'm shopping for some odds and ends now for our play – crepe paper and glitter and all that, if I can get any. I'm going to look in Woolie's.'

'If I remember rightly you weren't exactly looking forward to being a teacher, were you?' said Eunice. 'I mean . . . it was what your mother wanted, wasn't it, and you decided you'd better go along with it.'

'At the time, yes,' said Mavis. She smiled. 'I suppose there's something in the saying "Mother knows best". Not that I tell her that. She thinks she's always right, but in this case she was. I am enjoying my job.'

She certainly looked very well, thought Eunice, and attractively dressed too. Mavis was wearing a coat that looked like Persian lamb – rather too old for her, but very smart – with a close-fitting velvet hat and black suede wedge-heeled shoes. She doubted that a teacher's salary would run to Persian lamb; it might be an artificial fabric or the coat may have been passed on to her by her mother. She remembered the Foxtons had been quite well off and the mother often used to pass on scarcely worn clothes to her daughter. Eunice, in her old tweed coat, which she had had since the start of the war, and with a headscarf tied round her head, felt rather dowdy.

'All mothers think they know best,' she said now, in answer to her friend's remark. 'Mine always did. You remember her, of course?'

'Having a little grandson hasn't mellowed her then?'

'Oh, yes; quite a lot actually – at least as far as Sammy's concerned. She thinks the world of him.'

'And are you planning on having a little sister or brother for him?'

'Yes . . . we certainly hope so,' said Eunice.

'You were a librarian, weren't you, before the war?'

'That's right.' Mavis was smiling at her, but Eunice could not help thinking there was something patronising about her glance.

'Well, I'd better be going,' she said. 'Look, he's dropped off; it shows how tired he was.' Sammy was now fast asleep and looking the picture of innocence.

'Aah . . . bless him,' cooed Mavis, smiling sweetly at the little boy. 'We must keep in touch, Eunice, now we've met up again. Here – wait a minute – I'll give you my address.' She scribbled on a piece of paper from her bag and gave it to Eunice. 'If ever you feel like a night out, drop me a line and I could get a few of the girls round. I'm still in touch with Dorothy and Margaret and Joan . . .' girls who had been in their form at the grammar school, '. . . and we could have a get-together.'

'Yes, why not?' said Eunice. 'Cheerio then, Mavis. Lovely to see you. I'll keep in touch . . .'

She doubted very much that she would, although she had nothing against Mavis. It was just that they seemed to have grown apart and Mavis was very much a career woman now. One person to whom Eunice was still very close, however, was Gwen, but that was because they still had a lot in common: each of them had a husband and a baby. One big difference, though, was that Gwen and Bill had their own home and that was something that Eunice and Ronnie, as yet, had not achieved. As she had just told Mavis – making it sound better than it actually was – they were still living at her mother's boarding house.

Eunice was thoughtful as she hurried back home, walking quickly to get sleepy Sammy out of the cold early evening air. It was dark now at four o'clock and she had stood talking to Mavis longer than she had intended.

Strangely enough, she had got quite used to living at her mother's now, although she looked forward, of course, to the time when they would have a place of their own. Since that – now long ago – incident of 'Sammy and the potty', as she termed it to herself, she and her mother had rubbed along together reasonably well. Edith could not help being assertive, even bossy, at times; it was in her nature to be so. The two of them had occasional 'words', but on the whole she felt that they all got along quite well.

It was Ronnie now who seemed discontented. His bouts of depression, infrequent at first, had increased as the autumn gave way to winter. Eunice, as gently and tactfully as she could, had begged him to tell her what was wrong. She knew a lot of it was due to his war experiences – and that, she hoped, would diminish with time – but there must be something else that was making him so moody, so unlike the young man she had married. Eventually he had told her: he felt that he was a failure. He had not managed to get his little family a home of their own, in spite of his promises. He was saving up like mad, but still he did not have enough for a down payment on a house and he was determined not to ask his parents for help. And the council housing list, so far, had not come up with anything.

Eunice knew also that living with his in-laws was beginning to annoy him. He had used to be so tolerant of her mother and her little ways – her fussiness and bossiness, and her insistence, still, on calling him Ronald. He had used to laugh it off, but now she could see him gritting his teeth, unable sometimes to disguise his look of irritation. Edith, strangely, had appeared not to be aware of it, but then she had always 'flown the flag', as it were, for her son-in-law.

Eunice was glad to get in out of the increasing cold and

damp. Sammy woke up as she trundled the pushchair into the hall.

'Gran . . .' he shouted, holding out his arms as her mother came to greet them.

'Hello there, Sammy.' Edith kissed his cheek. 'My goodness, you're as cold as a little snowman! I'll get his things off, Eunice, while you make us a cup of tea. There's a few more cards come for you in this afternoon's post. I think that must be nearly the last, don't you? What a lot we've had this year . . .'

Eunice settled down by the fire with her cup of tea to open the Christmas cards. Sammy had soon come round after his nap and was zooming his cars about on the carpet with appropriate 'Brrr, brrr . . .' sounds. It was her mother's turn to make the evening meal today – they had decided, eventually, that just one of them should be responsible for it each day, giving the other a rest – and she had taken her cup of tea with her into the kitchen.

Eunice smiled as she opened the cards. It always made her feel happy to receive the age-old messages and pictures of Nativity scenes, robins, snowmen and Dickensian winters. One from Bill, Gwen and Belinda; two from old schoolfriends with whom she had – sort of – kept in touch; two from regular customers at the grocer's shop – how nice of them, she thought, to send a separate card to Ronnie and herself as well as to his parents; one from Phyllis, the friendliest one of the civil servants who had been billeted with them . . .

As she drew the last card from its envelope she noticed there was a letter enclosed inside. She did not recognise the writing as she had done with some of the other cards, but she had noticed that it was addressed just to her and not to both of them; but it said Miss Eunice Iveson, not Mrs. How very odd . . . She glanced first at the card, a stable scene with a donkey and oxen as well as the baby in the manger. Then, on opening it, she nearly cried out loud as she looked at the signature. 'To Eunice, With love, Heinrich.'

Heinrich! After all this time; after – how many? – more than three years. With trembling hands she opened the letter and began to read.

> Dear Eunice,
>
> You will be surprised to hear from me after so long, but I knew I must wait until the war had ended before I wrote to you. Please believe me when I say that I have never stopped thinking about you and I am so very sorry that we parted in such an abrupt way.

She reflected on how good his English was now. Of course he had been a clever and intelligent young man, already trying to improve his knowledge of the foreign language when she had known him.

> I loved you, Eunice. I believe that I still do, but I realise things might be different now, for you. The day after we met in the barn at Meadowlands Werner and I were moved unexpectedly to another farm. I expect Mr Meadows told you this, but I was unable to contact you myself. A week later several of us were moved to a different part of the country and that is where I am still working.

She glanced at the address at the top of the letter: High Tor Farm, near Ilfracombe, Devon.

> Devon is a beautiful part of your country and I have been happy here, as happy as I can be so far from

home and from those I love. Now we are at peace, Eunice, and how we thank God for that. Soon, maybe, I will be allowed to return to Germany. I think I will do so, but that depends on you. I would like to see you again if that is possible, or at least to hear from you and to know you have not forgotten me.

The farmer's wife here is a very understanding lady and she has helped me to write this letter. It was she who persuaded me to write to Mrs Meadows to ask for your address, also your full name. I had known you only as Eunice. But I needed to deceive her a little knowing that she might not have approved of our friendship. I said I was an old Land Army friend who wanted to get in touch with you and I called myself Harriet Miller. A good joke, yes?

I hope you are well and happy and that you have not forgotten me. You have always been in my thoughts. *With my love, Heinrich.*

Eunice sat there mesmerised for a few moments and then, coming to her senses, she shoved the letter and card back into the envelope and hid them away in her handbag. She could not understand why he did not realise she was married. Mrs Meadows had given him her married name, but she must, obviously, have omitted the Mrs. It was strange that she had known he was Heinrich Muller, but that he had known her just as Eunice.

But what was she to do? If the letter had arrived – say – three months ago she would have thrown it away without any hesitation. She was happily married to Ronnie and thoughts of Heinrich had seldom entered her head; even the feelings of guilt she had suffered for so long had been waning. But now . . . Ronnie was not himself. She knew it was only his depression and his feelings of inadequacy that were causing him to draw away from her, but she was concerned, and frustrated too, that they had not made love for several weeks. That had used to be one of the mainstays of their marriage. And so it was that her thoughts were straying towards Heinrich, recalling that golden summer and early autumn on the farm . . .

She shook her head and tried to pull herself together, realising it was time for Sammy to have his tea. He dined and was then put to bed before the rest of the family had their meal. And Ronnie would soon be home from the shop.

Her husband looked tired when he came in. The Saturdays leading up to Christmas were always hectic, but though tired, he seemed less tense and preoccupied. He chatted over the evening meal to Edith and Samuel far more than he had been doing of late. It was Eunice who was quiet, her thoughts drifting towards Heinrich and the letter burning a hole through the leather of her handbag. She felt, crazily, that everyone must know about it and must be aware of the change in her. But no one seemed to have noticed anything amiss.

During the Christmas period she was forced to pull her rambling thoughts back to the present. It was a happy family time. Little Sammy was wild with excitement and Ronnie was very much more like his old self. Eunice guessed that what he had needed more than anything at that time was a break from the shop routine; from the queues of customers, the home deliveries, the late working hours and all the extra work that Christmas brought.

They came together, at last, on Christmas Eve, and their lovemaking was just as wonderful as it had ever been.

'I'm sorry, Eunice,' he said as they lay quietly together. 'I've been such a grumpy old bear just lately, but I really will try, I promise, not to be so down in the dumps. I only want the very best for you, darling . . . and sometimes I feel that I can't do it. But next year, I promise, we'll have our own home. By hook or by crook, we will! Just . . . try to believe in me.'

'I do, Ronnie,' she replied. 'You must try not to worry about it.'

'Thank you for being so understanding,' he said, stroking her hair. 'I don't know what I would do without you. You would never leave me, would you, Eunice?'

'Of course I wouldn't, Ronnie,' she said. 'What a silly thing to say. We love one another and we've got our little Sammy, and that's all that matters.'

She had not answered the letter, still hidden away in her handbag. But, somehow, she felt that she couldn't destroy it.

It was at the end of February that she began to think she might be pregnant again. She did not say anything to anyone, not even to Ronnie, as she had been hopeful once or twice before, only to have had her hopes dashed. Her periods were still irregular, but the signs she remembered from before were there: the tenderness in her breasts and the slight queasiness in a morning.

In March her parents decided, at long last, to go away for a holiday. It was lovely and peaceful with them away. She felt a pang of conscience at the thought, but it was true. Edith and Samuel had taken some convincing, but at last they had been persuaded that a holiday would do them both a world of good.

'Nothing fancy, though, like Torquay,' her mother had argued. 'We can't afford them sort of prices; anyroad, it's too far. Morecambe or Southport would suit me fine.'

Finally they had booked on a coach tour with a local firm: seven nights in Scarborough, the resort almost opposite to Blackpool, but on the east coast, with excursions to Whitby, York and the North Yorkshire Moors.

There were no visitors booked in until the end of March and then, once Easter was over, there would be a lull until Whitsuntide. Bookings had been coming in steadily since January. Many were old faithfuls returning now the war was over, and Edith was well pleased that the business seemed to be picking up.

'We'll have our hands full this summer, Eunice,' she had said, as though taking it for granted that her daughter would still be there to help out. 'It'll be quite like old times. I remember when you were a little tot, you used to come round with me, helping me to clean the bedrooms, with your little dustpan and brush. That was when your gran was with us, of course. And now little Sammy will be doing the same. Yes, it'll be just like old times . . .'

But her mother did not know the good news. Eunice was sure now that she was pregnant.

She knew also it was time to get away to a place of their own, the sooner the better, before she and Ronnie and their children became entrenched there in the boarding house, as Edith and Samuel had been. Her parents too had never really had a home to call their own, at least not until her grandmother had died.

She told Ronnie her news when he came home that evening. He was more delighted than she had ever seen him, except, perhaps, for the time when he had first set eyes on his baby son.

'That's wonderful news, darling,' he said, throwing his arms round her, hugging and kissing her. 'You're sure about it, are you?'

'Well, as sure as I can be,' she said. 'You know how it is with me. That's why I didn't tell you earlier. But – yes – I'm sure. I'll go to the doctor, though, very soon, and make certain. You're pleased, then? Well, it's obvious that you are.'

'Pleased? I'm absolutely thrilled to bits . . . aren't you?'

'Do you really need to ask?' she laughed.

'I'm over the moon, absolutely.'

'Oh, Ronnie, aren't we lucky?'

He nodded. 'We should be in our own home, though.' He looked anxious again for a moment. Then he smiled. 'How about us going round to see my mam and dad tonight, to tell them the good news?'

'We'll have to take Sammy.'

'Well, yes, of course . . . Unless you think we ought to tell your parents first? You know what your mother's like; if she thought my parents had been told before her and your dad . . .'

'She won't mind. She's much more tolerant than she used to be,' replied Eunice. 'What does it matter? She'll know in a few days' time. I say, Ronnie, isn't it lovely having the house to ourselves?'

'Yes, I must admit it is. And you've managed to cook me a meal, all on your own.'

The idea was that the two women took it in turns, but seldom did Eunice manage to cook a meal without her mother's – well-meaning – assistance.

'Don't be so blooming cheeky! You know I can cook perfectly well, given the chance. Yes – liver and bacon and fried onions coming up, with my special mashed potatoes. Can't you smell it?'

'Yes, I can, and I'm starving too. Come on then, lass, get it on the table.'

She pulled a face at him as she returned to the kitchen. She knew he was only joking. But it was the first time since they were married that she had really had a chance to see what it was like to be completely on their own.

★ ★ ★

'Well, that's wonderful news,' said Mabel, kissing them both soundly on the cheeks, then picking up little Sammy and giving him a hug. 'A little sister or brother for you, young man. What about that, eh? He's just about the right age now, isn't he, to take notice of a new baby. Isn't it good news, Tom? And do your mother and dad know, Eunice?'

'No, not yet. They're away, aren't they, and I've only just told Ronnie. I wasn't sure, you see, at first. But now, well, all the usual signs are there.'

'Oh dear, you know what your mother's like,' said Mabel, just as Ronnie had said earlier. 'I won't let on that we knew first. Do you think that might be best?'

'Yes, maybe it would . . . We're going to move, though, Ronnie, aren't we, as soon as we can? My mother's very good really; I don't want to say anything wrong about her, but it's not always easy.'

'No, I'm sure it isn't,' said Mabel thoughtfully.

'I don't know about "soon",' said Ronnie. 'We've had our names on the housing list for ages.'

'You might still have a long wait, son,' said his father.

'Yes, I know, Dad, but it's the best we can do at the moment. Of course, if we were to hear of a flat coming vacant . . .'

Mabel and Tom looked at one another, and then Mabel began to speak. 'Listen, the pair of you, your dad and I have been thinking. Why don't you move in here with us? Well, actually I don't mean with us; I mean for you to have your own rooms. Our Chrissie won't be coming back, as you know . . .'

Chrissie had not really lived at home at all since leaving the WAAF. After she and Fiona had holidayed together they had paid a brief visit to Blackpool and then they had taken themselves off to Carlisle. They had found a flat there and both of them were now employed in the city as shorthand typists. Chrissie was working for a solicitor and Fiona for a firm of auctioneers and valuers. They had explained to Mabel and Tom that Carlisle, a city near the border of England and Scotland, was approximately midway between both their homes. It would be quite easy for them to travel either north to the Scottish Highlands or south to Blackpool. The two of them had spent Christmas in Blackpool, but Mabel and Tom seemed resigned to the fact that they would be seeing less and less of their daughter as time went by.

'Well, it's her life and I suppose we've got to let her live it the way she wants to,' Tom had said. Eunice wondered if he knew more about the relationship than he was letting on. It was never spoken of openly, and she guessed it would hurt Mabel dreadfully if she were to be made aware of the true situation. Mabel was still clinging to the belief that Chrissie would, one day, meet a nice young man and settle down to marriage.

'Our Chrissie's leading her own life,' she went on now, 'and I don't intend to keep her room for her, not if it can be put to a better use. She's moved most of her stuff out, anyroad.'

Mabel explained to Eunice and Ronald that they could have that bedroom. 'Chrissie always had a nice big double bed in there . . .' and the adjoining small room, which was commonly called a boxroom, for Sammy. Downstairs, the sitting room, usually referred to as the 'front room', was very rarely used except at Christmas or on special occasions. The family had always confined themselves to the room at the back of the house, which they called the kitchen. (Strictly speaking it was not a kitchen at all, because there was another small room, which they called the 'back kitchen', where the cooking and preparing of meals was done.) They dined in the back room and sat there in the evenings, listening to the wireless, reading, sewing or snoozing in the comfortable armchairs, and when the children were young they had done their homework on the table, cleared after the evening meal. This was the way of most folk who lived in terraced or semi-detached houses. The back room might be overcrowded with a dining table, four or six chairs, a large sideboard and a bulky suite comprising two armchairs and a settee, commonly called a couch, but it was the heart of the house.

The front room was special, usually quite sparsely furnished with another three-piece suite and a display cabinet containing the best china, EPNS silverware and various odds and ends, souvenirs and mementoes acquired throughout the marriage. Eunice recalled now that Mabel's front room had often smelled musty, and even felt a little damp, as a fire was only lit there on red-letter days such as Christmas and birthdays.

'And you can have our front room, just for the three of you; well, four of you quite soon, of course,' Mabel was saying. 'Tom and I never use it and it's daft, when you come to think of it, it standing there year after year, hardly ever being used. We'll start putting a fire in there to make it feel nice and cosy again; that fire draws just as well as the back one even though we've not used it much. And we might be able to get an extra coal allowance with two families living in the house. We'll get another table and a couple of chairs and . . . well, whatever else you think you might need . . . Just listen to me; I'm getting ahead of myself, aren't I?' She laughed. 'What do you think of the idea, then?'

Eunice and Ronnie looked at one another. He raised his

eyebrows questioningly. Ronnie spoke first. 'I think it's a great idea, Mam. Thanks very much. Don't you think so, Eunice?'

'Well, yes, I suppose so. It's just that—'

'I don't mean for ever,' Ronnie went on. 'Mam and Dad don't mean us to stay here for ever, do you, Mam? We've still got our names on the housing list and I'll still be saving up for our own place. But for the time being I think it would be great . . . Eunice?' He glanced at her a trifle anxiously.

'It's all right; I know what you're thinking,' said Mabel, looking at Eunice. 'You're wondering what your mother will say, aren't you, if you tell her you're leaving to come here?' Eunice nodded.

Her mother was much better nowadays, but the old rivalry between her and Mabel sometimes showed itself.

'It seems to me that it would do you both good, you and Edith, not to be living on top of one another,' said Mabel. 'They say two women can't share the same kitchen, but you're sharing a lot more than the kitchen, aren't you? It stands to reason you can't have your own rooms in the boarding house, except to sleep in, but we've loads of room here now there's only Tom and me. And as far as sharing the kitchen's concerned, I'll keep out of your way when you want to cook a meal, how about that? And you can do the same for me. We can work out a little timetable. I don't mean for ever, of course. Like Ronnie says, it would just be for the time being.'

'It sounds great,' said Eunice. 'Yes, I think I would really like to live here. It's been rather nice this week, being able to get Ronnie's meals ready without my mother inter— I mean, without my mother being there.'

'And Eunice is a smashing cook,' said Ronnie. 'That liver and bacon we had for tea . . .' He licked his lips appreciatively. 'Nearly as good as yours, Mam.' He winked at Eunice and she smiled back at him.

Yes, she thought it would work out just fine living there, and it was something that had never occurred to her at all.

Chapter 19

But what would her mother say about it? That was the thing that was worrying her. A certain amount of rivalry had grown up between the two sets of grandparents. It was the grandmothers really, most of it caused by her own mother. Edith never liked to think that she was being overshadowed by Mabel, either with the gifts she bought for the child – and Mabel could afford quite expensive ones – or the affection she showed him. At the moment Eunice was aware that her mother considered herself to be the leader in the grandmother stakes. She was the one who saw much more of the little boy, and she had had a share in his upbringing too, because the family was living with her. The boot would be on the other foot when Sammy lived in the same house as his paternal grandparents, and Eunice could see there might be friction ahead.

And then there was the fact that Mabel and Tom already knew about her pregnancy, whilst her own parents were still in ignorance. She would have to handle her mother with kid gloves when they returned from Scarborough.

They arrived back early on the Saturday evening. Eunice had been busy most of the afternoon cooking an appetising meal, as she was sure they would be hungry after travelling across the country. Edith kissed her daughter, but the hugs and coos of delight were reserved for little Sammy.

'I do believe he's grown,' she exclaimed. 'Don't you think so, Samuel? Just wait and see what Grandma's got in her case for you . . .'

'Leave your unpacking till later, Mum,' said Eunice. 'Come and have a meal first. I've made a steak and kidney pie; I expect you will be ready for it.'

They were regaled with tales of Scarborough as they ate their meal; at least Edith talked whilst Samuel sat quietly as usual, occasionally nodding, but sometimes making the odd comment that showed that he did not always agree with what his wife was saying.

'Yes, it's a very nice place, I must admit,' said Edith, as though unwilling to give any praise to the rival seaside resort. 'Lovely gardens and nice views from the cliffs.'

'Yes, grand views,' said Samuel. 'And you don't get that in Blackpool.'

'No, I know that, Samuel, but there was a biting east wind. It's much colder there than it is here. I certainly wouldn't want to live on the east coast, thank you very much. No, Blackpool suits me fine. Mind you, I'm glad we've been and we had some nice coach rides to York and to Whitby.'

'Whitby's a grand little place . . .' ventured Samuel.

'What! It stank of fish,' retorted Edith. 'No, I didn't reckon much to it myself. There's a harbour at Scarborough an' all. Your dad liked to go and watch the fishing boats, but that stank to high heaven as well.'

'Peasholm Park was nice,' said Samuel, trying again.

'Well, yes, I've got to admit it was quite nice; not a patch on Stanley Park, though. Our park here is much better and the lake is a lot bigger too.'

'And what was the hotel like?' asked Eunice, casting an amused glance at her husband. Her mother seemed determined not to concede that Scarborough had any charms or even to say they had enjoyed their holiday. She was longing to say, 'You might have done better to stay at home, Mother,' but she held her tongue. There was no point in getting on the wrong side of her when so much was at stake.

'The hotel? Oh, it was comfortable enough, I suppose,' replied Edith. 'We didn't have a sea view, though, like a lot of them did. That would be because we were late booking.'

'The food was good, though, Edith. You said yourself that—'

'I said myself that they put on a fairly decent spread, considering the shortages and rationing and all that. But no better than the visitors get here. Not as good, in fact.' She preened herself a little. 'I've got some new recipes I want to try out this summer. I was talking to a lady on the coach who has a boarding house at Morecambe and we exchanged a few ideas. We'll have to see what we can do, Eunice, to liven the menu up a bit. We should be able to get more foodstuffs before long. Goodness me; the war's been over for nearly a year.'

Eunice did not answer. She was waiting for the opportunity to tell her mother that, come the summer, she would not be here. There was silence for a few moments as they all ate the steak and kidney pie.

'Well, I must say this is very nice, Eunice,' said her mother, nodding approvingly when she had emptied her plate.

'Don't sound so surprised, Mother,' said, Eunice laughing. 'It was you who taught me to cook so well, wasn't it?' She realised that a bit of 'soft soap' would not go amiss before she told them the news; the two items of news. She decided there was no time like the present.

'We've got something to tell you, Ronnie and me,' she said. 'Well, two things actually. The first one is . . .' The good news first, she thought. '. . . we're going to have another baby.'

Her mother's mouth dropped open with surprise, although why she should be surprised Eunice could not imagine. 'Oh . . . oh goodness! Oh dear . . . Well then, that's—'

'That's very good news,' Samuel interrupted. 'Well done, the pair of you,' he added shyly. 'That's good news, isn't it, Edith? A little brother or sister for our Sammy, eh?'

'Yes . . . of course it is,' said Edith, smiling now. 'We're very pleased for you . . . if that is what you want.'

'Yes, it's what we want, Mum,' replied Eunice. 'Isn't it, Ronnie? We're thrilled to bits about it.'

'Well, that's lovely then,' said Edith. 'We'll talk about it while we have our pudding. I take it you've made a pudding as well, Eunice?'

'Yes, Mum; an apple crumble . . . made just the way you've taught me.' She went into the kitchen to dish it up, wondering how she was going to tell her mother the second piece of news: that they were to move away very soon to live with Ronnie's parents. But, as it happened, her mother gave her the very opening she needed.

'You could really do with your own place now your family is going to increase,' Edith remarked when she had taken a few mouthfuls of the pudding. 'This is a little tart, Eunice, if you don't mind me saying so. Baking apples need a lot of sugar . . . Now, what was I saying. Oh yes; there will be four of you before long. When did you say the baby was due?'

'I didn't say, but as far as we know it should be towards the end of September. That's what the doctor thought.'

Eunice had made certain of her condition with a visit to the family doctor a couple of days ago.

'Mmm . . . quite a while yet,' said Edith. 'But I'm beginning to think that living here won't be such a good idea, not with two children. Your daddy and I would never see you without a home, of course, but—'

Eunice smiled with relief. 'That's the other thing we were about to tell you, Mum. Ronnie and I are moving soon . . . aren't we, Ronnie?' She looked to her husband for support. 'As a matter of fact we are—'

'Yes, we're going to live with my parents,' Ronnie finished the sentence for her. 'Just for a while, I mean, not for ever,' he hastened to add. They had both caught a glimpse of the look of surprise – not very pleasurable surprise – on Edith's face. 'We've had our names on the housing list for ages, and I'm saving up to buy a little house of our own. This will be just for the meantime.'

'Mmm, I see. Well, I suppose that's all right then,' said Edith grudgingly. 'But I don't think Mabel will take very kindly to being woken up by a crying baby in the middle of the night. Don't forget she has a shop to run.'

'My mother will be fine,' said Ronnie. 'Don't worry about that. Anyway, as I've said, I do want us to have our own house quite soon.'

'Yes, you're a good lad, Ronald; I've never doubted that,' said Edith. 'I know I can rely on you to do your best for your little family. You'll need some help with a new baby, though, Eunice. You remember what a mess you got into with Sammy. Now if you were still living here . . .'

Eunice smiled to herself. She couldn't believe her mother sometimes. Edith had made it clear that she thought it was time they moved. Now, when it seemed as though the other grandma might turn out to have too much of a hand in bringing up the new baby, she was changing her tune.

'I'll be OK, Mum,' she replied. 'I'm three years older now, aren't I, and I'm much more experienced with babies. Anyway, you've said yourself that we should have a place of our own. Well, this is the first step. And Ronnie's mum will leave me alone; she won't interfere.'

Edith bristled slightly. 'I hope you're not implying that I do.'

'No, of course we're not.' It was Ronnie who spoke, with a meaningful glance at his wife. 'My mother will be there to help if she's needed, though, just as you will be. We'll only be round the corner, after all.'

Edith smiled, though still a little tight-lipped. 'Very well then. I hope you'll be very happy there, all of you.'

'I think it's wonderful news, all of it,' Samuel broke in, somewhat loudly and unexpectedly. 'And this apple crumble's really delicious, Eunice. Just as good as anything your mother could make.'

It was a wonder that the look Edith gave him did not strike him dead on the spot.

They were happily settled in their new surroundings by the end of April. They had acquired a second-hand drop-leaf table and four dining chairs from a saleroom; apart from that they made do with Mabel's furniture. The three-piece suite of brown moquette, which Mabel and Tom had had since the early days of their marriage, was made to look more homely with a few colourful cushions scattered around. Eunice did not consider herself to be much of a seamstress, but she quickly ran them up on her mother's Singer machine, from remnants of floral material she bought at Abingdon Street market.

Mabel had emptied the bureau bookcase-cum-display cabinet. The only books it had contained were tomes that were hardly ever read or even taken from the shelves;

neither Mabel nor Tom was a great reader. There was a Pears Encyclopaedia, Whittaker's Almanac, a cookery book by Mrs Beeton, the *Family Doctor*, a family Bible, a dictionary, and an out-of-date World Atlas, plus a few of Chrissie's old schoolgirl stories, mainly by Angela Brazil. The best cups and saucers, the silver tea service and the odds and ends of china from the upper shelves had been moved into the sideboard and cupboards in the back room.

Eunice had very few household possessions of her own as yet, but she displayed to their best advantage the rose-patterned tea set – a wedding present from Gwen and Bill – and a few small china ornaments and a cut-glass vase, which her mother had spared from her own display cabinet. The lower shelves, however, were quickly filled with Eunice's books, her old childhood favourites, and others she had bought recently, when she could afford them. Like Chrissie she had been an avid reader of the Angela Brazil stories; she had loved the schoolgirl heroines who turned out to be foreign princesses or long-lost relatives. But as well as these popular page-turners there were many of the childhood classics: *Black Beauty*, *Little Women* and *Good Wives*, *Treasure Island*, *Alice's Adventures in Wonderland* and *Through the Looking-Glass*, *The Railway Children* and, taking pride of place, *Anne of Green Gables* and several of the subsequent books, firm favourites with Eunice ever since, at the age of twelve or so, she had discovered this fascinating red-haired heroine.

Since Sammy had grown up a little and no longer occupied the whole of her time as he had done at first – it had amazed her how a tiny baby could completely take over one's life – she had rediscovered her love of reading. When she had worked at Boots Lending Library she had immersed herself in the light romances or the detective stories, chiefly by Agatha Christie, which had filled the major part of the bookshelves. Lately she had discovered not only the thrilling tales of such crime writers as Dorothy L. Sayers, Margery Allingham and Ngaio Marsh, but the works of other contemporary authors: J.B. Priestley, E.M. Forster, and Phyllis Bentley, whose sagas of Yorkshire millowners she found thoroughly engrossing. She discovered the classics too, many of which she had spurned as a schoolgirl, considering them to be dull and boring. Now she read for pleasure the works of Dickens, Thomas Hardy, the Brontë sisters, and the American writer Nathaniel Hawthorne. Many of the books she borrowed from the library, but she was gradually acquiring her own collection. When she could afford it she bought one of the classics bound in leatherette from Sweeten's or Coop and Naylor's bookshop on Abingdon Street.

When she had had time to browse in the town's bookshops it had strengthened her resolve to return eventually to her former job as a librarian. She had even dreamed, in her more fanciful moments, of having a bookshop of her own. But, for the moment, she was very contented.

She and Ronnie and Sammy had their very own space around them for the first time in their married life, and it was wonderful how much more at ease this made her feel. They had their own little place to dine in and to relax in of an evening, and Mabel had been as good as her word, staying away from the kitchen whenever Eunice wanted to prepare a meal.

Nevertheless, as the months drew on, time started to hang heavy for Eunice. There was only so much housework to be done in two rooms and her mother-in-law, with whom she might have spent the odd hour chatting and drinking tea, was always away working at the shop. Ronnie came home for his lunch occasionally, and always on a Wednesday as that was half-day closing at the shop; but most of the time he found it easier to take sandwiches as there were often odd jobs that needed doing whilst the shop was closed for an hour. Eunice had called to see her own mother a few times, but Edith had made it obvious that she had no time to stop and chat, not with a houseful of visitors due to return 'any minute now' for their midday dinner or high tea. Whichever time of the day Eunice called, it seemed to be inconvenient. Edith, of course, was still a little peeved by her daughter's departure and was determined not to be won round so easily.

Eunice took Sammy for long walks along the promenade. His little legs could not have coped with the distances she covered, north towards the cliffs at Norbreck or south towards the Pleasure Beach, and he was usually content to ride in his pushchair, shouting out in delight at the seagulls who swooped around in circles above his head. Very occasionally she took him on the sands, showing him how to fill up his little tin bucket and then upturn it to make a pie, but she would not let him paddle yet, not even in the rock pools left by the tide. There would be plenty of time for that in a year or two. By that time he would be able to appreciate the Boating Pool at North Shore, sitting up on the elephant's back on the automated ride, perhaps, as she had loved to do. She was looking forward, also, to introducing him to the delights of Fairyland at the end of the Golden Mile. By then, of course, his little sister would be here . . . or brother, she reminded herself.

She did not dare to think too earnestly about the daughter she longed for. She tried to convince herself, oftentimes, that another boy would be just as welcome; but she knew, deep down, that this was not true. She badly wanted a little girl, and no matter how much she tried to warn herself that she was just as likely to give birth to a boy, the longing would not go away.

She had already chosen the name for her baby daughter: Francesca, that was what she would call her. She hadn't discussed it with Ronnie, but she was sure he would fall in with her wishes.

By the end of her sixth month she was very tired, far too tired to take the long promenade walks, and she was rather concerned too about the amount of weight she was putting on. She had been large when she was expecting Sammy, but not as big, surely, she thought, as she was now. As the summer drew on, July, August and into early September, she felt as huge and ungainly as a whale. When she looked down she could not see her feet or her swollen ankles, only the elephantine protrusion which was making any movement a major upheaval: getting comfortable in a chair, going upstairs, using the toilet, making meals in the very small kitchen.

By mid-September she was longing for it to be all over. Even if it were a twelve-pound boy – which she felt it surely must be – she would not care, so long as she got her original shape back again. The doctor assured her that everything was in order and he could hear the baby's heart beat clearly. She was big, to be sure, but it was his guess that she was carrying a lot of water. He advised her to stop putting salt on her food and to rest as much as she could to ease her swollen legs and ankles. Just to be on the safe side he had made arrangements for her confinement at the nursing home on Whitegate Drive. She had argued that she wanted to give birth at home as she had done before, but the doctor – and Ronnie too – had insisted it would be for the best.

Sammy, now three years old, was becoming impatient that Eunice no longer wanted to play with him or take him for walks. He was playing up, to get her attention, unable to understand that she was tired and hardly able to bend down to play with him. This added to Eunice's longing for her pregnancy to be over.

Eunice went into labour, as predicted, towards the end of September. It was the early hours of Sunday morning.

'Well timed, darling,' said Ronnie. 'I don't have to go to the shop today. Isn't that lucky?'

He was only joking, as Eunice knew, but she was not really in a joking mood. Nor would Ronnie feel like making jokes if he felt like she did. Tom had bought a small second-hand van a few months ago to help with the shop deliveries, considering that both he and Ronnie were rather old now to be errand boys on bicycles. He and Ronnie had quickly learned to drive it and it was supposed to be used strictly for business purposes. The arrival of a baby, however, was considered to be an exception to the rule, and so Ronnie, having woken his parents to tell them that things were on the move, hurried round to the back entry behind the shop where they kept the van.

'Now, you've got everything you need in your case, have you, dear?' asked Mabel. Eunice had had her case packed in readiness for over a week now, as Mabel knew. 'For the baby as well as yourself? I dare say they will provide you with clothes and nappies at first, but it's nice to have your own, isn't it? Oh, I say; isn't it exciting?'

Eunice's answer was a grimace and she doubled up again as another spasm gripped her. She allowed it to pass before smiling weakly at Mabel. 'Yes . . . I suppose you could say it's exciting, but I'll be glad when it's over.' She usually managed to keep calm in her dealings with Mabel, who was far from the archetypal mother-in-law. A mite fussy at times, maybe, but never in an interfering way. Eunice knew she was only chattering away now in order to take her, Eunice's, mind off what lay ahead.

'Here, sit down, dear,' Mabel said now. They had been standing waiting by the front door, but Mabel ushered her back into the living room used by the young couple. 'My goodness, that was a severe one, wasn't it? I could tell, and here I am nattering away about nothing. I expect you feel like strangling me, don't you?

'Oh dear . . . how long between the pains now, Eunice?' she asked, seeing her daughter-in-law catching her breath again and gripping at the chair arms.

'About every five minutes, I think.' Eunice let her breath out again as the pain subsided. 'Oh crikey! I wish Ronnie would hurry up.'

'So do I,' agreed Mabel, sounding just a little panicky. 'Never mind, love. He'll be here in a minute, I'm sure.' She tried to smile encouragingly.

And so he was, but without the van. 'Goodness knows what's happened to the damned thing,' he said as he dashed in through the front door, his hair on end and his shirt, put on in haste, buttoned all wrong. 'I can't get it to start. I've even used the starting handle, but it's no good. It's refusing to budge. I'd better ring for a taxi. Oh, crumbs . . . D'you know the number, Mam, of that firm on Dickson Road?'

'I'll go and look at the van, lad,' said Tom. 'Happen I understand it a bit better than you do.'

'There isn't time, Tom,' cried Mabel. 'And never mind about a taxi, Ronnie. The baby'll be here soon unless I'm very much mistaken. Just take a look at your poor wife. In fact you'd best get her back upstairs and into bed again. I'll ring Mrs Wilshaw; I know she's not been seeing her regularly, with her supposed to be going into hospital, but she'll come, I'm sure. And I'll call Dr Everett an' all, just to be on the safe side. Come on, Eunice love, up you go. We haven't time to wait for a taxi.'

As soon as she got back into bed she could tell that the

pains were changing to what, she remembered from before, was the second stage of labour. She wanted to bear down, to push the baby out into the world, but she felt she did not dare to do so, not until some help arrived in the form of Mrs Wilshaw or Dr Everett. Ronnie, holding on to her hand, looked frightened to death. He winced each time a pain gripped her, partly in sympathy, but partly because of the vicelike grip in which she held his fingers.

'They won't be long, darling,' he tried to soothe her. 'Just hold on, Eunice.'

'Easier said than done,' she gasped, squeezing his hand so tightly it brought tears to his eyes. 'Oh, Ronnie, Ronnie . . . I think it's here . . .'

Mrs Wilshaw arrived just in the nick of time. Ronnie, exceedingly pale by this time, moved away thankfully from the bed to make room for her. He escaped into Sammy's room where the little boy, wondering what was happening, was standing up in his cot and rattling the bars.

The midwife took charge briskly but calmly, and Eunice felt she had never been so pleased to see anyone in her life. 'Good girl; you're doing splendidly,' she said. 'I can see the baby's head. Dark hair he's got this time like his mummy . . . Come on, now, there's a good girl. Just one more big push . . . There we are! That's done it.'

Eunice felt again, as she had when Sammy was born, the sensation that she was being torn apart, and then a feeling of immense relief. It was all over. But Mrs Wilshaw had said it was a boy. 'He's got dark hair.' That's what she had said. In spite of her relief she was aware of a moment of slight disappointment, before she heard the midwife say, 'It's a little girl . . .'

A girl! Eunice, with a feeling of exhilaration so intense she could hardly contain it, looked towards the end of the bed. Mrs Wilshaw had already released the baby from its umbilical cord and she was gently wiping away the mucus from a little face which, to Eunice's astonishment, looked just like herself. Dark curly hair, chubby cheeks, a tiny pursed-up mouth, and over all, a definite look of Eunice.

'Can I hold her?' she asked, filled with awe at the miracle of having the little girl she had wanted so much; her Francesca.

'In a minute,' said Mrs Wilshaw. 'Keep still, there's a good girl. There's still the afterbirth.' She put the baby, wrapped in a towel, into the Moses basket – a present from Mabel and Tom – at the side of the bed, and returned to Eunice. At that moment there was a knock at the door and the doctor entered.

'Ah, I'm too late, I see. Well, never mind. I can see everything has gone well, Mrs Wilshaw.' He came across to the bed, but as he looked down at Eunice his expression changed. 'Well, goodness me! I do believe . . .' He put a hand on her abdomen. 'Yes! Eunice, listen to me. There's another baby there . . . You're having twins!'

'Twins! Oh no, no, I can't be,' she cried. 'I would have known. Nobody said . . . You didn't say.' She looked at the doctor accusingly. 'Why didn't you tell me?'

Dr Everett smiled. 'Because I didn't know. It's not always possible to tell. Sometimes one baby lies behind the other in such a way that we can't hear another heartbeat. That's what must have happened here, but I did say you had put on a lot of weight, didn't I? Anyway, there's another one there, sure enough.

'Come on, Eunice. It looks as though you've some more hard work to do.' The doctor encouraged her whilst Mrs Wilshaw was busy with the first arrival. 'Another big push, there's a good girl. It won't be long now . . . And another. That's it; there we are; you've done it! Well, bless me, another little girl!'

Ronnie, on hearing the first baby's cry, dashed back to the bedroom. He hovered on the threshold as if fearful to go in. 'What is it?' he asked. 'Is it all right? Is my wife all right?'

'Everything's just fine, Ronnie,' said the doctor, who had known him, as he had known Eunice, since they were children. 'It's a girl. Well, two girls, to be exact. Come on in and have a look at them. You're the father of twins!'

Chapter 20

'Twins!' Ronnie's startled shout brought his mother and father dashing up the stairs. They had been hovering uncertainly in the hallway, occasionally venturing up a few steps and listening anxiously for the sound they were waiting to hear: the cry of a newborn baby. They lingered now in the doorway until the doctor called out to them.

'Come on in, both of you. Congratulations, Mr and Mrs Iveson. You've got twin granddaughters. Isn't that wonderful news?'

Eunice was propped up against the pillows, holding in her arms a tiny dark-haired baby. Ronnie, sitting in the basket-weave chair at the side of the bed, was holding the other child. It could be seen, from the top of the baby's head emerging from the blanket, that this little girl was ginger-haired, like her father. The faces of both parents were wreathed in smiles, but they were silent, as though this stupendous happening was too much for them to take in.

Eunice was totally bemused, but very, very happy. Not just one little girl, but two. This was something she had never ever dreamed of, even when she had known she was putting on a great deal of weight. Peering across the bed for her first glimpse of the child she had said, in some surprise, 'But she's got ginger hair. I thought twins were supposed to be alike.'

'Some are,' said Dr Everett, 'and some aren't. I'll explain to you later how it happens, but just now we'd better get this little girl cleaned up. And here's twin number one for you to hold.'

It was a few moments later, when the twins had been admired and exclaimed over by the proud grandparents, that Mabel remembered Sammy. Not that anyone had really forgotten about him, she was quick to point out, but there was so much going on and there was no sound coming from his room. She entered the boxroom, which had been converted into a cosy little bedroom, to find him sitting disconsolately in the middle of his cot, sucking his thumb. She quickly scooped him up into her arms and gave him a hug and kiss. He was getting quite heavy now and was really too big for the cot. A small single bed would be the next thing on the agenda, but Eunice and Ronnie had been so busy with other matters that they had not yet got round to it. Mabel, looking at the little boy's woebegone face, realised he was going to need some careful handling. Not just one little sister to get used to, but two of them; and Eunice would have her hands full looking after them. Not that she thought for one moment that either Eunice or Ronnie would neglect him, not intentionally; but perhaps it would be up to her, Mabel, to ensure that his nose was not pushed out and that he got his fair share of love and attention. It was difficult to know how to act, sometimes, lest she should be accused of interfering. That, she knew, had been the trouble with Edith Morton, and the reason that Eunice had wanted to move away from there. The little family had settled in very well in their new surroundings, to be sure, and Mabel prided herself on keeping her distance and not being a nosy mother-in-law.

'Sammy,' she said now, holding the little boy closer to her. 'You'll never guess what's happened. Mummy and Daddy told you, didn't they, that a new baby was going to come and live here?' The child nodded, a little uncertainly. 'A little brother or sister for you. Well now, something lovely has happened. You've got two little sisters. Two! Fancy that, eh? Come on now.' She put him down on the floor and took hold of his hand. 'Let's go and have a look at them, shall we?'

Sammy trotted into the bedroom with her.

'Hello there, Sammy,' said Ronnie, very cheerfully. 'Come and look at your new baby sister. And there's another one over there, see, with Mummy. Aren't you a lucky boy?'

But Sammy scowled and hid his head in his grandma's skirt. The expression on his face had clearly said he wasn't going to look at the silly babies – why should he?

Mabel quickly summed up the situation. 'Here, let me hold her,' she whispered to Ronnie, 'and you see to Sammy. He's feeling a little bit left out of things. It's not really surprising, is it?' Ronnie interpreted clearly the glance she gave him.

'Oh . . . yes, of course,' he whispered. 'I see what you mean. We'll have to be careful, won't we?' Hurriedly he handed the baby over to his mother, then picked up Sammy and gave him a cuddle. 'I think it's time for breakfast, isn't it, young man? Let's go downstairs, shall we, and see what we can find. What about a nice boiled egg and some soldiers to dip in? That's your favourite, isn't it?' He was relieved to see a tentative smile on his little son's face. 'Go and give your mummy a kiss first, then we'll go and get the kettle on.'

Sammy trotted across the room, still looking rather

unsurely at his mother. 'Hello there, Sammy,' she said fondly, rumpling his ginger curls. Then she put an arm round him, the arm that was not holding the baby, and held him close. 'Give Mummy a big kiss then.'

Dutifully he stood on tiptoe and kissed her cheek, but he did not look at the baby in her arms.

'We'd best be going as well,' said Mabel, tactfully, handing the baby she was holding back to the midwife. 'I expect you've some clearing up to do, haven't you, Mrs Wilshaw, and here we are, hindering you. We'll see you later, Eunice, love; and we're ever so pleased about the twins, aren't we, Tom?'

'I'll say we are,' replied her husband. He smiled a little shyly at his daughter-in-law. 'Well done, lass. We're proud of you.'

It was more than an hour before Eunice and Ronnie were able to be on their own with their two new baby daughters. The doctor and the midwife had both gone, promising to visit again soon to ensure that all was well. Eunice had eaten the toast and boiled egg that Mabel had brought up for her, as though she was ravenous. And now, holding her husband's hand, she looked contentedly at the two little bundles, asleep at the moment: baby number one in the Moses basket and baby number two in an improvised cot made from a large drawer filled with soft blankets.

'No wonder I thought I was carrying a twelve-pound lad,' she remarked. 'I thought it was going to be another boy, you see, but I didn't say so.'

'And you'd have been disappointed, would you, if it had been a boy?'

'Mmm . . . I might have been,' replied Eunice truthfully. 'Anyway, it wasn't, was it? Just imagine, Ronnie; twins! And each of them weighs nearly six pounds. That's quite a good weight, even if there was only one of them; that's what the doctor said. And they are what are called unidentical twins. Do you know, I had never realised there was any such thing. I thought twins were always alike.'

'No, not always,' said Ronnie. 'Sometimes there's one of each, isn't there? A boy and a girl.'

'Oh yes, of course,' said Eunice. 'I never thought of that. Would you have liked one of them to be a boy?'

'No, not at all,' Ronnie replied, smiling happily. 'I'm quite satisfied – well, tickled pink, really. It was quite a shock, I must admit, but a very pleasant one.'

'Anyway, like I was saying,' Eunice continued, 'Dr Everett said that identical twins happen when one cell divides into two, but when two cells are fertilised at the same time you get unidentical twins, like ours.'

'So you might say we've hit the jackpot,' Ronnie laughed. 'Clever, aren't we? Have you any idea what we are going to call them?'

'That one's Francesca,' said Eunice promptly, nodding towards the dark-haired baby in the Moses basket. 'I don't know about the other one. I wasn't anticipating two, was I?'

'My goodness! That was quick,' said Ronnie. 'Francesca . . . Yes, that's a nice name. It's got a sort of aristocratic ring to it. What made you think of it?'

'Oh, it's a name I read in a book when I was a little girl, and I've always liked it. I used to wish it was my name.'

'I've never heard you mention it –' said Ronnie – 'that you wanted to call the baby Francesca.'

'Is that OK with you?' She suddenly realised she had not given Ronnie much choice in the matter.

'Suits me fine, darling. And . . . the other one? We can't go on calling her the other one, can we?'

'You choose a name for her, Ronnie,' said Eunice. 'She'll

probably turn out to look like you; she's got ginger hair for a start. So you give her a name.'

'They are both our babies,' said Ronnie quickly. 'You mustn't start thinking of one as yours and the other as mine. They belong to us equally, darling. They are yours and mine, just as Sammy is. We will have to be careful not to neglect him, Eunice.'

'Neglect him?' Eunice sounded a little shocked. 'As if we would.'

'Not intentionally, of course,' said Ronnie. 'But you saw how he reacted earlier. Poor little lad; he must have felt as though his nose was being pushed out. It can happen when a new baby arrives if you're not careful. And we've got two.'

'Oh dear, poor little chap,' said Eunice. 'But he knows we love him, doesn't he? I'll have to have a little talk to him. Where is he now?'

'My mother has taken him round to tell your parents the news,' said Ronnie, giving a wry smile. 'Get ready for the onslaught, darling. We'll have your mum and dad here before long, I don't doubt.'

'Oh crikey!' said Eunice. 'I'd almost forgotten about them. Talk about somebody having their nose pushed out! That's how my mother will feel, with your parents knowing first about the twins.'

'Never mind, it can't be helped,' replied Ronnie. He was staring into space in a preoccupied manner. Suddenly he said, 'Eleanor . . . That's what we'll call her; Eleanor.'

'Mmm, that's nice. I like it,' said Eunice. 'It's a – what did you say before? – an aristocratic-sounding name as well. How did you think of it?'

'I don't know really,' said Ronnie. 'Perhaps I read it somewhere, like you did with Francesca.'

'Francesca and Eleanor,' said Eunice, in a voice tinged

with wonderment. She was still hardly able to comprehend the stupendous thing that had happened to them. 'We are lucky, aren't we, Ronnie?'

'Francesca and Eleanor . . . and Sammy,' said her husband.

'Francesca and Eleanor?' exclaimed Edith Morton, almost disbelievingly. 'Wherever did you get them fancy names from? Trust you, our Eunice. I might have known you'd come up with summat high-falutin. It's all them stories you read; you've always got your head stuck in some book or other.'

'As a matter of fact, Mother, Eleanor was the name of a queen of England; more than one queen, in fact. Have you never heard of Eleanor of Aquitaine, who married Henry the second?' Eunice knew it was very unlikely her mother would know anything about the Plantagenet king and queen, and she knew also that she, Eunice, was guilty of airing her knowledge. But her mother still annoyed her at times.

Edith sniffed. 'Can't say that I have. And you don't need to show off about all them folks you read about in history. What about Francesca then? Where did that come from?'

'We both liked it,' Ronnie interrupted, in a gallant attempt to stick up for his wife. 'Didn't we, Eunice? I think we might have read it somewhere in the beginning, but what does it matter? Those are the names we have chosen.'

'And very nice names they are, too,' said Samuel, 'for two lovely little girls. Well done, the pair of you. Come on, Sammy lad, let's go and have another peep at them, shall we? Your two little baby sisters. And what lucky girls they are to have a fine big brother like you.'

Sammy grinned up at his granddad. Eunice was relieved to see that the sulky look had gone from his face. When he had returned with his Grandma Mabel with her parents in tow, he had seemed much happier. He held tightly to his granddad's hand as he looked down at the dark-haired baby.

'This one's Francesca,' said Samuel. 'Can you say her name, Sammy?'

'Fran . . . chester,' said the little boy unsurely.

'Near enough, Sammy,' said Samuel, laughing. 'Give her a kiss then.' Obediently the child leaned over the Moses basket and kissed the sleeping baby's forehead. Eunice, watching the scene with extreme gratitude to her father, felt her eyes mist over with tears.

'And this one is Eleanor,' said Samuel as they looked at the baby on the other side of the bed.

'Ellie,' said Sammy; and Eunice realised, with an inward sigh of resignation, that that was probably what the child would be called by all and sundry. The twins, no doubt, would be Fran and Ellie, no matter how much she would try to insist on them having their full names.

'She's got ginger hair, like me,' Sammy said with a touch of pride, 'and like Daddy.' He reached out and gently touched a tendril of hair curling over the baby's forehead. 'Why is she in a drawer?' he asked, looking up questioningly at his granddad.

'Ah well, she came a bit sudden, like,' said Samuel, scratching his head.

'We've only got one baby basket,' said Eunice, smiling at her son. 'And there isn't room for both babies in it, so Eleanor is having to make do with a drawer, just for now. She's very nice and comfy, though.'

'She can have my cot,' said Sammy. 'You said I could have a bed, Mummy. Sammy's too big for a cot now. Not a baby.' He shook his head vigorously. He was talking very well, as he had done since he was two years old, but he still reverted, occasionally, to calling himself 'Sammy' rather than saying 'I' or 'me'.

'And so you shall,' said Eunice. 'Perhaps you could go to town with Daddy next week, to choose one?'

'And Eleanor must have her very own baby basket,' said Edith. 'Sleeping in a drawer, indeed! We can't have that. I shall go and buy her one tomorrow.'

'Thank you, Mother. That's very kind of you,' said Eunice. She knew her parents, and Ronnie's parents, too, would insist on showering the new babies with gifts, and there was little point in arguing with them. She hoped it would not escalate into too much of a competition between them, though.

'And you will need a bigger pram,' her mother continued. 'I think you can get twin prams to accommodate a baby at each end. I was saying so to Mabel on the way here, and we have agreed to share the cost of one between us. So if Ronald would like to go and choose one . . .'

'Thank you, Mother,' said Eunice again. 'Yes, I suppose that is what I will need. Goodness, it's going to take some getting used to. Two of them . . .'

'We had the shock of our lives when Mabel came to tell us,' said Edith, sounding a little put out, although she must have known she had not been kept in the dark intentionally, or for very long. 'Yes, the shock of our lives. I thought your daddy was going to have one of his funny turns. It was Sammy that told us, actually, bless him. "Grandma," he said, "Sammy's got two baby sisters." Well, you could have knocked me down with a feather. He's been such a blessing to us, Eunice, that little boy. I know in the beginning it was – well, never mind about all that now.'

'No, I should think not,' said her husband. 'He's a grand little lad.' He cast her a glance that said only too clearly, For goodness' sake, shut up, woman. He lifted the child up and put him on his knee. Sammy cuddled close to him in a way that Eunice never remembered doing with her father when she was a little girl. Samuel had become much more approachable and communicative since the birth of his first grandchild.

'Yes, he certainly is a grand little lad,' said his wife. 'But you'll have to be careful with him, Eunice. We don't want him to feel . . . you know.' She lowered her voice. 'Neglected. It can happen when new baby arrives. And you've got—'

'Yes, I know,' said Eunice. 'And I've got two. Don't worry, Mother. I know what I'm doing.' She felt annoyed – of course she wouldn't neglect Sammy – but at the same time she knew she should be grateful to her parents, and Ronnie's, for dealing with her little son so tactfully. His sulkiness and resentment at the arrival of the twins had been turned round into acceptance and a cautious interest.

'Thanks for looking after Sammy,' she added. 'I must admit he was overwhelmed at first. Like we all were,' she laughed. 'But he's going to be a big grown-up boy and help Mummy to look after his sisters, aren't you, Sammy?' The child nodded in a decided manner, but immediately afterwards he put his thumb in his mouth.

'And his grandma will help as well,' said Edith. 'His two grandmas, I mean. Don't forget that.'

As if I could! thought Eunice. But she smiled at the thought. She was very lucky to have both their parents so near and so willing to help.

It soon became obvious to her that it would have been difficult to have managed without the support of her mother and mother-in-law, and her husband, of course. She had worried, whilst she was pregnant, about breast-feeding the baby. She had disliked the procedure with

Sammy and did not relish the idea of going through it all again. With the arrival of the twins, however, Mrs Wilshaw had agreed – she had, in fact, suggested – that Eunice should put them both on to a bottle straight away. It would be difficult to breast-feed two of them and if she did not encourage her milk to flow then it would more or less disappear of its own accord.

Eunice was thankful that the problem had been solved so easily. It meant that Ronnie could help at feeding times. She fed one baby whilst he fed the other one, taking it in turns to hold either Francesca or Eleanor. But in addition to that there were two nappies to change, two babies to bath in the morning and evening, two hungry little mouths to feed, and two babies to comfort when they cried, often in the middle of the night. Ronnie assisted her when he could, but he had his work at the shop and he was often tired when he came home in the evening.

'I'm tired as well,' Eunice sometimes told him when she found him snoozing in the armchair, his copy of the *Evening Gazette* lying open on his lap. 'Good gracious, Ronnie; anybody would think you were an old man. That's what my father does, and yours: fall asleep over the newspaper. What about me? I can't take a nap, can I? And I've been on the go all day, seeing to these two, not to mention Sammy.'

'And I was up in the night seeing to Eleanor,' Ronnie reminded her. 'You said it was my turn to get up and so that's what I did. I agreed we'd take it in turns to see to them in the night and I don't mind. But surely you can see that's why I'm tired. And the shop's busy at the moment, with everybody dashing around getting ready for Christmas. I'll help you to bath the twins in a little while. Just let me have five minutes' peace, for goodness' sake, Eunice.'

This conversation took place in the middle of December when the twins were nearly three months old. They were sturdy-looking babies, steadily putting on weight with the Cow and Gate milk upon which Sammy, before them, had been reared. They were healthy too, as a rule, but Eleanor, of late, had been suffering with colic and was crying a lot more than usual. Eunice's initial euphoria, her delight in the twins, had lessened somewhat over the weeks. She loved them, both of them, more than she could say, but it was jolly hard work looking after the two of them day in and day out. And Sammy too. Although she had to admit, not without a twinge of guilt, that the little boy was often with one or another of his grandparents. She had not intended this to happen, but she was not going to turn down the offer of help when she did not know which way to turn with piles of soiled nappies to wash and two growing babies to feed and care for.

'All right, Ronnie; I'm sorry,' she said now. Tempers became a little frayed at times, and she and Ronnie were starting to snap at one another in a way they had never done before. She knew she must not allow this to happen. Ronnie was a husband in a million. 'I really am dead beat, though,' she added, 'and Sammy's been playing up again.'

'Where is he now?' asked Ronnie, as though he had suddenly realised the little boy was not there. 'With my mother again, I suppose.'

'Er . . . yes, he's with your mam and dad,' said Eunice. 'When your mother came home he dashed to meet her and she said he could have his tea with them.'

Mabel always returned from the shop a little earlier than Tom in order to prepare their meal.

Eunice sighed. 'To crown it all, this morning I found he'd wet the bed. And before you say anything, no, I didn't shout at him. It might just have been a little accident, so I didn't mention it. But it was the last straw, believe me, having to wash an extra sheet and pyjamas on top of all the nappies.'

'Oh dear! Poor you,' said Ronnie. 'Never mind, love. They won't be babies for ever. And that's all Sammy is, when all is said and done. He's only three; still quite a baby really.'

'He's certainly acting like one,' agreed Eunice.

'So he's with my mother now, and yesterday he was with your mother,' Ronnie observed.

'They both like having him, Ronnie,' she replied, 'you know they do, and, well, he seems to behave himself better for them at the moment than he does for me.'

'He's jealous, Eunice. Can't you see that? Because he thinks you're making too much fuss of the babies.'

'But I have to, haven't I, while they're so tiny? It isn't as if I don't love Sammy as well. He knows I love him.'

'Does he?'

'Here, hang on a minute. What are you trying to say?' Eunice was annoyed now. In spite of her best intentions they were beginning to fall out. 'Are you saying I don't love him, that I neglect him?'

'No, I know you love him, but does he know? If I were you, Eunice, I wouldn't be so eager to hand him over to our parents when things are difficult.'

'If you were me? But you're not me, are you?'

'You know what you've always said about your mother interfering,' he went on. 'Before we know where we are she'll have taken over completely, like she tried to do when Sammy was a baby. We moved from there, you remember, because you wanted to manage on your own.'

'It's different now. She's only helping.'

'Yes, but you know what she's like. She'll be boasting to her friends that she's brought Sammy up, and I don't want that. He's our responsibility. And my mother works full time at the shop; don't forget that. She's too old really to be looking after a grandchild.'

'It's only occasionally, and she enjoys having him.'

'Well, I'm going to get him now,' said Ronnie, jumping to his feet. 'I want to see him as well.'

'I thought you wanted five minutes' peace? And you said you'd help me to bath the twins.'

'Five minutes' peace?' He laughed a little cynically. 'Not much chance of that, is there? But I'm OK now; I've livened up again. I'll get Sammy and then we'll both help you to bath the twins. A real family activity, Eunice. That's what we should be aiming for.'

Eunice was worried. She and Ronnie had never used to quarrel like this, when they had had only the one child and were living at her mother's. She remembered, however, his bouts of anxiety and depression, and she wondered if that was what was ailing him now: that the recurring depression was causing him to find fault with her. She felt that his criticism, his hinting that she was neglecting Sammy, was quite unjustified. He had not actually said so, but the implication was there. She realised it would be better, for all their sakes, if they were able to move away from this immediate area, away from both sets of parents. Then they could really start to live as a proper family; just the five of them and no one else.

Fortunately they did not have very long to wait.

Chapter 21

They were granted a council house rather sooner than they had expected, in the spring of 1947. A slight snag, however, was that it was not strictly speaking a house, but a prefabricated bungalow – commonly known as a prefab. These one-storeyed aluminium structures, painted cream, had been erected on a piece of spare land at Bispham, within easy walking distance of Bispham village.

'It's rather small,' Eunice pointed out when Ronnie told her of the offer from the housing office. 'They've only got two bedrooms – not very big ones at that – and you know we need three.'

'Beggars can't be choosers,' he told her. 'Not that we're exactly beggars, of course, but I don't see that we're in any position to argue. If we turn this down we may well find ourselves at the bottom of the list again.'

'Hmm . . . I see what you mean. OK then, if it's what you want,' she agreed.

'We've no choice,' said Ronnie, 'and it will be a start. Just think, darling, our very own little home. What we've always wanted. And one day we will buy one, I promise you that. A nice three-bedroomed semi; that would do for us.' Ronnie never had big ideas beyond his station and he did not believe in pipe dreams that were clearly impossible. Like Eunice he had been brought up to 'know his place' in society. And to be the owner of a small house was the height of his ambition.

'All right then; tell them we'll take it,' said Eunice.

It was, as she had anticipated, very small, the rooms not nearly as large as the ones they had occupied at Tom and Mabel's. There was a living-cum-dining room, a tiny kitchen, a small bathroom and toilet combined, and two medium-sized bedrooms. They hummed and hawed about the sleeping arrangements, finally deciding that the three children would have to occupy the same room. It would be a tight squeeze for a single bed and two cots, but by the time the twins needed beds they might have been offered a three-bedroomed house, or they might even have enough saved up for a deposit on a house of their own.

The walls were painted in a uniform shade of cream, and the dark brown composition floors looked cold and bare. Very quickly, however, the place took on a more homely aspect. Eunice and Ronnie bought carpet squares in floral designs – all they could afford – for the living room and bedrooms, and with the odds and ends of furniture their parents gave them, plus the few items they had already bought for themselves, they had all the essential requirements. Eunice got busy again running up colourful curtains and cushion covers on her mother's sewing machine, and Ronnie laid a bright yellow and green checked linoleum in the kitchen to tone with the cream-painted cupboards and the cream enamelled sink.

They were happy there at first and their life entered into a contented and peaceful phase; they were far enough away from their parents to be independent, but near enough to call upon them if they wished to do so. Tom told Ronnie he could use the shop van to travel back and forth from Bispham. It was too far to walk, although they were all at the northern end of the town.

The inhabitants of Bispham village had always been proud of the fact that their village had been in existence far longer than Blackpool. It had been mentioned in the Domesday Survey, and the Anglian settlement was believed to have been in existence since AD 800. The name, Bispham, was generally thought to have been derived from 'Bishop's ham', meaning the home of the Bishop. Those days, however, were long gone and Bispham had become a suburb of Blackpool, and no longer a place in its own right, in 1917.

Very little remained now of the old world Bispham village. It had been a favourite trip out for visitors to Blackpool in Victorian times and for many years afterwards; for those who wished to seek a peaceful haven away from the bustle and noise of the seaside town. Ivy Cottage was a quiet retreat, a picturesque thatched cottage where afternoon tea was served in a Victorian parlour overflowing with ornaments and mementoes brought back from Africa during the Great War. It was still there in 1947, although the roof had been tiled in the early years of the century, as were a few more of the ancient cottages along All Hallows Road. All Hallows Church, about ten minutes' walk along the road, had been in existence since the twelfth century, the present building being the third to have been erected on the site. With its old graveyard and attractive lych-gate it was a popular place with visitors and for weddings, and the folk of Bispham were justly proud of it.

Eunice decided, all told, that Bispham was a very pleasant place in which to live. She had made friends with some of the neighbours, young women of roughly the same age as herself with one or two children, and Sammy had some playmates. Eunice shopped either in the quaint little village itself, or further down Redbank Road, the road that led down to the sea. The Dominion Cinema was there, and the tram sheds, the northern terminus for the trams that travelled along the promenade, and a wide variety of shops.

At the inland end of the road, only five minutes' walk from where they lived, was the school. This, also, had been in existence for centuries, the present building dating from 1878. Sammy would be four in July and was already talking about the time when he would go to school. Eunice had pointed the building out to him whilst they were shopping or taking the twins out for an airing. She decided she would wait until September and then make enquiries about when he could start. Not that she was wanting to hand him over to someone else, not at all; the little boy's behaviour had improved greatly since they had been living in their own home, and there had been no more bed-wetting.

A happy occasion had been the christening of the twins, not in the Bispham church, but in the one they had attended previously, where both Tom and Samuel were still sidesmen. The two little girls were named, respectively, Francesca Anne and Eleanor Jean. Eunice liked the idea of two names, having been forced to go through life herself with only one – and one she did not care for – and she felt the somewhat more ordinary names might appeal to her mother.

She remembered the slight altercation there had been before about godparents. This time she and Ronnie agreed that they should ask his sister, Chrissie, and her friend Fiona to stand for the children. Two godmothers and one godfather for the girls was the norm in the Church of

England, and so Ronnie decided he would act as godfather himself. No men had made an appearance in the lives of Chrissie and Fiona and it was unlikely they ever would.

The christening took place in the springtime when Sammy was almost four and the twins were about eight months old. The small party afterwards was held at Tom and Mabel's home. It consisted, simply, of christening cake and a glass of rich brown sherry, as only the immediate family members were present and Edith needed to get back to the boarding house to see to the visitors' high tea.

'I must say you left it long enough to have them done,' she remarked to her daughter. 'I thought the poor vicar was going to drop our little Eleanor Jean, she's got so heavy lately.' The second twin to be born had, indeed, overtaken the first one in growth, although they were both quite sturdy and bonny little girls.

'Better late than never,' said Mabel, 'and I might not have finished their dresses if it had been any sooner.' She had made each child a white silk dress, trimmed with guipure lace, and Edith, not to be outdone, had knitted lacy white cardigans finished off with satin ribbons. The day had turned out to be warm. Cardigans had been unnecessary, but Eunice had known it would be expedient for the twins to wear them nevertheless. 'And don't they both look lovely in their new finery?' The cardigans had been taken off now, but Mabel picked one up. 'I love this feather pattern, Edith,' she said admiringly. 'It looks very complicated; I'm not sure I would have the patience.'

Edith smiled complacently. 'Oh well, I've got plenty of that when it comes to my grandchildren. There's nothing I wouldn't do, for any of them.'

'Aye, we've got a darned sight more patience with our grandchildren than we ever had with our own, haven't we?' remarked Mabel.

'Er . . . yes, quite,' said Edith, a little taken aback. Eunice, hearing the interchange, suppressed a grin. It was unusual for her mother not to have the last word.

It was just after Sammy's fourth birthday – celebrated with a cake with candles and three new friends to tea – when Eunice saw the article in the daily paper. It was the headline that caught her attention, as, indeed, headlines were intended to do.

'EX-POW IN DRAMATIC SEA RESCUE,' it read.

And there, underneath, was a photograph of . . . Heinrich Muller. He was very much as she remembered him; his fairish hair now falling over his forehead, though, and not cut short as it had used to be, his wide smile and laughing eyes. He was standing next to a small boy, whom, the article stated, he had rescued when he had got into difficulties in the sea near Ilfracombe. The journalist praised his bravery and told of the immense gratitude of the little boy, Peter's, parents. It went on to say that Mr Muller had worked as a prisoner of war at High Tor Farm, and had decided to stay on for a while there because he had fallen in love with, and subsequently married, a local girl, Miss Jennifer Eaves. Mr and Mrs Muller, the article concluded, would be returning to Remagen on the German Rhine in a few weeks' time, where Mr Muller would take up employment in the family chemist's shop.

So . . . that is that, thought Eunice. He had soon forgotten her. It hadn't taken him long to fall in love again and get married . . .

Now, wait a minute, she told herself sternly, what do you expect? She had not replied to his letter, although it had burned a hole in her bag for several weeks. When she had discovered she was pregnant again she had thrown it away, determined to banish all thoughts of Heinrich for ever. But here he was again, the ghost of him intruding into her life when she thought she had said goodbye to him for ever. Would she never be free of the memory of him, she wondered.

She found herself wondering about all manner of things. He had met this young woman, this Jennifer Eaves, whilst working on a farm, just as, previously, he had met her, Eunice. If the circumstances had been different, would he have married her? she pondered. And would she have dared to marry him, a German, knowing of her father's antagonism to the race? At all events, his letter had arrived far too late, it was she who was already married to someone else. So why then was she even entertaining these useless, unprofitable thoughts? She knew the answer only too well.

It would have been easier to forget all about Heinrich, as she knew she really ought to do, if her life with Ronnie had been perfect. But, unfortunately, this was far from the truth. They had been happy enough for a while in their little prefab. She had found it peaceful – blissful, in fact – to have her little family to herself, even though she found it hard work looking after the three children on her own.

And then, out of the blue, or so it seemed, Ronnie had started with another of his fits of depression. She never knew what exactly was the cause of these bouts, but by now she knew the signs. The first sign was his drawing away from her, his disinclination to make love or, indeed, to want to chat to her in the evenings as he had loved to do when he returned from the shop. He was impatient with the children, although it was only Sammy who would notice this and he, bless him, did not comment. Sammy was such a good little boy now, doing his best to please both his mummy and daddy and looking after his baby sisters. What a blessing he had been to both of them. Eunice felt she was justified in feeling resentful when Ronnie started to hint – again – that she was neglecting their little boy. It was not true; Ronnie was imagining it. The truth was that Sammy had made new friends and sometimes went to play in a neighbour's house, and Ronnie seemed to object to this.

Her husband had become self-critical again, as well as criticising her. He was a failure, he said. They should have their own home by now, one that they owned, not rented. And the prefab was far too small, he objected. This had been Eunice's argument at first, but now she thought it was a cosy little home and she had grown to love it and the area in which they lived.

She just hoped and prayed that Ronnie's black mood would disappear as quickly as it had descended upon him. That was usually the case, but this one had been worse than usual. He had visited the doctor, but the medication he was supposed to be taking did not seem to be having much effect. The prevailing attitude was that there was little to be done about depression. You just had to help yourself to overcome it. Eunice feared they were drifting apart, but she felt helpless at the moment to do anything to stop the widening rift.

It was little wonder, then, that the article about Heinrich had given her such a jolt and caused her to reminisce when she knew she should be looking forward and not back. Especially as Heinrich, now, had gone for good. He was married and would soon be back in Germany.

But he had been her first love, she remembered as she looked again at the newspaper photo of him, the distance of time and space lending enchantment to what had been, in truth, little more than a flight of fancy. But she recalled only the good times now, not the heartache when she believed he might have betrayed her, or her panic and horror when she had feared she might be expecting his child.

She sighed and closed the paper. She was married to Ronnie now and she loved him so very much. She would try extra hard, she resolved, to get close to him again. But that was easier said than done.

Ronnie had known Mrs Cardwell ever since the end of the war, when he had returned to work in his parents' shop. She and her little son, Bobby, had moved from Liverpool to escape the bombing and had come to live in a small house not far from the shop. Her husband, at that time, had been in the RAF; a navigator, who had since been killed in a raid over Germany. All this Ronnie had learned from his parents, who had come to know the young woman quite well through her frequent visits to the grocer's shop. She was registered there for her weekly ration of essential foods and popped in at other times for this and that.

Their friendship had developed slowly, each of them scarcely aware, in the beginning, that the rapport between them was growing. Ronnie had noticed her initially because his mother had pointed her out to him; the young war widow with a little boy: 'So tragic it is, and she's such a lovely person.' And he had noticed her too because she had a certain bearing, an air about her that set her apart from many of the women who came into the shop. It was the time of 'make do and mend', when women were used to refashioning their old garments, if they were able; otherwise they wore their years-old tweed coat when shopping, invariably with a headscarf tied under the chin. Mrs Cardwell, however, was always immaculately dressed, even for shopping, in a well-cut suit or coat and a neat little hat, never a headscarf. It was believed she owned the house round the corner too; it was not rented, as many properties were.

'She must be quite well off,' said Ronnie's mother. 'Jolly good luck to her, though, that's what I say. She'll need every penny, left on her own like that, poor girl. And that little lad's a real credit to her; so polite and well behaved.'

The young woman was by no means snobbish or stand-offish, although she did not take much part in the chit-chat and gossip that was often exchanged in the shop queue. She kept herself to herself, and although by the end of the war she had lived there for the best part of two years, no one knew her very well. She had talked to Mabel, though, no doubt glad of a sympathetic ear and someone warm and friendly in whom to confide. She had told Mabel once that she reminded her of her own mother who had died just after the start of the war. And that was the reason, it seemed, that she had opened up to the older woman.

Her name was Thelma. Ronnie had learned this from her ration book, also that she had been born in 1921, the same year as himself. He thought her name suited her; an elegant sort of name, rather out of the ordinary, as she was. He did not use her given name, though – not at first – nor did she call him Ronnie as many of the customers did. His father was Mr Iveson, therefore it was only natural that the son should be called by his first name to avoid confusion. But Thelma Cardwell also called him Mr Iveson, as she did his father.

It was in the early summer of 1947, when little Bobby Cardwell came dashing into the shop. 'Me mum's sent me. She's hurt her leg and she can't walk – well, not very much. She's sent this list, and she says, can you please deliver these things sometime today?' His words were tumbling over one another as he stood there on one leg, anxious to be away from the shop as quickly as possible. 'I'll have to go, or else I'll be late for school.'

'Yes, you run along, Bobby,' said Mabel. 'Tell your mum we'll see to it for her, and we hope her leg will soon be better.'

'OK. I'm not going home though. I'm going straight to school now. Mum's written me a note to say why I'm late, but I don't like being late.'

'Hang on a minute, Bobby,' said Ronnie. 'I'll take you in the van. That's OK, isn't it, Mam? We're not too busy at the moment.'

'Yes, that's a good idea,' said Mabel. 'Off you go then. We can't have this little lad getting into trouble.'

'Oh, I don't think I'd get into trouble, Mrs Iveson. My teacher's real nice, but I don't want everybody looking at me. And if you're late three times you have to go to the headmaster and you get the cane.'

'Oh dear!' chuckled Ronnie. 'Well, that's not going to happen here. Come on, young man; we'll have you there in no time.'

The little boy was delighted to be having a ride in the shop van, sitting on the front seat next to Ronnie. 'I shall have a van like this when I'm grown up,' he said. 'Then I can take Mum out, can't I? My dad was going to buy a car, he said, when the war ended, but he died, didn't he? And I have to look after my mum, see . . .'

They arrived at the school yard just as the teacher was blowing the whistle, the signal for the children to line up and go inside. 'Ta-ra, then. Thanks for the ride,' said Bobby, scrambling out of the van.

'Cheerio, Bobby,' said Ronnie, smiling broadly. 'I'll see that your mum gets her groceries.'

Later that morning he put the items that Thelma Cardwell had requested into a large cardboard box and drove round to her house. He had not been there before as she invariably collected her groceries herself, as did most of the women in the area. Deliveries were mainly to the boarding houses or to elderly people who could not get about very easily. He walked up the path through the neat little garden and knocked at the door of the terraced house; knocked and then turned the handle as he guessed she would have left the door open.

'Hello there, it's only me, Ronnie,' he called as he entered. 'I'll pop this in the back kitchen, shall I, Mrs Cardwell?'

'Yes, thank you. The kitchen's at the back, the usual place. Just leave it on the table, please. And I'm in the living room.' She was sitting in an easy chair by the fire, her bandaged leg propped up on a stool. She smiled warmly as he came in. 'Thank you ever so much. I hate to be a nuisance, but there's no way I could have struggled to the shop and there were a few items I needed quite badly. I don't like to trouble my neighbour. She's doing enough as it is. She's said she'll see to Bobby's dinner today; her little girl's in the same class as Bobby.'

She explained how, the previous night, she had stood up suddenly when Bobby had shouted to her from upstairs and had twisted her ankle. Ronnie had noticed that her ankles were very slim and shapely. She had managed to hobble around, but by morning it had been swollen and very painful. She had seen to Bobby's needs – getting him a cup of tea and a bowl of cornflakes – and then sent him off to the shop with the list. She had then phoned the doctor – Ronnie was not surprised to learn that she had a telephone – who had called round and affirmed what she had guessed; that her ankle was badly sprained and she would need to rest it for several days.

'I can hobble around a bit,' she said, 'and he's brought

me a crutch to lean on. Honestly, I feel like an old woman! And what a stupid thing to do.'

'Accidents happen,' said Ronnie. 'And you've got a very sensible little boy. Now, can I get you anything while I'm here? A cup of tea? Something to eat? I'm not the world's best cook – in fact I'm hopeless; my wife would tell you – but I could rustle up some toast.'

'A cup of tea would be very welcome, thank you,' she smiled. 'And there are some biscuits in a tin in the cupboard; the tin with the London scenes on it. You'll have a cup with me, won't you?'

It amazed him how easily they conversed and how well they got along together. There had been a certain something between them when they had met in the shop, an awareness that they liked one another, and it seemed now as though that liking could develop, if they allowed it to do so, into something deeper. But Ronnie knew that would not – could not – be allowed to happen. He was married to Eunice and he loved her very much; he always would. There would be no harm, though, surely, in chatting to a young woman he liked and who so obviously liked him.

He learned that day that Thelma was from an ordinary working-class background; from a much less well-off family than his own, in fact. She was not – or had not originally been – a young woman of superior breeding, as he had once believed. Far from it; she told him she was the youngest of a family of five children, brought up in one of the poorer districts of Liverpool. Her father had worked on the docks. Unlike many of his ilk he had not squandered his wages or drunk excessively, but had been a good and reliable father to his family. He and her mother had been devoted to one another and they had brought up their children to be responsible and ambitious. They had all found the sort of jobs that their parents considered to be 'a step up the ladder'. Thelma had been a clerk in a shipping office until she had married at the age of twenty. Her husband, Raymond, had worked in the shipping office as well. He lived in nearby Cheshire, on the peninsula of land known as the Wirral. Over the years Thelma had lost much of her Liverpool accent.

'He taught me how to talk posh,' she said laughing. 'He liked me to dress well, and I learned to talk about all kinds of things – books and music and all that – like he did. I'm still an ordinary Liverpudlian lass, though, at heart. Raymond wasn't a snob; I don't want you to think that, but it was the way he had been brought up, you see . . .'

As Ronnie listened to her he could detect a trace of her original Liverpool accent, something he had not noticed before, as now and again she lapsed back into the vernacular of the region.

'I know folks round here might think I'm a bit stuck up,' she said. 'I find it hard to talk to people, and I sometimes give the wrong impression. I was all right when Raymond was with me. I suppose I came to rely on him, and after he had gone . . . well, it wasn't easy.'

'I think you're doing fine,' said Ronnie. 'And your little Bobby's a real credit to you, Thelma.' It was the first time he had used her name, but once he had done so it came easily to him. 'You're going to stay in this area, are you?'

'Oh yes, I think so,' she replied. 'I might get an office job if I can, now Bobby's settled at school; just part time, of course. I shan't go back to Liverpool now my parents have both died. I keep in touch with my brothers and sisters, but I wouldn't want to live there again. I like it here and so does Bobby.'

Ronnie realised he might have stayed too long. As far as he was concerned the time had flown by, and he believed it was the same for Thelma, but his mother looked at him curiously when he returned.

'You've been a long time.'

'Well . . . yes, I suppose I have. I made a cup of tea for Mrs Cardwell, and we got talking. Her ankle's badly sprained.'

'Oh dear! Well, that was kind of you, Ronnie. She's such a nice person, isn't she?' His mother didn't seem to think there was anything unusual about his neighbourly act. And that was all it was, he told himself: an act of kindness to a neighbour who was indisposed.

He called again, however, a few days later. Thelma was still having difficulty in getting around although her ankle, she told him, was less painful. It was during their chat that afternoon that she mentioned his wife, commenting that she had not seen her recently. How was she and how were the little boy, and the twins?

'Eunice has changed,' Ronnie found himself saying. 'She's changed such a lot lately. She's not like the girl I married.' But he knew, as he was saying it, that this was not strictly true.

He, Ronnie, had changed as well. He knew he was often moody and withdrawn and he could not see any real reason for feeling the way he did. He was told by the doctor, as well as by the members of his family, that it was the result of his wartime experiences. Yes, that was one of the reasons, he supposed. The traumas he had experienced did come back to haunt him, usually in the early hours of the morning when Eunice lay peacefully sleeping at his side; although he knew that, compared with many of his comrades, he had escaped very lightly. Some of them, indeed, were no longer here to tell the tale.

Eunice, however, seemed less patient of late with his state of mind. She was preoccupied with the children, or so it seemed to him; so much so that he, Ronnie, had begun to feel neglected. It was the twins she doted upon more than Sammy. They were, indeed, delightful little girls, the sort of children that everyone immediately felt drawn to. Their high-pitched voices, though, sometimes got on his nerves. They made his head ache, especially in such a confined space as their little prefab.

Sammy was growing up quickly, making new friends, and he was no longer the 'daddy's boy' that he had used to be, although he still resembled Ronnie very much in appearance. He was an independent little lad and did not cling to either of them any more. Ronnie knew it was wrong of him to accuse Eunice of neglecting the little boy. Of course she didn't; he was finding his feet and she, sensibly, was allowing him to do so. The truth was that Ronnie was sometimes so fed up with himself that he struck out verbally at his wife. If only she knew how much he really loved her. But they were drifting apart. And the less they conversed together, then the less they found they had to talk about.

What a refreshing change it was to talk to Thelma. He seemed able to shed all his worries when he was with her. But when she asked him, to his surprise, if he still loved his wife his reply was automatic. 'Of course I do,' he said, realising suddenly that he might be giving the wrong impression.

'I've changed too,' he said truthfully. 'Maybe we're just getting on each other's nerves a little. Nothing that time won't heal . . .' He knew, though, if he were honest with himself, that he was doing very little to heal the breach.

'Never mind, Ronnie,' said Thelma consolingly. 'I'm sure it will sort out in time. And you can always come and chat to me, you know . . .'

Chapter 22

The twins enjoyed riding in their double pram. They smiled at one another a lot – they had not yet got to the age of quarrelling – and chatted to one another in a language that no one else but they could understand.

Eunice put on their woolly cardigans, a recent present from Mabel. Not to be outdone, Edith had made them each a dress of soft velour, intricately smocked across the bodice. Fran's was red and Ellie's was blue, matching the cardigans. It had become customary to dress Fran in red or deep pink, which enhanced her dark hair, whereas Ellie was usually dressed in blue. Her ginger hair looked even brighter against the blue dress, and both twins had inherited Eunice's bright blue eyes.

She had never believed in dressing twins alike, thinking that to do so might stifle their individuality. Anyway, these two were by no means identical, either in looks or in personality, and it was fascinating to see them developing, each in her own way.

She tucked a tartan rug around the little girls' legs, locked the door behind her, and set off walking away from the cluster of prefabs, along Bispham Road. 'Let's go and see Daddy, shall we,' she said, 'and Grandma and Granddad Iveson.' It was a while since she had visited the shop and she hoped it would be a nice surprise both for Ronnie and for his parents. 'Daddy will be ever so pleased to see his two little girls, won't he?'

The twins smiled. 'Dada . . .' said Ellie, always the first to respond.

'Dada . . .' repeated Fran. 'Dada, Dada . . .' They were not one year old yet, but were trying hard to talk.

Eunice hoped that Ronnie would be pleased she had made the effort to go to the shop. It was quite a long way – the best part of two miles to North Shore – but she enjoyed walking. Sammy was not with them. He was playing happily with his little friend Billy next door, and Billy's mum, Mary, had begged her to let him stay there. It would have been too far for him to walk anyway, but Eunice hoped that Ronnie would not accuse her of neglecting the little boy.

I am right to make the first move, she thought to herself as she walked in the general direction of the sea. She knew she had to do something about their failing relationship before it was too late. She could not remember the last time she and Ronnie had made love. And yet it had used to be such a joy to them. Could it be so again, she wondered. Or had Ronnie's depression taken such a hold on him that he would not be able to shake it off?

As she drew near the street on which the shops were situated she saw a familiar grey van turn a corner just in front of her. 'Oh, look, there's Daddy's van,' she said to the twins. She talked to them all the time, whether they understood or not. 'He must be out doing his deliveries. Let's see if we can catch him up, shall we?'

She hurried towards the street into which the van had turned. Yes, it had pulled up beside the kerb and there was

Ronnie getting out, but he was too far away for her to shout to him. She recalled how, when she was a little girl, her mother had always said it was vulgar to shout out in the street. He opened the back door of the van and took out a large box. She slowed her footsteps, not altogether sure why she was doing so; and the next moment she stood stock-still, just watching. A young dark-haired woman had come down the garden path and was opening the gate. She looked very pleased to see Ronnie, and he seemed equally pleased to see her. He followed her up the path, the cardboard box in his arms, and into the house. The door closed behind them.

Eunice knew who the woman was. She was called Thelma Cardwell and she was a war widow with a little boy called Bobby. She did not know her very well. The young woman was reserved; Eunice had even thought her a little stand-offish. Ronnie will be out in a minute, she thought, when he has delivered the groceries; or perhaps Mrs Cardwell was settling the bill at the same time? She waited several moments but he did not reappear.

'Come along, we'll go and see Grandma and Granddad,' she said eventually.

Her mind was working overtime as she hurried towards the grocer's shop. Mrs Cardwell? Surely not; it was not possible. Ronnie would never . . .

'Hello, dear. How lovely to see you,' said Mabel as Eunice pushed open the shop door and she heard the familiar jangle of the bell. 'What a nice surprise. Did you think you'd come and see your gran, you two? And Granddad. Isn't this a lovely surprise, Granddad?'

'Aye, it is that,' agreed Tom, slicing bacon. 'Come on in and we'll have a cuppa, shall we, Mabel? We're not very busy this afternoon. You've just missed Ronnie. He's gone out delivering, but he shouldn't be long.'

'Yes . . . I thought he might've done,' said Eunice. She did not let on that she had seen him. 'Come on, you two; out of the pram. Sammy's playing with his friend,' she explained, 'so I left him with Mary.'

'Come on then; let's be having you,' said Mabel picking up Fran, whilst Eunice took Ellie out of the pram.

'I'll just rest me legs for five minutes,' said Mabel, when she had made a pot of tea. 'I can hear the bell from up here if anybody comes in the shop, but we've been dead quiet today.'

'Aye, well; there was a rush on earlier this week, wasn't there?' said Tom. 'You stay where you are, love. I'll take me tea downstairs. I want to finish off them bacon orders. I expect Ronnie'll be back soon. He might as well run you home then, Eunice, if you can get the pram in the back of the van. He's worked hard so we'll let him finish early.'

'Where has he gone?' asked Eunice, as Tom departed. 'Did he have a lot of deliveries to do?'

'Not all that many,' said Mabel. 'Mostly the old folk as can't get out. He's sometimes longer than we expect, 'cause they keep him chatting. Can't say as I blame 'em; he might be the first friendly face they've seen in a while.'

'Yes . . . I see,' said Eunice. She was thinking that Mrs Cardwell was by no means old, and she was quite capable, too, of collecting her own groceries.

Eunice chatted with Mabel about Sammy and the twins' progress, whilst the little girls played with the contents of their gran's button box, which she kept at the shop for them. The shiny buttons were scattered all over the carpet; Fran and Ellie, as usual, were fascinated by the different colours and sizes and shapes. But Eunice was preoccupied and restless.

'I'll have a walk round the block and see if I can find

Ronnie,' she said after a while. 'Then I can tell him we want a lift home.'

'All right, dear,' said Mabel, 'if you wish. But if you can't find him, come back here and wait. He can't be long now. I tell you what; leave the twins here. They're enjoying their little game. You'll be all right with Grandma, won't you?' She smiled lovingly at the two little girls.

Eunice's heart was in her mouth as she turned the corner into the street where she had seen the van. She told herself she was being silly and suspicious and that it was very wrong even to imagine such a thing about Ronnie. When had he ever let her down? But the van was still there. She stood still on the spot as she had done before, unable to believe her eyes. But there must be some explanation . . .

Then the house door opened and Ronnie walked cheerfully down the path. At the gate he stopped and waved to the woman at the door.

Eunice could not stop herself. 'Ronnie, Ronnie . . .' she called as she ran down the street towards him.

One look on his face as he turned and stared at her was enough to tell her that something was going on – or so she imagined – but he immediately tried to turn his look of alarm into one of pleasant surprise.

'Eunice, whatever are you doing here?'

'I've come . . . to meet you,' she stammered, out of breath. 'Aren't you . . . pleased?'

'Well, yes, of course . . .' He frowned slightly. 'Where's Sammy, and the twins?'

'Sammy's playing with Billy, and the twins are with your mother. I brought them to the shop to see you . . . but you weren't there, so I came to look for you.'

'Yes . . . I'm doing the deliveries. Didn't they tell you?'

'Oh yes . . . they told me. Your father says you can finish early today and take us all home. Come on then; let's get going.' She was trembling with the shock she had received. Ronnie was up to something; she was sure of it. But any accusations and explanations would have to wait till later that evening when the children were in bed.

He was very quiet whilst she made their evening meal, although that was nothing unusual at the moment. At one time he had used to come into the kitchen to help her, but he very rarely did so now. And to do so today would, surely, be an indication of his guilt? She had fed the children and put them to bed, and now she threw together some sausages, beans and chips; a makeshift meal, but that was all she felt like doing.

Ronnie did not appear to be aware of what he was eating. Eunice ate hardly anything.

'How long have you been friendly with Thelma Cardwell?' asked Eunice after a long silence. She guessed Ronnie had been waiting for the question. He looked pleadingly at her as he made an effort to reply.

'Eunice . . . let me try to explain. She's just a friend, that's all.'

'Yes, you'd better try to explain. I saw your van outside her house, and I saw you go inside. Yes, you didn't see me,' she added, at his look of surprise. 'You were too busy making eyes at her. And your van was still there getting on for an hour later. Oh yes, Ronnie, I think I deserve an explanation, don't you?'

'Eunice . . . you've got it all wrong,' he began.

But she didn't let him finish. 'You've been seeing her, haven't you?' she went on. 'Visiting her when you were supposed to be out delivering orders. Your mother says you're often late back because you've been chatting to old ladies. Old ladies, indeed!'

She had been determined to keep calm and not to raise her voice or to resort to tears. But she started to see red as an imaginary scene flashed through her mind. Her husband . . . with that woman. Her composure left her and she began to shout at him. 'What about the *young* woman, the one you've been . . . taking to bed? What about Thelma Cardwell, eh, Ronnie? How long has it been going on?'

'It hasn't!' He broke his silence, shouting back at her. 'There's nothing going on. I've told you, Eunice, we're just . . . friends.'

'You expect me to believe that?' She raised a quizzical eyebrow. She did, in fact, believe him, but she didn't intend him to get away with it so easily. She had a right to know what her husband had been up to whilst she was at home looking after his children.

'You can please yourself whether you believe me or not,' replied Ronnie. 'But it happens to be the truth, the honest truth. Thelma and I . . . I admit we've been friendly . . . and I'm sorry . . . That is, I'm sorry if I've hurt you, Eunice. But I can't honestly say that I'm sorry that Thelma and I are friends. She's been . . . well . . . a very good friend at a time when I needed somebody to talk to.'

'Oh, so it's "Thelma and I", is it? A friend to talk to, somebody you needed. What about me, your wife? Why didn't you try talking to me?'

Ronnie shook his head dejectedly. 'I don't know. Just lately it's seemed as though you haven't had time for me; not to talk to . . . or anything else.'

'That's not true, Ronnie,' she retorted. She was tempted to say 'It's all your fault!' but she knew that would sound childish. And it would be wrong to try and lay all the blame at Ronnie's door, even though she knew the rift between them was due, largely, to him and his moods, whether he could help them or not. 'It takes two,' she said, trying to speak calmly although she could not remember ever feeling so angry with him. 'We've drifted apart; I know we have, but I'm not going to take all the blame for that . . . It's obvious to me now why you don't want me any more.'

She didn't really believe what she was implying – that Ronnie had been unfaithful to her – but the words were out before she could stop them.

'That's just not true!' he shouted back at her. 'How many times do I have to tell you, Thelma and me, we're . . . just friends.'

'And you really expect me to believe that? Come off it, Ronnie! I wasn't born yesterday.'

'Oh, believe what you like then!' he yelled. She had never heard him raise his voice like that, not in all the years she had known him. This was not the Ronnie she knew at all. He stood up from where they were sitting at the table with such force that his chair toppled over. 'I'm going out,' he said. 'I need to get away . . . to think, to clear my head.'

'Where? Where are you going?' She felt scared, almost panic-stricken at his words. Whatever was happening to them? She had certainly not intended it to lead to this.

'Oh, I'll go to my mother's,' he said, a shade more calmly. But she could see he was very distressed and in no state to talk things over at the moment.

'I don't want your parents to know about this,' she said. 'Ronnie, please . . .'

'It's rather too late to be worrying about that, isn't it?' He went out and she heard him go into their bedroom. She did not follow him. The walls were thin and she did not want the children to hear them quarrelling, if they had not already done so. But fortunately there was no sound from their room.

About ten minutes later she heard the front door close quietly behind him. At least he had not shut it with a bang. She was tempted to run after him, but she did not do so. It would be dreadful to have an argument out in the street and perhaps he really did need time to sort himself out. Maybe these black moods he suffered were worse than she had imagined. But that was no excuse for him to get friendly with Thelma Cardwell.

'Oh, Ronnie, Ronnie . . . whatever is happening to us?' she said, aloud this time. And then she burst into tears.

Mabel was surprised, to say the least, when Ronnie knocked at the door at nine o'clock that evening. She could tell by his face there was something wrong. 'Good gracious, lad; whatever's the matter?' she cried. 'It's not one of the children, is it? Or Eunice? I thought she looked a bit peaky this afternoon.'

'No, Mam, they're all OK. Eunice – well, she's a bit upset to be quite honest, but . . . Look, can I come in? You're not going to keep me standing on the doorstep, are you?' He followed his mother into the living room where his father was settled in an easy chair, listening to the nine o'clock news. 'Actually, I've come to ask if I can stay here tonight? Eunice and I . . . we've had a bit of a row.'

'You've had a row?' Mabel stared at him in horror. 'So bad that you've walked out? Then you'd best get home, hadn't you, quick sharp, and make it up with her. Had a row, indeed! Whatever sort of a tale is that? Oh, for heaven's sake, turn that off, Tom. We can't hear ourselves speak.' Tom obediently turned off the wireless, smiling apologetically at his son.

'Let the lad have his say, Mabel. It must be summat quite serious, or he wouldn't turn up here, would he? Of course, I reckon nothing to walking out on yer wife—'

'And I don't believe in interfering in other folk's marriages, especially me own son's,' said Mabel. 'Anyroad, you'd best sit down and tell us what's up.'

'It's not been right between us for ages,' said Ronnie,

twisting his hands together agitatedly, until his mother told him to stop fidgeting and to get on with his tale. 'Eunice and me, we don't seem to get on any more, like we used to.'

'Then you've got to make more effort, haven't you?' said Mabel. 'I can't say I haven't noticed, 'cause I have. She was like a cat on hot bricks when she came here this afternoon. Restless, like; she wouldn't sit still. At least she had made the effort to come and see you.'

'Yes, that's what brought it to a head,' said Ronnie. He told his parents, very truthfully, about what had happened, about his budding friendship with Thelma Cardwell.

'So you've been carrying on behind her back, have you?' said Mabel. 'I'm not surprised your wife was angry. She was right to kick you out.'

'No, Mam, you've got it all wrong,' Ronnie protested. 'Of course I haven't been carrying on. We're just friends . . . but Eunice won't believe me.'

'And I can't say I blame her,' retorted Mabel.

'Listen, Mam, I know you don't understand it – I'm not sure I understand what is happening myself – but I just need to be on my own for a while, for tonight at any rate.'

'I know you haven't been yourself for quite a time, certainly,' said his mother, 'and I know you say you can't help this depression that you suffer from, but I don't think it's a very good idea to walk out on Eunice.'

'It's only for tonight,' said Ronnie. 'I can't go back now. Perhaps I was wrong to walk out like that, but I just felt I had to get away. It's all such a muddle in my mind.'

'Poor Eunice will be on her own,' Mabel told him, 'and she won't like that at all.'

'She's got the children. She's be all right, Mam. She's very competent, you know; much more competent than I am,' he added grimly. 'I'll see her tomorrow, and I'll try and think of a way to make things right again.'

Mabel sighed. 'Let's hope so. Eunice is a grand lass and I don't want to see her made unhappy.'

'And this is our Ronnie, remember,' Tom reminded her. 'He's a grand lad an' all, and we know he wouldn't do anything really wrong . . . don't we?' His wife nodded silently. 'We'd best let him stay here, just for tonight. It's their problem, but you can be sure they'll sort it out, given time.' Tom realised, possibly more than Mabel did, the effect that their son's war injuries had had on him. Depression could cause very strange reactions sometimes.

'Thank you, Dad,' said Ronnie quietly. 'It's all a muddle at the moment. But it'll come right . . . I hope . . .'

Eunice tossed and turned in her lonely bed until the early hours of the morning. She had half expected Ronnie to return, but he did not do so. Eventually she got up and took three aspirin tablets and then managed to sleep until the alarm clock woke her at seven thirty.

Maybe he will come round before he goes to the shop, she thought, but this did not happen. Perhaps it was worse than she had imagined . . . All kinds of thoughts started to spin round in her head. Maybe he really was having an affair with Thelma Cardwell; maybe he had decided to leave her, Eunice, for good. But his parents would never stand for that.

Her mind was in a turmoil as she got the twins and Sammy ready to go shopping with her. Life had to go on as normal – or as normal as was possible – and the children had not commented on Ronnie's absence. Sometimes he had departed for the shop before they had their breakfast so they did not notice anything unusual.

Sammy trotted along happily at her side, chattering away about his friend Billy, and about the school at which they would both be starting in a few months' time. They passed the school on the way to the shops, and to Sammy's delight the children were playing out in the yard. He did not seem to have noticed that his mother was quieter than usual.

As for Eunice, her thoughts were spinning round and round in her head. First and foremost, thoughts of Ronnie. Please, please, let him come back to me, she prayed silently. But she was thinking of Heinrich as well. Maybe she should have replied to his letter; she wished now that she had done so. But why? What good would it have done? Then she thought about Thelma, the woman who was stealing her husband. She tried to drag her mind back to the more mundane thought of what she and the children were going to have for their midday meal . . .

'Now hold on tightly to the handle of the pram while I go into this shop,' said Eunice to Sammy. 'I won't be long and the twins will be quite happy playing with their ball. You're such a good boy, aren't you, Sammy, looking after them for me?'

She disappeared into the butcher's shop and joined on to the end of the little queue of three or four people.

The little girls chuckled as they threw their furry ball from one to the other. They were sitting up, one at either end of the pram, their plump little hands grasping at the ball.

Sammy thought they were quite good fun now, but he hoped Mummy wouldn't be long. He glanced away from the twins, watching Eunice, who was now talking to the man in the striped apron. He heard Francesca give a little cry as the furry ball missed her hands and jumped out of the pram on to the pavement. It would have stayed there, because it wasn't a hard rolly sort of ball and Sammy would have picked it up; but at that moment a black and white dog came bounding up and snatched it up in his mouth. He lolloped across the pavement and Sammy let go of the pram handle and followed him.

'Stop it, you bad dog!' he shouted. 'That's my babies' ball. Put it down.'

The dog, tired of his game, dropped the ball by the kerb and scampered away. Sammy went to retrieve it; across the pavement he ran and over the kerb into the road, where he stooped down to get hold of the furry ball.

The driver of the van did not see him, a small figure crouching at the kerbside. As the poor man was to say, many times afterwards, the first thing he knew was a bang and a cry; then he saw a little form in a red coat being tossed away in front of his van and landing in a heap a few yards distant. Then the sound of voices and footsteps running, and one voice above all the others shouting, 'Oh no, no! My little boy . . . Sammy . . . Oh, Sammy . . .'

Chapter 23

It was like a nightmare to Eunice; the sudden realisation that the screech of brakes and the cry were connected with her precious little son. She fled out of the shop shouting his name, then she kneeled at the kerb at the side of his still and silent little form, the twins in the pram momentarily forgotten.

'Get my husband, please get my husband!' she cried. 'Ronnie, oh, Ronnie . . .' She needed him so very much.

'Give us his phone number, love,' said the concerned butcher and she managed to do so.

'Don't touch him, love; don't try to move him,' the anxious by-standers advised her. 'Leave to the ambulance men . . .'

After what seemed ages, although it could only have been a few minutes, an ambulance arrived. Sammy was lifted gently on to the stretcher and driven away with the lights flashing and the bell ringing. She could not go with him because of the twins. The two little girls were staring wide-eyed and open-mouthed at the scene.

And then, suddenly, her husband was there, with Mabel and Tom.

'Ronnie, Ronnie . . .' she cried, running towards him as he got out of the van. Then she was in his arms and they clung to one another, both of them knowing that that was where they belonged . . . together. 'He'll be all right, won't he, our little Sammy?' she sobbed fearfully. 'Oh, Ronnie, I'm so glad you're here.'

'They'll take good care of him,' said Ronnie. 'He's in the best hands, I'm sure . . .' They each knew of the other one's concerns and doubts, but they would be able to face it, together.

Mabel and Tom took charge of the twins whilst Eunice and Ronnie dashed off to the hospital. Eventually they were all there, waiting, just waiting. The only person missing was Edith. Someone was needed to look after the twins, and the boarding house as well. Even in a time of crisis the visitors' needs must be met.

Sammy was undergoing an emergency operation.

'He's in good hands,' they kept telling one another.

'The very best; he'll be OK. He'll pull through; he's a strong little lad.'

'Of course he will . . .'

At last the surgeon appeared. His face was solemn and he looked weary as he approached Eunice and Ronnie. They told one another afterwards that they had both feared the worst until he smiled; a very tired smile. Then he nodded. 'Your son is over the worst, Mr and Mrs Iveson,' he said. 'A broken arm and cuts and bruises of course, but the bump on his head is not as bad as I had feared; there is no brain damage. He's heavily bandaged and he'll be asleep for quite a while, but . . . he'll be OK.'

'Oh, thank you so much,' they both cried. 'May we see him?'

'Of course you may. Stay as long as you wish . . .'

The rest of the family went home to tell Edith the good

news whilst Eunice and Ronnie sat at their son's bedside in a private little room off the main ward. Sammy was sleeping peacefully after the operation. He looked pale, but he was breathing normally. Eunice and Ronnie smiled at one another, a little self-consciously at first.

'We're lucky,' said Eunice. 'We might have lost him. For one dreadful moment I thought we had.'

'So did I,' replied Ronnie. 'Don't, Eunice. We mustn't even think about it,' he shuddered. 'Sammy's still here, and we've got our two little girls as well . . . And we've got one another, and that's the most important of all.'

'Of course we have, darling,' she said. 'Ronnie, I'm sorry; for not believing what you said about Thelma. I never really doubted you, you know.'

The love shone from his eyes as he smiled at her. 'You will never need to doubt me, Eunice. There has only ever been you, and that's how it will always be.' He shook his head. 'I don't know what I was thinking of. I was flattered, I suppose.'

'And . . . what about her – Thelma?' asked Eunice quietly. 'Do you think she might have had . . . ideas . . . about you? I couldn't blame her if she had.'

Ronnie laughed softly. 'I really don't know. If she did, she'll get over them; she's a sensible woman. It's you and me, Eunice, and no one else, for ever and ever.' He leaned across and kissed her gently. Then, 'Oh look,' he said. 'Our Sammy . . . he's coming round.'

The little boy dazedly opened his eyes for a moment. 'Mummy . . . Daddy . . .' he said. Then he smiled and contentedly shut his eyes again.

Sammy recovered quite quickly. He started school in the January of 1948, and in the same month the family moved, at last, into their own home; their own in the sense that they really and truly owned it.

'Well, we will when we've paid off the mortgage,' laughed Ronnie, 'but it's good to say we own even a part of it. Just think, Eunice; it's ours – yours and mine. Isn't that wonderful?' His black moods seemed to have gone for good. They had both needed the short, sharp shock that had brought them to their senses.

Ronnie had worked and saved hard and had managed, with a little help from his parents, which Eunice had persuaded him to accept, to put down more than the minimum deposit required. The house, a three-bedroomed semi – such as had always been the height of his ambition – was in North Shore, the area with which they were both familiar, near to the Bispham boundary. There were gardens at the front and back and a garage in which to keep the shop van.

The following years were, on the whole, happy ones, but by no means uneventful and with their moments of sadness. It was in 1958 that Ronnie's parents decided to retire and hand the grocery business over to their son. Mabel and Tom were both still quite fit and active, but they wanted to enjoy their years of retirement while they were young enough to do so. Tom joined a bowling club, Mabel enlisted in night-school classes and took more part in church life and the Mothers' Union; and they both, for the first time in their lives, began to travel to the Continent on package tours, usually by coach.

Ronnie took over the management of the grocery store. He employed two assistants, a woman and a youth – a school leaver – to assist him. The business thrived for several years, but, alas for the small shops, times were changing. The change came slowly at first, but Ronnie could see the writing on the wall. Gradually there was becoming more and more competition for small businesses, with the emergence of supermarkets and self-service stores. By the start of the sixties, Ronnie began to notice a slight decline in his takings; not, as yet, enough to worry him unduly, but he realised he would have to start thinking about the future of the business.

They were what might be termed 'comfortably off', though by no means wealthy. Eunice was now working, as the children were at an age when she felt she could do so without neglecting them. Sammy was seventeen, in the sixth form at the Grammar School, and the twins were fourteen, both doing well at the Girls' Collegiate School. Ellie was still marginally ahead of her twin, academically and in other ways as well; livelier, more interested in boys, and cheekier too! Fran was gentler and inclined to be shy, but they were both very good girls at heart; and as for Sammy he showed signs of being a real 'go-getter'. Eunice, to her surprise and pleasure, had managed to procure a post at the local branch library. She was just an assistant, a part-time one to fit in with the children's school hours, but she was very happy and satisfied.

The future seemed rosy, apart from the little niggling concern about the grocery business. Eunice urged Ronnie to try out some new ideas, and he, who had needed persuading at first, agreed to do so. Instead of having all the goods behind the counter, they opened up the shop, had more shelving installed and put all the goods on display near to hand. The customers were supplied with wire baskets so that they could help themselves to whatever they required.

'You're encouraging folk to steal, that's what you're doing,' Edith argued, which did not surprise Eunice at all. 'Shop-lifting, they call it now, but it's stealing whichever way you look at it. How do you know they're not putting stuff into their own baskets as well as them wire things?'

'We don't,' said Eunice, 'but you've got to trust people, Mother. I think it's a good idea and so does Ronnie. It might encourage people to buy more. They'll see something they fancy – something that wasn't on their list – and decide to give it a try. Ronnie's ordered all sorts of new fancy biscuits, and sweets and chocolates; we're stocking more of them as well.'

'Oh, well, let's hope that husband of yours knows what he's doing,' said Edith. 'I shan't buy owt I don't need, I can tell you.'

Eunice wished at times that her mother would retire, as Mabel and Tom had done. She was sure the boarding house was getting to be too much for her. Her father was due to retire soon and she wanted them to be able to enjoy their time together, as her parents-in-law were doing. Bookings were down, Eunice admitted, as more and more people – seemingly much more affluent these days – were travelling abroad or to more exciting destinations in England or Scotland. Holiday flats, too, 'self-catering', as they called them, were becoming popular. The boarding house was just ticking over, as Edith put it, but she never talked of giving it up.

Ronnie noticed a slight improvement in the takings as folk who, for a time, might have gone elsewhere, returned, lured by the self-service idea. He did not notice any pilfering either, although sweets and bars of chocolate were kept near the counter where he could keep an eagle eye on the children who now, more than previously, frequented the shop.

The shop next door, a run-down drapery business, was put up for sale. It had been closed and empty for several months as the elderly lady who owned it had become ill and died. It had been a quaint establishment of the sort that rarely existed any more. Miss Parkin had sold – or tried to sell – old-fashioned underwear and aprons, rolls of material – mostly in checked gingham – and sewing and knitting requisites, many of which had faded over the years. Ronnie looked at the 'For Sale' sign thoughtfully. It would be ideal for expansion of his own premises. He had a germ of an idea he would love to put into practice . . . But he could not afford it at the moment and he was determined not to ask his parents to help any further.

In the January of 1963 Eunice's father died suddenly. He had been retired from his post at the Water Board for just a year. Samuel had long been a 'creaking gate', and so his death came as rather a shock. The trouble with his chest, from his old war injuries, had flared up again as it did periodically, but this time it turned to pneumonia, which proved fatal.

Edith was distraught at her husband's death. As it was wintertime there were no visitors in the boarding house. This was fortunate in one sense, although Eunice felt that looking after guests might have given her mother an incentive to keep going. As it was, she seemed to lose all will to live. Three months later, Edith too had died from a heart attack; a condition, the doctor said, that had lain undetected; Edith had seldom needed to visit a doctor. But Eunice was convinced that her mother had not wanted to go on living without her husband.

Over the years Eunice had wondered about her parents' marriage. They had taken one another so much for granted; Edith, undoubtedly, had been the boss and Samuel had seemed content to have it that way; but they had never appeared to be really enjoying their life together. But Eunice supposed, now, that in their own way they must have been contented, maybe even happy.

She was the sole beneficiary, something she had not even

considered, although common sense should have told her it would be so. The property was sold very quickly; the new owners were to convert it into holiday flats. It was the end of an era, thought Eunice. Grandma Gregson's boarding house that had been in the family for so long was, in essence, to disappear. But she, Eunice, had never had any desire to be a seaside landlady, like her mother and grandmother. She was, in point of fact, now quite a well-off woman.

The run-down draper's shop was still not sold. She had heard of Ronnie's tentative plans to expand, but not the exact details of them. As he had thought it to be little more than a pipe dream he had not talked about it overmuch. Now, however, it seemed as though it might be possible. Eunice, without any hesitation, had offered to plough her inherited money into the business. Share and share alike had always been their byword through the latter, very contented, years of their marriage.

She listened, enthralled, as Ronnie outlined his ideas. The grocery business would, he hoped, keep going – his parents would not wish to see that disappear – but he had great plans for the shop next door. They would knock through so that it became, basically, one shop. The new part would become a newsagent's, selling sweets, tobacco, fancy goods, papers, magazines and – he told her in great glee – a section for books, which would be Eunice's special domain; that was if she was willing to leave her job at the library . . .

She was thrilled and fell in wholeheartedly with her husband's plans. It was what she had long wanted: a bookshop of her own. It would not be on a large scale, of course – not like Sweeten's, the booksellers in the centre of town – and it would only be part of the shop, but she was sure she could make a success of it. Paperbacks, she decided; that was what she would concentrate on. Mostly new ones – she loved the feel and smell and the whole concept of new books – but maybe second-hand books as well. And a lending library, maybe . . .?

It did not happen overnight, but within a year the combined business – grocery, newsagent's, stationer's, confectioner's and tobacconist's, and bookseller's – was up and running. Eunice was in charge, not only of the books, but of the whole stationery and newsagent's department, including the sweets and tobacco. They employed extra staff. A man who lived near to the shop had offered to open up early each morning to see to the delivery of newspapers, and, in addition, there were two young women to help Eunice, and Ronnie's original staff on the grocery side.

More and more people were buying paperback books now, as well as borrowing from the libraries. They were reasonably priced and easy to handle; ideal for reading on the train or in bed, or slipping into your holiday luggage. Eunice ordered quite large numbers of Penguin books, the mysteries and thrillers with green backs and the orange-backed novels, as well as books with bright illustrations on the jackets; children's books too. It was encouraging to see children spending their pocket money on something to read, and the annuals she had in stock at Christmas time made ideal presents. There were also second-hand books at a fraction of the cost, although this did not seem to affect the sales of the new ones. And a small lending library of hard-backed books, mainly from the Companion and Foyle's book clubs, which she had purchased from customers; although how they could bear to part with their books, she could not imagine. Her own shelves, at home as well as at the shop, overflowed with them.

In the spring of 1968 Eunice and Ronnie celebrated their Silver Wedding. They had said that they didn't want a fuss making of them, but their three children had insisted that the family should celebrate by having an evening meal together. This took place at the Cliffs Hotel, one of the more prestigious establishments, situated on the promenade opposite the cliffs, as its name denoted, near to Gynn Square. And afterwards they all returned to Eunice and Ronnie's home to finish off the evening.

They were still living in the same semi-detached house. Even though their business was thriving and they could have afforded to move to a detached house or a larger semi, they had decided to stay put. Most of their earnings were ploughed into the business; besides, it seemed as though, quite soon, they might have the house to themselves.

The twins were now twenty-one. Fran had been married soon after her twenty-first birthday and was expecting her first child. Eunice and Ronnie were bemused at the thought that they would soon be grandparents. They were fond of Mike, Fran's husband, and could see that he was devoted to her. She had worked in the accounts department at the newly opened Lewis's store after she left school, but on marrying Mike and soon becoming pregnant she had shown no hesitation in giving up her job and settling down to domesticity.

Ellie had trained to be a nurse. Officially, she still lived at home, but her shift work meant that her parents never really knew when she would be there or if she would be elsewhere. She always had a boyfriend in tow, a different one each week, Ronnie laughed. Every month or two, certainly. Fran had settled down with the first serious love of her life, but Ellie seemed to be playing the field. She had been talking recently of getting a place of her own; sharing a flat, maybe, with another nurse.

Sammy, to their amazement, was an architect. He lived and worked in Manchester. He was twenty-four years old, not yet married, but with a steady girlfriend. His parents were very proud of his achievements and they wondered how the two of them had succeeded in producing such a clever son.

And so the nest was now empty. That made Eunice a little sad, but she knew that she and Ronnie were still young enough – in their mid-forties – to look forward as well as back. The future looked full of promise although one never knew, of course, what might lie ahead of them. They were truly happy together now, and if they looked back to reminisce it was to remember the joyful times and not the sad ones.

And then, in the early October of that same year, Eunice suddenly came face to face with a ghost from the past.

She was standing in a queue at the post office in Blackpool, one of several short queues of people waiting for attention. It was her half-day off from the shop. She and the other assistants took it in turns to have time off. They were even opening Wednesday afternoons now – which had long been Blackpool's official half-day closing time – to catch the holiday trade. This was still continuing during the illuminations season.

She became aware of the woman in the next queue looking intently at her. She looked back and half smiled. Was it someone she knew? At first she did not recognise her although she thought she looked vaguely familiar. About the same age as herself, Eunice surmised; greyish-blonde hair and a pale thin-featured face. A worried expression in her eyes . . . which cleared as she recognised Eunice. At the same moment Eunice realised who she was. It was Olive; Olive Pritchard – although she would not now be called Pritchard, of course – her colleague from the Land Army days.

There came a fleeting thought that she had never wished to come into contact with the young woman again, but this was hastily pushed away as Olive greeted her like a long-lost friend.

'It's Eunice, isn't it?'

Eunice nodded. 'Yes, that's right. And you are Olive?'

'So I am. What a surprise, eh? Although I don't know that I should be all that surprised. You lived in Blackpool, didn't you? Well, obviously you still do . . .'

'Yes, we do . . . What are you doing here, Olive? It certainly is a surprise . . . a very pleasant one,' she added.

'Oh, Ted and I are having a few days' holiday here. We wanted to see the illuminations. We used to bring the children when they were younger, but it's several years since we were here. I'm just getting stamps for these cards . . .' A view of the Tower and an illuminated tram was uppermost in her hand. 'Oh, see, it's my turn now. I'll wait for you outside, Eunice . . .'

All previous animosity appeared to have been forgotten as they chatted on Abingdon Street outside the GPO building.

'So you married Ted, then?'

'Of course,' Olive giggled. 'Just after the war finished. We've two children: a boy and a girl; grown-up now, but still living at home.'

'And . . . where is that? You were from Wigan, weren't you? And Ted was a Gloucestershire lad, wasn't he?'

'Yes, that's right. We've got a smallholding not far from where he used to live. His parents died, and so did mine, but his roots were down there in Gloucestershire so that's where we settled. We're doing very nicely,' she said, with a touch of pride. 'What about you? What was your boyfriend's name? Roy . . . Raymond . . .? Did you . . .?'

'Ronnie,' replied Eunice emphatically. 'Yes, we got married. We have three children, all grown-up like yours, but none of them is still at home. My husband and I run a business in North Shore. Groceries, newspapers, books, sweets, tobacco – you name it, we've got it.'

'Oh, very nice. And you live over the shop, I suppose? I remember, Ronnie worked for his parents, didn't he?'

'He used to. No, we don't live over the shop; we never did. We have a house not all that far away . . .' What could she do then but invite Olive and Ted to come and have a meal with them that same evening, if they wished. It would be good to see Ted again . . .

Olive jumped at the chance and she knew Ted would agree. They were staying at a small private hotel near to North Pier, where an evening meal was included. But it would be lovely, she enthused, to dine with Eunice and Ronnie instead. At the moment Ted was taking a walk on the promenade whilst she was having a meander round the shops. Eunice gave her their address and directions as to how they were to find it. They agreed to meet at six thirty, and Eunice planned, in her mind, that they would dine around seven fifteen.

It was when Olive departed, with a cheery wave, that Eunice began to wonder what she had let herself in for. Olive seemed as though she was remembering only the good times they had shared together, but Eunice knew her of old. She could not entirely forget the young woman's insecurity, and how that had led to jealousy and suspicion, and then to snide insinuations about the child that Eunice was carrying. Her suspicions had, in fact, not been unfounded, but she, Eunice, had denied and had gone on denying that she had been too friendly with Heinrich, the POW. What else could she have done?

She suppressed a shudder. She had not thought of him for years, except in passing; perhaps when one of the World War Two films appeared on the television, as they did with alarming regularity. Was no one ever to be allowed to forget the war? Then she would remember him briefly, and just as quickly forget him again. She had seldom thought of Olive either; and now, here she was, back to haunt her with remembrances of things that were best forgotten. It would be all right, though, she told herself. The woman she had just met seemed friendly and quite at ease with herself, much more mature and confident than the graceless, rather peevish, girl she had once been.

More to the point, what should she give them to eat? She decided on a casserole dish, so that she could prepare most of the meal in advance and not have to stand watching chops grill or carve a joint of meat at the last moment. She popped into the nearest butcher's shop for some beef steak, which looked juicy and tender, and then into Abingdon Street market for a selection of vegetables. She had baked a large apple pie the previous day. There was plenty of that left, and she would call at the shop on the way home to collect a carton of fresh cream to accompany it; and to tell Ronnie that they were to have company for their evening meal.

Ted was very little changed from the kindly and helpful farmhand that Eunice had remembered. A little grey now at the temples and a tiny bit stooped, no doubt with all the strenuous digging and planting; but she thought she would have recognised him, more than anything else, by the pleasant Gloucestershire intonation in his speech.

Ronnie had not met either of their guests before, although Olive hastened to tell him that she had heard a lot about him. 'Haven't I, Eunice?' she asked coyly, giggling a little. 'Honestly, Ronnie, she never stopped talking about you – did you, Eunice? – when we were at Meadowlands. I used to be quite jealous, I can tell you, because I hadn't got a boyfriend. And then, of course, I met Ted . . .' She gave him a glance that Eunice felt was more proprietorial than affectionate. 'We had some good times together, all of us, until Ted had to go into the army. Do you remember that Young Farmers' Dance that we went to? And the dresses that Mrs Meadows tarted up for us? Talk about "make do and mend"! We thought we were the belles of the ball.'

'As I recall it, we were,' said Eunice. 'There weren't all that many young people there. Most of the young men were in the forces, so it was mainly middle-aged farmers and their wives. We enjoyed it, though. I remember it was a pleasant change from slogging away on the land.'

'Yes . . . Ted and I danced the night away, didn't we, Ted?' Olive smiled at her husband and he nodded and smiled back, but without any comment. 'You didn't have a special partner did you, Eunice? With Ronnie being in the army, I mean.'

'I expect she did OK for partners, didn't you, love?' said Ronnie, grinning at his wife, but casting an ever so slightly annoyed look in Olive's direction.

Eunice laughed. 'Yes, old farmers who trampled all over my feet, from what I can remember.'

'Let's see – were we engaged then?' asked Ronnie.

'Er . . . no.' Eunice hesitated a moment. 'It was before . . . all that, I think. Yes, quite a while before.' She felt herself getting a little hot under the collar as the memories, so long stifled, started to return. 'Anyway, what does it all matter now? We are all here, and you two men managed to get through the war all in one piece.'

'Almost,' said Ronnie.

'Oh yes; you were wounded, weren't you, Ronnie?' said

Olive. 'In the desert . . . I remember now.' She half closed her eyes and nodded. Eunice feared she might be remembering rather too much.

'And I escaped scot free,' said Ted. 'I took part in the D-Day landings; not a bullet wound, not even a scratch. I was damned lucky and I know it.'

'Oh, let's forget about the war, shall we?' said Eunice. They were sitting in the front room of the house, the lounge – which they always made full use of, unlike their forebears – enjoying a glass of sherry before the meal. 'Tell us about your children. You have two, you said, Olive?'

Olive was only too happy to talk about Brian and Myrna. Brian, aged twenty-one, worked with his father at the smallholding – a market garden, they explained, with several poultry, but no large animals. And Myrna, aged eighteen, was at a secretarial college in Gloucester, but still living at home. From the photos they proudly displayed it was obvious that the young man resembled his father and the girl looked very much like Olive had looked at nineteen.

'And what about you two?' asked Olive. 'Three children, you said? You've done a bit better than us, eh? And they're all off your hands? That must be nice for you – to have time on your own, I mean. Although I can't imagine our two ever wanting to fly the nest, can you, Ted? They know which side their bread's buttered, the pair of them.'

'No boyfriends or girlfriends?' asked Eunice, bristling a little.

'Well . . . yes. They come and go. But our two are too comfortable at home to want to get tied down.'

'Oh well, we're soon to be grandparents,' said Eunice. She reached for the wedding photo of Fran which, with several others, stood on top of the bookcase. 'This is Francesca – Fran we call her – and Mike on their wedding day.'

'Oh, yes, she's lovely,' said Olive. Eunice felt pleased about that, but it was the comment everyone made when they saw the photograph. 'And isn't she like you? Like you used to be, I mean,' she added, which Eunice felt was rather a back-handed compliment.

'And this is Eleanor – our Ellie. They're twins, but not identical ones. She's more like her father, as you can see . . .' She explained that they were twenty-two and that Ellie was a nurse. 'And this is our eldest, Sammy. He's twenty-five. He's an architect in Manchester.'

Olive looked at the photo, a coloured one taken earlier that year when Sammy had been holidaying in the Lake District with friends. His auburn hair stood out like a beacon, which was no doubt what made Olive exclaim, 'Goodness me! Isn't he the image of his father?' Ronnie's hair, though it had faded, was still unmistakably ginger. 'Not just his hair, though, his features as well. I didn't know you, Ronnie, when you were his age, but you must have looked just like that.'

'So he did,' smiled Eunice. 'The very same.'

'Yes, there's no mistaking who he belongs to, is there?' said Ronnie, chuckling.

'He was the spitting image of his daddy, and he still is,' said Eunice, smiling as she looked at the photo Olive handed back to her. 'Everyone said so.' She looked intently at Olive, who looked back just as keenly at her.

'Yes, so I see,' she replied. 'Like you say . . .' she gave a little laugh, 'there could be no doubt who his daddy was.' She stopped, putting her hand to her mouth as though she might be misunderstood. 'Not that there *would* have been any doubt, of course. I don't mean—'

'It's all right, Olive,' said Eunice. 'I know what you mean.' She stood up. 'Now, if you'll excuse me I'll go and put the finishing touches to the dinner.'

They had sailed rather close to the wind, she thought, as they ate their meal, but the awkward moment seemed to have passed. Their conversation afterwards was pretty general: the state of the country and the Government and the economy in the 'swinging sixties', and the changes they had seen. They did not reminisce too much about the war or the Land Army, but Eunice was pleased to hear that Mr and Mrs Meadows were still alive and well, although now retired. Olive called to see them occasionally and Eunice sent them her love and very best wishes. She knew she should have kept in touch with them, but she had not wanted any memories from the past to disturb her. Now it seemed as though all ghosts were well and truly laid to rest.

She stacked the dinner plates to be tackled later when their guests had gone. There was an awkward moment – or was she imagining it? – when she returned to the lounge. Ronnie and Olive were sitting there on their own as Ted had gone upstairs to the bathroom. It seemed, to Eunice, as though they stopped talking when she entered the room. There was silence for a few seconds before Olive spoke, commenting on the curtains and how much she liked the contemporary design. Eunice was learning that Olive was not one to keep her thoughts to herself. She chattered much more than she had used to do and had an opinion about everything.

Eunice could not help being relieved when they had gone. The two women promised to keep in touch; it was dreadful, they said to one another, the way they had drifted apart over the years, but they would write . . .

What had Olive said whilst she, Eunice, had been in the kitchen? She felt sure there was something, but, if so, Ronnie would be sure to tell her. She certainly would not ask. But he made no comment, except to say that it had been an enjoyable evening on the whole. 'That Ted seems a nice chap, but I'm not too sure about her. She'd be hard going to live with, that Olive. Anyway, I doubt if we'll see them again, eh, love?'

'No, I shouldn't think so, Ronnie,' Eunice replied.

The two women exchanged a couple of letters, then Christmas cards for several years. And then even that dropped off. Olive and Ted were never mentioned again.

Chapter 24

1993

How the years had flown . . . It was a well-worn cliché, which Eunice heard so often nowadays from people of her and Ronald's generation. When she looked back it seemed no time at all since they had celebrated their Silver Wedding. It was incredible to think they had now passed their Golden one, that they had been married for fifty years.

They had had a good marriage; not without its upsets and sorrows, but the good times and the happiness they had shared had far outweighed the bad times. Ronald had had a heart attack two years ago, which had given him a scare and frightened her as well. Whatever would she do if she were to lose him? And yet she knew it was inevitable that, one day, there would come a time when they would be parted. She had come to realise she owed such a lot to Ronnie, and now, fifty years on from their hasty marriage, she still loved and cared for him in a hundred and one different ways. In spite of his tendency to grumble, to repeat himself, to fall asleep in front of the television – and she was sure that she too had a lot of annoying little habits – theirs was a truly devoted partnership. They now had five grandchildren and, amazingly, a great grandson. This little boy, to their delight, had been christened Ronald, but was always known as Ronnie. She had started, then, to call her husband Ronald – as her mother had always insisted on doing – to avoid confusion and in deference to his maturity.

They were passing by the site of the old bridge of Remagen now. As they had driven through the outskirts of the town Eunice had found herself peering through the window at corpulent German gentlemen – of a certain age – in their distinctive dark green jackets and ribbed knee stockings, and she had wondered . . . Don't be such a fool, she told herself. How could she recognise him after so long, always supposing he was still living in the same town . . . or was still alive. And how much of the beautiful dark-haired girl remained now in the seventy-year-old, somewhat buxom, matron that Eunice had become? Very little, except the memories.

She had never been able to forget Heinrich entirely, even though months and years might go by with her hardly giving him a thought. When she did find herself thinking of him she remembered him as a loving, sometimes serious, sometimes jovial, companion in those late summer days of 1942. When, towards the end of the war, dreadful things had begun to emerge about the Nazis and names such as Belsen and Auschwitz and Dachau were spoken in hushed voices, Eunice had found it hard to accept that the polite handsome young man she had known could belong to the same race. But most of them, she guessed, had been caught up in something of which they really wanted no part. And now . . . it was all such a long time ago, and Germany was a very pleasant place in which to spend part of their holiday. They had visited Germany before on their trips abroad, but this was the first time they had been to the Rhineland.

Gary, the tour guide, was telling the story now of how in World War Two an American unit reached the western bank of the bridge at Remagen to find that the bridge had not been demolished by the retreating Germans, the only Rhine bridge to have been left intact. The Americans had established a bridgehead there, and Hitler, consumed with rage, ordered all those in charge of the bridge defences to be shot. Ten days later the bridge collapsed into the river with considerable loss of life. Now nothing remained except two massive towers, like castles, one on each bank, one of them being a museum of peace.

Eunice knew the story. The film *A Bridge Too Far* had been shown on the television only recently, and she had half watched, as she did with all those old films, whilst Ronald had been engrossed. Even though he professed not to live in the past he was, for all that, an avid viewer of these wartime exploits.

They stopped for lunch at Boppard, a popular tourist centre; then they boarded a pleasure boat for a short cruise whilst Gary and Mike took the coach to an appointed place further along the route. It was a picturesque part of the Rhine with pastel-coloured houses and steepled churches on both riverbanks, and on every craggy hilltop yet another castle. They listened to a commentary in heavily accented English . . . Here was a village church you could only enter through the pub, the vicar being both publican and priest! Here was Maus – Mouse – Castle, and here was St Gaur, which took its name from the patron saint of innkeepers. Facts to be listened to idly and generally forgotten.

As they rounded the bend approaching the Lorelei rock the boat was suddenly filled with the sound of a German choir singing the song of the famous legend. Eunice, in her mind, substituted the words she had learned long ago at school.

> I know not what comes o'er me, or why my spirits fail,
> Strange visions arise before me, I think of an ancient tale . . .

There, on a spit of land running out from the cliff, was the bronze statue of the Lorelei maiden. According to the legend, sailors at twilight were lured to a watery grave by the maiden singing her song and combing her golden hair. A siren, thought Eunice, with a secret smile – half happy, half sad – luring young, maybe innocent young men to their doom. She and Ronnie had given way to their feelings in a moment of love and passion. Sammy had been the result. Sammy . . . and a very happy marriage.

Ronald joined her as she stood at the ship's rail. His next words came as a tremendous shock. 'You were thinking about him back there, weren't you?'

'What? Who? What are you talking about, Ronald? I don't know what you mean.' But she did know, of course. He meant Heinrich. But how could Ronald possibly know about him? She hadn't breathed a word to anyone, not for years. She was sure her secret would go with her to the grave.

Anyone, that was, except Gwen . . . and Olive. Yes, Olive. She remembered the woman's visit with her husband – but that was twenty-five years ago, not long after they had celebrated their Silver Wedding. She recalled how Olive had been very eager to hear about their children, and they had talked about Sammy and about how he resembled his father. But surely she wouldn't have said anything to Ronald about her illicit friendship . . .?

'Oh, come off it, Eunice.'

She glanced at him warily, but to her relief he was looking quite unconcerned.

He smiled at her. 'I know you were friendly with a young POW. I've known for ages, but I guessed you have never wanted to tell me, knowing how I've always felt about the Jerries. And it's all water under the bridge now, isn't it? You can't live in the past.'

'How did you know?' she asked, staring at him in amazement. 'Who told you?' Although she already knew the answer.

'It was that friend of yours; Olive; that lass that was at the farm with you. That time they came to have a meal with us.'

'Yes, I remember,' she said. 'But it was ages ago.' Olive and Ted had scarcely been mentioned since their visit, all those years ago. She had been glad to put the woman, and all the unpleasant memories she evoked, out of her mind.

'To be honest, I didn't like her,' said Ronald. 'I don't know why; there was just something about her. That's why I didn't take any notice of her. I don't think you were all that fond of her either, were you?'

'No, I wasn't; not really,' agreed Eunice. 'We were never bosom pals . . . What did she say?' She tried to make the question sound casual, but she felt quite sick and her stomach was turning somersaults. Surely Olive wouldn't have told Ronald of her suspicions . . . about the baby? It wasn't as if she had had any real evidence, and the photos they had shown her of Sammy had made it obvious he was Ronald's child.

'She didn't say very much,' replied Ronald. 'Just that she was pleased to see we were so happy together . . . and that she was glad it had all come to nothing with that German lad, Heinrich. She mentioned he came from somewhere on the Rhine; I remembered that. You were busy in the kitchen and her husband had gone up to the loo. I thought to myself that she'd picked her moment. Aye, aye; this one's a troublemaker, I thought. She was sounding me out to see if I knew about it; so of course I cracked on that I did.'

'Yes, that sounds just like Olive,' said Eunice, still feeling a fluttering of unease. 'She was always a sly sort of girl. What else did she say?'

'Nothing at all. Like I said; she was trying to stir it, but she didn't succeed. Jealous, more than likely, seeing how contented we were. I certainly didn't get that impression of her and her husband. He was henpecked, that poor chap.'

'And you never let on that you knew, all this time.' Eunice couldn't get over the fact.

'There didn't seem to be much point. I knew it couldn't have been much of a thing with you and him; I know you so well, Eunice.' She felt a stab of guilt, but she kept quiet . . . as she had done for more than fifty years. 'We were getting on so well, you and me, and I didn't want to rock the boat. Tell me, though, you didn't decide to marry me on the rebound, did you? I know it happened all of a sudden, with you and me.'

'I came to my senses, Ronnie,' she said, returning to her old familiar name for him. 'That's all. Let's say no more about it, eh? I realised I love you . . . I still do,' she added quietly.

'That's all right then.' He smiled at her. 'We've been happy, haven't we?'

'Very happy, my dear . . .'

'And we're going to have a grand holiday.'

'Yes, I'm sure we are; now you've stopped grumbling.' She nudged him playfully and he laughed.

'Well, you know me, don't you? I have to have my say . . .'

She had thought she knew Ronald inside out; but he had kept quiet about that, all those years. She realised he still had the power to surprise her. And that, after fifty years of marriage, must be quite something.

There's a Silver Lining

Margaret Thornton

It's 1918, the war is finally over, and Sarah Donnelly and her cousin Nancy are filled with hope for the future. In particular, Sarah eagerly awaits the safe return of her cousin Zachary, whom she has adored since childhood. But when Zachary returns to Blackpool, shattered by the horrors of war, he can barely face his family, let alone reciprocate Sarah's affections.

Refusing to be thwarted by rejection, Sarah throws herself into her job at Donnelly's tea rooms, where her father, the owner of Blackpool's most popular department store, has allowed her to work. Then Sarah spys a run-down building to let near North Shore, and decides to set up in business, running her *own* tea rooms.

Meanwhile, Nancy, forever a dreamer, has chosen to follow in her mother's footsteps on to the stage. But it is not long before her youthful naivety lands her in trouble.

There's a Silver Lining is an evocative saga, steeped in warmth and nostalgia, in which heartache, happiness, tragedy and triumph lie in store for a close-knit Blackpool community.

0 7472 4875 3

headline

For the Love of a Soldier

June Tate

Maggie Evans is living with her parents at their Southampton pub when the GIs arrive to support the British troops. Maggie's never met anyone like American Steve Rossi, and it's hard to resist his good looks and easy confidence. But there's another side to Steve, and when he pulls a knife during a fight, Maggie begins to wonder what other secrets he's concealing.

Steve's true colours show when Maggie is seen chatting to another GI, Joshua Lewis. Joshua is everything Steve is not: kind, considerate and honest. And he's black. Steve's a bigot – not the only one in Southampton, Maggie learns – and he warns Joshua off, even though Maggie swears they're just friends. Joshua's no pushover, and as Maggie sees the strength of the quieter man she wonders if her feelings are as platonic as she says . . .

June Tate's previous novels are available from Headline:

'Excellent and gripping . . . compelling' *Sussex Life*

'Her debut book caused a stir among Cookson and Cox devotees, and they'll love this' *Peterborough Evening Telegraph*

'A heart-warming tale with a vividly drawn central character' *Coventry Evening Telegraph*

0 7472 6318 3

headline